T0165054

Nancy Holder's 'The Sea Ghost' (artist Vicky Adams)

DRACULA
UNFANGED

Devised and Edited by

Christopher Sequeira

Foreword by

Leslie S. Klinger

A Dark Phases 'Imagine That' Title

This is a work of fiction. The events and characters portrayed herein are imaginary and are not intended to refer to specific places, events or living persons. The opinions expressed in this manuscript are solely the opinions of the author and do not necessarily represent the opinions of the publisher.

Dracula Unfanged

All Rights Reserved

ISBN-13: 978-1-922556-83-7

Anthology Concept Copyright to © 2022, Christopher Sequeira

V1.0

All contributions (story, and introduction and afterword) to this anthology are copyright ©2022 the authors of each contribution, with the exception of the following works used by permission of the current copyright holders:-
'The Legend Of Dracula Reconsidered As a Prime-Time TV Special' originally published 1992, copyright © 1992 to 2022, Christopher Fowler.
'Drawing In' originally published 1978, copyright © 1978 to 2022, Ramsey Campbell.
Frontispiece and Endpiece Art Copyright © 2022, Vicky Adams.
Cover Art Copyright © 2022, Dave Elsey. Design by Catherine Archer-Wills.
This book may not be reproduced, transmitted, or stored in whole or in part by any means, including graphic, electronic, or mechanical without the express written consent of the publisher except in the case of brief quotations embodied in critical articles and reviews.
Printed in Garamond and IM Fell DW Pica.

IFWG Publishing International
Gold Coast

www.ifwgpublishing.com

For my brother, Jonathan. Not just loyal, loving family; but a friend and support whenever I've needed one. And, from time to time, an artistic collaborator, of exceptional talent and insight. Jonny, dude; something to entertain you before we do our own vampire project one day (soon, I'm sure)!

Acknowledgements

Thanks to Catherine Archer-Wills for the brilliant design work on Dave Elsey's killer image for our cover; and to Gregory Stewart for proofreading.

Table of Contents

Introduction

LESLIE S. KLINGER

"The only good vampire is a dead vampire"

Vampires have had a bad reputation for a long, long time. Accounts of vampirism may be traced to the Mesopotamians, the Hebrews, the Greeks, and the Romans, among other old cultures, and in virtually all cases, the vampires are revenants—essentially the "walking dead"—of evil persons, including witches and suicides. Although Bram Stoker's *Dracula* was not the first depiction of the vampire in the 19th century, its appearance in 1897 cemented the popular idea that vampires were inherently evil monsters.

It took over three-quarters of a century before any writer dared to challenge that idea. That pioneer wasn't Stephanie Meyers, whose *Twilight* series was first published in 2005, nor was it Anne Rice, whose 1976 masterpiece *Interview with the Vampire* and its sequels and prequels achieved enormous popularity as the *Vampire Chronicles*. In fact, it was a rethinking of *Dracula* itself, a book called *The Dracula Tape* by Fred Saberhagen, first published in 1975, in which the Count himself sets the record straight.

Saberhagen dared to consider what we really know of Count Dracula, taking a fresh look at many of the "facts" of the Dracula legend. Saberhagen points out that when the villagers who live around Castle Dracula leave Dracula an offering of a bag containing a squirming being, is it a baby—or a piglet? We never actually see Dracula attack Jonathan Harker—or Lucy

Westenra or Mina Harker, for that matter. Jonathan fantasizes a lovefest with a trio of women. Dracula borrows Harker's clothes not to trap him but rather to have them copied for his own use. The crew of the *Demeter* was ravaged by a mad Roumanian , as the captain concludes, not a vampire. Lucy drugged her servants, not Dracula, to find some private time with the attractive Count. When she develops anemia, Van Helsing—an incompetent doctor at best—kills her by administering blood transfusions from four different men. Mina actually sucks Dracula's blood, not vice versa! Van Helsing is the man of evil, pursuing a vendetta against the Count, forcing Dracula to fake his own death in order to run off with Mina. In short, as Dracula explains at length in this recorded conversation with a reporter (a full year before Anne Rice's Louis is "interviewed"), he has been terribly wronged and his character besmirched.

So, was Dracula lying to the reporter in *The Dracula Tape*? What do we *really* know about vampires? Despite countless accounts of vampires and vampirism, in hundreds of tales, there is a lack of consensus about the characteristics of vampires. In folklore, only a few traits of vampires are common to virtually all reports: the vampire drinks blood, usually that of a carefully selected victim, which not only sustains the vampire but produces a youthful appearance or "rejuvenates" the creature, creating near-immortality; vampires are affected by holy artifacts; and they can be destroyed by decapitation, burning, or a wooden or iron stake.

Stoker's account of *Dracula* introduced additional ideas, including that vampires lack shadows, are un-photographable, have supernatural strength, shape-shifting abilities,* and the power of telepathic command. Post-*Dracula* accounts of vampires have borrowed freely from Stoker's canon, accepting some characteristics and rejecting others. In the world of *Buffy the Vampire Slayer*, for example, created by screenwriter Joss Whedon, vampires have no souls, while those who appear in Rice's *Vampire Chronicles* have souls to the same extent as humans. Rice's vampires are unaffected by religious symbols, while both the *Buffy* and Rice vampires can be photographed or filmed.

Still another well-developed "universe" of vampires are Chelsea Quinn Yarbro's more-than-two-dozen novels about Le Comte de Saint-Germain, a 4,000-year-old vampire who always exhibits a depth of humanism in his struggle to aid mankind. In Yarbro's books, Saint-Germain must combat

---

* Some folkloric accounts conflate vampires and werewolves, so the idea of shape-shifting was not wholly original to *Dracula*.

evil or depraved humans, in a war that has spanned centuries. Yet Saint-Germain displays most of the other characteristics of traditional vampires, including, of course, blood-drinking for his sustenance.

The origin of the vampire is unexplained in folklore. Rice's books posit an ancient lineage, beginning with Egyptian rulers who were possessed by a spirit. Her vampires, however, are not malevolent or bent on world conquest; rather, they seem to seek peaceful coexistence with non-vampires. In *Buffy* lore, demons, who once populated Earth alongside humans, fled to another dimension in ancient times. Some returned to our dimension through magical portals. Once here, they took up occupancy in mortal bodies and now seek world domination for the benefit of the race of demons. In contrast, Yarbro's Saint-Germain became a vampire when his tribal god, also a vampire (of unexplained origin), 'turns' him. While he has the power to create more vampires, they are much shorter-lived than Saint-Germain, and he generally refrains from doing so.

Rice, Whedon, and Yarbro are only a few of the hundreds of writers who have explored vampires and vampirism in their work, and many have played freely with Stoker's "rules," imbuing vampires with additional "superpowers" or weaknesses, inventing a hierarchy of vampires, and, often, establishing Dracula as the supreme leader of a unified army of vampires. It is this very plasticity of the concept of the vampire that has fostered the growth of vampire literature. It is this freedom that has allowed writers to use the vampire—and Dracula—to examine the human condition, in all of its infinite variety. "We all know Dracula, or think we do," wrote Nina Auerbach in her brilliant study *Our Vampires, Ourselves*. "[B]ut there are many Draculas—and still more vampires who refuse to be Dracula or to play him."* The simple truth of this observation is nowhere more evident than the multiplicity of versions of Dracula on display in this volume.

As far back as 1751, Dom Augustine Calmet, a French theologian and scholar, unsuccessfully attempted to classify, categorize and explain vampires and the sources of vampire tales in his *Treatise on the Apparitions of Spirits and on Vampires or Revenants*. Later scholars, such as Montague Summers and Paul Barber, have similarly failed. And so, in the absence of hard scientific facts, one writer's conception of vampires is just as valid as another's. Just as Saberhagen and others have shown, the figure of Dracula can be viewed in

---

* Chicago: University of Chicago Press (1995), p. 1.

many lights. So long as humans remain fascinated by the secrets of death, the lure of immortality, and the magic of blood, an infinite variety of vampires will continue to walk the pages of books like this anthology— and who is to say where else?

Leslie S. Klinger
February 2022

Prologue: Still Waters
CHRISTOPHER SEQUEIRA

The Year 1477. Mount Csindrel, Transylvania.

S atan stood upon the actual surface of the waters of Lake Hermannstadt—a massive artificially created reservoir housed by a large circular
stone dam that had been built by slave labour an eternity before. The
Devil smiled at his students, who stood in a line at the grassy edges of the
mountainside around the dam looking into the centre of the lake. Lucifer
then stepped across the lake's radius until he reached the flat grass, walked
onto the area in front of his acolytes, and beckoned to his prize pupil, the
Wallachian Prince.

"Dracula," said Satan. "You have graduated in first place in my school.
There have been others under my tutelage who have lived long lives and
ruled nations with the black arts as their arsenal. But you, so well have you
learnt, that not only shall you become Lord of the Undead; Monarch of
Vampires, but I also have another signal reward for you."

Vlad Dracula III, whom some feared as The Impaler, or Butcher of
Poenari, or Voivode of Death, stepped forward. He was a striking-eyed
figure of lean muscle and agile stance, and he turned to his fellow members
of the Scholomance; less than a dozen they were (as the most of the One
Hundred who commenced the studies had died horrifically in the trial
examinations).

"You are correct, Lord of Lies. I am the greatest of your pupils. But the
German, he who mastered not just alchemy but the scientific arts. I have

watched him. He has a secret. He lives to be subjugated. This is a man I would retain."

The German, who was a student named Klausen who'd survived many a challenge though application of marvels of chemistry and the physical sciences (where his occult skills were too shallow to have aided him), came forward and knelt before Vlad. He was a bizarre figure, certainly. He dressed like an impoverished monk, and had a strange optical glass over one eye, literally affixed there by a brass frame he had embedded with pins into his own skull. "My Lord", said Klausen. "I create, but more than this, I serve thee."

Vlad was pleased. Klausen had perfected mechanical iterations of some of the more pronounced methods of torture that often Vlad grew quite annoyed with seeing his soldiers try to do by hand, for they were oft too squeamish and too slow. Klausen had also used the benefit of journeys to the East where amazing applications of some volatile black powders could produce means of devastating physically concussive weapons; an alternative to catapults. Many were the working models Klausen had created of these; and Vlad wanted these to be his, and his alone.

Satan actually clapped his hands together several times in joy.

"This is apt, this is a perfect moment! Klausen, you proved wise beyond your years as I schooled. Again, you discern the future is with my star scholar. Prince Vlad will become not just Lord of the Grave, but his is to be a unique testamur indeed."

Vlad walked towards Satan, and there was nothing of deference in his approach. There was only certainty.

"Teacher. When my graduation concludes, I will pursue a small list of desires over coming weeks: I shall have the Sultan of the Ottomans brought to me for extreme sentence. I shall identify and gather the last of the Boyars that saw myself and my brother imprisoned as children for years and make they and their families dust, and I shall raise a new civilisation, that of the Undead, and we will make the world our prey. Never again will Dracula be a prisoner, forever he will be beyond any enemy, and any empire's power. But, to ensure this, I must have no rivals here."

"Granted," said Satan, and he gestured at the other students. They were instantly enveloped in flames, and every one of them died in a protracted torrent of agony; for the Devil's fire was not swift to end their lives. Fully five minutes elapsed.

The German watched all, he alone unhurt. Although he tried, drool could not be prevented from spilling from his open mouth. Satan and Vlad both saw this and actually exchanged smiles.

Satan walked towards the last dead student and ground out a small piece of burning grass near one smoking eye socket.

"Vlad, you know what I am about to give you. I have been the Adversary since human life began. Some have tried to wrest that role from me—not as many as have sought to destroy me for Heaven's Favour—but many. Only you have the mixture of dark intent, and the essential venal humanity that provide me any hope the role can be carried out adequately by someone else. And, as Lord of Vampires, you will bring new glory to the Great Works."

Vlad bowed his head, and there somehow was not a single note of subservience in that gesture when he made it. "I shall, Teacher."

Lucifer raised a fist in triumph. "It is DONE. I pass my mantle to you. I feel the core of my energies begin to transfer already. You know there will be pain? Great pain?"

Vlad snorted. "Pain has been with me since the childhood tortures of the Sultan."

The Devil continued. "Then it is so. I will slay you, here and now. Your body shall be taken to your citizenry and laid in state. Three nights will come, and you will arise, as Undead."

The German, who had been enraptured by this dialogue, began to fondle his reproductive organ under his cassock, but thought better of it and stopped.

"But on the fourth night," Satan said "I will cease to exist and at that moment YOU will be given my throne to the Underworld, and all my powers in addition to those of your own as Bloodlord. It will change this world's destiny."

Dracula stood tall. "Let us not delay, then." he said.

Satan gestured, and a sword, a Turkish sword, flew from the skies and impaled itself in Dracula's chest. He fell awkwardly, heavily—and yes, there *was* great pain—and he died. A Wallachian troop—who had no idea how they had wandered into this part of the country—appeared over the horizon, and, seeing the banner of Dracula flying from a pole, dashed forward. Klausen rubbed his hands together with delight.

Satan walked the mountain to a town nearby. He went to a tavern and he paid for a sumptuous feast. After dining, he engaged two women and two men who had experience as prostitutes to perform a variety of sexual acts with him. The prostitutes later agreed amongst themselves that Satan paid about ten times their customary rates (although, within a day, they all suffered a unique venereal infection that was unprecedented in the agony-levels of its symptomology).

One Night Later

Vlad lay dead, during the day, in a secret chamber in his fortress at Poenari. But those destined to become a vampire do not lie in death peacefully. They dream, and they dream the nightmares of the damned.

Vlad dreamed that first daytime of an Englishman, with odd clothes and manner unlike any Vlad had encountered, and Vlad, as a prince, was well acquainted with many foreign cultures and customs. Diplomats and couriers that Vlad had met, or dined with, or impaled, had given him many insights into varying traditions, but the figure in this vision was unlike any of these. A huge, red-bearded fellow, Vlad realized the man was using an unusual set of tools to write words onto parchment of a sheen and texture new to Vlad. Vlad realized the bearded man was writing about Vlad, and…praising him. Just as many a European had pamphleteered about Vlad's exploits as a powerful and wise ruler who punished transgressors deservedly by impalement and other means; the bearded man was doing the same but describing Vlad's yet-to-be achievements as a Vampire Lord. Vlad then began to understand, however, that he was seeing a fate where the fame of the pamphleteers was completely annulled by the work of the bearded man: It was his celebration of Vlad that would resound, for not just the few months of a war with the Turks, and no, not just Vlad's mortal years, nor even the extended lifespan of a vampire. No, Vlad understood (and knew this was no fantasy): *The bearded man would make Vlad known—perhaps in* every *crevice of the world—forever!* A magnificent, global acknowledgement of Vlad, Lord of the Grave, and soon also to be Adversary. *Unstoppable. Unkillable. Unable to be restrained in any prison built by the mind of man ever again.*

The clarity of this forthcoming truth was beyond question. It was everything Vlad could have sought the day he took his first lesson at the Scholomance.

So, Vlad did not understand why he was stricken with *absolute fear* by this revelation. And who had sent him this portent?

Vlad awoke at sunset and sat in his secret chamber. His body was cold, but he was filled with power. He saw his fingers were becoming like powerful, razor tipped talons, he could feel strength unlike anything merely mortal pulsing through him. But the visions he'd had disturbed him. He had no hunger, no desire—not yet—so he remained in his dark chamber, turning all over in his mind, until a force gripped him and made him become dead again; as, outside, the sun rose.

Two Nights Later

Vlad had dreamed again in the daylight hours, and his questions from the previous day had been answered.

His brother Radu—dead these eighteen months—had appeared to him. It was he who had sent the images.

Vlad had demanded to know why. Radu had advised him to beware a serious danger, a danger that would take victory and turn it into bitter, rotten fruit. Radu had warned Vlad that—as it had ever been in the lives of the children of Dracul—those you believe you may trust are exactly those who will betray you. And the best protection against such is the fierce punishment of a Dracula: Excruciating death.

Sunset came and Radu vanished. Vlad sat up, and pondered (although his body was distracting him during his thinking, for he was continuing to change; still greater sense of strength; his senses were amazingly alive and magnified; complete vision even in darkness): His brother, Radu, had held jealousies at times against Vlad; could this be a manifestation of that, or was there merit in the warning? Vlad clamped his mind down hard and concentrated, concentrated just as he had in the past done to get past the scheming liars of the Wallachian Court, or to survive meetings with assassins disguised as visiting nobles; Vlad used the great mind that had saved his life so many times to wrestle with the nightmares and their significance. He thought back to all he knew of Radu, all they had been through together; all Radu's foibles, and his attributes.

Finally, after two hours, Vlad summoned a captain of his guards, gave him some very explicit, detailed instructions, and then made that captain bring Klausen to him; and then gave Klausen his own, separate instructions away from the captain's hearing.

Morning came and Vlad returned to death.

Three Nights Later

Vlad pushed himself up from his bier—no longer in a secret chamber in Poenari but within a gleaming, black, horse-drawn coach. Vlad sat, senses sharp, as sharp as…the canine fangs in his mouth that he ran his tongue over that now jutted from his jaws. His transmogrification, his attainment of dark sacrament, was final. And the additional role as Adversary required but one more day's passing.

However, Dracula had made an oath aloud, to achieve his list of desires swiftly, so instructions he gave last night had been acted upon accordingly, to address some of this list.

Dracula had ordered his dead body be loaded upon a carriage and transported to Lake Hermannstadt during the day and he'd ordered other preparations to be made during that day, as well. He was pleased to see these appeared to have been carried out.

A simple ritual wooden platform had been instructed, leading from shore to lake waters. There, a small retinue of guards stood over a man dressed in Ottoman finery but with a black bag tied over his head. Klausen was there, too, preening over the shining brass and steel shaft of his invention, which was little more than a massive cylinder designed to discharge a powerful projectile—by use of combusting black minerals—sending that missile through a hoop-shaped scaffolding that would hold a man vertically suspended by his arms. It was because of this rather obvious arrangement that the guards kicked and snarled at the bag-headed one; telling him he was to be shockingly torn into pieces by a powerful weapon their Master had brought into creation.

Vlad flicked his cloak back from his shoulders and moved onto the platform and watched as his guards forced the hooded man into the straps in the hoop. The German—at a simple wave of Vlad's fingers—carefully examined his device, and used a calibration rule of his devising to assure the projectile's destination was assured; he twirled wheel-cranks and adjusted the height and angle of the cannon.

Vlad waved his guards away and they left the platform, and Vlad pulled the bag off the man's head. The Sultan's enraged face glared at him, and the ruler spoke in flurry of spittle and mania. Vlad let him curse, then grasped both cheeks of the man's face with his two hands. Vlad pulled and the Sultan's face was literally ripped from his skull.

"Reveal your true self," said Vlad, quietly.

And the Sultan's skull laughed and his face *grew* back, flesh and fat and sinew formed anew instantly, from nowhere: His *real* face grew back.

"Well done, my greatest pupil", said Satan. "How did you know?"

Vlad nodded. "In my youth, in captivity", he said "I had naught to do but scheme, and plan, and dream of bloody revenge. It gave me a keenness of mind, that I have foolishly neglected to use in adulthood when supported by an army of soldiers with swords and stakes. So, I used that old wisdom, that depth of thought, that allows me to calculate what motivates a being; a lust-filled woman, a cruel man, a venal cleric, a greedy courtier. And, even you. You wanted...freedom."

Satan transformed into his more customary raiment and a physique more intimidating than the simulated Sultan's dimensions, and stepped away from his restraints. "I do", the Lord of Lies said. "You have given me that. Willingly. You will be an Adversary perhaps greater in renown than I. I thought it might please you to think you had dispatched your greatest mortal enemy tonight; I thought it might solidify your resolve. I knew your men could not breach the leader of the Ottoman's security, not yet, so I faked this event, for, it may be a while before you do capture him, even with the powers of Vampire King, for you have a Vampire King's weaknesses, too. Thus, with regards your new form, whispers have reached the Sultan, he is fortifying his palace with protective relics and icons, so it may be a while yet before he is in your grasp."

Vlad nodded, and grabbed Satan's shoulder with affection and they both stepped off the wooden platform and onto the surface of Lake Hermannstadt. "So, Teacher, you thought to do me a kindness on the night before my Ascencion to your position. A gesture you say—lies, naturally—but still a gesture of congratulations, I do see. You honour me, but perhaps even more greatly than I had originally believed? For, I have intuited something. Am I, in truth, the *only* one to ever graduate from the Scholomance? Were the tales of other successful classes also simply lies?"

Satan clapped his hands and bowed his head in genuine admiration. "Of course."

Vlad stretched his arms outward. "Tonight I am lord of the Undead, and tomorrow night I will become the complete iteration of the anti-God. Where He bequeaths with generosity, I will literally steal life away; leading a race that will drink life-fluid of the millions of Yahweh's sheep—unless of course they bow to me. And with my achieving that status, YOU, you can end your existence, which is as you desire."

Satan shivered for just a half-second, but it was enough. "Yes," he said. "I was Lucifer, but my light must dim, for I tire. Only you have aspired for more than I; only you have ever earnt the role."

Vlad sighed, and waved his hand again, but in a different way. "Hence this entire little charade with the Sultan's image: You wished that I be so filled with evil joy at my greatest mortal enemy's demise that I would do nothing to stray from the path, and I would allow the clock to tick to my Fourth Night beyond humanity; to that moment when the mantle of Adversary would irrevocably pass from you to me."

The German had seen Vlad's odd little wave and had turned to his machine.

And Klausen fired the cannon at the southern-most wall of the dam; which is where it had, of course, been aimed all the time.

The wall ruptured as the sound of the explosion filled the night. Masonry flew outwards and crashed down the mountainside. And water followed it. Satan and Dracula still remained standing on the water's surface but the level of the water swiftly began to fall relative to the remaining walls of the dam. Millions of litres of liquid gushed down the side of the mountain.

Satan glanced at his protege, and saw Dracula's posture slump, and Vlad's proud face shuddered in pain as his body literally began to collapse upon itself; he became a twisting, curdling, melting thing.

"Running water, that which can destroy a vampire," said Satan.

They stood together, and Satan felt his invincible core of evil become aflame solely within himself again, as Vlad III, Prince of Wallachia, extraordinary Count Dracula of the Székelys, recently anointed King of the Undead, literally dissipated into unexistence. The Lord of the Vampyr was become Dracula Unfanged; he had rejected coronation as Adversary and became instead miniscule particles of potential, of mere fragments of being. His glorious, vile, future history as supreme titan of evil, scourge of Transylvanian legend, horror of Europe, plague of the new worlds, all ended before they could begin. Dracula's disaggregated essence mingled with the disappearing Hermannstadt streams falling to the earth, to soak disparately into soil and foliage, or escape as vapour into the air. Never to become a vampire, he was just the potential idea of centuries-living evil plaguing a reality now.

Satan stood in the air above the lake. He spoke—just to Klausen, for the others had all fled.

"He realized if he took my place on Fourth Night he would be chained to that specific existence, and the rigid confinements it carries, far beyond being Lord of Vampires. As simply King of Undead, he might be predator, but he might evolve, even learn mercy, he might choose many a path. But to be Adversary, he realized it was a role one cannot vacate, there are traits that cannot be adjusted. Choices I am forever denied to even try to make. Shackles unlike those that any thinking being wears."

Klausen looked at the waters that were almost gone, as Satan walked on empty air back to the grass. Dracula's body was long gone. "Indeed, Dark One. I cannot imagine what millennia had passed before this first chance for you to abdicate by appointing a successor, and, even then, this one chance has not borne fruit. If Dracula had taken your place, he must have known it might be a role he would never find his own successor for should HE tire of it, too. And you heard my Master, my Prince of Wallachia: *'And never again will Dracula be a prisoner.'*"

Satan then spoke an absolute truth. "Yes. Even a prisoner of his own ambition."

The Sea Ghost
NANCY HOLDER

July, 1968

You will cross land and sea to do my bidding.

His sea serpents and sea witches mobbed the submarine. They clung to the diving planes and ripped, ripped, ripped with talons and fangs. Sea sprites kept hold of the snorkel so that the seawater could pour into the vessel. Sharks rammed the hull. Orcas pushed the sea forward with the force of a massive, breaking dam.

The sub tumbled end over end, spiraling down to the crushing depths where the dark void devoured it. Five, four, three…the explosion sent shockwaves through the water. Towering undersea mountains shook and broke apart. His subjects shrieked as they flew along the currents, he along with them, screaming and cheering and laughing as all hands aboard died. Clouds of sardines and anchovies whirled like comets. Swordfish jousted. Tuna glittered as they danced.

Then the chaos subsided.

Some of the newly dead would haunt the sea as his subjects. Others would simply rot. Did their minds and souls go somewhere? He had lost his own soul six hundred years ago. When he had ruled as the human Prince of Wallachia in the fifteenth century, he bargained with the Devil to save his people from the Ottoman Turks. As a result, he had become Dracula, the dread vampire. He still called himself Dracula, because he didn't know himself by any other name. In Transylvania, he was still revered as a savior. In the waters of the world's oceans, multitudes of the sea's own and the land's drowned bowed down to him as king. He was mighty; he was strange.

As he savored the afterglow of the attack, crimson puddles circled him, phantom blood. It had no taste, no scent. He had no idea where it came from. Eerie blue light bathed him as electric eels slithered and slid over his chest and around his neck and limbs until he looked like the statue of Laocoön the Trojan priest, whom the gods attacked with snakes. He telescoped into a gargantuan copy of himself—the Colossus of Rhodes—and then he became man-sized once more. He shifted with the tides and the currents and he caused the tides and the currents. He changed and changed and changed; he had no permanent shape. Next he was a solid being of coral coated with barnacles and sea anemones; and then his skin was pale, as it had been in his lifetime, and smooth. Through it all, he was never a vampire again.

But he was always a warlord, presiding over a war, this one in the divided country of Viet Nam. Powerful foreign nations were battling for supremacy, destruction spilling over her borders into the countries of Cambodia and Laos. Two superpowers, Russia and the United States, were burning the land and the people for supremacy that they did not need, in lands that did not belong to them. They threw their garbage into the waters, poisoning, polluting. Their cause was unjust. They had no honor.

He had become a vampire to fight the Ottoman Turks. Now he fought these invaders. He conjured storms that sank their destroyers and tenders, and jammed their electronics with St. Elmo's fire, sending their battleships to shallows and reefs. He toyed with them, terrified them. He prolonged their agony, and reveled in their destruction.

For a moment, their deaths would ease his fury, quell his rage. But his lust for violence always returned magnified. All these wars...they were not his to fight, and yet he fought them. He had been a warrior, but he was not at heart an avenging angel. He had been a demon, and he had lost his own last battle to a handful of puny, anemic humans: Jonathan and Mina Harker, Quincy Morris, Abraham Van Helsing, and Arthur Holmwood. How he hated them.

Hated them still.

The tides turned. The moon rose and fell. The excitement of the submarine attack faded, and his subjects awaited the next rout. He sat on his throne of coral and shells and brooded as his trio of brides, the sea witches, loved him, caressed him. They were naiads , beautiful mermaids with streaming hair—scarlet, blond, brunette—and iridescent tails. He was their lord, and that was their constant. He ruled their world, their shallows and deeps, and he knew they believed he always had. Who would not twine themselves around such a one?

"Oh, Neptune," the scarlet witch, the most beautiful one, burbled at him. He wasn't Neptune, but he didn't correct her. All his subjects called him Neptune. He never corrected any of them. He knew he wasn't Dracula anymore, but he wasn't sure what he was—a god? A force? He wasn't a vampire, but he felt like a vampire. He was still a hunter.

After all this time—how much time?—five of the sub's dead had clawed their way up from the debris field, which had settled over several miles of ocean bottom in a chasm. Two of them were fully formed skeletons; a third was missing a hand, a foot, and his head; a fourth, the left half of his body; and the fifth was enrobed in charred flesh. He had a theory that the dead appeared to him in the state in which they had died, but he wasn't sure. It didn't matter. He had created graveyards everywhere. Whether they were filled with wraiths or corpses or kelp was immaterial to him. He didn't care about adulation.

"Neptune," the sea witch gushed, her eyes the color of oil, her hair fiery, her body covered with scales. Her fingers ended in talons, and her mouth was filled with sharp, pointed teeth.

He cocked his head. "When you look at me, what do you see?"

"I see my radiant king," she cooed. "I see my god." He waited, and she added, "So brown and muscular. A mane of golden hair, a beard that reaches to your massive chest, eyes the color of a lagoon…"

He was astonished. Golden hair? Blue eyes? He had seen himself in the mirrors of sinking pleasure boats, in pools of water when he broke the surface. The fact that he had a reflection again had made him laugh, and he had studied himself long and hard. He was as he had been six hundred years before: lanky, sinewy—by no means did he have a massive chest—pale skin, dark-haired and dark-eyed. He didn't look at all as she was describing him.

"And how long have I been your master?" he asked her.

The scales on her forehead wrinkled as she frowned, confused, and said, "Forever." She kissed him with her rough lips. "You are eternal."

His other two witch brides swam over, encircling him, enticing him. They jostled each other to be the one to coil into his lap. Irritated, he pushed all three of them away. As he watched them go, he scrutinized the floating ends of his long hair. Dark brown, practically black.

After the sea witches withdrew, the submarine dead wafted toward him, seeking audience. Their jawbones clacked. The ones with heads lowered them in obeisance. He wondered if the headless one could see and hear.

He said to the charred one, "When you look at me, what do you see?"

"John Paul Jones," the man replied, and Dracula threw back his head and laughed.

Then something sizzled through the water and struck him, hard; a bolt of electricity, a live wire, a detonating bomb. A blinding flash lit up the seas around him, and he tumbled like the submarine—or thought he did: the charred seaman hadn't so much as flinched; his trio of brides were placidly watching from a bower of giant kelp. Sharks zigzagged; tiny sea horses bobbled along. Whatever had touched him, it had touched no one else.

But he *knew*. With every fiber of his being, he knew:

Another vessel was approaching, and a Harker was on board.

A Harker.
A direct descendant of Jonathan Harker, who had cut off the head of Dracula, and Mina Harker, whom he had almost succeeded in turning into a vampire bride. Almost eighty years had passed since that fateful dusk on the Borgo Pass. But the blood of his enemies called to him. The blood, after all, is the life.

How long since I have fed on the blood of the living? Was that also eighty years?

He turned his back on his subjects and propelled himself in the direction of the ship. He swam like a shark, a predator again, a hunter. Sensing his violence, fish darted away. Octopuses panicked, releasing ink.

He had no idea how long he swam, but at last he zeroed in on the vessel like a torpedo. As he headed for the surface, sea lions panicked and barked warnings to each other. Dolphins chittered in fear. Seagulls squawked.

Steaming underway, a passenger ship with two stacks sailed through the troughs between the waves. The portside bow bore the name *S.S. President Wilson*. An American ship, then. The Harkers had been English. It would be interesting to discover what a Harker was doing here, now.

A human couldn't have managed to get aboard the *President Wilson* from the surface of the wild ocean, but he shimmied up chains and ropes and ladders with ease. Contrary to the beliefs of some, vampires were able to cross running water. He had murdered the entire crew of the *Demeter* on the initial voyage from his castle to his new properties in London, had he not? But that didn't matter anyway. He wasn't a vampire any longer.

He moved through the maze of the vessel, breaking into passenger cabins to shower and steal pieces of men's clothing and shoes, hoping to delay discovery by taking an item from each one and repairing the damage he had done to the locks. In each of the mirrors he was pale, dark-haired and dark-eyed and he looked utterly human. It pleased him to see his reflection, and to be reassured that there was nothing eye-catching about him. He could pass among these humans.

Though presentable, he kept to the corners and shadows. The din was overwhelming; there were so many people. This was the Swinging Sixties. He chuckled at the short skirts, the flamboyant makeup, the lacquered hair of the women. Many of the men wore garish floral shirts and light brown or white trousers. He had on such a shirt himself.

He scanned the throngs as they bustled about. They were awash in busy-ness. There was a map on a wall with a little black ship attached to a dotted line: their route. They had sailed from Tokyo to Oahu and were now on their way to the west coast of the United States. He squinted. San Francisco was their destination. They were closing in.

"Hey, Mark," a man said as he clapped Dracula on the shoulder.

He turned and the man's smile altered. "Oh, sorry, I thought you were Mark," he said. "Mark Cameron. You know him? He has a shirt just like that." He laughed. "I swear, that gift shop in Waikiki made a killing off this ship." The man peered at him. "Haven't seen you around. You must be in the early meal seatings. We're in the late. Where were you stationed?"

Stationed, Dracula thought. *He's asking for a location for something.* It didn't really matter if he gave a wrong answer. He wouldn't be aboard for very long. All he had to do was find the Harker descendant aboard and kill him.

He glanced at the map. "Tokyo." He mimicked the accent of the American Quincy Morris, whom he had killed when the Harkers' band of vampire killers had attacked him.

"In the thick of it, then," the man said sympathetically. "The people back Stateside have no idea what we've been going through." He grimaced. "Peace marches. You know the Commies are organizing them. Say, I was just about to meet some of the guys in the bar. Care to join us?"

"I wish I could." He smiled. "Another time?"

"Sure." The man extended his hand. "I'm Terry Haugen."

He was caught unawares. He had to think of a name. "Vla…er, Brad. Counter. Brad Counter." Vladimir was a Russian name and the Americans were usually at war with Russia.

They shook hands. It was the first time he had touched a living human since his vampiric death. He found the man's skin curiously pleasant: warm, dry. The sea was always so cold.

Terry Haugen moved on down the corridor, leaving him free to roam. He overheard snippets of conversation and soon put together the details of this particular ship: these were American military personnel and their families returning from tours of duty in Japan. Some of them had fought in Viet Nam, and some of them were doctors who had stitched the wounded back together and returned them to Viet Nam. Many of them were worried about their reception in the United States, where non-military citizens protested violently against the war. The passengers talked about "dirty hippies," high prices, and where they would be stationed next. He compared their bodies to those of his fierce Magyars and shook his head. Too soft and fragile. No wonder it was so easy to send their vessels to the bottom of the ocean.

He could do that now. Kill this Harker person by killing everyone aboard in a shipwreck. But he wanted to meet them, terrify them, draw out the act so that they would suffer as he had. And there were other considerations—did this individual have siblings? Offspring?

As he contemplated hunting them down, a sense of purpose thrummed in his veins as thick and hot as living blood. He meandered on, feigning nonchalance, all senses on alert. The days of connection to Mina had been fraught with erotic tension and the thrill of domination. She would have been his if he had won that last battle. But here was another chance—he was pleased to learn that their bond had never been completely severed. He would find her descendant. And this time he *would* win.

A three-toned chime hummed through the corridor; he quickly discerned that it was a call to dine. More formally dressed passengers separated from the others and began to head in the direction opposite to his. He turned around and scanned the crowd, walking slowly, waiting for that same shock of connection that had enticed him to the ship. *A Harker, a Harker, my kingdom for a Harker.*

The crowd was filtering through a double doorway on his left. He peered into a vast dining room filled with tables covered in white cloths and beige padded chairs. Eager though he was eager to investigate, his attire was incorrect and he wasn't expected. He stood beside the door as the diners entered, observing, waiting. The smells of food curled under his nose. In the ocean, he didn't eat. Was he hungry? He wasn't sure.

A thin woman in a green dress passed close by him. He smiled at her as she went into the dining room. Most of the groups were families.

Then the bolt struck him again—an electric shock running down his spine that rattled his teeth. He jerked, hard, startling a man to his left.

A small boy and girl came toward him. Both were blond and blue-eyed. The boy was dressed in long khaki pants, a white shirt, and a dark blue sports coat. The girl wore a frilly pink dress and shiny white shoes. Pink cheeks. A man in a suit followed behind them. Tallish, early middle age, military haircut. Also well attired.

And behind the man…Dracula's quarry.

So the Harker was a woman.

She was a woman of Asiatic heritage, with black hair swept up and dark brown eyes. She was wearing false eyelashes and heavy eye makeup, light pink lipstick, and a simple long-sleeved black dress that ended just above her knees.

As soon as she met his gaze, she froze in her tracks. Her eyes widened and those pink lips parted, and everything fell away. It was as if there was no one else on the ship. She backed away, and he came toward her. She walked quickly, almost running, and he followed. Oblivious, the man and the children went on into the dining room. Dracula swept after her.

She hurried outside onto the deck. It was dusk, and the crowd was thinner, but it was still a crowd. She kept looking over her shoulder as he closed the space between them; then she turned and pressed against the railing, facing him, hands gripping the varnished wood. As he approached, she instinctively reared back her head. Her neck was thin. Easy to snap. Her gaze darted left, right, as if she were seeking escape. She was afraid. This was delicious. This was better than he had anticipated.

"Good evening," he said. She remained silent. "It appears that you know who I am."

She swallowed. Gripped the railing. From her expression, he guessed that her mind was racing. When he had been a vampire, he would have been able to smell her fear, hear her racing heartbeat.

"Do you speak English?" he asked her.

She raised her chin. "I was born in San Francisco."

"Ah. And how did the Harkers wind up in America? I'm curious."

There was a beat, and then she said, "The Harkers. Oh."

"You *are* related to Jonathan and Mina Harker, are you not?"

Another beat. "They were my great-grandparents." She was watching him warily.

"Then you know what happened. What they did to me. In Transylvania."

Her knuckles white, her back ramrod straight, she ground out, "I've heard the story."

"Well, if they told you that they destroyed me, then clearly that is false."

She was trembling. "They didn't *tell* me anything. I never met them."

"It was nearly a hundred years ago," he conceded. "So the story has been handed down in the family?"

"What do you want?" she said.

How abrupt. "You thought it was a crazy family legend. But... somehow you knew me, didn't you? I saw it on your face." He inched closer. "I scare you."

"Go away."

"You *know*. You feel it in your blood."

"I'm going to call for security *now*."

"That's a bad idea." He smiled. "You'll be dead before they can stop me."

She sagged a bit. So she believed him. How exciting.

"Tell me about your family. I want to know what happened to them after our last encounter. Your grandparents. Your parents. Your brothers and sisters." He cocked his head as he studied her. She looked as if she was about to faint. "Your children."

Now she sidled sideways, taking a step away from him. "My stepchildren. I have no children."

"I see. What about brothers and sisters? Uncles? Aunts? Cousins?"

She looked down. "I have to go to my family." It was a plea.

He waved a hand over the waves and they rose up, crashing against each other in the waning light. Whitewater spray billowed above the railing and a few of the passengers stepped back. Someone said, "Oh, God, I hope we're not going to have a storm. I spent the first half of this trip throwing up in my bathroom."

"I have the power to send this vessel to the bottom of the ocean. To kill everyone aboard."

She ticked her attention from the waves to the deck; he reached for her arm, but she dodged his grip. She was really struggling to make sense of this.

"It isn't just Harkers I am after. Any other descendants of my enemies… I have sworn revenge. And as a nobleman, I must keep my vow. And to be honest, it is one I relish fulfilling."

"Revenge…"

"To kill those who tried to destroy me. To end their lines forever."

She stared at him long and hard. It was a lot to absorb, he knew. Surrounded by modern technology, standing in daylight beside him. But she had responded to her first sight of him.

He waited. She might be unaware that she kept glancing in the direction of the dining room. Her husband might be looking for her right now. Dracula didn't need any trouble. Maybe he should just grab her and jump overboard. No one would be able to stop him.

"So you are here to kill *me*."

He said nothing, allowing his silence to serve as his answer. Another long pause. She didn't scream or burst into hysterics. She looked out at the horizon. The sun was sinking and twilight cloaked them in a cocoon of privacy. He half-expected her husband to arrive on the scene because she hadn't gone in to dinner, but perhaps he was stuck because of the children. His children.

He moved his fingers, and the waves rose again. The deck shifted, but only slightly. Commercial vessels were installed with systems designed to keep their passengers' discomfort at a minimum. Still, she noticed.

"Tell me if you have brothers," he said. "Sisters." The deck canted again.

"All right, damn it." She didn't look at him. "We're going to dock in two days. Let me finish the trip with them. I'll tell you about my relatives. Then…" she trailed off and gazed at the dark waters. Her profile, her expression of dismay…it was like feeding.

"*Then*," he said. "Hmm." He was intrigued. If he made this bargain with her, and left her little family alive, there was zero chance for a reunion if she appeared in his realm of the briny deep. It would be the better form of vengeance. "What is your name?"

"Dana Cameron."

He raised a brow. "Oh, that's your married name, then. Your husband is Mark?"

She jerked, caught off guard. So it was. To that passenger Dracula had met, he appeared as her husband. How ironic.

"Someone aboard mistook me for him," he clarified.

"That's ridiculous. You don't look a thing like him." She caught her breath, as if realizing she'd said something to offend him.

He shrugged. "It doesn't matter, does it? What's your maiden name?"

"Dana Harris."

"How prosaic. Where is his first wife?"

Her expression clouded. "She died."

"How did you come into the picture?"

"I don't need to answer all these questions."

"But you do." He smiled. "It's part of the bargain."

She shifted her stance. "Please let me go to them now."

"How did you meet him?"

She threw back her head, huffed, and folded her arms over her chest. "I tutored him in Japanese before his tour."

"And you fell in love and went back to Japan."

"I had never been to Japan before."

"You tutored him in Japanese and then you married him. He has two children, and you and he have none together."

"We have no children," she concurred. "And you swear you won't hurt his."

He nodded. "Agreed. So to be clear: I will spare everyone else; you may have the rest of the voyage; and then you will die by my hand. You give me permission to cause your death."

She walked away without looking back at him. But he could tell that she was still trembling.

He bought himself some clothes in the shipboard shop and returned everything he had borrowed to their respective cabins. Nothing seemed to have been missed.

Though he kept his distance, he watched her. She in turn hovered around Mark Cameron's children and ignored Mark, who didn't seem bothered in the least by it. It was not a happy marriage. The children would miss her more than the husband. They had already lost one mother...

I will not back down, he thought, irritated with himself. *Those bratty peasants are not my concern.*

The hours passed as the ship traveled the waves. Did the sea witches miss him? Would Dana join his court? Would he appear as Neptune to her then?

She ignored him too, which he supposed was her right. He admired her grace under pressure. He knew what it was like to exist under the constant threat of death. If he were still a vampire, he might consider changing her, finally accomplishing what he set out to do with Mina. Maybe, unaware that he was no longer a vampire, she was hoping that he would. It was a kind of afterlife. There seemed to be all sorts.

He smiled as he watched her trail after the little boy and girl. There was no harm in enjoying these sweet family tableaux. He was not a monster, after all.

The *President Wilson* was due to dock at six o'clock in the morning. He jerked from a sort of reverie, not really a dream—he didn't think he slept anymore, but maybe, after all, he did—and in the dream he had raised the waves by moonlight until they towered over the *President Wilson* and brought thunder and lightning down from clouds as thick as clamshells. The ship pitched and yawed and the crew fought bravely, but she turned stern up and as she slid into the raging sea, the front two-thirds of the vessel broke off. Men, women, children pitched into the sea, flailing; no one could swim well enough to survive that.

Before that, a scarlet dawn: he bobbed in the water as he clung to a curved wooden ship fitted with gold. Banners streamed and arrows flow splashing with his free arms to bring the waves, bring the waves; and Japanese *samurai* rolled and skidded along the deck in heavy plated armor. A few, regaining their footing, shot arrows at him.

"*Funayure!*" one of them shouted, his voice ringing above the chaos. The dawn was blood-red, or maybe it was blood, dripping down from the heavens and feeding him, feeding him at last.

A succession of images cascaded one after another, over another: the destroyers and cargo ships and tenders he and his sea minions had taken down; their recent kill, the submarine—

"*Funayurei!*"

He jerked out of his trance as the ship's horn blared. The sun was up. Passengers were chattering and laughing. Many were carrying small satchels and bags, suitcases. The ship had docked, and they were preparing to leave.

It was time.

He surveyed the long queue for many minutes before he found Dana Cameron with her husband and stepchildren. Mark. The children were Noah and Marianne. Noah was holding his father's hand and Marianne was clutching a doll to her chest while she bounced up and down on her heels. They were chattering, and their father was smiling. Facing away from them, Dana gazed straight at him.

He approached. She turned to her stepchildren, then moved from her family and walked back to his side. She looked at him steadily. He reached for her arm and again, she avoided him. He had imagined her death, played and replayed that sweet vindictive moment a hundred times. Maybe a thousand. And now that it was here, he was reluctant to go through with it, because then it would be over.

That must be the reason.

He said, "Well. Here we are."

"Yes." She was surprisingly calm—or at least, appeared to be. The line of passengers was moving. Husband Mark was unconcerned about her absence. Maybe she had told him that she had to use the facilities and would rejoin them.

He led the way back to his shadowy corner. "I had the strangest dream," he said. "I kept hearing a word. Maybe it was Japanese. *Funa*-something."

Her expression shifted slightly. He moved more deeply into the shadows. No one could stop him, of course, but this was just between them.

"I am an only child," she said, "and I have no aunts or uncles. I'm the last of my family."

He flared. She wouldn't *dare* such a clumsy lie.

"All the Harkers are *gone*," she said for emphasis.

Heat swept up his body as rage began to simmer. He balled his fists and made a show of looking from her to the line of passengers. It had been moving; they were disembarking. He couldn't see her husband and the children any longer. Perhaps they had agreed to meet on the dock. But he would find them, kill them now. Right now.

And yet, he did not move.

"Was *funayurei* the word in your dream?" she asked. "It's Japanese. It means 'sea ghost.' A sea ghost can raise storms to sink ships. They do it for revenge."

Why couldn't he move?

"You aren't a vampire. I don't know who you really were—if it was a delusion of yours—but you are *funayurei*. A sea ghost. I knew it as soon as I saw you." She smiled now, and it was a bitter, victorious smile. "And you can't hurt me."

"Oh, you think so?"

"The ship has docked. You're helpless to do anything to it. Or me."

"Helpless? I've killed hundreds! Thousands!" He sneered at her. Advanced. Or tried to. "Our bargain—"

"I'm already dead."

She walked toward him, and then *through* him. The cold she brought was like the ocean depths, the darkness—

He whirled around, and there she was. "We were scuba diving. He drowned me. It was ruled an accident, even though I was the second wife of his to die."

"What? What the *devil?*" he shouted.

"This is the dress I was buried in. Marianne and Noah picked it out. I'm a sea ghost too, of a sort." She looked wistful as she gazed at the harbor. The passengers were all gone.

And then, in the next instant, so was she.

"Wait!" he called. "Wait! Were you a Harker, at least?"

Sea lions barked. Seagulls squawked. He heard their calls: *You are the shape of water. That is all you are, and nothing more.*

The Lost Warlord

LEVERETT BUTTS & DACRE STOKER

I. The Professor Plays It Square

"**A**nd so in order for the body and the soul, or *ka* meaning 'vitality,' to be reunited in the afterlife, ancient Egyptians had to find a way to preserve their mortal remains and prevent decomposition." Dr. Clark August "Tennessee" Phillips, assistant professor of history at Miskatonic University, sat cross-legged on his desk and bit into a ham sandwich behind his face-shield, chewing as he continued. "They dehydrated the corpse with natron, a natural salt found in northern Egypt, and then drained the rest of the liquids from the body and removed the organs." Tennessee took another bite of the sandwich and wiped his face with the back of his sleeve. "They removed the brain through the nose, did you know that?"

The students did not respond, though one or two visibly winced behind their masks.

"They threw out the brain, but they often preserved the rest of the organs in these clay jars, canopic jars, in case the deceased wanted to use them in the afterlife. He'd just, I don't know, put 'em back when he woke up? This is a great sandwich." Tennessee held up the remaining half of the sandwich. "You folks tried that sandwich shop on the corner of Parsonage and Lich?" Apparently, no one had. He took another bite. "Great stuff. Anyway, where were we?"

"The resurrected mummies could put their organs back if they needed them." This was Joe Manton, sitting as usual off to the side by the door. Could always be depended on to answer the questions if no one else did and keep the course on track. Best teaching assistant Tennessee had ever had. From a long line of educators. Tennessee thought he remembered the kid saying his grandfather had been principal of a high school, or maybe it was his great grandfather. Maybe an elementary school.

"The canopic jars, yeah." Tennessee smiled and mock saluted Manton. "You know the voodoo priests in Haiti and the American Delta use the same canopic jars to store souls of the deceased, what they call loa, until they can be put into their descendants. Pretty cool, huh? But the Egyptians: So next they'd rinse out the body cavity with wine and spices then stuff it with flowers and more natron before sewing it back up." Tennessee stopped, looked at the flow chart for mummification he had brought up on the projector screen. "I'm forgetting something." He tapped the sandwich against his chin. "Oh yeah." He snapped his fingers and turned back to the students. "They left the heart in the body. Can you believe that?" He smiled. "It had to stay with the body so it could get weighed against a feather in the Halls of Judgment to see if the deceased was worthy of passing through."

Joe cleared his throat and pointed to the clock. Tennessee gave him a quizzical look, glanced at the clock and back to Joey. Joey pointed to his wrist and nodded to the class.

"Is it time already?" Tennessee heard the students in the back failing to stifle the sound of their packing up. He sighed. "I guess so." Students were almost magically already making their way through the door. "Finish reading Chapter Twelve for next time," he called after them, "We're talking about coffins and funerary boats!"

"**D**r. Phillips?" The middle-aged man at the door to Tennessee's office had hair almost as gray as his three-piece suit and tie. He looked like he had just stepped from a Victorian novel. He had the most impressive walrus mustache.

"People call me Tennessee, Frank." Tennessee held up the remains of his sandwich. "Wanna bite? It's really good. Came from that new joint out by the cemetery."

Dr. Frank Whitmer, chair of the history department, looked at the sandwich as if it had just fallen from Tennessee's trouser leg. Then looked at Tennessee perched atop his desk.

"No, Dr. Phillips, I would not…care for a bite of your sandwich."

"You don't know what you're missing." Tennessee put the rest of the sandwich in his mouth and began to chew.

"I'm quite sure I do."

Tennessee shrugged.

"I'm not here to discuss your questionable culinary tastes, Dr. Phillips."

"Tennessee."

"I'm here to…You're not wearing shoes." Dr. Whitmer looked across the room at Joe entering today's attendance into the computer. "Why is he not wearing shoes, Mr. Manton?"

Joe shrugged and continued typing.

Dr. Whitmer turned back to Tennessee. "Why don't you have shoes?"

Tennessee swallowed the last of his sandwich. "I have shoes, Frank. They're right over there." He nodded to his bookshelf where a pair of scuffed brown brogans sat on the third shelf between Gibbon and Lovejoy.

"Why aren't they on your feet?"

"I don't want them to scuff the desk."

Dr. Whitmer sighed. "You *could* try sitting behind it in the chair."

"I don't want to scuff the floors. Is there something I can help you with, O captain, my captain?"

Dr. Whitmer reached into his inner coat pocket and retrieved a small pink slip of paper. He handed it to Tennessee.

"You firing me, chief? I have tenure."

"It's a note." Dr. Whitmer placed it on the desk as far from Tennessee's offending toes as possible. "A man came asking for you, and Jenny told him you were in class."

Tennessee looked at the memo:

> Drs. Clarke Phillips & Savannah Ford
> 396 North Garrison Street, 7:00 PM

"Did he leave a name?"

"No, or else I'm sure Jenny would have noted it."

"What'd he look like?"

"I don't know," Dr. Whitmer sighed again. "He was…foreign."

"Well that narrows it down."

"I'm sorry Dr. Phillips, but I'm afraid my actual job requires me to spend my time running the department; I scarcely have time to be your secretary. Perhaps you should hire someone."

"Nah." Tennessee nodded at Joe. "Shorty does fine."

"I wish you wouldn't call me Shorty," Joe said after Dr. Whitmer left. "What's wrong with Shorty?" Tennessee hopped off his desk and handed the note to Joe. "Look at this."

"It's not my name for one, and I'm hardly short." Joe examined the memo and handed it back. "That's the Community Theatre."

"Any idea what's playing tonight?" Tennessee pulled his shoes from the bookshelf, then sat on the floor to put them on. "Shorty was the best research assistant in all of cinema history. You should be honored."

"Shorty," Joe said swiveling back to his monitor, brushing a stray lock of red hair from his eyes, and typing, "was a nine-year-old pickpocket and getaway driver."

"He also gathered a shit-ton of intelligence on the Chinese mob." Tennessee smiled. "Best. Research. Assistant. Ever." Tennessee emphasized each period with a tap on the floor then began lacing his shoes. "They should have used him in the fifth movie instead of that *Transformers* guy."

"On that we agree." Joe swiveled the computer screen to face Tennessee. "Some guy named Dacre Stoker is presenting on the dude who wrote *Dracula.*"

"Huh." Tennessee looked at the note again. "Wanna come with?"

"It clearly says you and Dr. Ford."

Tennessee shrugged. "Savvy's got the late shift at the hospital tonight."

I awoke in a void, unable to see, unable to hear. The first thing I remembered was darkness. Cool sterile air gently wafted around me. My arms and legs remained numb. [Where am I?] *My mouth refused to move. I tried to scream but heard only silence.*

II. A Little Knowledge

"As you know, Bram's Dracula was inspired at least in part by Vlad the Impaler, a Romanian warlord also known as Vlad Dracul." Dacre Stoker clicked to the next slide showing a painting of Vlad the Impaler staring into the audience with his dark eyes and hawk nose.

Tennessee leaned over to Joe. "That's an impressive mustache."

"In Bram's notes for the novel, he has even written the name 'Dracul' in the margins as you can see here." The next slide revealed a page of scribbles that Tennessee assumed could be considered handwriting if you squinted your eyes. The name, however, was clearly legible as Stoker claimed. The next slide revealed another painting of Vlad. "Vlad was even rumored to have many of Dracula's qualities: Though it was debunked later, some critics claimed he drank the blood of his enemies, for example. He could also, according to some reports, enthrall you to his will using only his gaze, though some stories link this mesmeric power to his bloodline."

"Seriously," Tennessee whispered, "looks like he should be stomping mushrooms in a Nintendo game."

"Interestingly enough," Stoker continued, "No one is really sure where Vlad's buried. We know his head was taken to Constantinople, but no one knows for sure where it is. And the rest of his body was thought to be taken back to Romania, but recently historians have found evidence that it may have been taken to Naples after his daughter ransomed it and was buried at the church of Santa Maria La Nova."

"You could scour a sink with that mustache."

"**D**r. Phillips I presume?"

The olive-skinned man in the dark suit and black surgical mask approached Tennessee and Joe during the intermission.

Tennessee eyed him smiling behind a gray neck gaiter. "People call me Tennessee."

The newcomer looked at Joe. "And this is…Dr. Ford?"

"No, no." Tennessee clapped Joe on the back. "Savvy couldn't make it. This is my assistant, Shorty."

"Joe," Joe said sticking out his hand.

The man merely nodded at Joe before turning to Tennessee. "My name is Dr. Belshazzar Farkus, professor of archeology at Pázmány Péter Catholic University."

"That's a mouthful. What can I do for you?"

"Perhaps, we can help each other" Dr. Farkus nodded toward the back of the hall. "If you will come with me." He began weaving between small groups of the audience standing several feet from each other. "You may come as well … Shorty, was it?"

"Joe."

Farkus led them to a small office. Inside was a desk with several manila folders and a stack of papers bound in twine. He moved behind the desk and motioned to two chairs across from him. Tennessee leaned against the wall while Joe took one of the seats.

"What do you know about Vlad Dracul?" Farkus asked.

"Vlad Tepes?" Tennessee shrugged "Fifteenth century Romanian warlord. Had an affinity for homemade lawn decorations and impressive facial hair."

"He was one of the inspirations for Bram Stoker's Dracula." Joe added. "Very charismatic. It was said he could control the minds of his followers with only his sheer willpower."

"All of this is true," Farkus waved his hand dismissively, "but there is much more to the story. Have you ever heard of John Hunyadi?"

"Sure," Tennessee replied. "He was the governor or king or grand poobah of Hungary about the same time. Killed Vlad's pop, right?"

"And his brother, yes." Farkus nodded. "Vlad allied with the Ottoman Turks to retake Wallachia."

"Southern part of Romania, Shorty." Tennessee murmured. "Right under Transylvania and Moldovia."

"I got it," Joe muttered back. "And my name is Joe."

Farkus sighed. "Suffice it to say that Vlad's enmity toward Hunyadi never faded, though he allied with him more often than not when it was militarily convenient. Both houses spent years exacting revenge on each other. You cannot imagine the bloodshed."

"Don't be so sure," Tennessee interjected. "I've seen all three *Godfather* films and most of Tarantino's stuff."

"After his death," Farkus continued, "Vlad was beheaded and his head was sent to the Ottoman Empire to prove his death."

"I thought the Ottomans were Vlad's allies," Joe interrupted.

"It was…complicated," Farkus shrugged. "Allies are rarely permanent in politics or war. Less so with Vlad. He had a tendency to play both sides against each other. Besides, Vlad was a devout Christian and spent more of his time allied with Hunyadi against the Ottoman Turks, than allied with the Turks against Hunyadi."

"Okay," Tennessee clapped his hands together. "So his head goes to the sultan or whatever. What happened to his body, and why should I care?"

"Officially, no one knows where his body wound up. Tradition has it buried in the Monastery of Snagov, but excavations have found nothing other than bones of horses. A more likely grave would be in the first church of the Comana Monastery, which Vlad founded and which is near the battlefield in which he died, but we have found no evidence of his burial there." Farkus nodded outside. "We suspect, however, that the writer out there is correct. Vlad's daughter received his remains and buried them in Naples."

"Who is 'We'?" Tennessee asked. "And you still haven't explained why I need to know any of this."

"We are the Farkus clan, direct descendants of Vlad's daughter, Maria Balsa, and it is our sworn duty to protect our noble ancestor from those who would besmirch his honor."

"Probably not too happy with that guy's uncle then." Tennessee nodded toward the door.

Farkus blinked. "We do not concern ourselves with folklore, Dr. Phillips."

"People call me Tennessee."

"What care we of werewolves or vampires or Frankenstein monsters?" Farkus shook his head. "Let the peasants hide from shadows. We have more…tangible worries. It would seem that the Hunyadis or the Turks desire to find our ancestor, for what we do not know. His head disappeared from the Ottoman Empire long ago, but we must find his body."

"Great." Tennessee pushed off from the wall and turned to the door. "I'm a historian. Tell me all about it when you do, and I'll be happy to write a paper on it."

"Your specialty is ancient burial customs, is it not?" Farkus stared Tennessee back from the door. "We need your help navigating the tombs and making sure all appropriate disinterment and reburial rites are followed."

"Why me? I am sure there are far more well-respected historians you could call on."

"Do not sell yourself short, Dr. Phillips, you are quite accomplished in your field, and you have one quality other more well-known specialists do not have."

"Yeah?" Tennessee chuckled. "What's that?"

"We desire to maintain a low profile," Farkus explained, "and you are a nobody."

"You sure know how to flatter a girl." Tennessee mumbled.

"We'll arrange a leave of absence with your department, pay your expenses, and give you $250,000 when you have completed your work."

"What time is our flight?"

"I don't know how long I'll be, Savvy." Tennessee shrugged and tossed a pair of boxer shorts in a suitcase on the bed. "They're paying me to find a centuries-old corpse, so however long that will take."

"I presume it'll take longer than a day. You may want to pack a few more of those." She brushed a strand of dark hair from her face and nodded to the dresser. "Another pair of pants and a shirt wouldn't be too extravagant either. Maybe some more socks."

"If you'd just come with me," Tennessee stretched his arms beseechingly, "I wouldn't have to worry about this. You could pack for both of us."

"Aren't you a bit modern to be relying on traditional sexism?"

"It's not sexist if it's ironic."

"It's not ironic."

"That's where my argument always falls apart. Nobody understands irony anymore." Tennessee shrugged and threw a few more t-shirts into the suitcase. "I blame Alanis Morissette. Look, if I agree to pack my own clothes, will you come with me?"

"You're already packing them, and I can't leave the hospital, and unless you've forgotten, there's a pandemic." She nodded to the television in the next room, which was discussing the latest death toll of the C-19 virus and announcing that HTG, some kind of pharmaceutical or chemical or weapons developer or something, was the latest company working to develop a vaccine.

"There's a pandemic in Italy, too."

"I'm needed here." Savvy sighed. "I have surgery in two days. Remember the conjoined twins? They won't separate themselves. Take Joe. He'll be more help to you anyway, and he could actually use the experience."

"He doesn't kiss as well as you do."

In the darkness I became aware of cool air brushing my face. I could hear muffled voices echoing hollowly around me but could make out no words, save that they spoke a foreign tongue.

[Who is there?] *I tried to yell.* [Show yourself and face my wrath!] *No words left my mouth, though I was aware of my mouth moving.*

III. The Burial Place

"**W**here is Dr. Ford?" At the airport, Dr. Farkus looked beyond Tennessee to see if she was, perhaps, coming up behind him.

"Can't come," Tennessee sighed. "Something about having to help heal the sick or something."

"That is," Farkus paused as if searching for the right word, "disappointing."

"You think you're disappointed? I'm stuck taking an all-expenses paid trip to Italy with Shorty here."

"My name is Joe."

"Doctors," Tennessee shrugged, "what can you do?"

"If it cannot be helped," Farkus said with a resigned shake of his head, "it cannot be helped. We make do with who we have."

"I'm right here," Joe muttered.

"Come," Farkus continued, "the plane is waiting for us."

Tennessee had never ridden on a private jet before, and this one, a Gulfstream GVI, was the height of luxury complete with a full bar, movie theater, and seats that converted to surprisingly comfortable sleeping berths. Tennessee felt like an underdressed James Bond entering the cabin, which was a shame, he later thought, since he spent almost the entire transatlantic flight asleep.

It was just as well that he did sleep, as once they landed in Naples, he and Joe were met by a limousine which took them directly to the Church of Santa Maria La Nova.

"What about our stuff?" Tennessee asked.

"It will be taken along to the hotel."

"I had hoped to change clothes and freshen up a bit before getting started."

Farkus cast a glance over Tennessee's Atlanta Braves baseball cap, faded jeans, gray t-shirt, and brogans. "You look fine. Time is pressing."

Tennessee sighed. "It's only these are my good brogans is all," he muttered.

"D amn." Tennessee whistled as he stepped out of the limo and saw the front entrance to the church and it's attached monastery. "I didn't expect it to look like every other church in Italy. Truly amazing."

Farkus ignored him.

"Won't the Vatican have a problem with us tromping around their church?" Joe asked.

"Yeah," Tennessee added, pulling his backpack from the trunk and slinging it over a shoulder. "I'm sure they're not too keen on us tapping walls and digging up dead Romanian warlords on their holy ground."

Farkus shrugged. "It has been deconsecrated."

"Probably a good idea since they have a vampire buried here." Tennessee murmured.

"Still," Joe continued, "Somebody owns the property. Won't they have a problem with us excavating?"

"The city uses the monastery for municipal offices now and generates money by offering tours of the church. We merely offered them a…" Farkus rubbed his thumb across his fingers. "rather sizable revenue. Come," he moved through the church doors, "The tomb we want is in the small cloister."

T he tomb was in the Cloister of St. Giacomo della Marca in one corner of the garden. It was marble and stood at least six feet in height. A bas-relief took up the side facing visitors depicting two sphinxes on either side of a knight's helmet and shield below a dragon. Extending from the sides of the helmet were several tentacles, four of which ended in tassels. Atop the tomb rested the figure of a man, unshaven and dressed as a knight.

"He looks smaller in person." Tennessee frowned. "I miss the mustache."

"That is, of course, a depiction of Matteo Ferrillo, Maria Balsa's father-in-law, who is supposed to be buried within."

"Of course." Tennessee nodded.

He set his pack down and moved to the bas-relief. And ran his fingers across the carvings. "Farkus," Tennessee's voice was all business now.

"Reckon you can round us up a stepladder or something? We're going to need to see the top."

"Certainly." Farkus left them alone in the cloister.

Joe joined Tennessee at the tomb. "What do you see?"

Tennessee tapped the dragon's head then tapped the helmet. "The knightly Order of the Dragon," he said. "Vlad Tepes' order. Romanian. Not likely something an Italian noble would join, but an order we know Vlad was the head of. Interestingly, his surname *Dracul* is Romanian for 'dragon.' Also," he pointed to the two sphinxes, "those represent the Egyptian city of Thebes."

"So?" Joe shrugged. "Vlad was Romanian. What's an Egyptian city have to do with anything?"

"The Egyptians would pronounce *th* as a hard *t* and *b* as a *p*."

"Tepes." Joe murmured.

Tennessee grabbed the top of the tomb, pulled himself up and straddled the carved figure of Mattia Ferrillo.

"I thought you sent Farkus to find a ladder."

"I just wanted him out of the way. I don't trust him."

"Why?"

"Later. Look at this."

Joe pulled himself up enough to see over the lip of the tomb.

"Put your hand here." Tennessee grabbed Joe's hand and placed it on the knight's chest.

"It's warm."

"It's warm," Tennessee nodded. "Much warmer than it should be in a shaded alcove. Now, hop down."

Tennessee climbed down after Joe and began examining the bas-relief again. He looked at the four tassels and traced a line below each one. Then he ran his fingers over the dragon's opened mouth, just below one of the tassels. Next he felt along the top of the left-hand sphinx in the vicinity of another tassel and the bottom of the right-hand one just above the third tassel. Finally, he ran his hand across the top of the bottom molding below the final tassel.

"Latches." He smiled at Joe then grabbed his hands putting one beneath the right-hand sphinx and the other on the molding. "Feel them?"

Joe nodded, and Tennessee placed his own hands inside the dragon's mouth and atop the left-hand sphinx. "Let's press them together."

The top of the tomb opened with a groan, and Tennessee grabbed his pack, then scrambled back up to peer in.

"Hey, Shorty?" He stuck his head further into the tomb. "Grab a flashlight and get up here. You ain't gonna believe this."

I do not know how long I listened to the voices before their gibberish became intelligible. Time had no meaning in this infinite darkness. I know only that gradually I understood the voices.

"Dr. Victor," said one, "has there been any change in the patient?"

"Minimal." Dr. Victor's voice seemed older than the other. "The EEG sometimes shows minimal electric activity, admittedly more than the none you'd expect from a specimen this old, and when this happens, the MEG shows an almost infinitesimal magnetic field."

"Both could," the first voice interrupted, "be due to equipment error."

Dr. Victor grunted in agreement.

"What about the Govi jar?" the first voice seemed closer now. "Any change?"

"He's still in there, Dr. Bert, if that's what you're asking." Dr. Victor's voice had a tinge of irritation.

"And when the instruments measure brain activity? Where is he then?"

"I'd not even thought to check."

"Do so next time." Dr. Bert sighed. "Have you fed him yet?"

"I was about to."

"I'll do it."

There was change in pressure and a faint light. Then warm liquid surrounded me, and I tasted copper.

IV. The Tomb

Joe clambered next to Tennessee and handed him an ancient floating lantern that looked like it had once worked the coal mines of West Virginia. Joe shrugged and shined the light into the tomb.

There was no body. It wasn't even a tomb. Instead, where the bottom should be, they saw a short platform with a stone ladder leading down into darkness. A dank smell of must and moisture rose from the stairwell. Tennessee climbed in and began testing the top stairs with his feet.

"You're not going down there?" Joe wrinkled his nose.

"Sure we are." Tennessee set the lantern down and helped him climb inside. He handed the lantern back as soon as Joe regained his feet.

"This thing made from an entire Buick?" Tennessee lifted the lantern with a grunt and handed it to Joe. "You're carrying it. Come on."

The ladder led to a stone tunnel about six feet high and five across. Something on the wall glittered in the lantern light, and Joe swung the beam to reveal a bronze plaque.

"That's not English," he said. "What is it? Greek?"

Tennessee leaned to see it better. "Close. It's Cyrillic." He ran his finger across the text, translating. "'Whosoever would meet the voivode must avoid his wrath,'" Tennessee moved his finger to the second line. "'and offer unto him his life.'"

"I don't like the sound of that." Joe shuddered.

Tennessee gave Joe a mirthless smile, "I'm sure it's fine. Nothing to do with us." He slapped Joe's shoulder and moved on down the tunnel. "Step carefully, though," he called over his shoulder, "you know, just in case."

"So why don't you trust Farkus?" They had been walking about five minutes, the silence driving Joe to speak.

"He's a liar," Tennessee shrugged. "By omission at the very least."

"How so?"

"He doesn't need me for this job. Any idiot who's ever watched an Indiana Jones film or read Allan Quatermain could do this. He needed me to get to Savvy."

Joe chuckled. "What the hell are you talking about?"

"He was too concerned with my bringing her. Did you see how disappointed he was that she didn't come with me to the Stoker presentation? Then when she didn't come with me to Italy, he looked like a teenage girl stood up for the prom. No, he wanted Savvy, not me."

"But why?"

"What would he want with an accomplished neurosurgeon on a quest for Vlad the Impaler? No idea. But he damn sure…didn't…need…" Tennessee's voice faded, "…me. Shine the light over here." He indicated one of the cobblestones on the floor. Joe shifted the beam and Tennessee dropped to his knees placing his right eye even with the floor.

Joe bent over keeping the light on the tile in question. "What is it?"

"This one's higher than the others." Tennessee ran his finger lightly against the side. "See?" He looked just past the stone and pointed. "About three stones forward and to the left. See the other one?" He pointed further along the passageway. "Another one there."

"They seem random," Joe added. "No real pattern to them. And look at this." He shown his light between the first and second stones then swung further up the passageway to the left. In each place, at the corner where the stones met was an opening that was slightly larger than the other corners in the path. "What do you make of that?"

Tennessee looked up at Joe then shook his head. "You really need to watch more movies, kid. That or play more D&D. Stand back." He pressed the cobblestone, and nothing happened.

"Huh." Tennessee sat back and rubbed his chin. "I really thought it was some sort of..." Half a dozen meter-long iron spikes shot out of the floor. "Never mind."

"What the hell?" Joe's voice broke a bit.

"'Whosoever would meet the voivode must avoid his wrath.'" Tennessee rose. "What do you think Vlad the Impaler did with his enemies?"

Joe ran his hand over the nearest spike and winced as it drew blood. "Still sharp as a razor."

"I don't imagine they've had use enough to dull them." Tennessee pulled a roll of bandages from a side pocket of his pack and handed it to Joe. "Wrap your hand, and let's move on." He readjusted his pack and began weaving through the spikes. "Watch your step there, Shorty. All the spikes may not have been triggered."

A few yards further on, the corridor turned to the east and widened into a chamber with an ornate door on the other side behind an ornate altar. Tennessee tried the door. The latch didn't move. He turned to the altar.

A deep golden bowl sat in the center. It looked very much like a goblet without its stem.

"What's that?" Joe asked.

"It's a crucible." Tennessee tried to lift it, but it wouldn't budge. Grabbing the lantern from Joe, he examined the inside. "There's a hole in the bottom."

Joe leaned in, motioning for Tennessee to angle the light differently.

Sure enough, light seemed to reflect through the hole and off the walls of a kind of pipe or tubing. "Looks like it goes all the way through the altar itself." He muttered. "What are we supposed to do with this?"

"Your parents really did you a disservice, Shorty." Tennessee shook his head. "Did you read no horror as a kid? Surely you've read *Dracula*."

"When you've lived in Arkham long enough," Joe replied, "you'll understand why we prefer romantic comedies and sitcoms."

Tennessee sighed. "'Whosoever would meet the voivode must offer unto him his life.'" Tennessee gestured to the chalice. "Had you read *Dracula*, you'd know that blood is the life. Fortunately," he took Joe's hand and unwrapped the bandage, "you came prepared."

With a resigned sigh, Joe held his hand over the bowl and let blood drip in. First a few drops fell, then Joe tensed as the drops became a trickle. Then a stream.

"That should be enough," Tennessee looked into the bowl, but nothing seemed to change as the blood went straight down the drain without touching the sides. "Save yourself enough to get back."

"I can't move," Joe's voice seemed strained, and the trickle of blood became a stream. "Feels like something is sucking it straight from the hand."

Tennessee looked at Joe's stricken face then tackled him, grabbing the younger man by his midriff and shoving him to the floor. He then took the bandage from Joe and began re-wrapping the wound. The two men sat with their backs against the door catching their breath.

"I better get an A from this," Joe wheezed.

"At least a B plus," Tennessee spoke between breaths. "We still have to get back home."

Behind them they heard a click, and the door they leaned against slowly opened under their weight. Tennessee rose and offered Joe his hand, helping him up. He swung the light into the newly opened chamber. The room was small, only about ten feet deep and the same across. The walls appeared to be the same stone as the rest of the catacomb, but the air was cool and dry.

At the center of the room lay a stone coffin.

"I guess this is the place," Tennessee stepped into the room with Joe following. They moved to either end of the coffin, Joe feeling the edge of the lid.

"There's a latch here," he dug his fingers under the lid and squeezed. They heard a click that seemed to echo throughout the catacomb, but the lid didn't budge. "See if there's one on your end?"

Tennessee nodded, set the lantern down. and felt under his end of the lid. He smiled at Joe as another click sounded and the lid rose as pressure was released from within. Tennessee and Joe gently removed the lid and set it aside.

"What is that smell?" Tennessee pulled his t-shirt over his nose to mute the earthy-sulfur smell coming from within.

Joe retrieved the lantern and shone the light on the interior. It was filled with a brownish green spongy substance. "It's peat moss."

"Like the stuff they found all those ancient Irishmen in a few years ago?"

Joe nodded. "I have no idea where this came from." He gestured to the coffin. "As far as I know there aren't any peat bogs this far south."

"If I had to guess," Tennessee slung his pack on the floor and began rummaging inside, "I'd say Romania. There's at least one bog there I know of, the Mohos."

"Why Romania?"

"You really should read *Dracula*, kid." Tennessee pulled out a roll of sheet plastic and spread it across the floor. "Native soil. It's pretty important to vampires." He moved back to the coffin and began digging in the moss. "I think I found his feet," Tennessee tried to speak without inhaling and was only moderately successful.

Joe moved to the other end and began digging. "But this isn't a vampire." He grabbed something and lifted. The upper torso of a headless body emerged from the moss. "It's just a corpse."

Tennessee lifted the body's feet from the moss and together they carried it to the plastic and began rolling it up. "Legends have to start somewhere."

"Quite right, Dr. Phillips." The voice came from behind them. Dr. Farkus stood inside the door to the chamber flanked by four very large men. He nodded, and the men entered the chamber. Two of the men lifted the plastic wrapped corpse and carried it from the chamber. The other two moved to stand behind Tennessee and Joe. "I want to thank you both for helping us retrieve the voivode, but," Farkus nodded at the two men behind them, "I still require one more service from each of you."

Tennessee had always hated when, in novels, a narrator described the protagonist being knocked unconscious as "everything went black," so he was particularly annoyed when this is exactly what happened.

I could feel my extremities. Cold metal beneath my back and legs and arms. The world was still dark, but cool air washed over my whole body now, not just on my face. Something had changed.

"Is this the donor?" Dr. Victor's voice was tinged with doubt.

"His blood has already interacted with the patient's, so yes." Dr. Bert sounded irritable. "How did the reattachment go?"

"As well as can be expected given the rate of decay."

"The body was almost perfectly preserved." Dr. Bert's voice was closer, something brushed across my left hand, squeezed the meat between my thumb and forefinger. "The flesh is quite pliable."

"Well," Dr. Victor sounded as if he stood above me. Pressure on my cheeks. "A pity the head wasn't stuck in mud for centuries. It's practically desiccated."

"The transfusion should fix all that."

"Has the specialist arrived?"

"Soon. I believe they are taking her from the airport as we speak." Dr. Bert's voice moved further away. I heard the sound of ceramic touching metal. "Lunch time, Vlad."

I tasted copper.

V. In the Castle of the Devil

Tennessee found himself in a small room. He was lying on a cot bolted directly into the rear stone wall. Across from him was a heavy wooden door with a little iron grate about head high. He sat up, placed his feet on the stone floor. And ran his hand through his hair. The room was dimly lit by a gas lamp suspended from the ceiling. He saw his phone placed on a small writing table along the right-hand wall and a slops bucket placed in the corner of the left and far walls.

Besides his phone, the only sign that he was, in fact, in the twenty-first century was flat-screen monitor attached to the left-hand wall and a security camera mounted at the top of the left-hand corner of the front wall. Pressing his fists into the small of his back, he stretched, twisting his neck to the left and right with an audible crack.

The door, he discovered on inspection, used an old mortise lock. Putting his eye to the keyhole, he was able to see through to the hallway beyond. He stood up and looked through the grate.

"Anybody there?" he called, futilely trying the door. "I seem to have gotten myself stuck in here."

No answer.

He banged on the door with his fist. "Hello?" He looked back at the camera. A red light flickered underneath beneath the lens.

"Ah, Dr. Phillips." The light changed in his cell. Tennessee turned to find Dr. Farkus staring at him from the monitor "You're awake."

"Where am I?"

"Are you familiar with the Princely Palace of Bucharest?"

"Sure," Tennessee turned from the monitor and moved to the writing table. "Vlad Tepes' place, yeah?"

"Indeed." Farkus nodded. "I did not think you were familiar with Vlad's history, yet at every turn you have impressed me."

"Mama told me it was impolite to brag." There were two drawers beneath the tabletop. He opened them both, finding a stack of lined paper in one.

"You are in its dungeon."

Tennessee turned to face the monitor again. "So why am I here? I got you the body you needed. This is a hell of a way to say thank you."

"Make no mistake, Dr. Phillips," Farkus chuckled. "While your help retrieving Vlad's body is appreciated, it was never what we needed you for."

"I told Shorty that." Tennessee shrugged. "I am at a loss as to what you did need me for, though."

"Why, insurance, of course," Farkus spoke as if this were self-evident. "We will set you free as soon as your girlfriend has completed her task to our satisfaction."

"Savvy?" Tennessee felt his face pale. "She's here? How? What do you want with her?"

"Sit tight, Dr. Phillips, I will send someone for you directly and your questions will be answered." The screen went dark.

A few minutes later, Tennessee heard footsteps in the hall, and one of the large men from the catacombs unlocked the door.

"Oh, good," Tennessee muttered, pocketing his phone, "it's Conan the Hungarian." The man made no reply other than to motion for Tennessee to follow him.

Conan led Tennessee through a series of stone corridors lit by gaslight, but monitored by oscillating cameras mounted over the hallway junctions. Tennessee wished he had breadcrumbs to drop, but instead he counted corridors and memorized the turns. Finally, they arrived at a metal door with a small, eye-level window and a keypad lock. Conan punched in a number, and the door swung slowly open on a room that seemed equal parts a mad scientist's laboratory and state of the art operating theater.

In the center of the room were two parallel surgical tables supporting blanketed bodies connected by tubing. At the head of each table stood a man in a white lab coat. The younger of the two, was a gangly, bespectacled blonde man in his early to mid-forties. The older appeared to be in his seventies.

Savvy stood between the tables checking the pulse of what looked like a mummified arm sticking out from the left-hand blanket. When she saw Tennessee, her mouth fell open and she dropped the arm. "Tennessee," she gasped. "You're okay?" Then she ran to him, throwing her arms around him.

"Savvy," Tennessee asked as she leaned back from him and hooked her hands into his jean pockets, "what's going on here?"

"History, Dr. Phillips." The voice came from the other side of the room, behind Savvy. Tennessee looked past his girlfriend to see Dr. Farkus with a rictus grin, one hand caressing a primitive looking clay jar on a table. "You are in the presence of history," he continued, "and the future."

"You do realize that doesn't sound nearly as calming as you'd think, right?" There was a television playing silently on the back wall showing scenes of pandemic victims being wheeled into mobile morgues followed by a political rally in Middle America.

Farkus chuckled. "Dr. Ford here and your little assistant are helping Drs. Bert and Victor," he nodded to the two other men in the room, "bring about the end of disease and world strife."

"Yeah," Tennessee shrugged as Savvy pulled her hands from his pockets, "still not feeling any more sanguine about this."

"There are those who believe," Farkus continued, "that *Dracula* borrowed much more from Vlad Tepes than simply his name, that like his literary counterpart, Vlad was, for all intents and purposes immortal."

"I just pulled a headless body from a crypt that would seem to argue otherwise."

"On the contrary, if these believers are correct, Vlad was beheaded because nothing else would kill him." Farkus' grin widened. "Injuries healed too quickly, poison ran through him like water. All because his blood was strong enough to fight off anything but decapitation." He looked at Savvy as he moved from the clay urn to the surgical tables. "Dr. Ford, would you be so kind as to show our guest what we are working on?"

Savvy patted Tennessee's thighs just above his pockets and kissed him. "It's up to you to get us out of this," she whispered before returning to the covered bodies. She grasped the blanket of the left table and pulled it back.

"What in the Hammer Horror hell?" Tennessee found himself staring at a mustachioed desiccated head surgically stitched to the mummified body Tennessee had last seen emerging from peat moss in the crypt.

"The subject shows every sign of revivification. He even has a slight pulse." The younger doctor, Dr. Bert, spoke with a New England twang.

Tennessee stared incredulously at the body. "How?"

"The reanimation process is quite simple, actually, assuming you can obtain the correct substances for the serum." He shrugged. "Ordinarily, I require a fresh body, but this one is preserved surprisingly well, and the head was intact enough that Drs. Victor and Ford were able to reattach it."

"The blood transfusion," The older doctor interrupted. He sounded as if he were from Germany or Austria, "should help immensely with rehydrating the head."

Tennessee stared from one man to the other. He had apparently forgotten how to close his mouth. "To what conceivable end?"

"As I said," Farkus answered. "We are going to save the world, from disease and heathenry."

Tennessee blinked and noticed the clay pot Farkus had been caressing. "Is that a canopic jar?"

"For loas, yes."

Tennessee stared at the jar in disbelief. "And who do you think you have there?"

"An old friend, Dr. Farkus. The founder of our organization in fact."

"Who even are you people?"

Farkus chuckled: "You know of HTG, yes?"

"Sure." Tennessee answered, staring at the thing on the table. "They're a pharmaceutical company, like Pfizer, right?"

"Among other things, yes." Farkus smiled. "The Hunyadi Tepes Group also dabbles in traditional and chemical weapons as well as global government consulting. We are quite diversified."

"They've been working on a virus vaccine," Savvy said as she lifted the second blanket and began checking the pulse on what appeared to be the arm of a young male. "It's been on the news."

"Indeed," Farkus gestured to Vlad's body, "and the blood of our voivode here is going to provide us the key to a cure and so much more. The world lacks cohesion, you see. It must be unified under a single rule, and we have the means to do that here. Once we have injected our vaccine, made from Vlad Tepes' blood, we can control the masses through the power of suggestion, mesmerism."

"That's insane." Tennessee chuckled. "You know that's crazy, right?"

"Time will tell," Farkus shrugged. "Once we have the Western world under our influence, we can turn them to humanity's true enemy. We can finish the work Vlad started and erase heathenry from the planet."

"Heathenry?" Tennessee watched as Savvy rechecked the pulse on the younger arm then turned to Vlad's and checked his.

"The Muslim, the pagan, the atheist, the Jew." Farkus counted on his fingers. "The world will not know true peace until we have used the blood of the voivode to ensure the survival of the only true religion."

Dr. Bert nudged Savvy out of the way, turned the blanket down again and checked Vlad's pulse at his neck. The face, Tennessee noted did look significantly less withered. Savvy turned back to the other patient.

"So your plan is to turn the Western world into an army of mindless zombies?" Tennessee shook his head. "Even if the vaccine works as you claim, half of America think they're microchipping the vaccine to control them. They'll never take it."

"But don't you see?" Farkus guffawed. "Anyone gullible enough to believe the government is microchipping them doesn't need to take the vaccine. They can already be controlled."

"Why are you telling me this?" There was something familiar to Tennessee about the arm Savvy was holding. "What's to stop me from telling?"

"Nothing." Farkus stated. "Tell me, Dr. Phillips, what is your honest opinion of those who claim there's a microchip in the vaccine?"

Tennessee said nothing.

"Indeed." Farkus smiled. "Go ahead. Tell anyone you want."

By this time, Dr. Victor had moved to the younger patient's table opposite Savvy. He lifted the blanket, blocking Tennessee's view of the face. "The pulse of der Junge is quite thready, Herr Farkus."

Savvy dropped the arm and ran to grab the defibrillator from the wall.

"Vlad's pulse is much stronger. We did it!" Dr. Bert's voice cracked with excitement. "He's alive!"

"He's dead!" Savvy yelled as she ripped the blanket from the other patient and began charging the defibrillator.

Tennessee tried to scream when he saw the lifeless body of Joseph Armitage Manton lying on the table, but he found his throat quite unable to make a sound.

I woke in darkness again. I heard muffled voices alternately arguing and laughing but could make out few of the words. A man yelled a name. Joe? Shorty? Perhaps he was yelling to two people. Perhaps they were Bert and Victor's Christian names.

"Herr Gølstrup, please take Dr. Phillips back to his cell." This new voice was vaguely familiar. "We cannot work with his racket."

I gradually grew aware of a low-pitched thumping as the shouting seemed to grow further away. I felt warm and aware of my limbs.

Steady thumping moved me along and I felt…different. Aware of my arms and my legs but also different, like someone was standing right behind me, staring.

[Who the fuck are you?]

Was that me? Did I ask that?

[And where in the seven hells am I?]

VI. Worse Things Waiting

Back in his cell, Tennessee reached into his pockets. Savvy had slipped him two hair pins.

"That's my girl." He opened the writing table drawer and removed several sheets of paper, folding them and shoving them into his hip pocket. The camera appeared dormant, no light beneath the lens. Tennessee reached up to adjust a valve on the gas lamp then approached the door, just out of the camera's line of sight, and sank to his knees.

Removing the bobby pins, he bent one into a corner, and spread the other out before inserting them into the lock and working the tumblers. After two minutes, he felt a satisfying click as the last tumbler fell into place.

"Getting rusty." Turning the lock slowly, he inched the door open and glanced both ways down the empty hall. Timing his escape around the rotating cameras, Tennessee scurried down the hall, remaining low and ducking into open cells to avoid cameras and adjust the lamps.

When he reached the metal door, Tennessee glanced into the window. Savvy was alone, sitting by Joe's table with her head in her hands. The air at this level smelled faintly of methane as Tennessee crouched down and punched in the door code: 031537.

"Savvy," Tennessee spoke low but Savvy looked up. Her eyes were red. "We gotta split, dollbaby."

"What about Joe?"

Tennessee looked at Joe's body on the table. Someone had replaced the blanket over his face and tucked his arm back under it. "Is he…?"

"He's dead, Tennessee," Savvy's voice broke again. "I couldn't save him. He just," she shrugged, "went."

We gotta leave him, darlin'." Tennessee hated himself for saying it. "We can't carry him and get out of here safely." He looked at the other body. Vlad had been strapped down despite his body seeming to shrink into itself.

Savvy saw Tennessee's glance. "He seems to be deteriorating. I don't know what happened there either. His pulse was strong and steady one minute and the next, nothing." She rose from her chair and kissed the blanket over Joe's forehead.

Tennessee stepped into the lab and grabbed a flask and pushed a bottle of alcohol into his other hip pocket with a sigh. "I am really going to miss my backpack." Savvy joined him at the door. "You know the way out?"

Savvy nodded. The television screen on the back wall was still on. Tennessee saw the president waving his hands and yelling at a crowd of supporters.

"Lead on." Tennessee took a spark-lighter from the counter and gestured toward the door, sniffing the air seeping into the lab. "And stay low."

They continued down the halls, crouching low, Savvy leading and Tennessee indicating when to duck into an empty room. In each room, Tennessee adjusted the light valves until a steady hiss could be heard.

"Take a right at the next junction," Savvy whispered as they moved back into the hall. "There's a stairwell at the end leading to a tunnel that ends in a garden house outside of town."

Tennessee nodded and moved to the lead, pausing at the stairwell and motioning Savvy back into a room.

"People ahead," he explained as he joined her behind the door. He pulled the alcohol and papers from his hip pockets. Taking the flask, he poured alcohol to the halfway mark then stuffed several sheets of paper in the neck, allowing them to soak up the liquid. "We're going to need a distraction."

Tennessee flicked the spark lighter over the paper before tossing it down the hall. The air in the hall erupted in flames. An alarm blared, and they heard startled yells with the stomping of running feet up the stairs and past the door.

"Drop to the floor!" someone yelled. "Get to the lab before Farkus kills us all!"

Tennessee and Savvy counted to fifty before slowly making their way out of the room. Above them, the air glowed with yellow flames as they reached the stairs. At the first landing, they were able to stand. They encountered no one else as they made their way to the tunnel and found their path to freedom.

I looked around at the destruction and carnage surrounding me. Several large men in dark suits lay strewn about the floor like discarded scarecrows. I looked down at my bloodstained hands and stretched the fingers, then curled them into fists.

The air smelled of smoke, and I could still hear an annoying ringing coming from outside the laboratory. Most of the flames, however, had been doused by streams of water from the piping in the ceiling.

[Will somebody tell me what in God's name is going on?]

"Go to sleep." I told the voice in my head. "And do not blaspheme." The voice fell silent.

A picture on the wall attracted my attention. It seemed so realistic and appeared to move magically. A large man in a red hat gesticulated at a crowd of minions. I recognized his intent and immediately understood his failure: He was too concerned with how the minions viewed him instead of how the world viewed his minions.

The picture changed to an image of white uniformed soldiers moving shrouded bodies into metallic wagons. Then a man in gray clothing speaking to me, but I could not make out his words. Next there was an image of villagers pillaging a town that could be in my own Wallachia except the villagers wore strange clothing.

Buildings exploding and men, women, and children running from soldiers took over the picture before something else grabbed my eye.

A polished silver tray leaning against the wall reflected my image. I looked nothing like I expected, significantly younger and with red hair hanging in my eyes.

I smiled at my reflection before turning back to the magical picture.

"I can work with this."

Drawing In

RAMSEY CAMPBELL

No wonder the rent was so low. There were cracks everywhere; new ones had broken out during the night—one passed above the foot of his bed, through the elaborate moulding, then trailed towards the parquet floor. Still, the house didn't matter; Thorpe hadn't come here for the house.

He parted the curtains. Act one, scene three. Mist lingered; the lake was overlapped by a ghost of itself. Growing sunlight renewed colours from the mist: the green fur of the hills, the green spikes of pines. All this was free. He'd little reason to complain.

As always when he emerged from his room, the height of the ceiling made him glance up. Above the stairs, another new crack had etched the plaster. Suppose the house fell on him while he was asleep? Hardly likely—the place looked far too solid.

He hesitated, staring at the ajar door. Should he give in to curiosity? It wasn't as simple as that: he'd come here to recuperate. He could scarcely do so if curiosity kept him awake. Last night he'd lain awake for hours wondering. Feeling rather like a small boy who'd crept into this deserted house for a dare, he pushed open the door.

The room was smaller than his, and darker—though perhaps all that was because of the cabinets, high as the ceiling and black as drowned timber, that occupied all the walls. The cabinets were padlocked shut, save one whose broken padlock dangled from the half-open door. Beyond the door was darkness, dimly crowded. Speculations on the nature of that crowding had troubled his sleep.

He ventured forward. Again, as the cabinet loured over him, he felt like a small boy. Ignoring doubts, he tugged the door wide. The padlock fell, loud in the echoing room—and from high in the cabinet, dislodged objects toppled. Some opened as they fell, and their contents scuttled over him.

The containers rattled on the parquet as he flinched back. They resembled pillboxes of transparent plastic. They were inscribed in a spidery handwriting, which seemed entirely appropriate, for each had contained a spider. A couple of dark furry blotches clung with long legs to his sleeve. He picked them off, shuddering. He couldn't rid himself of an insidious suspicion that some of the creatures were not quite dead.

He peered reluctantly at them. Bright pinheads of eyes peered back, dead as metal; beside them palpi bristled. The lifeless fur felt unpleasantly cold on his palm. Eventually he'd filled all the containers, God only knew how correctly. If he were an audience watching himself, this would be an enjoyable farce. As he replaced the boxes on the high shelf, he noticed a padlocked container, large as a hatbox, lurking at the back of the cabinet. Let it stay there. He'd had enough surprises for one day.

Besides, he must report the cracks. Eventually the bus arrived, laden with climbers. Some of their rucksacks occupied almost as much space as they did. Camps smoked below the hills.

Outside the estate agent's office, cows plodded to market. The agent listened to the tale of the cracks. "You surprise me. I'll look in tomorrow." His fingertips brushed his hair gently, abstractedly. He glanced up as Thorpe hesitated. "Something else?"

"The owner of the house—what line is he in?"

"Anarach—narach—" The agent shook his head irritably to clear it of the blockage. "*An* arachnologist," he pronounced at last.

"I thought it must be something of the kind. I looked in one of the cabinets—the one with the broken lock."

"Ah yes, his bloodsuckers. That's what he likes to call them. All these writers are eccentric in some way, I suppose. I should have asked you not to touch anything," he said reprovingly.

Thorpe had been glad to confess, but felt embarrassed now. "Well, perhaps no harm's done," the agent said. "He went to Eastern Europe six months ago, in search of some rarity—having fixed the amount of the rent."

Was that comment a kind of reproof? It sounded wistful. But the agent stood up smiling. "Anyway, you look better for the country," he said. "You've much more colour now."

And indeed Thorpe felt better. He was at his ease in the narrow streets; he was able to make his way between cars without flinching—without feeling jagged metal bite into him, the windscreen shatter into his face. The scars of his stitches no longer plucked at his cheeks. He walked part of the way back to the house, until weakness overtook him.

He sat gazing into the lake. Fragmented reflections of pines wavered delicately. When mist began to descend the hills he headed back, in time to glimpse a group of hikers admiring the house. Pleased, he scanned it himself. Mist had settled on the chimney stacks. The five squat horned blurs looked as though they were playing a secret game, trying to hide behind one another. One, the odd man out, lacked horns.

After dinner Thorpe strolled through the house, sipping malt whisky. Rooms resounded around him. They sounded like an empty stage, where he was playing owner of the house. He strode up the wide stairs, beneath the long straight crack, and halted outside the door next to his.

He wouldn't be able to sleep unless he looked. Besides, he had found the agent's disapproval faintly annoying. If Thorpe wasn't meant to look in the cabinets, why hadn't he been told? Why had one been left ajar?

He strode in, among the crowd of dark high doors. This time, as he opened the cabinet he made sure the padlock didn't slip from its hold. Piled shelves loomed above him as he stooped into the dimness, to peer at the hatbox or whatever it was.

It wasn't locked. It had been, but its fastening was split: a broken padlock lay on top. On the lid, wisps of handwriting spelled *Carps: Trans: C. D.* The obscure inscription was dated three months ago.

Thorpe frowned. Then, standing back, he poked gingerly at the lid with his foot. As he did so, he heard a shifting. It was the padlock, which landed with a thud on the bottom of the cabinet. Unburdened, the lid sprang up at once. Within was nothing but a crack in the metal of the container. He closed the cabinet and then the room, wondering why the metal box appeared to have been forced open.

And why was the date on the lid so recent? Was the man so eccentric that he could make such a mistake? Thorpe lay pondering that and the inscription. Half-dozing, he heard movement in one of the rooms: a trapped bird scrabbling in a chimney? It troubled him almost enough to make him search. But the whisky crept up on him, and he drifted with his thoughts.

How did the arachnologist bring his prizes home—in his pocket, or stowed away with the rest of the livestock on the voyage? Thorpe stood on a dockside, awaiting a package that was being lowered on a rope. Or was it a rope? No, for as it swung close the package unclenched and grabbed him. As its jaws closed on his face he awoke gasping.

In the morning he searched the house, but the bird seemed to have managed to fly. The cracks had multiplied; there was at least one in every room, and two now above the stairs. The scattering of plaster on the staircase looked oddly like earth.

When he heard the agent's car he buttoned his jacket and gave his hair a rapid severe brushing. Damn it, the bird was still trapped; he heard it stir behind him, though there was no hint of it in the mirror. It must be in the chimney, for it sounded far too large to be otherwise invisible.

The agent scrutinised the rooms. Was he looking only for cracks, or for evidence that Thorpe had been peeking? "This is most unexpected," he said as though Thorpe might be responsible. "I don't see how it can be subsidence. I'll have it looked at, though I don't think it's anything serious."

He was dawdling in Thorpe's room, perhaps to reassure himself that Thorpe had done it no injury. "Ah, here he is," he said without warning, and stooped to grope beneath the bed. Who had been skulking there while Thorpe was asleep? The owner of the house, it seemed—or at least a photograph of him, which the agent propped curtly on the bedside table, to supervise the room.

When the agent had left, Thorpe peered up the chimneys. Their furred throats looked empty, but were very dark. The flickering beam of the flashlight he'd found groped upwards. A soft dark mass plummeted towards him. It missed him, and proved to be a fall of soot, but was discouraging enough. In any case, if the bird was still up there, it was silent now.

He confronted the photograph. So that was what an arachnologist looked like: a clump of hair, a glazed expression, an attempt at a beard—the man seemed hypnotised, but no doubt was preoccupied. Thorpe found his dusty presence disconcerting.

Why stand here challenging the photograph? He felt healthy enough to make a circuit of the lake. As he strolled, the inverted landscape drifted with him. He could feel his strength returning, as though he were absorbing it from the hills. For the first time since he left the hospital, his hands looked enlivened by blood.

From the far end of the lake he admired the house. Its inverted chimneys swayed, rooted deep in the water. Suddenly he frowned and squinted. It must be an effect of the distance, that was all—but he kept glancing at the house as he returned along the lakeside. Once he was past the lake he had no chance to doubt. There were only four chimney stacks.

It must have been yesterday's mist that had produced the appearance of a fifth stack, lurking. Nevertheless, it was odd. Doubts clung to his mind as he climbed the stairs, until his start of surprise demolished his thoughts. The glass of the photograph was cracked from top to bottom.

He refused to be blamed for that. The agent ought to have left it alone. He laid it carefully on its back on the bedside table. Its crack had made him obsessively aware of the others; some, he was sure, were new—including one in a downstairs window, a crack which, curiously, failed to pass right through the thickness of the pane. The staircase was sprinkled again; the scattering not only looked like, but seemed to smell like, earth. That night, as he lay in bed, he thought he heard dust whispering down from the cracks.

Though he ridiculed thoughts that the house was unsafe, he felt vulnerable. The shifting shadow of a branch looked like a new crack, digging into the wall. In turn, that made the entire room appear to shift. Whenever he woke from fitful dozing, he seemed to glimpse a stealthy movement of the substance of the room. It must be an optical effect, but it reminded him of the way a quivering ornament might betray the presence of an intruder.

Once he awoke, shocked by an image of a tufted face that peered upside down through the window. It infuriated him to have to sit up to make sure the window was blank. Its shutter of night was not reassuring. His subconscious must have borrowed the image of the inversion from the lake, that was all. But the room seemed to be trembling, as he was.

Next day he waited impatiently for the surveyor, or whoever the agent was sending. He rapidly grew irritable. Though it could be nothing but a hangover from his insomnia, to stay in the house made him nervous. Whenever he glanced in a mirror, he felt he was being invisibly watched. The dark fireplaces looked ominous, prosceniums awaiting a cue. At intervals he heard a pattering in other rooms: not of tiny feet, but of the fall of debris from new cracks.

Why was he waiting? He hadn't felt so nervously aimless since the infancy of his career, when he'd loitered, clinging to a single line, in the wings of a provincial theatre. The agent should have given his man a key to let himself in; if he hadn't, that was his problem. Thorpe strode over the slopes that surrounded the lake. He enjoyed the intricately true reflections in the still water, and felt a great deal healthier.

Had the man let himself in? Thorpe seemed to glimpse a face, groping into view at a twilit window. But the only sound in the house was a feeble scraping, which he was unable to locate. The face must have been a fragment of his dream, tangled in his lingering insomnia. His imagination, robbed of sleep, was everywhere now. As he climbed the stairs, he thought a face was spying on him from a dark corner of the ceiling.

When he descended, fallen debris crunched underfoot. During his meal he drank a bottle of wine, as much for distraction as for pleasure. Afterwards he surveyed the house. Yes, the cracks were more numerous; there was one in every surface now, except the floors. Had the older cracks deepened? Somehow he was most disturbed by the dust beneath the cracked windows. It looked like earth, not like pulverised glass at all.

He wished he'd gone into town to stay the night. It was too late now— indeed, the last bus had gone by the time he returned to the house. He was too tired to walk. He certainly couldn't sit outside all night with the mists. It was absurd to think of any other course than going to bed, to try and sleep. But he drained the bottle of whisky before doing so.

He lay listening. Yes, the trapped bird was still there. It sounded even feebler now; it must be dying. If he searched for it he would lose his chance of sleep. Besides, he knew already that he couldn't locate it. Its sounds were so weak that they seemed to shift impossibly, to be fumbling within the fabric of the walls.

He was determined to keep his eyes closed, for the dim room appeared to be jerking. Perhaps this was a delayed effect of his accident. He let his mind drift him out of the room, into memories: the wavering of trees and of their reflections, the comedy sketch of his encounter with the piled cabinet, Carps, Trans.

Darkness gathered like soot on his eyes. A dark mass sank towards him, or he was sinking into dark. He was underground. Around him, unlit corridors dripped sharply. The beam of his flashlight explored the figure that lay before him on dank stone. The figure was pale as a spider's cocoon. As the light fastened on it, it scuttled apart.

When he awoke, he was crying out not at the dream but at his stealthy realisation. He'd solved the inscription in his sleep, at least in part. Eastern Europe was the key. Carps meant Carpathians, Trans was Transylvania. But C. D.—no, what he was thinking was just a bad joke. He refused to take it seriously.

Nevertheless, it had settled heavily on his mind. Good God, he'd once had to keep a straight face throughout a version of the play, squashed into a provincial stage: the walls of Castle Dracula had quaked whenever anyone had opened a door, the rubber bat had plummeted into the stalls. C. D. could mean anything—anything except that. Wouldn't it be hilarious if that was what the bemused old spider-man had meant? But in the dark it seemed less than hilarious, for near him in the room, something was stirring.

He groped for the cord of the bedside lamp. It was long and furry, and seemed unexpectedly fat. When he pulled it the light went on, and he saw at once that the cracks were deeper; he had been hearing the fall of debris. Whether the walls had begun to jerk rhythmically, or whether that was a delayed symptom of his accident, he had no time to judge. He must get out while he had the chance. He swung his feet to the floor, and knocked the photograph from the table.

Too bad, never mind, come on! But the shock of its fall delayed him. He glanced at the photograph, which had fallen upside down. The inverted tufted face stared up at him.

All right, it was the face he had dreamed in the window; why shouldn't it be? Just let him drag clothes over his pyjamas—he'd spend the night outside if need be. Quickly, quickly—he thought he could hear the room twitching. The twitches reminded him not of the stirring of ornaments, but of something else: something of which he was terrified to think.

As he stamped his way into his trousers, refusing to think, he saw that now there were cracks in the floor. Perhaps worse, all the cracks in the room had joined together. He froze, appalled, and heard the scuttling.

What frightened him most was not how large it sounded, but the fact that it seemed not to be approaching over floors. Somehow he had the impression that it hardly inhabited the space of the house. Around him the cracks stood out from their surfaces. They looked too solid for cracks.

The room shook repetitively. The smell of earth was growing. He could hardly keep his balance in the unsteady room; the lines that weren't cracks at all were jerking him towards the door. If he could grab the bed, drag himself along to the window— His mind was struggling to withdraw into itself, to deny what was happening. He was fighting not only to reach the window but to forget the image that had seized his mind: a spider perched at the centre of its web, tugging in its prey.

The Artist Formerly Known as Vlad

JIM KRUEGER

Q. Is he actually the Lord of Vampires, Vlad the Impaler, Dracula himself?

That's really going to be your first question? Your first? Really?

I thought this was actually going to be a serious interview. Oh, "Interview About A Vampire," that was your working title? It's a little condescending, isn't it? Or at least a little "been there, done that." It certainly lacks some creativity. Let me suggest something better. How about, "Is the former hypno-hop performer Vlad growing a little long in the tooth? Or is this a bold new era in the life of the seemingly unkillable superstar?"

No?

Okay, very well. I'm certain this won't be the last time I have to say this; he is not a vampire. But he is a real prince of a guy.

This whole Vlad thing is just a gimmick. A way to reach the post Emo, Goth, Glam...you know, the Gerard Way, what's under the Umbrella Academy, crowd. I don't even know what they call themselves anymore. There doesn't seem to be a new word for it. Maybe, similar to Vlad...or, I mean, "The Artist formerly known as Vlad," they seem to prefer to be not-so-defined anymore.

I know our speaker systems and the staging are shaped like giant coffins, and castles of old, but that's part of the gag.

Again, he is not a vampire. At one point he was going to call himself the artist formerly known as Prince Vlad, but it seemed too close to Prince, who, forgive me, doesn't even know what it means to be a prince. We're also not using a symbol, either. No. It's just a name. Or the lack of one. And symbols collect too much, I don't know, residual resonance. They stop being people and become causes. So again, he is not Dracula and he is not even Vlad. He's not the "Impaler" in any sense of the word. I realize that an "unfanging" seems to be happening here, but I did promise a tell-all. And in the end, no matter what you write, there will still be those, like you, who really need there to be a Dracula in this world.

You really need there to be ultimate evil, don't you? So, you've begun this interview already doubting my answers.

Q. Who am I, you ask?

That's not an important question. But it does sort of have its own sense of irony. The truth is that I'm pretty certain that even HE still probably doesn't know my name. Not my real one at least.

Nope. It's all about him.

He's such an artist. All he talks about is himself. So vain.

You saw what I did there, right?

But it's also not that true. He's a good guy. No matter what he seems like on the stage. A good guy. And no matter what some say, there are no rodents that are actually harmed during a show. That sort of thing went out with KISS years ago.

As for my name, I usually find myself answering to "buddy", "you there", "hey", "uh", "now", or even "dipshit." And let me tell you right now, I have never called him "Master," even when he went by the name of Vlad. He is a master of music, to some of course, and a real performer, but that's all. He's kind of a slave, actually. You know, to his fans.

You can call me Fred. My full name is Fred Lien. But again, I only agreed to this if you promised not to use my real name. And Fred is like Friend, isn't it? If you mix up the letters in my name, you do get friend anyhow. With a couple letters left over, but who cares, right? Word Games, that's my thing. Accents too. I think it comes from touring with the band. A guy has got to do something to pass the time, you know.

As you can see, once I get going, I'm more than willing to talk without stopping. You can "count" on that. See, I did it again.

Anyhow, I've been with the band since the beginning. You might even say that Vlad, when I could call him that, and I, are pretty inseparable. And that's why I know he is no Dracula. Or Alucard, if you mix the letters up again like they did in at least a couple movies.

As for my job for "The Artist," I wear a lot of hats. Sometimes I'm a roadie. Especially during set up and take down. Sometimes I work security, holding the crowds back, which isn't as hard as you would think thanks to all the muscles I have from being a roadie. And sometimes, like right now, I'm the guy that fields interviews. At least when something is as impromptu as this meeting. You know, an interview on the fly.

Yum.

Oh, please excuse me. Lost my concentration. What was I saying? Just got hungry for a moment.

What are you writing down? Are you playing a word game? You know how I love them.

What's that? You did an anagram of my name.

And you got Renfield out of Fred Lien?

You are clever. A word-duelist yourself. How wonderful.

What gave it away? Oh, the word "fly." Oh, not just "fly" but my yum that followed it. I can certainly explain this, of course.

What makes you think that as a part of a band inspired by vampire mythology, that I wouldn't also have a…well, a stage name? Or even a false persona? We've all been waiting for one of the fans to put it together. To be part of a band like this, one enshrouded in mystery with its hypno-beats, shadow-vids and all, well, having layers and mysteries to us all, things to discover…and, and…

Yes, yes, yes! What a perfect word you just suggested. Mysteries to "unearth."

Well.

Done.

You.

I'm a nobody. A guy who works behind a curtain is all. Doesn't even matter who I am. You're here to talk about the music of "The Artist."

You're not? What? Why are you here?

Q. What about the missing girls?

Oh, I see. This isn't about music at all. You want to talk about girls. The missing girls. Those presumed dead by unnatural causes or missing.

There's a…well, let me first point out…let me first say that over half a million people go missing every year. Most of them are teenagers. I want to also encourage you to be cautious. "The Artist" has not exposed his sexual identity and orientation to the world, so suggesting that these missing girls are somehow linked to him and some sort of sexual depravity is careless and insulting. Your magazine would hardly approve of such shaming tactics. Or even such insistence to label things that even US passports no longer label. Your readers will not be happy with you if you continue down this road that will only bring you condemnation. The greatest and most unforgivable sin is certainly that of intolerance.

Oh, so you say that blood is blood. It doesn't matter the sexual identity or whatever gender they claim or don't claim? Blood is blood. Is that what you said?

Hardly. Blood carries strands of DNA, pieces of knowledge, it is the thoroughfare of the soul. But in times like this, times that have to define every mystery according to hashtags and content, definitions are necessary, I suppose. No matter how much a person tries to deny them.

You think I'm lying, or sidestepping the issues? You want to talk about the missing girls? You think I'm part of a cover up for "The Artist."

Okay, let's talk about the girls. As you will see, I am more than prepared for you and your "digging" into the past of Vlad.

Let's talk about "Janice Tyson." You could have just read the police reports. I spoke to the police at length, of course, when she first disappeared. Her father was a celebrity and our concert in Bryant Park, in Manhattan, was the last place she was seen.

Her body, where did we dump it? That's a big assumption. Perhaps I hoped for a little too much when I assumed you worked for a conservative news outlet. You're more of a *National Enquirer* reporter, it would seem.

How should or could I know where she went? Between 1.5 and 2.8 million teenagers run away from home every year. Why do you think we are trying to get away from the name Vlad? It puts a target on him. It puts him in a certain light that when things happen, everyone points their fingers and rushes into the dark of what they don't know. After all, he has his reputation at…

"What?"

Yes…at stake. Very good. Wish I had a Scooby Snack for you. You're quite a Velma. But why I should reward such disrespect is beyond me. I can end this interview at any point.

As for Janice, who knows where she went. Maybe she was just sick of her father's celebrity. Maybe she wanted some privacy. I know I wish that I had it right now. Did you know that social media has effected the well-being and personal regard of so many people that those that quit "posting" almost never go back? This impudence, it's in your blood. That's what I'm guessing.

"Abbie Groves?" Another so-called victim? Yes, of course, there were puncture wounds on her neck. Go back to the report. Abbie Groves. Puncture wounds in neck. And so many more in her arm. She was a heroin user. She was an addict. You are forgetting that a band that spends so much time performing, it has followers, it has groupies even. Ours are often called the "Grateful Undead." Do they use drugs? Yes, yes, of course they do. They are trying to escape the reality of their lives. In other words, the "news," Miss Reporter. The news. People, like me, want an escape from people, like you.

"Emma Grace." Really? Our concert in Orlando? Of course, her body was missing blood. She was found in the water. It could have been any number of coast-based sea urchins. Or gators. Or crocodiles. From what I remember, there wasn't much of her left at all.

Did you know that the crocodile, as a species, dates back to 200 million years ago? That they have outlived the dinosaur by over 65 million years? And unlike every other species on the planet, they look exactly like they did then? Also, very interesting is this—crocodilians have four-chambered hearts, just like people. But unlike "normal" people, blood does not have to flow to the lungs when underwater. In fact, it's not uncommon for the heart rate of a crocodile to fall to a beat or two a minute.

I think this interview is over. Let's just say, "See you later."

Oh. You have pictures there to make your argument more convincing. Let me see.

I see "The Artist" over and over again. Often with fans. That should prove he's not a vampire. In my understanding of vampire lore, a vampire can't be seen in a reflection. And some of these pictures have been taken during the day. Again, a big no-no according to the stories.

Oh, and by the way, here's something you may not have known about Vlad.

The Artist formerly known as Vlad, someone whose real name is also on a missing person's list, he has a name tattooed on his heart. It's a sacred name, I suppose. Hardly what you would expect from one such as him. But clearly, it's a symbol that would be death to him if indeed he truly was a vampire.

There's never been a picture of me, though? Well, I told you. I'm a nobody. I work in the shadows.

Yes, of course, where the sun doesn't shine.

I'm not going to fool you, am I? That's what you're saying.

Oh, very well. Maybe someone really should indeed know the truth. The truth may set you free, but it might also do the opposite. Sometimes there are truths under truths. And more truths beneath those. Sometimes the truth, like a conspiracy with evidence, becomes a black hole. It intoxicates and demands every part of a person. Sometimes the truth is too large. But, if indeed, you would like to proceed, let us continue.

Q. So are you, the Renfield anagram, actually Dracula?

Let me begin by saying that there is no Dracula. There never was, and there never will be. He is a work of fiction. A rather necessary fiction, but fiction nonetheless.

Bram Stoker, who wrote the book, he and I met and talked many times. And I understood his situation, and was…let me put it this way, sympathetic to his blood disease. But more on him later.

Wait, what? A warning? For me? If you do not return unharmed, you have a document that will be released to certain authorities citing your suspicions and conclusions? You have no intention of becoming another missing person?

As I said before, aren't you the clever one?

Let me continue by saying that immortality is not all it's cracked up to be. Especially for someone like me.

Again, there is no Dracula apart from the fictional creation. But there are vampires. And I am one of them. When I was bit, when my blood was tainted, I no longer really recall. It's not because I suffer from a form of memory loss, it's more like the longer I exist, the more there is to remember. And the less each memory matters as the years pass on.

Many of your kind hold onto a faith in eternal life as a way to deal with the tragedies of your existence and the slow, slow death that comes of age. For beings like myself, it is just the hunger. It's new every day, and brings with it sensations and desire and thirst as magnificent as the first time. It's not the feeding that brings newness and a sense of life, it's the hunger. It's the yearning for new life and the anticipation of having it immediately available. It has been this way for many, many years and has not, will not, change.

Old people tend to eat less as time goes on. But a newborn child's first breath is followed by a cry for hunger. A desire to live. An obsessive wail to be satisfied, knowing full well that there will be hunger again. Our very presence is an affront to your churches and your philosophies. There need not be concern for tomorrow if there is a hunger to be satisfied today. To be a vampire is to live in the moment. Every moment. And to know each one as if it were the first gulps of life.

Do I believe I'm a monster? No. Do I believe that I have been cursed by God? No. This is who I am. And while it might be argued that this is not what your God made me, this is what he allowed me to become. And to remain. Surely, your churches would say that he has a reason for this. Is this not also how they have covered up the atrocities of their fellow man? Or the selfish acts of those within their own parishes?

But there are those amongst you that believe that I, and others like me, are monsters. And they have hunted my kind for more years than I ever thought they would or even could. Even in this modern age of universal acceptance, when no one is allowed the "freedom" to condemn anyone, my kind is still the stuff of imagined nightmares. We are still the targets of religious bigots and the hunters of the supernatural, all of whom have their own hungers and their own thirsts. None of which, I think, are actually for a so-called God.

This brings me back to Bram Stoker. And God, to a degree. Right now we exist in a world of celebrity overload. But when Bram wrote Dracula, the celebrities of that day were limited to Kings and Queens, Presidents and assassins, and authors. Even then, the desire to be a celebrity, or worship at the feet of them, was a thirst that brought me not only amusement, but the answer to the problem that dogged my heels—the self-proclaimed vampire hunter. I needed a target for the hunters.

With Bram, I was able to create a false target. A celebrity monster and mythology for men to hunt and fear. And maybe even secretly aspire to. There are no secrets in that book, though. Not really.

The rules for killing a vampire are not in that work. It's the survival of the vampire, actually, that this literary creation encourages. You see, I love the cross. It brings me encouragement and a sense of comfort.

I may actually be the only true evidence that there even is eternal life.

As for a stake through the heart, my heart hasn't beaten for hundreds of years. This is why I mentioned the crocodile before. To drink from another's blood, is to enter into the ebb and flow of that person's heart beat. It's their heart that allows me to drink, not my own. It's their heart that aids the sucking of their throat. I drink, but it is a person's heart that pushes the blood to satisfy my thirst. Even in this, I am entering the very process of the natural order. Not a supernatural one, but a natural one.

A vampire's thirst is for life, though I fear I am repeating myself too much.

Back to Dracula. It's your want for celebrity, your desire for a god to worship, or fear, that has led to Dracula's popularity. The story says that I can't handle the image of a god. As I said, it's quite the opposite. You can't handle the image. Your need for celebrity, for significance, for specialness has condemned you and your entire small history on the planet. How many great men has your kind murdered because they tried to bring peace to the world? How much violence has been wrought in the name of religion, or business, or freedom?

Stoker's book and other books like it, the movies, the TV shows and cosplay, it all allows you all to become the celebrity, to play-act at your own desire to be special. To be significant. To be God. And in so doing, you become less than you are. You are like people trying to catch birds because you fear how quickly time flies. You want eternal life and significance but fail to live in the right now. You can't enjoy the moment.

Your kind has condemned mine for years. Why should you be surprised that I now condemn yours?

What's that?

There are marked moments in history when Dracula has been killed, and when he has returned to life?

No, not Dracula.

I've hired many "Draculas" over time. You really think he's dying and being resurrected? He has never resurrected at all.

You've heard of the Day Men who guard his coffin while the sun shines? Do you really think I wouldn't also have Night Men?

I hire actors, all of the same basic type, to be Dracula. Or actors to be vampires of European decent. Now granted, in this day and age, in light of social media, it is more difficult because photographs can be compared, and the many differences can be seen. But there are lawyers who can take things off the internet. There are ways to alter even the most zealous entry into Wikipedia. The world wants someone in the spotlight.

It's a temptation.

And there are so many who want to be Dracula. They sometimes think it's a movie they are trying out for, or a promotion for a new book, or a theme hotel, or a commercial. Years ago, many believed it was part of a way to bring the stage to the streets.

Believe me, though, each of my "Draculas", at least for a moment, thought they were special. Thought they were part of a story that was bigger than them. And each died at the hands of the so-called righteousness of those so quick to believe the story, and their own cause. Each wanting the glory of ending true evil. I laugh every time your kind has an election, and both sides refer to the opposite candidate as a new Hitler. As if cutting spending or opening borders could be compared to genocide. It's "Hitlarious" if you ask me. Did you see what I did?

Q. Then who are you, really?

Just as there have been many false "Draculas", there has only been one true Renfield. There has to be a target. Like a transplanted heart, the goal was always to make the hunter look elsewhere.

No one ever looks at the little guy. No one ever notes evil minion member #5. Or the not-quite-as-attractive-but-funny best friend. That's the thing about magic, isn't it? It's about diverting the eye. Showing what we want to show, so that people can make their assumptions and take it on faith that they understand.

Think about it this way, it is believed that there are 57 billion worms below the surface for every human life on the planet. Do you care about all they eat, all they consume? They have a mass of 300 million tons. But do you care? No. Of course not. And that is because you can't see them. There is nothing to draw notice to them. But they are essential to the world's health.

It's also the little people that have worked to change this world. Not the celebrity. The inventors of industry throughout history only became celebrities after they created something that changed the world. It's rare that they ever created anything of worth after. Your race's greatest discoveries have always catapulted the discoverer into such a limelight that it's impossible for them to ever search the shadows again. There are exceptions, of course. Even in the music industry. Which brings me to today's interview.

As for my newest "Dracula," the artist known formerly as Vlad, I'm afraid his time is coming to an end. It's not because you have gotten too close to a few missing people which, of course, are not because of Vlad, but because of me. No, his time is over for another reason.

I simply hate his music. It is not the music of the children of the night.

I especially hate his lyrics and how small and unimportant they are. I do have to admit, though, that there is something to the beat I can't help but think about. It's steady pattern. House music, they call it. So much like the human heart. So much like the rhythm of blood and the pulsating of human vessels through which it flows.

And it does indeed make me thirsty. It even calls me, to a degree.

Incidentally, not everything Bram Stoker wrote was wrong. I know you are wondering if I am going to kill you. This is the reason that you mentioned that if anything happened to you, certain evidences and conclusions would be made known to the local authorities. But let me state right now that I don't have to kill you. Not today at the very least.

I keep my promises, you see. I promised a "tell-all" interview. But, at the same time, for you, it's also going to be a sort of "forget-all."

Look at my hands again. Watch how the fingers move. How they stretch out like the spider's legs, moving towards you, reaching, but for something beyond the need to touch. Look at how I fold them over each other. How I let them arch their backs, almost, how they seem poised to spring at your throat. Keep watching. They are reaching into your mind, now, into your heart. I see in your eyes, that you are completely within their grasp.

So, repeat after me, and say the words. They must be your own. They must be said with conviction. There are no such things as vampires. There are no such things as vampires. Your beliefs that somehow these missing children are associated with Vlad are unfounded. And you are never even going to mention them in this interview, or anywhere for that matter.

And in the end, your article will speak to your love for the monster of Dracula and how the world needs this mythology to make it feel good. To make your small lives all the bigger. By huddling together in the dark and thrilling to another stake through the heart, another smoking cross that cannot be gripped by the vampire, another wafer-tainted coffin that will never hold the undead again.

There. I want to thank you for the interview. Oh, you have some questions? You can't seem to find your notebook?

If you want to keep the interview going, I suggest we go somewhere dark where we can get a drink.

Oh, you don't drink? You have a past, you say? So do I. And it's not a short one.

But I do. I most certainly do drink.

But in the interest of respecting your former thirsts, I'll just take a little one this evening.

Jonathan Harker: Witch Hunter

BRAD MENGEL

Letter from Lucy Westenra to Mina Murray
5 May 1891

My Dearest Mina,

It has been far too long since you last wrote, I fear that your Jonathan thinks that I am a witch or some sort of bad influence on you and has forbade you to write me.

You would remember Artie Holmwood? The youngest son of Lord Godalming, he was so dashing in his Army uniform with his fine moustache. He asked me to marry him. I told him I had to think about it. I mean how could I ever leave poor ill Mama?

He invited me into Town to whisk me off my feet. We were dining at the Palatino and he had just proposed when we were greeted by an old friend of Artie's, a doctor no less. Doctor John Seward. He was in town to take over the running of the sanatorium after the previous chief doctor Abraham Van Helsing had suddenly died of a brain aneurysm. Dr Seward looked so young to be looking after madmen.

It was the strangest thing, Artie congratulated Seward and the doctor said that the Lord helps those that help themselves. The doctor left and Artie became such a bore, he barely paid me any attention. Surely, it wasn't that I had smiled at the doctor?

Your confidant,
Lucy Westenra.

Letter from Mina Murray to Lucy Westenra.
8 May 1891

Dearest Lucy,

You may recall that that Papa forbade me from seeing you when we were girls and I ignored him then. Were Jonathan to do the same I would simply ignore him too. For I could not abandon my blood sister so easily. No, I have simply been busy. If Jonathan were to ever propose, I would be the wife of a solicitor. To assist in his practice after we marry, I have been learning shorthand in secret.

I can hear you now as you read that, calling me a dull secretary, but I think that a wife should be an asset to her husband. Listen to me, I sound like an old married woman and Jonathan can barely hold my hand.

I do recall young Artie Holmwood, the blighter pulled my pigtails, one hopes that he has gained some better manners since then. I thought you had sworn off 'pretty boys in pretty uniforms' after that summer in Bath. I think that was when your mother developed her heart condition.

As to why Artie became a bore, maybe he knew this Van Helsing chappie?

Anyway, I must run, Jonathan is taking me to see a play.

Love,

Mina Murray.

Letter from Arthur Holmwood to Lucy Westenra
12 May 1891

My Dearest Lucy,

I fear that I was poor company the other night. Talk of death is so mournful, it always saddens me. You must think me such a terrible bore. Allow me to make it up to you and take you out for a picnic in Hyde Park. I know a delightful spot on the banks of the Serpentine. There will be magic in the air.

My heart sings at the thought of the mere sight of you again. I still await your answer my dear, but I have a feeling that I shall be a happy man with the world at my feet in no time at all.

All my love,

Sgt Arthur Holmwood. 5th Berkshire Rifles.

Letter Lucy Westenra to Arthur Holmwood

My Dear Artie,

I would be delighted to join you for dinner. I simply haven't had time to think about your question with Mama being so poorly.

Love,

Lucy

PS Do wear your uniform.

Letter from Lucy Westenra to Mina Murray
13 May 1891

Mina,

You will not believe it, I was dressing to see Arthur when there was a knock at the door. Imagine my surprise when the maid brought me the card of Dr Seward. I finished dressing and met him in the parlour.

He looked so stern and serious, with his wire-rimmed glasses and a gaze that seemed to reach right into my brain and understand me maybe better than you do. I could see that he was nervous. We talked the very small talk that people do and I asked about his new job. Did you know that head doctors earn some twenty thousand pounds a year?

The next thing I know he declared his ardent love for me and he dropped to one knee and proposed marriage. He was so nervous that he nearly stammered and asked to marry Mama. He was so sweet and awkward.

Two proposals in two days, whatever is a girl to do? I, of course, appeared overcome as a good young lady should be, having the vapours and fainting into his arms.

It was very forward of me but I wanted to see how keen he was to get his hands on me. When I recovered I told him that I would have to think about it.

I'll have to think about who to accept.

Love,

Lucy Westenra.

PS I had just finished penning this missive and was about to seal it and send it when Dr Seward appeared again. He was so apologetic. He realised that his proposal was so sudden and I barely knew him and he took me out to the Lyceum theatre where we saw Sir Henry Irving. During the interval there we chanced upon an acquaintance of his, Lord Vlad Dracula from Transylvania. Lord Dracula was so mysterious and exotic. The strange thing was that Dr Seward seemed displeased to see his friend. At the rate I'm going Lord Dracula will visit to propose tomorrow.

Letter from Lucy Westenra to Mina Murray
14 May 1891

It appears that my words went from my pen to God's eyes for Lord Dracula did indeed appear and propose. I was sitting in the parlour and again the maid advised that I had a caller. I could tell by the look on her face that she did not approve of this visitor. I told her quite sternly and firmly that I would see the caller as I set aside my needlepoint. I marked my place with a brass pin.

In walked Lord Dracula. How do I describe such a man to you? He is so different to the men I normally meet. He was exotic. He wore his hair longer than typical for Englishmen, nearly down to his shoulders, no wonder Miranda hated him. He is a tall man, taller than your father, who we both know is quite tall. He has a long, lean face with an aquiline nose. He is commanding and yet compassionate. He was the type of man who would have ruled nations and lead armies a few hundred years ago.

He sat near me and looked deep into my eyes. They were the blue of the ocean and I could feel myself diving into their depths. He told me that I was haunting his dreams. I first appeared to him when Arthur mentioned me and appeared each night. It was when he saw me at the theatre that he knew that I was the woman who had invaded his dreams and that I must be his wife.

I had joked about this in my last letter to you, but it was a shock for it to become real. I was speechless for a second, almost like I was drowning in those sea blue eyes. He seemed to be about to say more, when his hand came to rest on my cross stitch. It was as if he had touched a red hot poker, the way that he jumped to his feet.

I felt like I had come out of a trance, and I stammered that I had to think about it as he left the room. Had I offended him in some way? Or was he overpowered by the enormity of his affection?

Oh, I sound terrible and selfish but I have the best of all types of problems. For I have had three proposals of marriage, and I must choose only one. Oh, why can a woman not have multiple husbands like a man can have multiple wives?

I met a Mormon gentleman on the train who told me that a man of his faith can have as many wives as he wishes. He said that he had four wives and twenty-eight children. Mama was completely scandalised when I asked if he was in London to find wife number five.

Don't worry, I'm not planning on running off to Utah Territory with Quincey Morris. He had the most abhorrent habit of spitting tobacco juice out the train window.

I wish you were here to talk to, dear friend. I would talk to Mama but she is so frail and her heart simply wouldn't take the strain.

Please come and visit soon.

With affection

Lucy

Letter from Lucy Westenra to Mina Murray
15 May 1891

Dearest Mina,

What am I to do? I find myself at a loose end. I dreamt of Vlad last night, he appeared in my room as happens in dreams and he kissed me. In more places than my lips. It felt so real, like a sign or something to tell me that I should marry Vlad.

Even now beside the fire, wide awake I find myself thinking of Vlad, Lord Dracula. It's like part of me is bewitched by those blue eyes. I want to think about Artie and Dr Seward and their proposals but my mind keeps turning to the exotic Transylvanian. Indeed, had he not run out yesterday, I think what might have happened.

Is this love? You told me that you love Jonathan, is it like this? I laughed at the silly plays with love at first sight but has it happened to me? I want to jump in a hansom and ride to Vlad's lodging but I have no idea where he is staying. The two people who are likely to know where that would be are his two rivals in love. Vlad not being an Englishman had no card, I checked with Miranda. She clucked her tongue disapprovingly.

Lucy

Clipping from *The Daily Gazette*
Bizarre Death of Lord and Heir
By Fergus McArdle

The peerage mourns the loss of Ian Holmwood, Lord Goldalming, who died in the most unusual way.

Eyewitness reports indicate that Lord Goldalming, something of a political power broker, had called several of his party's members to his house for a meeting. Partway through the evening, Lord Goldalming left the meeting to retrieve some papers and while walking slipped on one of the steps and fell over the railing and onto the floor below.

In a cruel twist of fate, his Lordship's heir and man about town, Philip Holmwood was about to ascend the stairs himself and was struck by his father's falling body. Both men were declared dead on the scene.

Inspector Bradstreet of Scotland Yard made the following statement, "After a thorough investigation, there is no evidence of foul play at the scene and this is a doubly tragic accident."

Lord Goldalming is survived by his wife, May, and youngest son Arthur. The younger Holmwood is currently serving as a sergeant in the Berkshire Rifles. He is expected to resign his commission to become the new Lord Goldalming.

Letter from Lucy Westenra to Mina Murray
17 May 1891

Oh, Mina, you simply will not believe it, I had partially resolved my issue and I was set to see Artie and tell him that I could not marry an Army man as my poor Naval officer father would be rolling in his watery grave, when I heard the most bizarre news. The old Lord Goldaming slipped on the step of the ancestral keep. As he tumbled down the stairs he broke his neck. Arthur's older brother Philip tried to catch his father and fell over, dashing his brains out on the solid stone bannister. Both men died instantly.

Arthur is now the new Lord Goldalming with an income of fifty thousand a year, and he must resign his commission. I am back to three suitors.

I told Mama of the proposals and she took a turn, worried that I would leave her all alone.

Letter from Mina Murray to Lucy Westenra
17 May 1891

Dearest Lucy,

There was such a flurry of mail from you that I had no sooner finished reading one letter than another would arrive. I barely know where to begin responding to you. Three betrothals why that is nearly unheard of. Don't be too hasty with your decision. After all, you barely know these gentlemen. But don't take too long either, as they may grow bored and may be stolen away from you. Besides, as you say your mother is in poor health and who knows how much longer you will have her around. I wish I could have had more time with my mother, and for her to see me marry and have little Harker grandchildren.

This has left me maudlin, dear heart.

Mina

Telegram 18 May 1891 Lucy Westenra to Mina Murray

MINA STOP MAMA DYING STOP COME AT ONCE STOP LUCY STOP

Letter from Mina Murray to Jonathan Harker
18 May 1891

Dear Jonathan,

Mrs Westenra has taken ill and may not have long. The dear woman was a second mother to me when my own mother was taken from me far too soon. I know the low regard you feel for Lucy but she is a sister to me and I must be at her side in these difficult times.

Mina

19 May 1891 letter Jonathan Harker to Mina Murray

Dear Mina,

I hope your trip to London went well. The firm is quiet and I believe that I can take time to come to the City to support you and Miss Westenra in your trying time.

Jonathan Harker Esq.

25 May 1891 Newspaper clipping *The Times* morning edition
HORROR IN HYDE PARK
By Kate Reed

Not since the horrors of Jack the Ripper in 1888, has London been held in the grip of such terror. Horrified park goers in Hyde Park were traumatised by the sight of not one but two bodies burnt at the stake near the banks of the Serpentine.

Another two bodies were located nearby dressed in strange robes. The names of the deceased have not been released. Inspector Athelney Jones of Scotland Yard was on the scene and he advised that the Yard was investigating and an arrest was imminent.

Rumour abounds that one of the bodies is the new Peer, Lord Goldalming, but that is unconfirmed and the Goldalming Estate has been telegraphed for comment.

Readers of our social pages may be aware that Lord Goldalming, a suddenly very eligible bachelor was seen on the town with a mystery redhead after the sudden death of his father and older brother. There were reports that Godalming was talking spiritual advice from Lord Vlad Dracula, a European nobleman.

Headline from *The Telegraph*
HYDE PARK KILLER CAPTURED
by Hamish Blundell

In a sensational turn of events, the fiancé of one of the women burnt at the stake in Hyde Park has been arrested for the heinous murders. Jonathan Harker, a solicitor in Whitby was captured by Inspector Athelney Jones as he was about to board a train to Whitby.

Harker will be held at Broadmoor Prison until his hearing.

The Confession of Jonathan Harker

In this the year of our Lord 1891, I, Jonathan Harker, stand before this court charged with the deaths of Mina Murray and Lucy Westonra. I stand accused of the murder most foul of two of England's fairest roses, plucked in their prime and burned at the stake.

The truth is that neither were fair roses having been seduced and turned away from our Lord and protector part of the coven of Dracula. That European blasphemer and defiler of our women. He took my beloved Mina away from me. No doubt that slattern Lucy Westenra brought the devil to her bosom.

It so happened that Mina had left my side to comfort Lucy upon the death of her mother. Mrs Westenra was a good God-fearing woman who took my Mina in and raised her like a daughter after the death of Mina's mother and her abandonment by her father who ran off to the far corners of the Empire to avoid his duty.

Mina went to comfort a woman who was like a sister to her. But that woman was tainted by the sin of Eve and dragged my pure Mina into a hedonistic life of sin and debauchery. I found Mina's correspondence with Lucy and discovered the death and debauchery that orbited Lucy Westenra and her social set and the centre of the solar system was Dracula, a name that I had dealt with in the past.

I immediately made arrangements to leave my law practice as quickly as possible and I arrived some three days before I was expected. This was my chance to catch the devil in the act and send him back to the very hell that spawned him.

My cab dropped me at the Westenra house and instead of a house of mourning I found the house empty. The lone weeping maid told me that Miss Lucy and Miss Mina were out with Miss Lucy's suitors.

I knew that it was a matter of urgency to find Mina before it was too late. From the letters I knew some of the places they frequented. I went to the Lyceum theatre, and several restaurants and bars before I recalled the picnic on the banks of the Serpentine River. What better place than a river named for the creature that corrupted Eve to corrupt my dear Mina.

I found the five of them performing unholy rites in a pentagram formation. I was too late. Lord Dracula had formed his coven. I could see the pattern forming the sudden and mysterious deaths, that served as good fortune for the members of the coven. Seward gets a big promotion, Arthur Holmwood become a peer, Lucy Westonra free of her ailing mother and Mina. Mina was weak-willed, she always followed Lucy into trouble. I could see them dancing around a fire – not a waltz but rather a paganistic, wild frenzy of a dance. The Englishmen had taken off their shirts and undershirts and I could see the sweat glistening off their chests.

Lucy was in some sort of trance and she was dancing completely naked, her pale skin almost luminescent in the firelight, her hair wild and loose. As she writhed and danced, her scarlet locks flicked around like it was a simulacra of the flames.

I could see Mina across from her. She was still dressed and hair was still in a sensible bun but I could see her swaying to a music I couldn't hear.

"Resist," I thought. "Resist." I wished the thought could fly from my head to hers. I prayed that I could lend my strength to hers to reject the seduction of Dracula.

But my thoughts and prayers went unheard and unanswered as I saw Mina reach for her hair and remove her hairpin. Her long ebony locks flowed from her head, cascading down her back. She began to unbutton her blouse. I watched in horror as she unbuttoned further buttons. For the first time, I saw what should be first seen on my wedding night, her undergarments. She continued to undress.

I was about to avert my eyes from this scene of depravity when I glanced to Mina's left. There stood Lord Dracula. He wore only a long cloak, I could see his bare chest and his manhood. At least the Englishmen were decent enough to retain some modesty.

I looked at his face. His eyes emitted a red glow, clearly a reflection of the fire or a mere trick of the light. Then I swear, he looked right at me, threw back his head and laughed. He moved to his right and kissed Mina, who was now naked.

She responded in kind and in a moment the pair were fornicating on the ground. As I looked away, I saw that vile harlot Lucy taking not one but two of her suitors. The corruption was complete and total and I admit that I wept. I wept for my beloved Mina—the woman who I loved and engaged to make my wife.

As I dried my tears, I felt my resolve harden. Since Mina left, I knew this was a possibility, the corruption of her immortal soul and the actions I might be forced to take. I know the evil of that man, Lord Dracula, if man is the right word for that tool of Satan. The only way to stop the spread of his evil is to burn out the infection at the stake.

I reached into my pocket and pulled out my revolver. I made my way towards the fire and the trio engaged in their depravity. I pulled the trigger twice; both men fell to the ground dead. I struck Lucy Westenra with my pistol, sending her into unconsciousness. You may accuse me of ungentlemanly behaviour and say that I should not have struck a lady. Lucy Westenra was no lady, there was no purity or chasteness to her soul. She was no lady but rather a harlot of hell, damning men's souls to the underworld.

I turned to the pair on the other side of the fire but Lord Dracula was gone. Mina was there on the ground. Dracula had corrupted her immortal soul and then cast her aside like yesterday's collars and cuffs. He had fled having achieved his goal.

I raced to my fiancée's side. She lay there, as naked as Eve. There was no shame or unease. As she saw me she smiled.

"Jonathan." She greeted me as she rose. "Come and lie with me, Jonathan."

I could feel the heat of the fire behind me and the heat of her lust before me. There was a huskiness to her voice, similar to the slatterns and whores that walked the streets. Her naked form moved towards me, tempting and testing my immortal soul.

I would like to say that my will was strong and steadfast, but in that moment I weakened. I lowered my gun and moved towards her bewitching embrace. I moved as if in a trance and lowered my face towards hers. I inhaled as I went to kiss her and caught the scent of him: the vile seducer who corrupted my fair beloved into a jezebel. I jerked away and swung the pistol. The hard metal barrel smashed against the side of her head and she dropped before me unconscious.

I was tempted to chase the architect of this depravity and corruption but I had to cauterise the infection that he had left behind. There was little to be done for the men I had shot. I pulled them to one side and covered their bodies in the discarded cloaks I had found .

Next I moved the two women together, propping them back to back as I built their pyre around them. I bound them together with the suspenders and belts I salvaged from the discarded clothes. I pulled out my medicinal brandy and took a sip before dousing the women and the pyre.

Lucy began to stir as the liquor splashed her, her breasts jiggling, trying to break my determination. Even unconscious, the demon temptress was still trying to seduce and beguile me. I grabbed a flaming stick from the small fire and lit the pyre.

The brandy soon caught fire and it was like the flames of hell leapt to the Earth to claim that which belonged to it. Flames leapt and spread. engulfing the women, their screams blending with the crackle of the fire. It was a hideous sound as I could hear their screams rise and fall as the fires claimed their lives. This was the worst part of burning a witch.

I know this first hand, for Miss Westenra and my beloved Mina were not the first witches I have had cause to burn at the stake. That cursed devil wizard haunts me, turning all the women in my life to the left hand path. He seeks to torment me, seeking revenge for killing him in another life.

You scientific Victorians may scoff and boast that ghosts need not apply but I know better. There are many things not dreamed of in your philosophy. Shakespeare stole that from me.

I sense your confusion, Shakespeare lived some three centuries ago. How might I have known the man and still live? In truth, I was near on a century old when I met Shakespeare. Impossible, I hear your cry now. But does not chapter 5 of Genesis tell us that Adam lived to nine hundred and thirty years, Seth was nine hundred and twelve and Methuselah lived to see nine hundred sixty and nine? For in God, it is possible to live nearly a millennium. And does not Jesus our Lord and Saviour grant us eternal life?

I was born in the year of our Lord 1411. I was a pious man and joined a holy order. In my first year, a lad of just fifteen who had not even taken my holy vows, I uncovered my first witch. 'Twas St George's night, when I was awoken by the hand of our Lord just in time to see the glow of a candle under the door. I rose from my cot and moved swiftly to the door. I looked on the now empty hallway and I noted that Brother James' door was ajar. I moved to his cell and placed my eye to the gap. It was then that I saw the temptress witch. I recognised her in the flickering candlelight; Brigid, a girl of my age from the village. She had wild and unruly raven locks and when I saw her I felt something in the pit of my stomach.

Brigid was untying my brother's robes as he pulled the clothes off her. James's cassock and vow of chastity were soon discarded on the floor. James pulled the now-naked woman to him and kissed her on the lips. She moaned in earthly pleasure before offering the temptation of Eve. I could see her naked body and hear Satan whispering in my ear, telling me of impure thoughts, inviting the sin of lust.

As if guided by Satan, Brigid turned and I could see her womanly figure, the curves of her breasts, her feminine mystery. All the better to lead me into the path of temptation and sin. To forget the vows I was training to take before God and his son, sacred vows.

I took hold of the simple wooden cross I wore around my neck and ran to the Abbot's cell. The Abbot found Brother James and the girl engaged in carnal sins. The pair were tried for witchcraft and the worship of the dark lord Satan. Brother James repented and his immortal soul was saved from Satan's fiery pits of damnation – he was hung by the neck and given a Christian burial. Best to speed him to heaven, while his soul was clean.

The girl on the other hand, denied her sins and the sins of Eve, but she had been caught in the act. I bore witness to her sinful arousal of lust in my brother. For that she was found guilty and she burnt at the stake that very day.

I shortly thereafter took my vows and renounced the outside world. My life soon became the monastic routine, though every so often I would recall the powerful magic of the witch Brigid. I prayed that I would have the strength to resist such temptations should they ever be directed towards me.

I studied well the sacred texts in my monastery and became an expert in the ways of witches. Does not Exodus 22:18 command "Thou shalt not suffer a witch to live"?

I dedicated myself to hunting and finding witches, warlocks and other magic users. I had gained something of a reputation and my king called me to court. He had need of my services as the French were at war and their army was commanded by an arrogant witch. Unlike her English counterparts, who would hide their sinful natures in the vestige of a pious woman until they turned their wiles on you, this Jeanne d'Arc shamefully wore the armour of a man, proudly exposing her deviance. The French were so corrupt that not only did they tolerate it, they worshipped her and followed her. It was only a matter of time before she emboldened others of her ilk and the French would turn their eyes to England.

This heretic could not be suffered to live and I was dispatched with orders to stop the Maid of Orleans. I captured and tried her for the blasphemous abomination she was. What she called the voice of God, I called the whispers of Satan.

As I went to her cell to collect her for her punishment, Lucifer the Lord of Lies spoke through his willing vessel. Oh, first she tried to charm me, show me her womanly charms. The same charms that Eve used to corrupt Adam but I was immune.

Seeing my resolve the beast turned. Her eyes rolled back in her head and flecks of foam spat from her lips. "In the land beyond the forest, I shall rise as the scion of the dragon and lay waste to you and yours."

At that point, I ordered the beast to leave the girl. The demon cursed at me but fled as I slapped its vessel across the face. At point, I saw the devil's final illusion, a scared young woman. She refused to come with me and I dragged her to the waiting pyre. She burnt as well as any witch that I had sent to the fires.

In the years that followed, that day—May 30, 1431—was etched into my memory. I continued hunting witches and was eventually called to Rome. His Holiness had heard of my prowess and sought to reward me with a Cardinal's robe. I refused. I was not one for a position of such power.

While I was at the Vatican, an emissary from the country of Transylvania arrived seeking audience from his Holiness.

"I come from the court of Vlad Dracul, Order of the Dragon, King of the Land Beyond the Forest," the man introduced himself.

It had been nearly two decades since I burned that witch Joan of Arc at the stake but I remembered her prophecy. I must admit witches, wizards, warlocks and other magic users had spat curses at me but the Lord did protect me. This was the first time such words had come back to haunt me.

His Holiness, for his own reasons, denied the entreaties of Vlad Dracul but I made it my mission to befriend his emissary, Alexandru and to join him on his journey back to Transylvania. Alexandru was the head of Dracul's personal guard, a giant figure standing several inches above me. He wore his hair long and was clean shaven except for a long droopy moustache.

As we journeyed, in our shared tongue of German, I learned everything I could about the Transylvanian court. I discovered that there was a son also named Vlad Dracula or the Scion of the Dragon, born on May 30, 1431. When I heard that, I felt a chill pass through my body. For that was the very date that I had sent Joan of Arc to hell and the day that she had cursed me. Alexandru told me that at age ten, the boy and his brother were sent to the Ottoman Empire as hostages for his master to not declare war on them.

Before long we were in the land of Transylvania. In Alexandru's absence, things had taken a turn for the worse. Dracul's sons had escaped their captors and the Ottomans had declared war and tried to install a puppet government with a cousin of Dracul, Vladislav.

There was a civil war brewing and I was there in the thick of it. Alexandru took me to Dracul's castle, a massive stone structure that appeared to have been built centuries ago atop a mountain. Three towers rose out of the main building giving the castle's defenders a clear view for miles. As we rode to the castle we stopped at the end of the road. A large chasm stood between us and the castle. Alexandru gave a cry and the drawbridge was lowered.

Once in the castle, a servant girl lead us to the great hall where I met Vlad Dracul, a stocky, swarthy man with a flowing moustache that no doubt formed the inspiration for Alexandru's facial hair. He looked every bit the fearsome warrior that my new friend had made him out to be.

Dracul greeted me warmly after Alexandru's introduction and as a proud father introduced me to his three sons, Mircea, Vlad and Radu. Looking at the three boys with the same stocky build and swarthy complexion, it was like seeing their father earlier in his life. When the middle son looked at me with his dark piercing eyes, I swore there was a flicker of recognition in his eyes.

Dracul called to the servant girl in their Transylvanian tongue. I could pick a word or two but not enough to follow the conversation. The conversation switched to German and I was introduced to Irena. The girl was fair with a porcelain complexion and blonde locks. She was to be my personal servant during my stay.

As a man of God, I settled into a simple routine in the castle. Rising early for morning prayers in the chapel before partaking in a simple breakfast in the kitchen, I soon picked up enough of the local tongue to hold a simple conversation and began to explore the castle. Dracul stocked an excellent library and I spent much time there. Irena followed me everywhere: she was my guide, translator, companion. She was a pure soul. I think the poor girl was lonely as the rest of staff appeared to shun her.

It was during breakfast that I was talking with Ion, a young boy who arose before the cook and stoked the fires. The boy stopped mid-sentence. His eyes rolled back into his head and he dropped to the hard, stone floor. He had no sooner hit the floor and his body convulsed and writhed on the floor; a sure sign that the lad was bewitched. I prayed over the poor soul and after a few moments he returned to normal. Irena was amazed at the work of the Lord and fell to her knees in prayer and worship.

I began to see the signs and portents of witchcraft around the castle.

An apple outside a door, which on examination had been sliced in half horizontally revealing the devil's pentagram, put there after the serpent gave the fruit to Eve in the Garden of Eden. Drops of wax where you wouldn't expect them to be. Small bags left in hidden corners, known as hex bags. There was witchcraft afoot.

In my conversations with Irena, I discovered that she was infatuated with young Vlad. With a hint of bitterness she informed me that the prince would sneak out of the castle on the night of the full moon, "to fornicate with the village whores." I kept my eye on young Vlad Dracula. While he may be tomcatting, I knew the full moon was a strong time for witchcraft. The next full moon, I followed him sneaking out of the castle, through an escape passage.

I followed his trail into the forest. We began to head into the mountains. It seemed as if Irena may be wrong. As we ascended I could see Lake Hermanstadt in the valley below. I recalled that I had read something of that lake. As I struggled to recall, I felt the temperature drop with an unnatural suddenness. I could feel the short hairs on my body stand to attention.

I pulled my dagger, an athame I had taken from a witch in London. As I recalled that particular witch was very powerful. She had owned a copy of the Key of Solomon, a book reportedly written by King Solomon, telling of spells and magic, that the son of David had learnt from the various demons and jinn he had enslaved. The Key told of Solomon's school – the Scholomance, built in the Carpathian mountains overlooking Lake Hermanstadt. After Solomon's death, the demon Asmodeus took over the school and handed it over to his master Satan. Legend has it that in a single night one may learn magic directly from Lucifer himself.

I'd never encountered a witch that had claimed to have ever studied there and had considered it to be a myth. Perhaps I had been mistaken. I wished that I had the Key with me, but the delivery of that particular tome had been one of the reasons I had recently travelled to Rome. Such a book was not intended for the hands of mortals. The Vatican's Library of St John the Beheaded was the safest place for such a book.

I made my way through the tunnel within the mountain, that athame in my hand feeling tiny as I held in front of me, making my way through the darkness. Suddenly the darkness was not infinite and I could see a pinprick of light in the distance. As I moved closer it grew and flickered. There was a fire ahead. Could it be the flames of Hell reaching up from the pit to strike at one of its most feared enemies? Was the witch's curse that led me here an elaborate trap conceived and executed by the Master of Lies?

With the dim light, I could see the path before me and began to move faster. I sent a prayer to the Lord to keep me safe. The tunnel suddenly opened to a large chamber. Torches lined the walls. Underneath each lamp was a desk. At the far end of the chamber was a larger table marked with symbols arcane and profane. I moved closer and I recognised the seal of Solomon. I had found the Scholomance.

There was part of me that wished that I could study the details, for to know one's enemies is to sow the seeds of their defeat, but at the same time that could be the devil whispering in my ear, distracting me from the task at hand.

I glanced around the cavern. Vlad was nowhere to be seen. Could he have continued through the cavern into the darkness or have stepped into a side tunnel that I stumbled past in the Stygian darkness? A prayer for protection slipped from my lips and I saw a vision of Irena, so sweet and innocent. At the same time a chill crawled long my spine and I turned and fled this cursed cave.

I raced through the forest, pine needles stabbing and whipping me in my headlong dash. I found the hidden doorway and returned to the interior of the castle. I returned to my room to find Irena lying naked on my bed, her throat slit and a pentagram carved into her lower torso.

To my eternal shame I fled, for I knew that Vlad Dracula was a powerful wizard, one who had learnt the art of teleportation. He had led me, the great and glorious witch hunter on a merry caper and framed me nicely for his own debauched rituals.

I fled into the forest and at dawn sought to return to the Scholomance. Despite following my tracks and my own memory, Dracula's witchcraft had hidden it from me. I made my way across Europe. No matter what guise I adopted he would find me. I married several times, in different countries, hoping that might confuse him , but he found me and either killed my wife or corrupted her to the left hand path.

I still hunted witches where I found them for several centuries until I realised that he was tracking me through the signs I was leaving. My time in Salem, America was particularly fruitful. As the 19th century dawned, I no longer hunted witches; science seem to be far more effective than magic and it was harder to find witches.

It had been nearly three lifetimes since Dracula and I had crossed paths. I thought I had lost the demon for good. I had made a life and again was to marry. Imagine my surprise to see his name appear on the deed of sale for Carfax Abbey. I had convinced myself that it was merely a coincidence when the name appeared in Mina's letters. We all know the end of that story. It was his ultimate trap.

I was about to put down my pen, when I felt the temperature drop. A sure sign of witchcraft and the sensational capture of the Hyde Park Killer would have told him of my location. This will be our final battle.

From the private journal of Inspector Athelney Jones

I arrived at Newgate Prison with the intent of interviewing Harker about the crime. The guard assured me that no one had visited the prisoner. I took the key and opened the cell…a cell that was empty. There was no sign of escape – the bars were intact and far too close for anyone to pass between them. All I found were two piles of dust and a handwritten note. Clearly, Harker was setting up an insanity defence.

I am tempted to summons Holmes to see what he can make of this mystery.

Hothouse Crush

LEE MURRAY

Aimee,

Be more careful! Your last note was sticking out from behind the radiator. Anyone could have gone past and seen it. Miss Beady-eyes Bartlett, for example! You're in this too, remember?

Anyway, Annabelle and I need you to post these two letters to Zoe, in Nice, so Zoe can send them on to our parents. You can read them if you like—the envelopes are still open—just make sure you put them back in the right envelopes (they're already addressed) because our olds will recognise our handwriting. The letters are both the same, except mine mentions Greer, and Annabelle mentions her brother James. We figured it was safest if our stories were identical. We used our French textbooks from last term to add the other touches, things like the Promenade Des Anglais and the creaky parquet. All French apartments have parquet, right? It was Annabelle's idea to add *les mots français* for extra authenticity.

(Ha! Like my parents will care. Last time I was home, they spent the entire holiday arguing. I wouldn't be surprised if they get divorced.)

The money is for stamps. Tell Zoe, if she can, to put a train ticket or a restaurant napkin into each envelope. Touches like that will make our parents believe we're there with her. And remind her to take some snaps of her holidays; Annabelle and I will go into town and get some prints made when she gets back next term. If anyone asks, Miss Bartlett, or Ms Edbrooke, best to keep it simple and tell them you're writing to find out how Zoe's holiday is going on the Côte D'Azur, although I doubt anyone will even ask, seeing as you're spending the entire summer at school. So sucky! Anyway, it'd be great if you could get these off today because they're going to take a couple of weeks to get to France and back again.

Also, make sure you push your note *all* the way into the gap next time. Meanwhile, this paper will self-destruct in ten seconds, after you've read it—haha!

Thanks, Aimes! Gotta go; Annabelle's mooning over the new grounds-man. See you tomorrow night.

Marjie

Hi Zoe,

I hope your holiday is going well.

God, I wish I was there in France with you instead of mouldering in this hellhole. Second summer in a row that my step-monster has dumped me here at school. It's good for me, apparently. Creates independence. *Empowering* and all that. Well, she's not the one stuck here, is she? Bloody cow.

I should have done what Marjie and Annabelle did, and made my own arrangements. Empowered myself, you know? You wouldn't catch me staying at school, either—I'd be off to Auckland or Wellington. Somewhere where I could disappear and not have to answer to anyone. The freedom to come and go as I please; that'd be amazing. Seriously, why would anyone want to hide out in the school basement? Although, at least they're not likely to get caught. Since the caretaker retired, no one ever goes down there. Marjie and Annabelle have been sleeping on mattresses in the store cupboard. They must be positively cooking at night; it's been so blimmin' hot. Not that they're there much. Too busy going to clubs and hanging out with boys. They sneak out in their school uniforms and get changed later, in case anyone glances out the window. You have to admit as much as we all hate the scratchy maroon sack, it offers a veil of anonymity, especially from a distance.

The big news is that Marjie has snagged herself an actual boyfriend. Some guy she met in town. Mikey, his name is. Get this: he's twenty-six. *Twenty-six.* That's a whole decade older than her. He gave her a photo, which she carries in her bra and takes out occasionally to swoon over. "He's so hot. Isn't Mikey hot?" she goes.

It's true he looks a bit like Rick Springfield. In the photo, he's in this old leather jacket—it's hanging open—he's not wearing a t-shirt, and he's straddling a motorbike. I get why she likes him—I mean, he does look like Rick Springfield—but what does he see in her? It has to be about sex. They'll be doing the deed. They have to be. Explains why she's been so full of herself, lording it over Annabelle, who hangs on her every word, you know?

Poor Annabelle.

I can't really talk; the pair of them have turned me into a first-class thief, stealing food for them from the breakfast buffet, stuffing it into my pockets to deliver to the basement later. I've been nipping to the kitchens so often that Mrs Pederson is getting twitchy. Marjie says I don't have to do it anymore, that Mikey can get her whatever she wants. I don't want to get on the wrong side of her—you know how bitchy she can be—but I have to think of Annabelle. I can't let her starve. There's still another six weeks 'til the school term starts. Anyway, here's the next bunch of letters to send off. I owe you.

Write to me! I'm dying of boredom.

Love Aimee. xoxoxo

Dear Simon,

In response to the board's request, I am writing to follow up regarding the two new appointments to Hamilton Girls' school staff.

Tracey Bartlett took up her role as a junior teacher of English two months ago, nearing the end of last semester. You'll recall that at the time of her appointment I had misgivings about hiring such a young teacher, particularly one not long out of teachers' college. I'm happy to report that my concerns were unfounded. Ms Manssen, the department head, assures me Miss Bartlett has a sound knowledge of English literature, has slotted herself onto the staff with very little fuss, and in the short time she's been with us has established a reading group amongst the summer-stay girls (of whom there are around a dozen). A nice addition to the programming. Without their regular scheduled classes and sports fixtures, hostel girls who stay on can find the summer especially long. Perhaps it's because she's so young—barely much older than the senior students herself—that

Miss Bartlett has a feel for the kinds of texts which will engage them. Ms Manssen suggested we order Orson Scott Card's newly released *Ender's Game,* but when I approached Miss Bartlett for her view on the matter, she said they were already studying Lawrence's *Lady Chatterley* and were up to Chapter 2. Pleasing, since the school already possesses a class set of the literary classic. The hallways have been full of the girls' lively chatter. Of course, summer shouldn't be all about work, and Miss Bartlett has been accompanying some of the older students on evening excursions into town, either to the movies or to see the occasional stage show. So far, discipline has been maintained, with the girls all very appreciative of the extra freedom, and as we've had no reason to call in any parents, I see no reason not to continue the practice.

With regards to the new groundsman, Mr Dracul, apart from glimpsing him striding across the lawn to the hothouse one evening just after dinner, I've not seen him at all. You'll recall that the previous groundsman, Jim Carysfort, carried out the induction before he retired. As it happens, Mr Dracul's insistence on working flexible hours hasn't bothered us in the slightest, and given his rare skin condition, it's the least we could do. The board was worried about late night and early morning noise, but I've not noted any from my principal's quarters, and the school grounds remain immaculate. Mrs Pederson tells me that Mr Dracul has been leaving produce in the school kitchens each morning before she arrives—beetroot, radishes, runner beans, even some out-of-season varieties appearing like magic on the benches—an unexpected bonus, which should help to reduce our summer catering costs. Board members will be able to sample the 'fruits of his labour' at our Parent-Board luncheon in the new term. I hope this note lays to rest any residual concerns. I'll provide a fuller report at the next meeting of the board. Wishing you all a wonderful summer.

Yours,

Pamela J Edbrooke
Principal, Hamilton Girls' High School

Tracey's Journal, Summer 86

●●● **t**his morning the principal approved my summer reading progr-amme. I have the senior girls studying the provocative Constance

Chatterley. It's a small group—just seven girls. Already, they're thumbing ahead to the smutty bits and swooning over Mellors's muscles. To be fair, the aging school texts practically fall open on those bits. All the 'fucks' and 'cunts' are underlined. I don't think Pam Edbrooke has the slightest idea what the book is about. Jane Manssen said the principal had been a math teacher before being promoted into management. Doesn't surprise me. I told Pam that *Lady Chatterley's Lover* was a classic and that, seeing as the school bookroom has a class set, we should make good use of it. Jane raised her eyebrows at that, and quickly suggested a sci-fi, but I held my ground. Isn't it my job to open the girls' eyes to these things? What's the point of literature otherwise? I didn't say that, of course. I told her we were already up to Chapter 2, and I could hardly ask the girls to swap at this late stage, and that was that.

I like the girls. They're sassy, vibrant, funny. They haven't yet had the spark beaten out of them, which, from what I can tell, appears to be a key goal of the education system. Poor things. I've been taking them to the movies on the weekends, even stopping in at a local bar with them on the way home. No one suspects a thing. Made-up, and in their civvies, you'd think they were office girls and all old enough to drink. Only two of them are, but I can hardly leave the others out; they'd be wild with envy. I've sworn them all to secrecy and they're only too willing to comply for that illusory whiff of freedom. Youth, freedom: it's all so fleeting. They'll learn that soon enough. Although, these girls probably already know that, since they're still here while their schoolmates are holidaying in Australia, or France, or wherever. Life's such a disappointment; they may as well find their pleasure where they can.

That's my plan at any rate…

Hi Aimee,

That was a close call the other night at the bar! Thanks for distracting the summer stay girls, or we might have gotten caught. Go to jail. Do not pass go, and all that.

As it was, me and Annabelle and Mikey were giggling so much, we nearly gave ourselves away. The barman must have thought we were off our rockers, hiding in the booth trying to stifle our laughter. I wasn't too worried about Miss Bartlett recognising us—she arrived so late in the school year that she barely knows us, and especially not with us wearing our civvies—but Sheryl and Karen are in the same French class as Annabelle and me, so it was just as well you knocked over that wine glass when you did. Anyway, well done for doing that, and sorry about your skirt.

Thanks for these tomatoes by the way. After you saw me, I went back to Mikey's flat and stayed the weekend (his flatmates were away at a concert), so I didn't find them until I snuck back into the storeroom this morning. Looks like they've gone ripe a bit in the heat.

Hey, have you seen Annabelle? I don't know where she's got to. Probably out stalking the school groundsman. Talk about desperate. I mean, the school *groundsman*. Did you know he works at night? Annabelle has a thing for him.

"He's a dreamboat," she says. "All bare chest and muscles."

It's been so humid that she's been slipping out after midnight, peeking through the panes of the hothouse in her nightdress, no doubt hoping Mr Dracul will get a glimpse of her luminous white skin and heaving breasts. Haha! As if.

One time, though, she came back with this story...

"I was out in the gardens, desperate for some breeze."

(Desperate to get laid, more like!)

"It was stifling in the storeroom, so hot I couldn't get comfortable. Sweat was running under my breasts and in the creases between my legs, so I escaped into the gardens. It was freeing to be out in the open. The air was cool, and the wind was delicious, intoxicating. Just being out there in the darkness felt dangerous. Rebellious. I hugged the sides of the school building, keeping to the footpath so Ms Edbrooke wouldn't see me if she happened to glance down from the second floor. Her curtains swelled and twitched, but only because the windows were open and the breeze was drifting in, gently lifting the gauzy fabric and letting it drop. I kept on, lurking in the shadows, like a pale ghost in my night dress.

"The path led me down to the hothouse. I couldn't help it; it was as if I was being called there. I was drawn to the building, as helpless as a moth and my heart as fluttery as its flour-dust wings. The lights were on, glowing a soft yellow and flickering every once in a while. I slipped off the path, the damp grass tickling my bare feet, and circled around the back of the building where no one would see me.

"There was a wheelbarrow parked against the side, near the rear door.

I hunted around a bit, found a brick to wedge under the wheel, then climbed up and peeked through the panes.

"Dracul was there, inside working. Shirtless.

"I nearly died right there.

"His back to me, he was bent over a raised wooden garden bed, his shoulder muscles flexing as he turned the soil, plunging his arms into the earth scooping it up, lifting it, then letting it drop back. He was preparing the earth for planting a new crop: tomatoes or red peppers or something. Even through the grubby panes, his skin glistened with sweat. I couldn't hear through the glass, but I imagined him breathing, the sound of him inhaling and exhaling, and the patter of the soil as the clumps hit the bed and tumbled away.

"At that moment, if someone had come by, most likely I wouldn't have been able to pull myself away. The whole scene was mesmerising, like I was watching something illicit, erotic even. The way he was sifting the soil by hand made me wish I were laying in that bed, that I was the earth itself; he touched it so tenderly, like a lover.

"I would've stood there all night, balanced like a garden gnome in the wheelbarrow, but after a while, he stopped and brushed the dirt off his trousers. I ducked back quickly into the shadows and held my breath as he turned. The glass was dirty, and the grounds behind me were shrouded in darkness, so I don't think he saw me, but the thought that he *might*, the knowledge that he could be aware of my presence, was thrilling. My skin tingled with gooseflesh, and I shivered in spite of the heat. A dribble of sweat cooled and trickled down my front. Perhaps he did see me, perhaps I didn't just imagine it and everything he did was with the knowledge I was there.

"When Dracul crossed to another raised bed, I breathed again. Several stakes emerged from the soil, and one of them had a label that peeped out from between the leaves: Carysfort, it read. I recognised the previous gardener's name. He must have planted the bed before he retired.

"The crop was flourishing. Lush green foliage thrust upwards from the mound of dark earth. Even with the tent of support struts reaching to the hothouse roof, hundreds of the twisted tendrils reached out towards the sky and across the aisle, like fingers grasping and clutching at the air. They would not find a handhold, the spindly stems too weighed down with crooked runner beans. Mr Dracul took up his secateurs and snipped the beans from the vine, relieving the plant of its burden. Snip, snip. When he had enough—I guess for the school kitchens—he put the secateurs down. Then he bent over and turned the earth beneath the plant, as he had in the empty bed, only this time I saw what looked like a wrist, and *fingers*, in the clump that fell away. Grizzled mangled things.

"I gasped, and perhaps he heard me because he looked up, his dark brows coming together. I leapt out of the wheelbarrow and crouched behind a bush, my poor legs stiff from hours peering through the glass. I realised then it was almost morning and Mrs Pederson could arrive at any moment to begin the school breakfast. It was all I could do to force myself to turn away and creep back to the storeroom. What I'd seen was horrible, gruesome, and yet only the promise of coming again the next night allowed me to leave."

Annabelle said that when she got back to the storeroom, I was still snoring.

I feel a bit sorry for her really. She's so jealous of my relationship with Mikey, that she's made it all up of course—the furtive midnight excursions and that weird peep show with the groundsman. She must think I'm stupid. I reckon that's why she's not here. She'll have got the pip because I didn't come back all weekend, and now she's taken herself off to lick her wounds somewhere. Such a baby. Can I help it if I have a proper boyfriend? She just can't bear the thought of me engaged in an adult relationship. Still, we've been best friends since intermediate school, and I've gotten used to her sulking by now. She'll come around eventually. Or maybe she *has* got something going with Dracul; I don't know. Still, us hiding out over the summer was supposed to be the two of us. If she gets caught, we'll both be in big trouble. We could get expelled. You too, Aimee. So, do you think you could maybe check her room in case she's gone back there? I'll look for your note behind the radiator later today, so let me know if you find her.

Oh wow, these tomatoes are amazing. Did you try them? Bring more if you can. They're divine. I've been devouring them as I write this letter, and red juice is dripping everywhere. It's like blood, the liquid running down my fingers and soaking into my clothes. There's a big red stain in the middle of the mattress. I've already eaten six of them. I hope Annabelle isn't hungry when she gets back because they'll be gone.

Anyway, check her room, will you? Thanks.

Marjie. xoxox

Mrs Pederson,

Quick note to thank you for the Niçoise salad you served at lunch today. Absolutely magic. The beans, the tomatoes. Delicious. If you see him, please also pass on my thanks to Mr Dracul for the vegetables.

Pam.

Hi Aimes,

Annabelle still hasn't turned up. I'll check out the hothouse, see if she's there. If you hear anything, let me know.

Marjie.

Nice, France. Summer 1986

Hi Mum and Dad!

Sorry to take so long to write. I would have phoned, but toll calls are really expensive, and I'm trying to save my money for the art galleries.

I'm having *un temps merveilleux* in the south of France with Zoe and her family. Thank you so much for letting me come! Right now, we're staying in an apartment in the old town, *la vieille ville*, near Les Promenade des Anglais. The apartment has creaky old parquet floors. You can't move without making a noise. Zoe's mum insists they are *charmants*! The apartment has *une vue fantastique* of La Place Rosetti and the *cathédrale* (which would be even more fantastic if only we didn't have to climb four flights of stairs to see it).

Each day, Zoe, Marjie, and I go downstairs to the boulangerie to buy brioche for us all for breakfast, so I'm learning lots of French *vocabulaire*. Mlle Hourdin had better be impressed when we get back to Hamilton Girls' next term. I'm an expert at converting my money to French francs now, too. I'll write again soon. Don't bother to reply as we will be moving around a lot and the mail probably won't reach me in time. I'll show you the photos when I come home for the winter break.

Tell James if he touches any of my stuff, I'll come back to haunt him. Haha!

Love Annabelle xx

Tracey's Journal, Summer 1986

I took the senior girls to the pub again tonight. This time, we
• • • skipped the movies and went straight there. Weeks on, we've got
a favourite booth now. The girls are so deep into the subterfuge, I don't
even have to pay for my drinks. And one of them brings peppermints
to suck on during our walk back to school in case we're waylaid by Pam
Edbrooke and her gaolers.

These girls. No flies on them.

They're still engrossed in *Lady Chatterley's Lover* and, poor kids, they're
so starved of affection, they're seeing Mellors everywhere. Take the new
groundsman, for example. With the exception of Aimee, who I suspect
might be gay (probably too early to tell), they all have a massive crush
on him. Gushing over his muscles. His forearms. Raving about how
handsome he is. Quoting Connie Chatterley and using words like 'turgid'
and 'quivering'.

Well, it's like that mountaineer Mallory said, isn't it? Because *it's there.*
Dracul might not be their teacher; they might only have seen his shadowy
form going in and out of the hothouse or glimpsed him crossing the fields
at dawn, but his elusiveness has only served to make him more enigmatic,
more mysterious. The way they talk about him, he could be Heathcliff, all
dark brows and full of foreboding. They'll have cast themselves in the role
of Cathy, of course, every one of them a romantic heroine imprisoned
behind the walls at Hamilton Girls' and denied her life-giving force. And
meanwhile, Mr Dracul, their Mellors, their Heathcliff of the moment, has
been hovering at the edges of their everyday, tantalisingly beyond their
reach.

He's too old for them, of course…

But I'm not a student, am I? And I've been thinking that as a consenting
adult, I might just stroll down to the hot house one of these nights and
sample the produce myself!

A my. Marjie was supposed to meet me last Friday, but she never turned
up. If she didn't want to hang out with me, she should have just said
so. Tell her it's over. I don't have time for effing schoolgirls, anyway. Mike.

Zoe,

Oh my god, I don't know what to do. Everything has gone wrong. First, Annabelle went missing. Marjie thought she was miffed because Marjie has a boyfriend—well, I told you how Marjie was being a cow. Anyway, Marjie says Annabelle was making up stories about sneaking down to the hothouse at night and spying on the new groundsman, Mr Dracul. Marjie thought the stories were bogus. Now I'm not so sure because Marjie's missing too. And before you ask if she's hanging out with Mikey, I saw him in at the pub last night and she wasn't with him.

I was at the counter with Miss Bartlett, ordering in the drinks for the group like usual, when he brushed past me, stuffing a scrap of paper into my hand. I couldn't read it then, but a bit later I excused myself and went to the Ladies to read it. It made my blood go cold. You can probably see how shaky my handwriting is. The thing is, Mikey hasn't seen Marjie for a week. A whole week!

I decided then and there to tell Miss Bartlett. You don't know her very well, but she's not like the other teachers. She really gets us. I know, I know, we could all get expelled, you included, but what if something bad has happened to Marjie and Annabelle? I had no choice; there was no one else.

I was going to tell her on the way back to school, but when we reached Tristram Street she pulled up, telling us she thought she might have left something at the pub. She insisted that we girls go ahead, saying she'd catch us up later.

I lingered near the school gates, under the trees, waiting for her. But when she came back, she didn't go up to her room. Instead, she skirted the school grounds. My heart skipped a beat when I saw she was heading for the hothouse. I followed her, keeping to the bushes where I wouldn't be seen.

She went straight in. She left the door ajar, so I snuck in behind her and hid behind a stack of plastic sacks filled with potting mix. My heart was beating so hard it nearly burst out of my chest.

Dracul was there. He was just as Annabelle described him, tall and lean, with dark green eyes under his black fringe. He wore no shirt, and his body was slick with sweat. His face was pale, though, and there was a scar on his forehead.

"Mr Dracul," Miss Bartlett said, strolling around the ring of raised garden beds. The plants were so profuse, their foliage spilling everywhere, that Miss Bartlett slipped in and out of my line of vision, although I could still hear her.

Cutting tomatoes from a sprawling vine, Dracul looked up and smiled out of the side of his mouth.

I shuddered and squeezed myself further into the darkness.

Miss Bartlett, though, wasn't concerned. Running her fingers along the wooden edge of bed of flowering marjoram, she lifted her chin to show him her throat. "I thought we should meet," she said, teasingly. "Tracey Bartlett. English Department. I believe we started our tenure here at Hamilton Girls in the very same week."

He inclined his head, his fringe dropping over his green eyes. "Is that so?"

She grinned. Lifting her head and showed him her throat. "It is indeed. It makes us kindred spirits, don't you think?"

Sashaying about the hothouse, she picked up a trowel caressing the handle in her palm.

His hands still busy snipping the ripened fruit, Dracul followed her with his eyes. "If you say so."

Passing by an empty bed, she stabbed the tip of the trowel into the mound of dark earth. "I thought you might like to know that you're driving the girls wild."

"Really?"

She approached him. "Oh yes. They've been reading *Lady Chatterley's Lover*, and they fancy you as Mellors."

"Is that so?"

"Do you know the book?"

Abruptly, he stopped his snipping. "It was as if thousands and thousands of little roots and threads of consciousness in him and her had grown together into a tangled mass…"

I recognised the words; it was a quote from the novel.

"Ah, an intellect," Miss Bartlett exclaimed. "How interesting! So, tell me, are the girls correct? Are you a Mellors, Mr Dracul?"

He shrugged. "I'll admit that I like it down here, in the darkness and seclusion of the trees," he said, "I like the potency of silence." Then he resumed his snipping, accidentally piercing the flesh of one of the tomatoes. Red juice gushed from the punctured skin. Dracul raised his fingers to his lips and sucked the fruit-blood from his fingers. When he had licked them clean of dirt and juice, he said, "And you, Miss Bartlett? Do you fancy yourself as the lady?"

Miss Bartlett grinned from under her lashes. "You know, Mr Dracul, a woman has to live her life, or live to repent not having lived it," she replied, running the tip of her finger across his shoulder. Then she leaned in and whispered, "So then, shall we fuck a flame into being?" She was looking right at him, staring into his eyes, as she undid the top button of her blouse.

But Dracul stepped away from her. Shook his head. "I'm sorry, Miss Bartlett, but I prefer younger flesh myself. It's why I came to Hamilton Girls. To sample the students. The girls. The *children*."

"What?"

"Don't play coy. You understand me completely: '*only youth has a taste of immortality—*'"

Miss Bartlett's eyes flashed, and her mouth twisted. Her eyes narrowed. In that moment, she didn't say a word, but I could tell she was furious. Even in the sultry air of the hothouse, I felt her rage; it poured off her in hot waves. Here she was offering herself up to him, and he was rejecting her. She whirled then, lunging for the empty bed. She grabbed up the trowel.

Raised it above her head.

But Dracul, simply plucked it from her fingers, and laid it beside the mound of soil. "A strange weight was on her limbs," he said. "She was giving way. She was giving up…she had to lie down there under the boughs of the tree…"

Miss Bartlett's eyes widened as he spoke, but she was paralysed. She didn't resist, just stood there, as limp as a day-old lettuce leaf. It was as if he were enchanting her with his voice.

"She felt weak and utterly forlorn," Dracul went on, still calmly quoting Constance Chatterley. "She wished some help would come from outside. But in the whole world there was no help."

He used the secateurs to slice and snip her body into tiny pieces. Miss Bartlett simply stood there, while he hacked and tore at her, only falling to the ground when he severed her hamstring, yanking out the white tendons with the curled blade.

She was still alive. I know she was because her lips parted like a fish and tears leaked from her eyes, at least they did, until he gouged out the orifices with the tool.

Zoe, the hothouse ran with her blood. There was so much blood that I could taste it. Dracul reduced her to shreds of muscle and bone, then ploughed her into the newly readied bed. Afterwards, he patted a seedling into the mound, Miss Bartlett's blood seeping between his fingers.

All the while, I crouched behind the potting mix, useless. I was shaking so hard I was afraid he would hear my bones rattle. I thrust my fist in my mouth to prevent myself from crying out. I didn't attempt to help her. I watched him chop and dice her into a salad and yet I did nothing. I could have run—the door was open—but I remained there, like a mouse, crouching in my hiding place. Now, I wonder if I was enchanted, too.

When at last he'd completed his gruesome task, Dracul straightened. He arched his back slowly, then turned in my direction.

My blood ran cold. He *saw* me. I know it. He looked right at me, and said, "Vitally, the human race is dying. It is like a great uprooted tree, with its roots in the air. We must plant ourselves again in the universe."

I leapt up, pushed past the sacks of potting mix, and ran. Planter pots clattered behind me. I didn't stop. I sprinted into the night, up the path, to the school. I looked up, praying for someone, anyone, to look out the windows, a teacher or student, some witness to what was happening, but there was no one. Behind me, Dracul's laughter carried on the balmy air.

That was two nights ago. When I reached the school, I locked myself in my room and hid under the covers, too terrified to sleep. The next day, I went down to breakfast, wide awake and yet convinced I'd dreamed it, but Miss Bartlett wasn't in her usual place.

I asked Karen and Sheryl, but they hadn't seen her since she'd hurried back to the pub. They giggled.

Karen nudged me with her shoulder. "Maybe Miss Bartlett got lucky," she said.

"Honestly, Aimee, are you blind, or what?" Sheryl added. "I wouldn't be surprised if we don't see Miss Bartlett today."

"Or tomorrow, for that matter," Karen said slyly.

My heart flipped, hope surging in my veins. They knew!

"Yeah," Sheryl went on, "that guy in the leather jacket was totally eyeing her up." She gave me a shove. "Get a life, Aimee," she said, and, laughing, the pair of them left the dining room.

Leather jacket?

My heart sank when I realised they meant Mikey.

Zoe, it happened. It did. Everything happened exactly as I've written. I wasn't dreaming and I'm not making it up. Dracul's the devil. A demon. He killed Miss Bartlett, and maybe Annabelle and Marjie, too. And now he means to kill me. He does! If only to ensure my silence.

Last night, I heard him, calling to me in the night, urging me to join him. I can't sleep. I don't dare. I know my body will betray me; that it will creep from my bed to follow the path to the hothouse. I won't go. I won't. I dig my fingernails into my palms and will myself to stay awake, but I can't get the snip-snip of his garden shears out of my head.

Now he's climbed the tree outside my window, and waits, crouching in the branches. I know it's him. I recognise the scar on his forehead.

Zoe, please. Help me. I don't know what to do.

Dear Simon,

Quick note. I'll send a formal letter to the board in due course, but I just wanted to let you know that our young English teacher hasn't turned up for several days now. Nor has the school received any phone call to explain her absence. I contacted the address she gave on her application, but her parents haven't seen her either and I didn't want to sound alarmist. I very much doubt anything sinister has happened to her. The thing is, she was last seen by our senior girls when she took them to the pictures last Friday night. No one is saying anything much, but from the sideways glances and mentions of a 'friend', I gather she left the theatre with a young man. None of our business what she does with her own time, of course—she's an adult—but seeing as she's employed by the school as an overnight supervisor, a task she hasn't fulfilled for days now, I've had to organise one of the other staff to step in. If we haven't heard from her by the end of the week, Jane Manssen and I will pack up her room and start the process to terminate her contract—which will likely mean another round of job interviews before term starts. Shame, as the girls really liked her. I should have listened to my gut; I did say I thought she was flighty. Still, if I unearth anything in the meantime, I'll certainly let you know. On the other hand, Dracul, the groundsman has been a godsend. You should have tasted the Bartlett pears he sent up last week. Bursting with flavour. I didn't even know the school had a tree.

Pam.

While You Were Out. Phone Message. Thursday, 2.30pm

Ms Edbrooke,

Stephanie Branch, here, returning your call. I appreciate your concern regarding my stepdaughter's rapid weight loss and her recent night terrors. Teenage girls tend to be overly dramatic, don't they? I'm afraid Aimee has a bit of a track record on that score. Her distress over Zoe's parents' decision to have their daughter stay on in France is regrettable, I agree, but we cannot give in to Aimee's ridiculous threats to run away. My husband is currently out of town, but I have spoken with him by phone, and he agrees with me on this. Aimee will see out the term at school as planned, and we will revisit the situation again during the winter break. Hopefully, by then, this nightmarish behaviour of hers will be over.

The Legend Of Dracula Reconsidered As A Prime-Time TV Special

CHRISTOPHER FOWLER

JOURNAL OF J.H.

16 July – NYC

I figured with a name like mine it was the best thing to do, kind of like an omen, y'know? I started it while I was at school—just about the only thing I *did* start at school apart from a fuckin' fight. I got maybe seventy, seventy-five pages finished before they threw me out. Most of the guys in my year were taking advanced business studies, high-risk trading in non-government approved chemicals, how to improve your yield by cutting your shit with powdered laxative. Lemme tell you, I stayed out of *that* stuff 'cause I'm a dumb white boy and I just don't got the connections. So if I didn't live down to the neighborhood expectations, sue me – I walked outta school with bigger plans.

I wanted—I *want*—to write. I knew that much when I was five. Not classical stuff, 'cause let's face it a guy like me ain't ever gonna get to college given the fact that if my Ma ever got hold of enough money without turning tricks or robbing a bank, only the latter of which is unlikely, she'd blow it on a trip to Vegas to see Wayne Newton before she turned it over to me. So I figure I have to do it the other way around, which is write something first then sell it to the Big Boys. And hence the thing about my name, which is Harker, John Harker like the guy in *Dracula*, which gives me what to write about.

See, a guy with a pothole in his head can figure out the future is in media. You got more leisure time, you got more technological hoozis to play with, satellites and hi-definition and sixty 'leven channels, you're gonna need more programming to put out on the air. These network guys are strip-mining the past for black-and-white sitcoms no one watched the first time around 'cause they were so crummy, anything they can slam out into the ether, build themselves some ratings and get a channel profile, get advertisers knocking at their door with thirty-second spots for haemorrhoid ointment, and a guy like me, written off in the third grade as one of the Future Losers of America, stands a real chance of selling them something. First a pilot, then a series, then ninety-eight shows stripped weeknights coast to coast, bouncing off into space for the rest of eternity. Immortality, man. Immortality.

But first things first. I just finished writin' a sure-fire script, a new version of *The Legend of Dracula* told from my viewpoint, John Harker's angle on the battle with the Lord of the Undead, and let me explain here that this script cost me on account of I got caught writing it in the store and they threw me out, so as of today I got no job.

Which means, according to this Self Help book I'm readin', it's time to take stock of myself.

I got my health, my height and my happiness (if a lifestyle scenario which excludes fun, sex and money can be called that). I got an apartment in Queens. I'm renting with these two guys who're never home, but findin' the rent keeps me working my butt off half the night at the store, only now I don't have that job.

So I'll get another, no big deal, and meanwhile it allows me the time to go through the phonebook calling the networks to find out who's the big cheese in each organization that I can send my script to. The script's a second draft for a feature-length TV movie, but it's all there, they can make out what it's about, so I outlay a fucking grotesque amount of money on photocopying and postage and send off twenty-three separate envelopes in the Manhattan area, 'cause I ain't sendin' it out on no flash drive just so's it can end up as someone else's meme.

And then I sit back and wait.

Which is what I'm doin' now.

9 August – NYC

A guy can die from waiting.

After sending those packets I'm really glad I didn't splash out on a new cell phone 'cause to be absolutely frank my old one has not been ringing off the wall. At first I think maybe they don't like the subject matter, it's kind of ghoulish although there is what you'd call a subtext on the human condition, and the subtext is the reason for doing it.

I mean Dracula's been done to death, backwards, forwards, male, female, black, white, straight, trans, gay, musical, comedy, soap, kid's stuff, and every version available on every format ever invented. See, I got this theory. Times have changed; we don't die in the bosom of the family no more, we die in the arms of efficient strangers. It's 'cause we've become scared of death. And the more scared we get, the more sanitized we make the process of decay, the more we sugar up the Dracula legend to give us a palatable handle on dying.

So Dracula's been turned into some kind of upscale Eurotrash salesman, and he's everywhere, soft drinks, breakfast cereal, you name it. New York has vampires up the wazoo, but the Undead have been totally emasculated. They're clowns now, an' that sure takes the sting out of death.

So my script, my own *Legend of Dracula*, puts that life-draining shock of mortality back where it should be. It returns physical gravity to the material, provides us with a fear of death so real and deep and strong that we have to embrace it, and through catharsis allow it to exist in our lives once more.

Listen to me, I'm sitting on the john thinking my script is gonna change the fucking world and the truth is I can't get a network executive to read it. Not one reply so far, can you *believe* that?

Time for me to literally shit or get off the pot. So I ring around, try and get to speak to these guys.

Now, I ain't so naive to think I can just zip through the chain of command and reach Mr Key-Decision-Maker straight off the bat, but I figure that sending out the script gives me a talking point, an edge even, and out of twenty-three packages one must have eventually landed on the right desk. I start at the top of the list an' I call each one: NBC, ABC, CBS, HBO, Ted Turner, Cable, and not only can I not reach the busy-busy PA bitches with the English accents, I cannot get beyond the fucking switchboards of these places.

I presume my script reached one of your readers, I hear myself saying, to which some girl wearing a plastic headset asks me if it was a solicited manuscript, and if it wasn't can I come and collect it 'cause they don't get returned no more on account of so many being received and cluttering up the place.

I just thought I'd start at the top. Start with the Big Guns, y'know? I never really expected it to get picked up at that stage. Time to move down the list to the smaller independent companies, people who handle specialist material. No need for somethin' like this to have big names in; it's the idea that counts. I sit and compile a new list and do the same thing again with the photocopies and the mailings, 'cause if I give this up I sure as hell ain't got anything else to look forward to. Only it used up all my money, and I'm still lookin' for a job. So I go to see Frankie at the AcuPak Night Storage way down on 3rd, but it don't pan out. I thought you said you'd always have a job for me, Frankie, I say, but he grinds his cigarette on the floor of the stockroom and looks dumbly at me. Every-where's cuttin' back, John, he replies. There's a major recession on, ain't you heard?

Yeah, I heard all right. Which is why I just left Queens for this unair-conditioned shithole apartment on Bleeker that's cheap on account of the guy who owns it is a total burned-out fuckup and his lover needs someone there to keep a watch on him and stop him from sticking stuff in his arms every chance he gets and turning the joint into a shooting gallery. So now each night I have to close the bedroom door to block out the sound of Tina Turner singing *Break Every Rule* for the four millionth time before I can concentrate on getting the script out. This time I will get it to the right people.

I have faith.

Probably 'cause that's all I have.

20 September – NYC

What is it about Robert De Niro's name? I cannot *believe* this shit. Once again, no replies through the mail but then I can't be sure if Mr Manic Depressive Disco-Dolly don't reach the mailbox before me and set fire to the post. (I empty uppers and downers out the bathroom cabinet as fast as he puts 'em in, but I can't always be sure what he's taking 'cause he lies about it. Right now he's dancing around in the next room to some old Diana Ross album. He's not happy—it's a high. It's 11.00 a.m. By my estimation he's peaking about twelve hours too early.)

This time I figure why wait longer and start calling around almost immediately, and now I get a new kind of standard reply. I mean, it's obvious that small TV companies can't afford a fancy Upper East Side address, but just because De Niro put TriBeCa Films in a street full of warehouses don't mean every two-bit TV exec in town should evoke his name like a fucking talisman. Well, they say, we're small but we're very selective, situated near Bobby (Get this, *Bobby* De Niro, as if the exec goes over to his place for cocktails) De Niro's place.

I'm thinking listen, you could be workin' out of eastern Turkey for all I care so long as you read the goddamn script, and *this* is the crunch—for all the talk they give out, usually about themselves and the saintly regard the industry has for them, for all the smooth dialogue it emerges that none of them, not one, has read the damned thing. There's too much stuff coming in all the time. Too much loose paper around. Every dickhead with a desktop and an hour on his hands thinks he's got a script inside.

An' you know, maybe that includes me, but I still have faith in the script. That's what I tell myself as I type out the 'C' list and set about borrowing more postage money. My name is John Harker and I was born to battle the Prince of Darkness. And that's what I'm gonna do.

27 September – NYC

Well, the Disco Diva took a dive.

Yes, my room-mate managed to set fire to himself while enjoying the intoxicating effects of several noxious substances, which means he's in the hospital and I'm out of my watchdog job and out on the street. I think his lover was more pissed that the sound system got burned up than anything else. I don't even have the money to phone around the networks, 'cause these companies keep you on call-waiting systems for fuckin' hours, so I just did something I said I was never gonna do and that was, I sold a pint of blood. Under the circumstances, it seems appropriate.

It's hard conducting business from a callbox, but it's paying dividends. I start early, catch 'em before they got a chance to think. And guess what, someone has read the script and likes it. Two people, in fact. Both of them say they're interested. I got me a pair of meetings to take. Oh, I *like* the sound of that. Priorities first, though. At the moment I got nowhere to sleep, and no good clothes. It's still hot at night, I can rough it for a couple of days until something turns up, take the meetings—after all, they're interested in the quality of writing, not whether I shop at Armani—and maybe get an advance.

Round Two to the Harker family.

Good shall prevail.

October – NYC

I should know better by now.

The first meeting's at a place called Primetime Product, situated, natch, near *Bobby's* building, and is taken in an office the size of a basketball court by a guy who's coping with premature baldness by growing a ponytail. He gives me the once-over, wrinkles his nose as he lets me sit down and hunts out the script. Then he asks me how I'd feel about turning it into a half-hour sitcom featuring Dracula as a funny superhero. I give the idea careful consideration, then tell him I don't think it'll work, and remember, I say this with an image of me sleepin' on a park bench in mind. But he wants the bones without the meat and it really *won't* work, a child of five could see that. End of meeting, shown to the door, thanks for comin' in—and I have to ask for the fuckin' script back because he's returning it to the shelf behind his desk even as he's talking me out.

Sleepin' in the park is okay because the cops don't run you in anymore – these days there's too many people an' nowhere to put us all. I could have done without some drunk puking his guts up on the next bench all night, but right now it don't pay to be fussy, and besides I'm already thinkin' of the next meeting. I got two shirts, one pair of sneaks and one pair of shoes, one T-shirt and a pair of ratty jeans, plus a nylon backsack containing a shave bag, a blanket and the scripts. There's other stuff at my Ma's but she's in Atlantic City underneath some loser and I don't got the keys to her apartment.

Next day's a real hot one, so I go for a swim an' use my last five bucks to get my shirt laundered so maybe I won't look like a total bum.

I get to PowerVision (I'd like to meet the guy who sits in a room thinkin' up these names) at twenty before the meeting, an' I'm still sittin' there at twenty after. The woman who sees me is dressed so severe that first of all I think she's wearin' a grey cardboard box. She looks at me funny even though I don't smell and my shirt looks great. Then she tells me she hasn't read the script but she's been instructed to buy it. Although I'm gettin' excited this alarm bell is goin' off inside me, and I ask what she would like to do with it.

And she says I want to give it to our writers to see what *they* can do. I ask her what she means. *I'm* the writer. I mean, if they like what I've written, why get someone else to fuck with it? I guess I'm not supposed to speak at this stage 'cause she looks at me as if I just took a shit in her fruitbowl. Well, she says, the piece is way too downbeat. It can be Gothic, but it's got to be fun. We could liven up Dracula by giving him a wacky sidekick. I point out that there's one in the book we can use, and I see her flinch at the word we. Renfield, I say. He's an interesting character. What's he like? she asks. He's insane, I explain, and he eats flies. Not on television, she replies, not if we want a family audience. Also, the title has to go. We've already got a new title. *Fangs A Million.*

You can figure out the rest. At least this meeting lasted longer than the first one, mainly 'cause she was late gettin' it started.

On the way back I gave blood again, which gives me some ready cash, but I gotta tell you this is depressing the hell out of me. Tomorrow I'll maybe try to tap some guys I know for a loan. Then I guess I'll start calling again.

It's a setback for the Harker family as the Lord of the Undead goes into the lead. Where the hell is Van Helsing when you need him?

19 October – NYC

In the last couple of days the weather has turned. Central Park never looks fresh at the best of times. Even in spring the greenery has a kind of dusty look about it, an' now it's just brown. There's nothing lyrical you can write about autumn in this city. New England maybe but not here. I can't believe I'm still sleeping rough. It's gettin' too cold to stay out all night. I did one smart thing while it was hot – I kept out of the sun. You get a tan in New

York, you automatically look like a bum unless you're wearing good clothes.

Nobody I know has any money to spare, but I ain't going to panhandle for it. That's what I told CeeCee, you offer a service or no deal. I was always taught that nobody rides for free. He laughed an' said that's exactly what he believes. CeeCee used to work at the coffeeshop on Bleeker, but he got canned and now he's started hustling again, which I figure you have to be pretty fuckin' desperate to do these days, and I ain't that desperate. Yet.

Trouble is I can't get welfare 'cause I ain't been out of work long enough, and in theory my Ma can still help. Of course, she's in a garter belt on her knees in some motel workin' off her blackjack bill at the Trump Casino, but try finding a sympathetic ear for that one. I been workin' on some revisions to the script, some improvements I think they'll go for. Trouble is I got no access to any devices. It's all written longhand, and the networks won't read longhand.

I got the blood thing down to a fine art by loaning out my card to a rota system. See, they won't let you give blood again until you've made it up fully, and they date-stamp your card, but a bunch of us go to different clinics with each other's cards. It shaves off a few days and don't harm you none so long as you keep eating.

I guess this is the low point of my life right now. It can only get better from here. I even called around to my Ma but there was no one home. I've walked my ass off going to every single goddamned company on my list tryin' to get to see someone, anyone who could help. That's it; I've tried them all except the pornos, and out of the whole shebang I got me one decent new lead: I read that some rich NoHo gallery just financed a new TV company to develop independent projects for cable, so I dropped a script around to them, called them back a week later and they want to see me tomorrow. I'll go along, but I ain't expecting a miracle. It's starting to get dark out here, and the park is looking more and more like Transylvania to me.

October – NYC

Max Barclay has the same number of letters in his name as Van Helsing, and the same powers. I feel like he just jumped on the refectory table and pulled down the drapes, blasting pure morning light across the prostrate figure of the Count. And in a way, that's what he's done. He's saving my fuckin' life is what he's doing. Let me go back three days.

WorldView TV turns out to be a pretty snappy joint, located in an area where the only thing that separates power-dressed corporate executives from bums lying in doorways pissing their pants is a foot of concrete and a window. Their receptionist is hip enough to once me over without calling security, which is a relief as I am sporting that 'just attacked in the park' look, then this beefy guy who may be a pro-football player comes up and shakes the bones outta my hand and tells me how he loves the script.

And how he wants to make it.

Just the way it is.

An' that's where we are right now. It's gonna take a while to sort out the contract, but it's gonna happen. The bad news is, no loan until it does, but hey, it's always darkest before the dawn. That script is my stake, and now I've found someone with a hammer. Together we'll nail the son of a bitch.

27 October – NYC

No news yet.
Called Max today and we talked over problems with the script, all minor. He says he may be able to get some upfront money soon. I don't want him to know I'm still living in the park. It could fuck things up between us; he'll think I'm some kind of nut. I want this to be right. One day I'll be mixing drinks in my seventeen bedroom adobe-style Bel-Air ranch house telling kids how tough it was to break into showbiz, and at least I won't be lying.

My dawn will break.

11 November – NYC

I called Max and told him about my cashflow problem. It took a certain amount of pride swallowing, but I can't live like this much longer. He breezily suggested meeting over a drink but I can't let him see me, it's just too fuckin' humiliating. I got no clean clothes and no money. It is so fucking cold that even the seasoned park bums have all moved on, God knows where. Maybe they just froze up an' got covered over with leaves. Maybe that's what'll happen to me if I don't get a few regular meals soon.

Max says there's something he forgot to mention before, and that is he has to present the script to his board. There's no chance they'll turn it down so long as his recommendation stays, but it delays things. It ain't his fault, he doesn't know what I'm goin' through here. And I ain't about to tell him any more than I have to.

18 November – NYC

Just when I thought my 'income' couldn't get any lower, some attitudinous dude at the clinic finally figured out what we've been doing with the donor cards. A few days back, the temperature went out the bottom end of the thermometer, so I moved down into the subway. The smells here are warm and bad. You can taste disease in the air. But the people are worse. Dangerous, like regular laws don't apply to them underground.

CeeCee says I can stay with him, it's a nice place, he can get me some duds an' a spending roll. All I have to do is take a couple of the extra johns from him. He says I got a good body, I could earn two, three hundred bucks a night. I told him things are bad but I'm just not ready for that kind of stuff.

I tell myself I'm the one with the moral strength. A Harker. A defender of the faith. So instead of waking in a soft bed, I look up at the city through a fucking grating.

30 November – NYC

I know the number so well I punch it out in my sleep: Wait. Give the extension. Wait. Max Barclay please. Wait. Last Tuesday I spoke to the PA again, Stephanie from London. Very polite. Max is in Hawaii for two weeks, didn't he tell me he was taking a vacation.

No, he fucking didn't.

I try to explain I'm not badgering her, all I want is some reassurance, a sign of faith. I had—I *have*—faith in my script. Max says he has too but he don't ever prove it. It seems the board weren't entirely happy. There have to be a few small changes made. Okay, I'll wear the changes but let's get the contract through first, then we'll talk changes.

Changes. Dear God. I'm at CeeCee's apartment. When it started to snow an' the subway filled with crazies, the cops threw us back on the street an' I knew the time had finally come. I got no more blood to give. My weight was down to 120 pounds. I looked like a peeled stick. CeeCee's been good, at a price. I take no more than one john a night, and nothing too wild. If they won't wear a rubber they're out on their ass. I do it without thinking. I daren't let myself think. This is one part of my biography that's gonna stay in the drawer.

There's a new scene in the script.

By the dying light of the chamber's fire, the Count can be seen stepping forward. He stands a full head taller than the librarian. Gently, he takes Harker's face in his pale, tapered fingers and studies him, a spider examining a new kind of fly. The chill from his dead eyes sinks into Harker's bones. The young man is truly face to face with death. He feels the vampire's gaze killing off the cells in his body, and his brain starts to grow numb. He knows that if, at this moment, the Count chooses to let him die, he will indeed die. The numbness rapidly spreads. His will is drained away like blood leaking from a deep wound. Reason fades, to be replaced by a thrilling new sensation far beyond fear, an awakening ecstasy as Harker finally understands the night, the eternal night...

And the Count releases him, breaking off his gaze. He has granted his foe a steady, lingering look into the abyss. But the sight has made Harker stronger, because it has made death his friend. It has given him the power to free himself.

I hold on to that thought.

22 December – NYC

Max says I'm difficult, too idealistic, that nobody survives intact. I assume he's talking about the script. At least he's back from his vacation and we actually get to meet again now that I have some clothes. We drink red wine in a fashionable media joint on Amsterdam, surrounded by flickering TV monitors. Well, I say, this is the longest courtship I've had before somebody's fucked me, and he laughs. The contract's gonna be through after Christmas, he promises, when WorldView's legal department finally get to check everything out with the Bram Stoker estate, plus every other joker with a claim to the character who reckons they have exclusive copyright. It better come through, I say, 'cause right now what we have here is a failure to remunerate. He laughs again, tells me I'm really on form tonight.

If Max has noticed that I'm going quietly nuts waitin' for the green light, he ain't showing it. He wishes me a happy Christmas an' walks off into the snow with his scarf around his shoulders, that's how confident he is. Me, I don't wanna leave the bar. Leavin' the bar means leaving the warm an' going back to CeeCee's. Back to work. But at least I know now that I have the strength to get through it.

The Harker family will be avenged.

16 January – NYC

Why is it all the changes have to come from my side? He remains motionless, a silhouette on the ramparts, a shadow in the doorway. I adapt to survive. He lives on, unchanging, the eternal victor, the cape wrapped around his elegant form like a suit of armor. Impenetrable. Immovable.

It isn't fair.

CeeCee is dead. On Christmas Eve he went out to some fancy new club, and that was the last anyone saw of him. The cops say he got rolled by a john over at the Adonis around 2.00 a.m. Christmas morning. Ordinarily he wouldn't have died but he'd had a little booze and taken a few uppers, and the shock of hitting the ground did something to his neck. He never regained consciousness. The cops asked me if he had any family. It never occurred to me he even had a family.

Christmas morning. What a lonely fuckin' time to die.

CeeCee always said I could stay on in the apartment. He knew I didn't like taking the johns. He wanted to help me so he said I could stay. He never told no one else. I went in his bedroom to pack up his stuff and it was like a little kid's. Teddy bears and movie star posters. The next night

I came home and found the locks had been changed. I wish he'd told someone else I could stay.

I called Max to ask about the contract, but he wasn't there and the English PA wouldn't give me his home number. I found myself crying on the phone. Fucking pathetic.

Goin' back on the street was a shock. When I get ahold of Max I'm gonna ask him to put up or shut up. Hell, I'm gonna ask him if I can stay at his place while I'm writing the script. I should retitle the fuckin' thing *Out For The Count*, 'cause that's what I'm gonna be soon if he says no.

I'll do anything to get out of this situation, man.

Anything.

January – NYC

I am undead. That's how I think of it. Trapped in limbo. This is living death. Darkness reigns and Harker loses. Now and forever.

Fuck Max. Wherever he is, fuck him. He could have told me, he must have known. You don't leave a job without a little preparation. You don't just up and blow. The PA says he's gone out to LA, she don't know his whereabouts. She couldn't tell the truth if her fuckin' life depended on it. Lying is part of her job description.

The new guy's name is Feinstein.

I spoke to him after calling so many times he finally had to speak to me. He told me the first thing he did when he took over the job was freeze all of Max's projects. He needs to determine a budget floor and ceiling for next season, and he won't be rushed. It'll take some time to establish market windows. That's not to say the door is closed on my script. By this time I figure either he used to be a builder or he's incapable of gettin' through a sentence without using mediaspeak.

I tell him I am experiencing a downturn in my fiscal wellbeing at the moment and may not be alive by the time he gets around to perusing my masterpiece. Perhaps I can call him in a day.

Taken aback, he agrees. But not to a day. A week.

One week. Days, hours, minutes. Nights.

I don't work on the script no more. I can't 'cause some asshole lifted my bag on the subway, and the last copy I had was in there. It's 3.00 a.m., way below freezing, and I'm hustling for johns on 42nd St.

Man, this is so far below my dignity, it's horrifyin'. I got a cold that won't go away, an' a dream that won't die. Better if it did. Better to let it go.

Maybe I been fightin' on the wrong side all this time. After all, my namesake met his end in the book, but it was just the beginning of the Count's career.

They say people are attracted to him because of the darkness.

The dark never seemed attractive to me until now.

31 January – NYC

Another couple of days, he tells me. There are so many scripts to go through, and he must be fair to every one. Call him back at the end of the week and he promises to have an answer, this way or that. The PA tells him mine's one of the best scripts she's ever read, an' she's been in the business a long time.

I am standing in the phone booth listenin' to this.

It's so cold I can't tell where my feet end and the sidewalk starts. I have two dollars in my pocket, a coldsore on my lip, and there are no johns on the street. I stayed a couple of nights at this guy Randy's apartment but it turns out he really wanted to beat me with a studded strap, so I got out. It was worth good money, but hey, I have my pride. That's a joke, by the way. There's a sticker on the coinbox in front of me, some broad offering guys an enema and I'm thinkin' well, at least it would warm me up. I feel weird, like I passed beyond some kind of barrier.

I can't give blood no more. They don't want it. They said it's gone bad. I got bad blood now. I told the doc I'd been bitten, but he didn't get it. Two more days. The dark before the dawn. This is gonna be an eleventh hour rescue, I can tell you.

You should never have tried to fight him, Jonathan.

February – NYC

A foot of snow around the callbox an' I got sweaty hands.
I got a pocket full of quarters which it turns out I need 'cause they leave me on callwait for ten minutes, during which I get to listen to three songs from *South Pacific*. Then he's not at his desk. It takes them a couple more minutes to locate him. I'm thinking this is good, this is a buildup of tension, this makes the news stronger.

Well, it does do that, at least.

I really didn't like it, he says. Not *sorry for fucking you around* or *maybe you'd like to write something else for us*. Just I *really* didn't like it. But that's not the best part. He leaves a small silence while I'm supposed to make grateful noises for his opinion. Then he says I should remember the network buzzwords, which are *Feelgood* and *Reassurance*. The public don't want to see this kind of thing, he says, it's way too depressing. Times are tough for them. They need to be told that everything's okay. I should bear that in mind next time.

I guess I could have screamed and shouted at him, but I just said quietly, there isn't gonna be a next time, and hung up.

A t least it's over. I kind of feel better now. Not knowing was more painful than I'd realized. Yeah, I feel better now. I'm a little shaky walkin' out of the box, but the sun is shining. I should of asked him to return the script, but somethin' in me didn't want it back. The battle's ended. Dawn's here.

I gotta get myself a new jacket. This one's too thin. I'm freezin' my ass off. Pockets are ripped. Gonna get myself cleaned up. That's how I'll start. First the jacket. Then the life.

A t least I took the bastard on, right?
Maybe I didn't win, but I sure as hell held him at bay once more, until it's someone else's turn.

Isn't that all you can ever do?

J.H.

New York Post 6 February

MAYOR SLAMS 42ND ST
'SIN PLAYGROUND'

A fresh call to clean up the 42nd St and Times Square areas has begun following the death of a young hustler in the early hours of yesterday morning.

John Harker, aged eighteen, intervened in a fight during which he was stabbed in the throat by an unknown assailant and left to bleed to death in the street. His pleas for help went unheeded and he died before reaching hospital. Police have so far been unable to trace his family, and are appealing for witnesses.

The Mayor has called for an immediate crackdown on resurgent vice in the area, dubbing it a 'battleground where the forces of evil are nightly fought'.

Variety 18 September

DRAC'S BACK, AND
WORLDVIEW'S GOT HIM!

J ust when he seemed all played out, Dracula came back to wreak havoc with a record-breaking bite of the season's otherwise glum ratings last night.

WorldView Productions' three hour mid-season replacement *The Legend of Dracula* became the stuff of legends when it topped the Nielsen ratings with a tale that proved both a critical success and an audience smash. Worldview Veep Arnie Feinstein attributes the hit to a new slant on a very old tale, and promises a series to follow the special.

Legend sees the familiar battle of light and darkness unfolding through the eyes of a teen adversary, and seems set to sweep the board at Emmy time. Impeccable performances and stylish sets grace a powerhouse script of depth and subtlety.

Surprisingly for such an acclaimed project, the anonymous *Alan Smithee* tag conceals author credits, but with interest running this high, WorldView will have to name the source of their script to qualify for its inevitable awards.

The scene most singled out for praise features a struggle of wills in which the desperate Jonathan Harker is subjugated and lured to the brink of eternal darkness by his merciless captor. Given the fever pitch of worldwide sales interest, it looks as though the Prince of Night is once more set to reign – this time through the cable channels of the world.

Children of the Dragon

JASON FRANKS

NICK GANTO'S JOURNAL–OCTOBER 12TH

Today was my first day working for the Children of the Dragon.

Other cults would call their headquarters a compound, but since they're based out of Silicon Valley, the Children call it a campus. That's also the reason they contract out the drudge work: cleaning, catering, and, of course, security. Yay for gainful employment.

The Dragon himself came to meet me when I showed up at reception. "Nick Ganto?" he said, standing next to the ubiquitous potted ficus tree by the reception desk. Most clients are surprised to see a woman in the job. That's why I added the K: Nicola gets fewer security gigs than Nick.

"Yeah, I'm Nick."

The Dragon looked me over. I'm big enough that few people question my qualifications to do the job on the basis of my gender—unlike, for example, my time working at the newspaper.

"You can call me V." He wasn't friendly, but he spoke with an intensity that made you believe him. I could immediately see why people would follow him.

"Good to meet you, Mr. V." I was glad he gave me an initial, because Mr. Dragon was gonna get awkward quickly.

"You know who you are working for?"

V is difficult to place, and not even Google appears to know. He might be a Sephardic Jew, or Roma. Or maybe Spanish. Arab. There's definitely something Eastern about him. He has wavy black hair and olive skin and more mustache than is fashionable. Can't place the accent. I bet he was educated in some fancy international school.

What does the V stands for? Victor? Valentine? He's too foreign to be a Vance.

"I work for the security company, Mr. V, and they've contracted me to you."

He shook his head, spread his hands in a low-key movement to encompass all the people in his organisation. "Not me. Us."

"The Children of the Dragon." I kept my voice toneless.

"You know who we are?"

"A faith community."

"We're not a religion."

"Didn't say you were." I had Googled them before work, but I still wasn't sure what they were. While everyone with a message to sell is looking for virality, the Children are opposed to 'surveillance culture'. It's a sign of the times that such obvious cause-and-effect is counter-intuitive. How can you tell people to stop watching you, if they aren't watching you to find out?

The Dragon smiled for the first time. It was an honest smile, although a little on the toothy side. "We're a cult," he said. "Nobody here will deny it."

"Long as the agency pays me, I don't give a shit. What do you need me to do?"

V put his smile away, like it was a rare thing that might oxidize if shown too much air. "Monitor who comes in and out. Maintain the perimeters. Sometimes you will be my bodyguard."

"Any particular threats I should know about?"

"I will keep you apprised." He turned away. "Come, I'll show you around."

The campus stands behind a 20-meter electrified fence, with parking on all sides. A checkpoint with a boom gate is the only way in, but the booth is unoccupied unless V is expecting visitors. The Children use the same keycards for parking as they do to access the campus building: a five-storey office block, with converted living quarters interspersed with the work areas. The second floor has a gym and exercise studios. I estimate about thirty people live and work here, with more commuting in.

The fifth floor looks like a hotel. V was cagey about it but it's basically a place for weird sex and drugs. I'm actually glad that's part of the ideology, because the Children of the Dragon are more like a startup than a cult. Without the free love it's just a bunch of people sitting in front of computers or going to meetings.

Control room in the basement has feeds from all the CCTV cameras outside the building. There are no cameras inside, of course.

The basement has a storage room for weapons. V is an advocate of the Second Amendment, but nobody is allowed to be armed on the campus except me, so there's usually a lot of ordnance in there.

"What about the sub-basement?"

"There is no sub-basement," V replied.

I pointed at a door in a niche behind the elevators. "That's a stairwell."

"Oh," said V. "I did not know that."

He watched me as I went to the door. "Definitely a stairwell."

The door had a new-looking deadlock mounted above it, but no keycard reader.

"I suppose it's unused," said V. I didn't ask if he had a key. "Come, I'll walk with you back to Reception."

Back on the first floor, he just walked away without waiting for a final salutation.

I think he likes me.

OCTOBER 26TH

I've worked twelve shifts at the Children of the Dragon's campus now but today's the first time I've actually had to do anything.

Security work is mostly walking up and down and watching traffic. Boring, but exhausting from maintaining a state of vigilance for uneventful hours. Security for a cult is just as excruciatingly mundane as it is for any other client. Or maybe the Children are a boring cult.

Anyway, today was full of action and excitement. First, I rousted a paparazzo camped out in a car across the street. Sleazebag slept there overnight—I guess hoping to snap some celebs coming or going. Desperate, if you ask me. Anyone famous involved with the Children of the Dragon is not the kind of famous I recognize. Nerd celebrities.

Right after that, V asked me to escort a woman off the premises. Leaving the cult, apparently. V didn't seem angry but there were definitely bad vibes.

The lady was upset, but no more so than someone who had been let go from an office job.

After lunch I turned away a pair of reporters who showed up, unannounced. I guess that's what I used to be like when I was at the paper. Like those two creeps, only bigger.

I could have crushed them like a pair of bugs.

NOVEMBER 4TH

Today I escorted the Dragon to an off-site seminar.

V doesn't conduct regular sermons. He manages the Children quietly, but personally. Passing through the campus, I often see him hunched over someone's shoulder, looking at a screen, or sitting in a meeting room with a small group. He listens more than he talks. So a speech is a rare event.

We piled into a big Mercedes, driven by a silver fox type. I think the Merc is his personal vehicle. The fox drove us to a hotel, where a crowd of about a hundred was waiting for us in a conference room. There were no recording devices that I could see. I sort of recognized some of the audience from campus; some from the news media. Some I just recognized the look of. Silicon Valley types: engineers; product managers; data scientists. Startup founders; VC investors. Hustling writers, negotiating both sides of the increasingly hazy line between journalist and social media influencer. The same hustling that drove me out of the business after the newspaper shed 80% of its staff.

V stepped to the lectern. I stood behind him and to one side, scanning the crowd. They were watching him with an intensity that was unnerving. If it had been just one of them, I would have pegged them as unstable and dangerous, but here it was the whole room.

"We were promised freedom," said V, starting with some classic Americana. The audience was holding its breath.

I'm paraphrasing, but let me assure you, dear diary snoop, that V is a hell of a lot better speechwriter than I am.

"Freedom to be as we please, to build the future we please. That is why all of us came here, from all across the world. To build the future." The crowd was diverse, but no more so than you might from a tech business. A lot of white men and not nearly as many white women. As the demographic travelled eastward through Europe, the Middle East, the

Subcontinent, Russia, and East Asia, the proportion of women grew, but not to parity. Few people from south of the equator were represented among V's future-makers.

"Fifty years ago, this city was ground zero for the Summer of Love. But we have abandoned this legacy. Instead of elevating it, we have buried it, and left it to molder." ('Molder' is such a great word! He said it with a straight face!) "We have built a future of surveillance. Our data is mined and commoditized. Our behavior is cultivated and harvested without our knowledge or consent. We ourselves, the future-builders, made the tools that are used to exploit us. To sell us false comforts to fill the void of the freedom... the love... that we have given away.

"The data-mongers offer us convenience and a sense of community that comes free of commitment. They offer us a kind of immortality: a debased existence, rendered down to ones and zeroes, from which they have skimmed our human essence. They keep us like sheep, to fleece or to slaughter at will.

"But we are not sheep. We few, at least. I am the Dragon, and you are my blood. My children. You are dragons also. Together we will write a new future. We may bleed in the doing, and we may burn. Hard work is never easy. Love is not easy, but love is everything. We will prevail."

When he stepped down from the podium the trance gave way to ecstasy. "We love you, Daddy V!" "The dragon prevails!" "Bleed and burn!"

It sounds corny, written down. A pile of old hippy nonsense, rehydrated and microwaved until it steams. But I'll never forget the sight of all the Children chanting it with their bleached-white teeth showing, veins pulsing in their necks.

V turned from the lectern, impassive, and I led him down from the stage. I'm unsure if the crowd had parted for me or for him.

Crazy or not, the lecture did get me thinking. When I got home I went and deactivated my Facebook account. Maybe tomorrow I'll ditch Twitter.

DECEMBER 5TH

I caught a pair of ninjas during last night's shift.
They were pretty good. Little bastards had timed my perimeter checks and they cut the fence when my back was turned, so it was mostly luck that I saw them.

Lucky. I was bored and cold on a foggy San Francisco evening. I stopped to do fifty quick pushups under the fire escape to get my heart rate up.

Twice lucky. They didn't see me when I saw them, because I was low to the ground when they came out of the fog, all dressed in black, hoods up, gear slung behind them.

I flattened myself against the concrete and waited for them to pass. Then I followed, low and quiet. I loosened my sidearm and fingered the mike receiver clipped onto my cuff.

The ninjas worked their way around the building to the loading bay, then went up the ramp to the metal door beside the roller shutter. They judged their approach to avoid the exterior CCTV cameras. Slick.

One of the pair knelt down in front of the door. It's the only exterior door with an ordinary lock instead of a keycard reader. The other one turned to keep a lookout.

"Hi there," I said, resting one hand on my holstered Glock.

The lookout ninja raised his hands hesitantly. The second one turned around slowly without getting to his feet.

"Hi," said the lookout. His friend couldn't speak, on account of the lock-picks pursed in his mouth. "Hold steady. This is all a big misunderstanding."

"I understand this is about to progress from trespassing to breaking and entering," I replied.

"Actually, we're, uh, from the..."

I raised the mike. "Control, this is November Golf. I have two intruders at the loading bay, over."

"This is control," said a radio voice from the security company. "Do you need backup, over?"

The crouching ninja spat his lockpicks and lunged like a sprinter coming off the blocks. I don't think he meant me real harm—he just wanted to knock me down so he could run for it. I turned with him, hooked an elbow around his neck, and levered him face-first into the asphalt.

I stood away from the fallen ninja and drew the Glock. It must have hurt pretty bad. Apparently today's ninjas don't know how to breakfall. The second ninja put his hands in the air.

"I say again, November Golf: do you need backup? Over."

I kept the Glock on them one-handed and raised the mic. "I need the cops, Control." The ninja on the ground looked up at me with blood dripping in his eyes. "And probably an ambulance, over."

V surprised me by coming out to see them for himself. I'm pretty sure he waited until I had both ninjas face down and zip-cuffed. I had the impression he didn't want them to get a look at him.

He didn't say a word, just looked around the scene and gave me an appreciative nod. He'd gone back inside before the cops arrived.

DECEMBER 6TH

V tells me that the ninjas were actually private investigators, sent to plant some listening devices. Ninjas or PIs, those two creeps weren't amateurs. The Children of the Dragon must have some serious enemies.

I'm V's favourite, now. I think he must have spoken to the security company, because they bumped up my rate a dollar an hour.

Sure as shit beats working in the mall.

DECEMBER 8TH

Like all of the other contracted drudges, I've been more or less invisible to the Children up until now. Occasionally one of them will greet me if they saw me on my rounds, but usually not. That's perfectly okay with me.

Today, the silver fox who drove V to the seminar approached me as I was arriving for my shift. He's younger than I thought, and more handsome. "Ms. Ganto," he said. "I'm Rob Schmidt. A pleasure to meet you."

"Nice to meet you, Mr. Schmidt." I don't usually shake hands when I'm working, but he put his out and I couldn't politely refuse him. I've seen him around since the seminar and I don't think he lives on campus, but he seems quite senior in the organization. He has a good grip.

Schmidt smiled like he meant it. "Call me Rob."

"What can I do for you, Rob?"

"Look, I just wanted to thank you for your work yesterday," he said. "And I was wondering if I could buy you a cup of coffee?" He has that confidence that assumes you can't, or won't, say no. I wouldn't have minded the company of someone good looking, but I didn't think he was angling for a date. "I'm sorry, Rob, I'm about to start work." It was 1400—I had nine hours to go.

"Tell me when it suits you," he said. "I'll make myself available."

I guess we're on for tomorrow. Maybe it's a date, after all?

DECEMBER 9TH

It wasn't a date.

At 1330 Schmidt was waiting for me outside reception. We walked a couple of blocks to an Australian coffee shop on the ground floor of an office tower. Inside, it's all blonde wood, hanging lights and cool-colored tiles. It doesn't smell like Starbucks and it doesn't sound like Starbucks, which is pretty much the only kind of coffee shop I know.

"What'll you have?" The waiter had a disappointingly local accent.

"Americano, please?"

"Long black," he replied. I just nodded. Whatever he wants to call it. Schmidt ordered a decaf latte.

"So anyway, thanks for coming to coffee with me."

"Sure."

"You did some pretty great work with those private dicks the other night."

"It's my job," I replied. "Thanks for noticing I'm competent."

"They were good," said Schmidt. "And there were two of them. That was more than competence."

"Professionalism, then."

The waiter brought our drinks, which came in glasses. I was surprised they were so small. Schmidt spooned half a sugar into his and stirred it. I picked up mine by the rim, then set it down again. Too hot to drink.

"Anyway, you've done a service to the Children, and we'd like to reward you."

"Send me a gift hamper," I said. "Weird soaps and fancy preserves. I love that shit."

"That's not what I meant." Schmidt took a sip from his latte, licked the froth off his lip. "What I meant was…access."

"You want me to join up."

"There are benefits," he said. "And I don't just mean the insurance."

Insurance is something I definitely need, but I was sure there was a price.

"If you join, I can probably get you in at level four, and I'll personally pay the admission fee."

I hadn't expected the price to be so literal. Was this an Amway pyramid scheme or a cult? I snorted softly, and then tried to conceal it by drinking some coffee. It had cooled some. "I'm not much of a joiner, Rob."

"First time for everything," he replied.

The coffee was thicker than I expected, and the taste was fuller. Coffee is something I drank in quantity as a stimulant and, maybe sometimes, a thirst quencher, but this was something better. I couldn't see myself coming back for it, but I could sort of understand now why cashed-up techies were into it.

"You don't need a security thug to help with all that computer-y stuff you got going on."

"Nick, it's not just about who is valuable to the Children... it's about who understands the mission. Who is down for the cause. And I think you might be, if you gave it a chance."

"I'm not a peace and love girl, Rob."

He leaned across the table, his hands clasped together, and pressed them to his mouth. Then he raised his head. "I was the same," he said. "Hard-nosed pragmatist, I thought." I looked at him again. Now I looked I could see the military in him.

"USMC?"

"Army. A couple of lifetimes ago. I thought coming out of that was tough, but... real life turned out to be tougher."

I nodded.

"It got bad. My career, my family... you know."

I blew my own career, but I've never had a family—or wanted one. But Schmidt obviously thought it was a point of empathy. "Hard times. And then I met V, and..." There were actual tears in his eyes. "He changed my life, Nick. I know it sounds dumb, but...he saved me."

"Was there a baptism?"

"No. No." He smiled, dabbed away the tears. "No Jesus stuff, nothing like that. But V, the Children...they taught me how to love. For real and for true." He was completely sincere. I couldn't understand why an operator like Schmidt would embarrass himself like this, in public.

"I think I get it."

"No you don't." He just looked at me. "Nick, you said 'peace and love' before, but you're only half right."

"Yeah, look...thanks for offering, Rob. And thanks for the coffee. I've never had one like this before."

He could see that I meant it, too. He cleared his throat, and out came the salesman's smile again, though his eyes were still red. "It's cool," he said. "I'm sorry if that came out like some kind of pitch. But really... really truly...if you change your mind, come to me. We could really use someone like you. It'll change your life."

I put my coffee glass down on the table and stood up. It really had been a tasty drink, even if it was a bit undersized.

Wasn't 'til I was on the job that I remembered V's sermon and I figured out what he meant when he said I was half right.

Not peace and love. Love and war.

DECEMBER 13TH

Been out of sorts the last few days. The more I think about it, the less I appreciate Schmidt's attempt to bring me into the fold. Meanwhile, the Children have gone back to ignoring me. And the weather's been shit. Which is not an excuse for what I did, but it is a reason.

Tonight I was bored and lonely and cold and pissed off beyond the usual baseline rent-a-cop levels. I let myself in the fire escape door and took the stairs down, telling myself I was going in search of my thermos.

On the basement level there was no one using the gym. In the control room, I could see there was no movement outside the building.

I opened my locker, took out the thermos, and then took up the lock-picks I pocketed before the cops had dragged away the two ninjas.

It was unprofessional for me to go and look at the forbidden door. Out of character, too. But Schmidt's overture had unsettled me, and I was looking for some kind of answers.

I'm not a thief, but I have some friends who do physical pen testing— guys who get hired to break into buildings to see if their security is up to snuff. I've also watched a bunch of videos on YouTube. It took me about three minutes to open the deadlock and half that to pop the door handle.

As expected, the door led to a stairwell. I took out my SureFire flashlight and resisted the temptation to unclip my holster as I started down. On the landing, the smell of damp yielded to rust and diesel fumes.

I expected an old boiler room, but the sub-basement was a private car park. The SureFire revealed polished concrete floors marked with parking bays. There was only one vehicle, which was covered with a tarpaulin. On my left, tucked into a corner, was a fridge, a writing desk, and a chair. The far wall was obscured by a mess of pipes and electric cabling.

First I went to the car, my boots squeaking on the floor, and raised the tarp. A compact SUV, Japanese. Nothing fancy. No plates. Dark color, maybe black or blue.

I shone my SureFire around, following the perimeter until I saw a ramp leading out. At its mouth I found that it was blocked by a serious steel shutter. There were no controls for it on this side of the door. I wondered where it came out. Certainly not inside the campus carpark. Most likely under one of the buildings across the road.

I went back inside to get a look at the weird knot of plumbing. Lying inside a loop of copper pipe, webbed over with fat black DC cables, I found a rectangular box a little bigger than an adult human. The front of it opened like a fridge, but it wasn't an appliance. There was a glass viewport at one end, through which I could see it was lined with rubber. Red lights shone on the glass like the head-up-display on a fighter jet. I think it's some kind of sensory deprivation tank.

Was it a place where the Children were conditioned and/or tortured?

Probably not. They might be a cult, but none of them are zombies.

I'm pretty sure it was V's private chamber.

Creeped out by the tank, I went to investigate the desk. It was covered in books and papers, hand-written, in a mix of languages. I couldn't read any of them. Some used the Cyrillic alphabet, some Roman characters. There were a handful in Arabic and…maybe Hebrew? If I had bothered to take photos I guess I could stick them into Google Translate, but I'm a minimum wage security guard, not a spy. Anyway, I was more interested in V's paperweight, which was a weird bayonet.

The handle was made of wood and the whole thing looked very old. The blade was squarish and unpolished, but sharp. It was no Spyderco, but it was pretty cool.

I made myself walk back to the stairs and climbed them carefully, wiped the lock clean of prints with the tail of my shirt and closed the door quietly behind me. I didn't think V would be pleased if he'd seen me coming out of there.

AP WIRE–JANUARY 14TH
34 Dead at Rhubarb Shooting

This morning 34 people were killed when armed gunmen stormed the Cupertino headquarters of internet news site the Rhubarb.

All five perpetrators fled the scene. One of them is believed to be injured.

Police are treating this attack as an act of terrorism but have not identified any suspects. No terror-linked organizations have claimed responsibility at this time.

The Rhubarb is an online news site known for long-form journalism and aggressive advertising campaigns targeting rival publications.

The death toll includes bystanders not affiliated with the Rhubarb. An additional five people, injured during the perpetrators' escape, are in critical condition. There are no survivors among the Rhubarb staff.

NICK GANTO'S JOURNAL - JANUARY 16TH

The Children are taking the Rhubarb massacre very seriously. V put the campus into lockdown. Nobody in or out without his say. The cleaning and catering services are cancelled. With no visitors, I'm patrolling for my entire shift, so it's cold and shitty all the time.

I don't understand the lockdown. I mean, nobody knows who did the massacre. 4Chan neo-Nazis, still angry that their idol has been cucked? Charlie Hebdo jihadists? A hostile state actor? Why are the Children concerned?

In the week after 9/11, when I was still at the paper, the building was evacuated because some poor dick in a turban got off the elevator on the wrong floor. I just don't see why the Children would be a target. If they were, surely there would be cops here, not just me?

JANUARY 18TH

The campus is still locked down. The Children are talking to me, now, since I'm the only one who gets to come and go.

They are sympathetic to the dead and their families, but I also hear darker mutterings. Outlandish stuff: the Rhubarb was spying on them. Rhubarb journalists used hackers and social engineering to gain information. Rhubarb bought data from shady brokers. Rhubarb was planning a libelous story about the Children. Rhubarb deserved what it got.

Maybe the journalism business has changed, but I don't believe any of that. I'm damn sure those ninjas weren't working for the Rhubarb, or we'd have heard all about it.

JANUARY 24TH

Forgot my thermos at home, so I went back to the Australian coffee shop before work to caffeinate. Waiter must have recognized me, because he asked me where my friend was.

Hadn't realized it, but I haven't seen Schmidt around for a good couple of weeks. Kind of a relief, actually.

The coffee's still *mwah*.

JANUARY 28TH

Well.

Night shift. Come 0300, I knew something was wrong. It was just too quiet, even for the late hour. Not a single light on.

My keycard didn't work, which was another bad sign. I went around to the loading bay door and I picked the lock.

It was dark inside. Emergency lighting only, although none of the buildings adjacent to the campus were blacked out.

I took the stairs down to the basement. The fusebox looked fine, but the power stayed off no matter if I toggled anything.

In the control room, the console must have been on the emergency circuit. Maybe the card readers were on the mains? It didn't make sense. Camera feeds showed no movement outside.

The floor plan view of the campus showed a lock icon over every single door, in red. As I watched, the icon on one of the rooms on the fourth floor switched to a green, open lock. A couple of minutes later it went red again. Then next door along the hallway opened. I don't how many fire safety codes that must violate and I wondered where V had sourced this security system. A prison, I guess?

I grabbed the keys for the fire escape from the lockbox and took the stairs up to the first floor at reception level. Up again. Landing, turn. Up. Landing. Turn. Up. Landing. Turn. Up. I opened the heavy door as quietly as I could and emerged onto the fourth floor.

The emergency lights pulsed redly in the empty hallway. I unclipped my holster and put my hand on my Glock.

A door at the far end of the hall opened. A figure emerged.

No question it was V. He was dressed, as usual, in a suit, with a dark shirt open at the collar. He turned and looked directly at me.

"Nick," he said.

"Good evening, V." I started to walk towards him, hand resting on the butt of my Glock.

He came towards me as well, making no effort to conceal the bayonet in his right hand. The blade was clean, but I could smell blood as he drew closer. His hands were wet.

"You're up late," I said.

"When you're a leader, sometimes the only time you can get work done is when everyone is asleep. I'm just finishing up now."

I glanced at the bayonet again. "For the last time, from the looks of it."

"It's time the dragon took flight."

"And the dragon's children?"

He shrugged.

"They loved you," I said.

"They did."

"I thought love was everything?"

"Ah," he said. "I was not a good father, but perhaps I have learned something."

I looked at him standing there with the bayonet. I didn't know how many people he had murdered in their beds that evening, going room to room. Did he waken them first? Did any of them resist?

"Love isn't satisfying, if you don't love them back," I said.

He nodded once. He didn't make a show of it, but I could sense him weighing his options. He was a just as tall as me, but I was bigger. He had a blade, and I had a pistol and a good ten meters. Not good odds for him. V turned the bayonet over in his hand and tucked it away, concealing the blade behind his wrist. He raised his empty left hand, palm open, keeping it at waist level. Something happened with his face that wasn't an expression change so much as a change in *intensity*.

"Do you love me, Nicola?"

I frowned, surprised at the question, and found that I had to really think about it. I shook my head. "No, but I do think you're a nice guy."

The dragon nodded once, his decision made. "I'm leaving now," he said. "Feel free to call the police and emergency services. But in the meantime I suggest you hurry out of here. There will be fire soon."

I could have drawn my pistol. I could have told him to freeze. I could have shot him. But I knew I wouldn't, just as well as he did.

Maybe it was some strange cult leader charisma, maybe not. Truth is, I've never shot anyone. I'm a security guard, not a cop, or a soldier. It's not my job to shoot people who aren't threatening me, or to arrest those who've committed a crime. Why would I? The best outcome for me is a manslaughter charge.

V turned his back on me and went to the elevator. I did not know where the bayonet had gone, but both of his hands were empty by the time he reached it. The doors opened for him as soon as he pressed the button. The light inside was startlingly bright. Now I could see his bloody footprints on the carpet.

V went into the elevator and turned to face me, and I think that image will haunt me forever. V, reflected by mirrors on three sides, blood dripping from his cuffs, lit from above like a religious icon.

The doors closed and I turned and ran.

JANUARY 28TH - CONTINUED

Cops kept me for like thirty-six hours. I told them that V had a car in the sub-basement, but since I didn't know the registration and it was such a generic model they're probably not going to have much luck tracking it.

I supposed that V planned an escape route that avoided surveillance cameras. That was his thing, after all.

MARCH 2ND

I've been watching the leaked footage of the Rhubarb massacre for three days now. I've seen a dozen edits on YouTube: set to music, dubbed with dialogue, or plastered over with memes. At the moment they're being posted faster than they can be taken down.

I can't bear to look at it anymore, but it's there whenever I shut my eyes. I'm going to try to exorcise it by describing it here.

Whichever law enforcement agency is responsible spliced the footage together from many cameras, at different resolutions and aspect ratios. There are gaps in some parts of the coverage, while others are visible from multiple angles. Thankfully there's no sound.

Ok.

It opens on the ground floor of an office building. Couches, pot plants, elevators. Three people milling around in the waiting area and one more sitting behind the reception desk.

Six hooded figures come in through the front doors. They are wearing gloves, goggles, surgical masks—it's impossible to make out their faces. I think one is a woman.

One of them bends to set some device on the keypad that prevents the doors from opening. Four of the others draw Steyr assault rifles from inside their coats. The sixth individual, a tall man who remains unarmed, directs them to open fire. The receptionist ducks out of sight but the leader directs a gunman to move around the desk with a hand gesture. The gunman does so and fires three times.

The man who set the locking device guards the door as the other five advance into the building, reloading as they step over the bodies. The floor is littered with shell casings. These first four victims are collateral who just have the misfortune to work in the building that houses Rhubarb's main office.

The camera on the receptionist's computer gives a profile view of the killers waiting for the elevator. The camera in the elevator shows a view down to them. They keep their guns at ready. None of them look up. They file out of the doors when they open.

The killers fan out at their leaders' instruction and start shooting. The footage cuts between the overhead CCTV cameras and webcams mounted on individual computers and, in a couple of cases, cellphones. Some of these shake, or are strangely tilted, as the killers stalk through the cubicles, spraying the room on full auto.

One of the killers staggers. Blood sprays from an exit wound high on his back and he staggers against the glass window. An overhead view shows a balding man with a heavy caliber pistol in two hands, rising from a kneeling stance. A low angle shot from someone's cubicle shows him advancing on the leader of the killers. He's shouting.

The leader turns to face the balding man. He's still unarmed. He stands there, straight-backed, and raises his left hand to the man with the gun, keeping it at waist height, palm open. The footage cuts between three different cameras to show this moment. It's hard to tell with the mask, but I think he asks the man a question.

The balding man looks confused. The gun in his hand wobbles. Cut to an overhead view as a burst of automatic fire smashes him off his feet.

The leader turns on his heel, raises his hand above his head. The killers form up behind him and we watch them take the spiraling stairs down from a single high vantage. The stairwell brightens as the door at the bottom of the stairwell opens, but the killers are no longer visible. Their shadows flicker across it and it falls dark again when the door closes.

The footage cuts back to the images of carnage in the Rhubarb office, and down in the lobby. The only movement is the flickering of the timestamp at the bottom left of the screen.

Fuck this. I'm going to bed.

MARCH 3RD

Didn't sleep much. It's 0245.

I watched that fucking video a thousand times, but I knew from the first that the leader of the killers was V. How many of the others are people I was around every day for the last 5 months?

MARCH 3RD - AGAIN

Poring over every news article I can find about the massacre and I spotted something in the victims list. Neringa Karlsson. She's the former disciple I escorted off the campus in my first weeks. I remember the name, because V had me cancel her security access. Apparently she went to work for the Rhubarb.

I remember the Children saying the Rhubarb was going to run a story on them, but…I found Karlsson on LinkedIn. She's not a journalist. The Rhubarb hired her as an accountant.

What the actual?

REUTERS - MARCH 12TH
Cult Linked to Deadly Raid

The privacy cult calling itself the Children of the Dragon have been linked to the mass shooting that resulted in the murder of 34 people in the Cupertino offices of the Rhubarb, an internet news site.

Police have identified the remains of a man found on the slopes of Black Mountain in West Santa Clara as belonging to Robert Belmont Schmidt, who is believed to have been a senior member of the cult. The coroner's office says Schmidt had a sustained gunshot wound, but ascribe the cause of death to knife attack. Schmidt is believed to have been one of the shooters at the attack on the Rhubarb.

Most members of the Children of the Dragon died in January this year when their compound burned to the ground. Police are still investigating the fire.

NICK GANTO'S JOURNAL - APRIL 5TH

I can't seem to let this thing go. Maybe I shouldn't have quit the security company because now I have nothing to do but stew on it all day.

So I went back to the cops for another chat. Nobody in the station house would tell me anything, but I did convince the computer forensics nerd (his name is Brad) to come out with me for an Australian coffee. Brad says the whole thing was a hacking operation. They were stealing private information about the people who worked at the tech giants. V told the Children he was going to use it for leverage in his privacy wars. Getting them to let up on their surveillance so the Children could love free and clear. That's what he told them, while he was actually selling the hacked data on the darknet. So much for data privacy extremism...

I don't believe V will ever be found. The reality of the Dragon will fade until all that remains is his image, cast in grainy security camera footage, left to haunt true crime accounts and crank conspiracy theories.

I've been thinking about what to do with this journal. I've spent more time with the Children of the Dragon than anyone left alive. I was there at the end. Maybe I should turn this into an essay. Publish it somewhere. Sell the TV rights. Or maybe just earn some pizza money. Who the hell knows what journalism means today?

But this isn't some researched news article. This is my story. This is me. If I put it out there, I'm feeding V's legend. It's like inviting him back into my life. Do I want to spend the rest of my days in his shadow?

What frightens me most is that I don't know.

Meeting Brad again for coffee on Thursday. He's buying.

MEMORANDUM FOR THE DIRECTOR – JUNE 12TH
Special Agent Vanessa Helsing

Chuck,

Wish we'd moved sooner on Ganto, but her police statements were misfiled and now it's too late. She would have been a goldmine of information.

Some good news: whoever tossed her missed her journal when they took her computer and devices. Think you'll find the transcription (attached) illuminating. For one thing, we had no idea that one of the Rhubarb vics was a former cult member.

Neringa Karlsson was V's accountant. With her name we've managed to trace money from the cult to a series of offshore accounts (paper trail attached). The Rhubarb event was about her. The other 33 deaths were a smokescreen.

Have also made some progress on identifying V. He's likely a Romanian national named Vladimir Țepeș. Believed to have come up through an Eastern Bloc infosec academy at the end of the Cold War. When he was an active hacker his handle was 'Dracul'. Dragon.

No record of him ever entering or leaving the US. No information on current whereabouts. The offshore accounts we identified were cleared weeks ago.

We're still looking into Ganto's disappearance. The Sheriff's Office computer forensics team does not have any operators named Brad. CCTV footage from the station house the week of Ganto's last visit is missing and we're still trying to work out what happened.

Enjoy the reading,

– VH

Worlds of Wonder

RON FORTIER

The Brothers Dracula – Karl Ludwig Dracula (1785-1863) and Wilhelm Carl Dracula (1786-1859) were Transylvanian academics born in the village of Borgo Pass. They attended the University of Transylvania. They were devoted to researching the early history of their native language and literature including Germanic folktales. The Brothers Dracula established a methodology for collecting and recording folk stories that became the basis for folklore studies.

This is a story about stories. Actually, it's about the people who tell the stories. Storytellers for the most part, although in these modern times we simply refer to them as writers. Oh sure, there are a few folks who still love to spin an oral saga every now and then. If you lived in the wilds of some deep, dark jungle à la the Congo or perhaps Borneo, you might find an old tribesman who remembers how to spin a yarn with their words and keep an audience spellbound for hours on end.

Whereas our setting is New York City in 1934. We'll keep this story about writers. And like their savage, uncivilized brethren, they also knew how to keep their readers turning pages. Don't let anyone ever fool you into thinking storytelling isn't a gift. It really is.

If you were living in those days, you'd know this already. America was in middle of an economic collapse that historians would eventually come to label the Great Depression. People by the thousands had lost their life savings as bank after bank went bust. Factories closed by the hundreds and jobs were as hard to come by as pirate's sunken treasure off the Florida Keys. Keep that image in mind for later. Wall Street had crashed, the Roaring Twenties were kaput and Mr. and Mrs. America prayed in churches across the land for better days while unable to drop even a nickel in the collection plates.

Breadlines went around city blocks filled with weary, tired men in suits and ties still doing their best to look good; to put on a brave face and tough out another day. They had tons of self-respect and very little else.

Which is where we come to the subject of entertainment, what little there was available in 1934. If you were lucky enough to own a radio, you could at least sit around at night and listen to cheesy melodramas on the air or ridiculous comedies, skin-crawling tales of horror or simply tune in to some big band playing the latest melodies from high atop a Manhattan skyscraper.

The movies also provided momentary escape, if you were lucky enough to live near a movie-house and had quarter to your name. At least for a couple of hours you could forget the troubles of the world outside and get lost in the last cowboy adventure or applaud a new Busby Berkeley dance number with hundreds of gaily dressed hoofers all moving in elaborately choreographed syncopated rhythm.

But the cheapest, most readily available and clearly the most outlandish entertainment of them all were the cheaply-printed monthly magazines that miraculously appeared on street kiosks every week. An enterprising fellow from Maine named Frank Munsey had come up with the idea of using the new high-speed presses to print on inexpensive, untrimmed pulp paper in order to mass-produce affordable periodicals. Whereas those titles printed on clean, white paper were called the "slicks," and cost all of a quarter, the "pulps" were offered for one lousy dime.

Munsey then pioneered the first all-fiction titles. They were the direct descendants of the last century's dime novels and penny dreadfuls. These were aimed at the working class and filled with all kinds of action adventure stories from gun blazing westerns to high seas romances. Remember that pirate reference earlier? By the time of his death in 1925, Frank Munsey had pretty much guaranteed his place in the annals of American literature as the Father of the Pulps. Sadly, he really never got to see just how popular they would become. Just nine years after his passing, pulps proliferated and every kind of topic imaginable was represented in their coarse, brown pages.

By 1934 dozens of pulp publishers were giving their readers monthly doses of exhilarating fiction featuring such great heroes as the Shadow, the Spider, Doc Savage, the Phantom Detective and so many, many more. Street & Smith led the pack as the most successful of these publishers. Founded way back in 1855 by Francis Scott Street and Francis Shubael Smith, their offices were located at 79 Seventh Avenue in Manhattan and boasted some of the finest writers and editors in the business.

But the most famous pulp editor of them all hung his hat at another shop; Xanadu Press located two blocks north. Xanadu had been started in 1905 by Harvard graduate Thomas Amesbury Belmont to publish high school and college text books. What with the Industrial Revolution having spurred the advancement of education throughout the land, institutes of higher learning were popping up everywhere like wild mushrooms after a summer rain. Belmont, with his degree in Business Management, saw a buck to be made and soon was one of the wealthiest book makers in the country.

When the Depression hit, many schools were forced to close their doors due to lack of both funds and students. Who could afford an expensive degree when scraping up pennies to feed themselves? Thus Xanadu, like its publishing sisters, saw its own sales plummeting and most likely would have folded completely had not young Thomas A. Belmont Junior, having joined the company upon his graduation from Dartmouth, convinced his father to diversify their product line. He suggested they get into the magazine game and shortly thereafter established the subsidiary branch Wonder Press and its flagship pulp title, *Six-Gun Outlaws*.

Thereby saving the company.

Over the next few years, Belmont Jr. continue to add other titles to their line and for a while things looked good. Unfortunately, the grind of assembling and putting out half a dozen monthlies uncovered a very sad truth; that although Belmont Jr. may have been a good business man, he wasn't a very good editor. Which is where our tale is heading, if you haven't figured that out yet.

Who am I? Actually, that's really not important. You can call me the Narrator if you'd like. You see, who I am is part of the mystery of this particular tall tale and I promise you we'll get to that by the end. But for now, don't give my identity a second thought. After all, this story isn't about me. It's about our protagonist; the greatest pulp editor who ever lived. He's the real hero and he is just about to make his appearance. So let's get back to the story.

So where were we? Oh, right, Xanadu Press was in trouble and Thomas A. Belmont Jr. was getting an ulcer worrying about how much longer he could keep the company afloat. Desperate to turn things around, Belmont Jr. put an ad in the Daily New York Journal looking for an editor with the proper bonafides to take over the daily operations of Wonder Press.

Two days later, on a quiet August morning, a smartly dressed fellow walked into the Wonder editorial offices located on the fourth floor of the building. He looked to be in his mid-thirties, of average height and physically fit. His face was well defined with good, rugged manly features and he sported a thick black brush mustache that covered his upper lip. His eyes were gray and with a lively intensity that seemed to drink in his surroundings wherever he looked. Wearing a brown suit that had seen better days and carrying a black umbrella, he marched to the only desk in the small reception room and removing his gray fedora with the wide brim , bowed to the receptionist in what was clearly a grand, old school gesture.

"Good morning, Miss," he greeted her in a deep, bass voice.

The Miss he was addressing was Belmont's aide, secretary and all around receptionist, Wanda Rawlings. In later years, when recalling that first meeting, Wanda would describe the man as striking. On the other hand, she was nothing to sneeze at either. In fact the twenty-one years old Wanda was a stunningly beautiful woman who had turned many a man's head while growing up in Plattsville, Utah. She'd been born with her Swedish mother's honey blonde hair and her Irish father's stature and dazzling green eyes. Standing tall at five feet, nine inches, she had always towered over the boys she went to school with. Raised working on a dairy farm, by the time Wanda entered Thomas Jefferson High School, she was a statuesque beauty who would have given Aphrodite a run for her money.

And believe me, I should know.

Anyway, after graduating, Wanda had a rather important epiphany: unless she went and got herself a decent job, the men in her future would only be taken by her ravishing beauty and not her quick, brilliant mind. You see, she'd graduated the head of her class and was the Valedictorian at her graduation ceremony. The topic of her speech was "Women in the Business World." By the end of that twenty minute dissertation, half the parents in the hall had nodded off.

A week later Wanda boarded a train to Chicago where she enrolled in the Emma Browning School of Dictation. She earned her diploma as an Executive Secretary and then took another train; this one to the great metropolis of New York City. Two weeks after arriving she was hired by Belmont Jr., who couldn't believe anyone could type three hundred words a minute until he witnessed Wanda doing just that.

What really surprised the hard-working editor was how she looked when she arrived at work the next day. Attired in a formless, oversized, dull colored dress, Wanda had bunched her shining locks into a tight bun behind her head and stuck a pair of black rimmed glasses over her face. Note, the lenses were clear glass as she'd always had twenty-twenty vision. When Belmont Jr. commented on her appearance, she explained it was a social disguise that would put off the more cavalier of the men she would deal with.

"I'm sure you understand," she stated quite flatly, before leaving his office and for the first time taking the chair behind what was now her own desk.

Belmont guessed at her meaning, scratched his head and forgot about the matter. As long as the young lady did her work, how she dressed was none of his concern. Still, he always thought it was such a shame to hide such natural beauty.

"Good morning, Miss," greeted the striking visitor. "My name is George V. Dracula and I have an appointment with Mr. Belmont Jr."

Wanda glanced at her desk calendar where she'd jotted down the fellow's name.

"One moment, please," she said and then flicked on the intercom box.

"Yes, Wanda," Belmont Jr.'s voice sounding tinny over the small speaker.

"A Mr. Dracula is here to see you, Mr. Belmont."

"Ah…right, send him in, please."

Wanda shut off the speaker and indicated the door to the left behind her. "Please, go right in."

"Thank you," he replied politely, nodding his head. Then he entered her boss's inner sanctum and Wanda Rawlings went back to sorting all the

151

incoming mail for that day. Though not as popular as Thrilling Publications or Street & Smith, Xanadu did have its loyal following and hundreds of letters poured into the Wonder offices every week. It was Wanda's task to open them and then direct them to whichever magazine title they were referring to. Most were affable and she did enjoy reading them. Naturally a few were nasty and critical, but she merely shrugged their caustic comments away as the product of small, little minds. Wanda was a true optimist at heart.

"**C**ome in, come in," Thomas Belmont Jr. welcomed as George Dracula entered the editor's little square office. It was a corner room with windows to the right and behind the small desk opposite the only door. They were opened four inches to allow fresh air into the sanctum as well as the constant cacophony of music known as New York City motor traffic. To the left were several tables on which were stacked both completed the latest Wonder pulp magazines and next to those, hundreds of unopened manila envelopes. They were stacked so high, several appeared to be precariously close to toppling over. Behind them on that wall were several framed posters representing the better-selling Wonder titles, à la The Dakota Kid and Mrs. Homicide.

Now Belmont Jr., unlike his guest, was a roly-poly figure who simply loved food and couldn't avoid sweets. Add that to the fact that most of his day was spent sitting behind a desk, the poor soul never got any real exercise at all. In his fifties, he was of average height, with thinning gray hair, a round, doughy face almost pure white for lack of sunshine, a fat nose, and two surprisingly blue eyes beneath wire-framed round glasses. His chief distinguishing asset was his ready smile which, when on full display, seemed to illuminate his rather plain features and show the world a friendly zest that continued to reside within his large frame. Let's just say, physical appearance aside, Belmont Jr. truly had a good heart.

The desk he sat behind was cluttered with giant sized galley sheets, each containing the full copies of the newest issues ready to go to press. Beneath these were more manuscripts, note-books, city directories and somewhere buried beneath them all, his telephone and intercom unit. Guarding over the mess were two standing photographs: one of Belmont Jr. and Belmont Senior, in fishing togs, standing knee-deep in a Colorado river, a captured moment of love between father and son; the other a black and white picture of Belmont Jr., his better half, Gladys Marie Walters Belmont, and their eighteen-year-old boy, Jeffrey. When things got tough, the tired magazine manager would look at those two pictures and find renewed strength to persevere.

Now, as he stood and came around that overtaxed work station, he prayed Mr. George Dracula just might be the answer to all his prayers.

"So happy to meet you," Belmont Jr. beamed as he shook Dracula's hand.

"Likewise, Mr. Belmont. Thank you for responding to my resume so swiftly."

"Please, have a seat," the editor offered, pointing to one of two hardback chairs in front of his desk. "And please, call me Junior. Everybody does."

"Very well," Dracula smiled as he sat down. "And I'm George."

Now seated again, Belmont Jr. just stared at his guest for a few silent minutes until the awkwardness of the moment became apparent. For his part, George Dracula simply waited for the man to say something, which he finally did.

"Ah, yes," Belmont Jr. chuckled good-naturedly. "On to the interview. But before we start, would you like some coffee?"

"Yes, that would be nice."

Belmont Jr. brushed aside two inches of manuscripts and slapped the intercom switch.

"Yes, Mr. Belmont?"

"Miss Rawlings, would you be so kind as to get us some coffee?"

"Of course, sir," Wanda's musical voice was soft and pleasant. "How does Mr. Dracula like his coffee?"

Dracula made a small waving gesture with his hand. "Black is fine."

"Black, Miss Rawlings."

"Coming right up, sir." The intercom button clicked off.

Belmont Jr. smiled again. "Black, heh. I used to drink it like that. Back in my college days. But time's caught up with me some." He slapped his rotund belly. "Now I need sugar and cream or the caffeine will bother me all day."

"I was brought up drinking rich Italian espresso, myself," Dracula said. "At times I think my veins are filled with the stuff."

"Right. Most editors on the street practically live on the stuff." Belmont Jr. shuffled more papers about and then found a thin yellow folder which he picked up. "I was very impressed with your background, Mr. Dr...ah...

George. Says here you were born in Transylvania but grew up in Greece."

"Athens, to be exact. It will always be my home."

"You're not by any chance related to the famous Brothers Dracula, are you?"

"In fact I am. Apparently Karl Dracula was my great-great-grandfather. Or so I was told as a child when my mother read me their fairy tales."

"I must say, your English is excellent; you don't have any accent at all."

"I believe that's due to my many travels and education. I graduated from the University of Seneca where I studied English Literature. I am fluent in six languages and can read and write eight."

Belmont Jr. waved the folder in his hand. "You say here you taught at Oxford in England."

"Yes, after finishing my education, I applied for graduate studies there. Upon my arrival, the Dean of College asked if I might be willing to teach a course in Greek Mythology. Obviously because of my nationality and background."

"Fascinating. How did you like teaching?"

"Well I'll confess to being a bit apprehensive at first, but then again I'd grown up in the world where all these marvelous stories were born. I'd heard them all my life from my parents, grandparents, neighbors. You can't be a Greek without knowing everything there is to know about the Gods of Mount Olympus. The tales are timeless and the opportunity to share them with those young scholars was a rare privilege I will never forget."

"I can well imagine," Belmont Jr. commented. In his entire life, he'd never been west of the Mississippi and now here he was conversing with an experienced world traveler.

"So tell me, George, after teaching at Oxford and all, why did you come to America and why do you want to be a pulp editor?"

Before the interviewee could offer up an answer, the door behind him opened a crack. He looked over his shoulder to see Miss Rawlings kicking it wider with her foot while carefully holding two porcelain cups from which steam arose.

Dracula jumped to his feet and gratefully took one of the cups from her hands. "Thank you, Miss Rawlings."

"You're welcome, Mr. Dracula. I hope it's not too bitter for you."

Instead of answering, he brought the coffee to his mouth and took a cautionary sip. A smile appeared on his rugged features.

"It is excellent, Miss Rawlings. Strong, but flavorful."

She nodded and then turned to hand Belmont Jr. the second cup.

"Will there be anything else, sir?"

"No, thank you Wanda."

She gave them both a sweet smile and exited, quietly closing the door behind her.

"A very charming woman," George Dracula commented before taking another sip of coffee.

"She is indeed," Belmont Jr. agreed. "I'd have been lost without Wanda these past few years. She's a very organized, efficient secretary who keeps our little ship afloat most of the time."

"Yes, I can see that. Now, you wished to know why I am here?"

"Right. I mean, if I can be frank, George. There are a whole lot of other, more polished publishing houses you could have gone to. And with your credentials, they'd have fought like cats and dogs to hire you. So what on earth are you doing at a place like Wonder Press?"

"Hopefully helping to make dreams come true, Junior."

It was the last thing Belmont Jr. had expected to hear. Mind you, anything George Dracula said would have surprised him. The man was clearly a puzzle someone like Belmont Jr. rarely ever encountered.

Dracula was also highly astute in reading others as he could see the editor's obvious befuddlement.

"It's really no big secret," he continued. "You see, Junior, I love stories. All kinds of stories. From the wildest to the most tragic, from the romantic to the fanciful and even the hilarious. We live in a world that spins around the sun propelled by the stories we all tell each other every single day."

Dracula was just getting warmed up. "You walk down the street and see a friendly face. You ask, 'How are you doing, my old friend?' The fellow then replies, 'Well, my wife's mother is ill,' and just like that he has become a storyteller. Don't you see, all of us communicate with stories, be they small and routine, or exciting and thrilling. In fact our family motto is 'The stories are in the blood'."

Dracula swept his left hand out pointing to the table of magazines and manuscripts. "And where are the boldest, biggest, most entertaining stories found in the world today? Why right here, in your amazing, over-the-top, beautiful, bloody pulps! From western outlaws to pirate buccaneers, masked avengers to thrilling detective mysteries. Tell me, Junior, where else in this entire world can people find stories like these? Nowhere. This is the Holy Mountain of Tall Tales and it's here I wish to plant my flag. If you'll have me, that is?"

It was one of the most impassioned speeches Belmont Jr. had ever heard and it moved him. "Bravo," he started clapping his hands together. "Well said, George. Well said."

"Thank you, Junior. Now having heard my position, may I ask as to why you want to give it up? The editorship, that is."

For his response, Belmont Jr. pointed to the unopened manuscript envelopes. "Look at them, by the hundreds. They just keep coming in and despite that our sales are at an all-time low. George, as much as I love the publishing game, I'm really not an editor. We need someone like you, with your fire, your enthusiasm for the job itself. And were I to not address that problem, I fear we'd be shutting our doors within the month."

Belmont Jr. sighed deeply before continuing. "As it stands now, that's not much more than a few months away at best unless we can regain our readership, grow our profits and be able to pay both our creditors and staff etc. After much discussion with my father, both of us agreed my role should be as the publisher. I know business, George. I have as much love for numbers as you do for stories. Once I'm up on the top floor, all this will be left to you to manage and bring under control. Do you still want the damn job, George?"

"Indeed I do."

"Excellent." Belmont Jr. cheered happily. "When can you start?"

George Dracula thought about his response before answering. "Well, today is Thursday. Why don't I leave you to inform your people of my arrival and then I start bright and early on Monday morning."

"Yes, that would be just fine." Belmont Jr. stood and walked around his desk so the two could shake on the deal.

Note, they did discuss salary, but that's neither here nor there in regards to the crux of our tale. Let's just leave it that the sum offered was fair and Dracula was happy with it.

After shaking hands, Belmont Jr. escorted his new editor out into the reception room where Miss Rawlings was typing away in her usual brisk manner.

"Excuse me, Miss Rawlings," he interrupted her.

She swiveled her chair around. "Yes, Mr. Belmont?"

He smiled and indicated Dracula. "I have just hired Mr. Dracula here to be our new Managing Editor. He will assume the position next Monday morning and I am sure you will do all you can to help him get settled here at Wonder Press."

"But of course," Wanda Rawlings rose and extended her own hand to her new boss. "Welcome, Mr. Dracula."

"Thank you very much, Miss Rawlings. Can I ask what time the editorial staff comes to work in the morning?"

"At eight o'clock sharp, every day."

"Good." He gave her a mischievous grin. "I'll be here at seven."

True to his word, George Dracula walked into the office bright and early the next Monday morning. Only he found Wanda Rawlings already there, just starting to brew a pot of fresh coffee. Upon hearing the outer door open, she turned and welcomed him.

She wore a stylish dark blue dress that dropped below her knees, a yellow blouse and white kerchief about her neck. She had on tiny zirconium earrings and a touch of pink of lipstick was barely visible on her lips. He couldn't help but notice the same glasses and bun hair-do that she manipulated so skillfully to hide her natural good looks. He made a mental note that he would have to do something about that too.

"Good morning, Mr. Dracula."

"Miss Rawlings," he removed his fedora. "I suspected I might find you here ahead of me. That really wasn't necessary, you know."

"I know, but as it is your first day on the job, I didn't want you arrive to an empty place. That somehow didn't seem right."

Dracula liked the way she thought. As Belmont Jr. had indicated the previous Friday, Miss Rawlings was someone special.

The brewing mechanism came to a stop and she immediately took a cup from the serving table and poured it full.

"Black, correct?" she smiled, handing him the coffee. Most of the men Wanda knew were shorter than her. Thus having her green eyes at the same level as Dracula's gray orbs was an odd experience. One she could easily get used to, she thought.

"Yes, thank you." He set his hat and cane on the table next to the tray and then took the cup. "Please, pour yourself one and join me in…ah… my office."

"Is there some dictation you would like me to take?" she inquired politely.

"Actually, Miss Rawlings, I'd like to pick your brain, if I might."

She was undecided at first. Still she could see no harm in it and complied with his wishes. She poured herself a cup of java and the two of them entered his office.

"Please, have a chair while I get those windows open," he suggested. Once fresh air had joined the warm sunlight circulating the room, Dracula took his place behind the desk.

"And so, here we are," he declared matter-of-factly.

"Yes, we are," she was amused. He was a strange fellow. She was about to discover how strange.

"May I call you Wanda? I've never been one for formality."

"Very well," she relented . "But I don't think I can call you anything but Mr. Dracula."

He bit down on his lower lip and tapped the fingers of his right hand on his ink blotter. "Hmm, a conundrum. I have it. Simply call me 'Boss'. How's that?"

"Alright…Boss, it is."

"Good. Now Wanda, I'm sure you are well aware of just how much trouble our little house of dreams is in. And I'm sure you understand I was hired to save the day."

"I didn't realize things were that serious."

"They are, Wanda, and though I don't mean to alarm or worry you, I'm just laying down all my cards here. If I'm to save Wonder Press, then I am really going to need everyone's help. Including yours."

"Me? Mr..ah…I'm just the secretary."

"Oh, I don't believe that for a minute. Not one minute. And right now, I need you to fill me in on the rest of the team. The company's staff from the Assistant Editors, to the Art Directors and most importantly who are our Accountants. I take it you are familiar with these people?"

"I am."

"Then I need you to tell me everything you can about them."

"You mean their names and such."

"Of course their names, but I need much more Wanda. I need to know what kind of people they are. Their work habits, their temperaments, their characters."

She squirmed in the chair, clearly uncomfortable with where he was going.

"Is something wrong with that?"

"It sounds a little like I'm gossiping at best, spying at worst."

"Nothing could be further from the truth. Wanda, I can't properly lead people I don't know completely. If you can help me learn who they are, then it will go a long way toward helping me decide how I approach each of them as the unique individuals they are. An editor's job is to draw out the best from his people. Only then can the team work like a well-oiled machine. I'm asking you make that possible. Tell me who they really are and I'll do the rest."

From her earliest days as a child, Wanda Rawlings had an uncanny knack of recognizing horse-apples when they were thrown at her. She'd been lied to by some of the smoothest salesmen in New York ever since she'd stepped off the train from Chicago. So she knew hyperbole inside and out. Mr. George Dracula wasn't shoveling anything but pure, honest sincerity.

And she believed him.

"Very, well. Boss. Where do I begin?"

Dracula reached into his jacket and pulled out a long, fat cigar. He bit off the tip, spit it in the trash can. Then striking a wooden match on his desk, got the stogy going with some good strong puffs. He sat back and let a cloud of tobacco circle his head.

"The Assistant Editors. How many do we have? Who are they and what titles do they handle?"

Ninety minutes later, George Dracula's office was crowded with the four people responsible for keeping Wonder Press pulps going. He had asked Wanda to gather them after spending the first few hours of his day devising a strategy he hoped would shake things up and get the company moving again. As there were only three chairs in his office, he had John Baron, the Chief Accountant and oldest person in the room take one of the two in front of his desk. Baron was a small fellow, who wore vests and bowties all the time. His round face reminded people of an owl, particularly his eyebrows which always pointed upward at the ends. The man loved numbers.

What really surprised Dracula was learning that his two Assistant Editors were actually brothers; Steve and Sam Sweet. Twenty-five-year-old Steve was a former college football tackle and he looked the part, with square shoulders and a beefy face that appeared to have been chiseled out of stone. Whereas Sam, a year younger, was a movie-handsome rascal with curly brown hair and a dancer's graceful body. Both preferred casual clothes and the neckties around their collars were always undone. Sam also wore glasses and was easily the most personable of the pair. They had both graduated together from a small liberal arts college in Indiana with degrees in English Literature. Upon entering the office, Steve had positioned himself by the manuscript table; arms folded over his broad chest and allowed his brother to take the chair beside the bean counter.

The last member of the group was Art Director Leon Bearman, a tall, husky, brown fellow with a bald head. He wore comfortable canvas boat shoes, baggy slacks held up by suspenders and an old white, paint-stained smock over a blue denim shirt. Bearman's features were sharply defined and his skin was the color of rich maple syrup that set off his sparkling white teeth. Bearman's father was German and his mother Jamaican. They had immigrated to New York when he was five and early on recognized he had a talent for drawing people in the neighborhood. After years of hard work, he graduated from the prestigious Manhattan School of Fine Arts. Upon graduation he landed an apprenticeship with a marketing firm on 5th Avenue. He lasted all of six months. Drawing housewives next to washing machines, housewives holding tubes of toothpaste, and housewives holding jars of floor polish nearly drove him insane. And so one day he stepped away from his easel, threw his apron on the floor and quit. Two weeks later he was at Wonder Press doing his best to direct a dozen of the finest painters and illustrators in the city. His biggest problem: getting half of them to meet deadlines.

As Bearman was the last one to show up, Wanda began to close the door only to have Dracula wave to her from across the room. "Leave it open, Wanda. It'll let some of the air circulate in here with the drafts from the window. And grab your pen and notepad and join us please."

Surprised, Wanda rushed back to her desk, grabbed her writing tools and returned to the now packed room.

"Please, sit at my desk," Editor Dracula suggested, rising up and moving to the corner of his desk. "It will be easier for you to take notes."

Wanda moved past the others, circled the desk and sat. She flipped open the cover to her pad and held her pen at the ready.

"Thank you all for coming," Dracula began immediately. "As most of you already know, my name is George Dracula and as of today I am the man in charge of Wonder Press. Now, I've read all of your folders and am thrilled to have such a capable staff on hand. So without any further delays, let's get down to business, shall we."

Dracula looked at the Sweet brothers. "I know we are currently publishing six monthlies. What are they and who edits which?"

"I've got the westerns," Steve Sweet replied. "That's *The Dakota Kid, Six-Gun Outlaws* and *Wild West Adventures.*"

"And I handle the crime stuff," the dashing Sam Sweet continued. "Those are *Headline Mystery, Mrs. Homicide* and *Real Detective Stories.*"

"Thank you, gentlemen." Dracula pointed a finger at the mousy accountant who held a red leather bound journal on his lap. "Mr. Baron, are any of these six titles making us a profit?"

Baron coughed in his hand, and then swiftly opened the ledger. He ran a bony finger down several columns before looking up to answer. "Two, Mr. Dracula. *Six-Gun Outlaws* and *Mrs. Homicide.*"

"I see." Dracula leaned back against his desk and tugged softly on his chin. "And the others?"

"We're losing money on them, I'm afraid to say."

"It's not your problem, Mr. Baron. It's mine," Dracula corrected him. "And here's what we're going to do about it. Effectively immediately, the four titles are canceled."

"What!" Steve Sweet blurted out. "But what about all the work we've done on next month's releases?"

"Right," his brother chimed in from his seat, looking up in confusion at his new boss. "We've got dozens of stories in teletype and pages all laid out and ready to shoot."

"Never mind the artwork put together," Leon Bearman added angrily.

All of them had expected some kind of shake-up. With a new editor, it was to be expected. They just weren't ready for the floor to drop out from under them. Nor the next set of words that George Dracula uttered.

"I don't care." He balled his right into a fist and punched it down into his left palm for emphasis. "This company is finished publishing magazines no one wants to buy or read. All that stops today. Right here and now. As for the material collected for the next issues of those four titles, it's simple enough. We're going to fold their stories into the two remaining titles."

He pointed at Steve. "Everything slated for the next issues of *The Dakota Kid* and *Wild West Adventures* you now schedule as the content for the next two *Six-Gun Outlaws*."

Sam nodded approvingly. "I get it, Boss. And you want me to roll over the next *Headline Mystery* and *Real Detective Stories* into *Mrs. Homicide*."

"Exactly. That way we not only utilize what content we've already paid cash for but this allows us a two month publishing buffer in which to keep the company going."

"Geez Louise," Bearman shook his head. "Are things really that bad?"

"Yes, I'm afraid they are, gentlemen." Dracula looked at each of them and then a smile emerged on his face. "But I think we can save the ship, if all of you are willing to work with me. I've looked at the last few months of copies and we really do have a great bunch of talented writers and artists. The problem is we're not giving them the right material to sink their creative juices in."

"What's that mean exactly?" Sam Sweet inquired.

"It means that although we are canceling more than half our current line, I'm going to take a gamble and, by the week's end, will be sitting with each of you to discuss two possible new titles."

If his men weren't befuddled before, they were now.

"So let me get this straight," Sam Sweet tried to sum up what Dracula had just told them. "We are now going to cancel four titles because they aren't making any money."

"Correct," Dracula nodded.

"And we're going to use the material from four issues not being published to carry our remaining two titles for the next two months."

"That's right."

"And now, before I can wrap my head around all this stuff, you say you might want to launch some new titles."

"Three to be exact."

Sam Sweet scratched the back of his head. "That's nuts."

"No, Sam, it isn't. Our problem isn't that we don't have the right chefs. Our problem is we don't have the right recipes."

After the others had left, Wanda Rawlings picked up her notebook and stood up to vacate Dracula's chair.

"Well, that certainly shook them up," she commented moving around the opposite side of the desk.

"I hope so," Dracula sighed. "The days ahead are going to be challenging. For all of us."

He looked at the table with the multiple stacks of unopened manuscript envelopes. "What do you think, Wanda? How many stories are in there waiting for our attention?"

She eyed the piles and guessed, "Several hundred at least."

"Agreed, and every one of them contains someone's hopes and dreams. And it's up to me to decide which come true and which do not."

"I never thought of it like that before. You still happy you took the job?"

Dracula grinned wistfully. "Yes, I am. But I think you're going to have to make me a fresh pot of coffee."

"Coming right up, Boss. And this time I'll make it extra strong."

Another two days passed and Wanda quickly adjusted herself to her new boss's daily routine. George Dracula arrived at seven every morning, grabbed a cup of coffee and then sequestered himself in his office until ten. At that time he'd call for her and a second cup of the strong black brew.

It was during this first morning session when he would give her those manuscripts he had rejected with instructions to return them to their respective writers along with a polite note. With those set aside on the corner of his desk, he would then dictate letters of acceptance for those stories he had approved and would eventually print.

Below is an example of one of those early letters Wanda typed up and sent out with the afternoon mail.

To – Mr. Earl Stanley Gortner,
St. Louis, MO

Dear Mr. Gorner,
We are delighted to accept your mystery story, "The Reluctant Client," for publication in our Sept. issue of *Mrs. Homicide*. We would be very interested in more such tales from you as we think your lawyer protagonist, Larry Mason, has a great deal of series potential.

Sincerely Yours,

George Dracula
Managing Editor

Once done with those letters, Dracula would go back to reading until lunch, which he would always have at a nearby diner down the street called the Wooden Spoon. Back by one p.m. promptly, he'd take whatever calls had come in during his absence and then return to reading and editing.

On Thursday afternoon, just after two, he came out of his office and informed Wanda he was off to the Paste-Up room. This was the huge, wide open pre-production area where the Sweet brothers had their desks and graphic designers assembled the giant galley sheets that made up each magazine. Once completed, these stacks of pages were put on a cart and rolled to the elevator for their trip to the ground floor printing presses.

At the far end of this long bay was Art Director Bearman's cubicle where he met daily with his artists to either receive completed paintings or hand out assignments. Beside himself, the company had two other illustrators on payroll; Walter Baum and Allison Kirby.

When Dracula arrived in the Paste-Up room, Steve Sweet was at one of the art tables discussing the placement of black and white illustrations for a particular story. Sam Sweet was at his own desk, on the telephone. He spotted Dracula and waved to him to come over. After a few more words, Sweet dropped the phone back on its cradle with a look of frustration.

"Bad news?" Dracula began.

"Not really," the debonair Sweet grabbed an open pack of cigarettes off his desk top and offered one to Dracula.

"No, thanks. I'm a cigar man myself."

Sweet found a wooden match, scratched it to flame with his thumbnail and lit the tip of his cigarette. Then he extinguished the flame with a twist of his wrist and dropped it into a round steel ashtray already filled with butts and burnt lucifers.

"That was Max Sands," he blew out a puff of smoke. "One of our western writers. He wasn't thrilled with our holding off on his scripts for a few more months."

"I can imagine. Sam, you remember my comments about creating new titles during our Monday morning conference?"

"Yes, of course."

"Well, I've decided what they are going to be and I'm hoping we can find some new writers among the slush pile submissions to make them work."

"Alright, so what do you have in mind?"

"Sam, I want us to do a monthly devoted to pirate stories. I want to call it *Bloody Buccaneers* and I want you to edit it."

"Pirates!" Sam couldn't have been more surprised. "I don't know a damn thing about pirates."

"So, what did you know about cowboys and Indians before you started editing *Six-Gun Outlaws* and from what John Bacon tells me, it outsells most of the other westerns on the stands today."

Sam knew a back-handed compliment when he got one. "It's not the same thing, Boss. I mean, most kids grow up going to the flicks seeing Hoot Gibson and Tom Mix. It's American, you know. But pirates? Why pirates?"

"For the very logic you just put forth. So far all our titles have been focused on adventures right here in the good Old U.S. of A. With pirate stories, I want us to expand our scope and our readers' experiences. Think of it, Sam. We take the same wild and wooly trappings of Robert Louis Stevenson's *Treasure Island* and *Kidnapped* and give folks exotic island paradises, cold-hearted villains like Captain Blackbeard and pirate queen Ann Bonnie...tons of high seas battles between magnificent sailing ships. If done right, our readers will eat it up."

Sam Sweet took an extra long drag on his butt, held it in and then slowly blew it out.

"Alright, I see what you're saying, Boss. I just don't know if I can make it work."

George Dracula leaned over his Assistant Editor's desk and extended his right hand. "If I didn't have faith you could do it, I wouldn't have asked. Come on, Sam. Take a chance."

"Aw, hell." Sweet took hold of Dracula's hand. "Why not? *Bloody Buccaneers* it is!"

Two weeks later, Dracula approached Steve Sweet with his idea for *Ghost Agent*.

"He's a super secret government agent and master of disguise. No one has ever seen his face and his true identity is only known to the President."

Unlike his younger brother's initial reaction to *Bloody Buccaneers*, Steve saw the possibilities immediately.

"I like it, Chief. This guy could give the Shadow a run for his money."

"Exactly what I was thinking," Dracula slapped the big man on his arm. "Now go make it happen."

By the middle of October, both new titles were out and their first issues had each sold half a million copies. At the same time, both *Six-Gun Outlaws* and *Mrs. Homicide* had each seen a jump in readership, what with the canceled titles no longer dragging down the overall sales numbers. Accountant Mr. John Bacon was practically dancing around the editorial offices. It was safe to say George Dracula was getting the job done.

He was also having a decidedly strange effect on Miss Wanda Rawlings. It was Leon Bearman who first noticed she had stopped wearing those clunky old glasses of hers. Then one morning she showed up at work with the lustrous blonde hair draped down over her shoulders and she had applied a light touch of red lipstick.

It was suggested Dracula had somehow mesmerized the lovely Miss Rawlings and office gossip began to speculate just how far things would go between them. The only dissenting opinion was voiced by Sam Sweet, no doubt due to his own past failures in wooing the young lady.

"I don't know what's going on," Sam claimed one afternoon during a coffee break by the layout tables. "But I can tell you this, old George hasn't got a clue. All he ever thinks about is the damn magazines and stories. All he sees Wanda as is just another cog in his well-oiled machine."

Which was the truth. The two of them had become a very efficient team.

Here's another letter Dracula dictated along about this time.

To – Mr. H.P. Lovetrade
Mystic, Conn.

Dear Mr. Lovetrade,

Your new horror submission, "The Outer Gods" is a masterful work of vivid imagination and one we believe our readers will enjoy greatly. We trust this will not be your only foray into this new Bluth-Uth mythos you've created.

Sincerely Yours,
George Dracula
Managing Editor

"That'll be the last one for today," Dracula told Wanda.

"Alright, Boss," she folded the notepad on her lap and slid the pencil over her right ear, brushing aside her hair to do so. "I'll have these typed up and out with the afternoon mail."

Dracula pulled back his sleeve and glanced at his wrist watch. "Look, it's already after lunch. Why don't you wait on those and join me for lunch?"

"But who'll cover the phones?"

"Oh, I'm sure the world can get along without us for an hour, Wanda."

At first she was undecided. He came over to her and gently took the notebook out of her hands.

"It's my treat, please."

"Alright. If you insist?"

He grabbed his fedora and hurried to open the door for her. "Oh, but I do. Indeed I do."

In the outer office he dropped her pad on her desk and then helped her into her light green jacket. Winter had already established itself with several threatening snow squalls the previous week and New Yorkers were all bundling up. The last thing Wanda grabbed was her matching green cloth beret and then they were gone.

Wanda generally brought her own bag lunch to work as it was cheaper then eating out all the time. In the process she had passed the Wooden Spoon daily but had never once been inside. Now she relished the idea. Fortunately for them, the biggest part of the lunch crowd had dwindled by the time they entered the cozy diner.

A waitress name Carla recognized Dracula and led them to the furthest booth in the corner away from the kitchen.

"You're in luck, George," she said snapping her chewing gum. "Your favorite booth."

"Thanks, Carla," he replied helping Wanda remove her jacket before sitting. "What's the blue-plate special today?"

"Meatloaf and mashed potatoes with string-beans and carrots on the side."

"Sounds delicious." Wanda slid into the red padded seat.

"Then two blue-plate special it is, Carla."

"What'll you have to drink?"

"Coffee for me." Wanda removed her chapeau as Dracula squeezed in behind the table while dropping his hat on the seat beside him.

"Me as well," he added.

"You got it." Carla spun around and disappeared into the busy kitchen. She returned a minute later with their coffee and then once again vanished.

"She seems very efficient," Wanda commented as she cautiously tasted her coffee.

"Carla? Indeed she is. Quite the character. She's a huge baseball fan and keeps telling me we should devote a title to sports."

"What do you think?" Wanda took another drink.

"Maybe some day, but for right now I want to do a magazine devoted specifically to all kinds of fictions. Everything from mystery, to horror, fantasy and whatever else those wonderful writers can envision."

"It sounds like something you've given a lot of thought to."

"I have Wanda." Dracula took a sip of coffee then smiled. "I mean we're Wonder Press and we don't even have a title with that word in it."

"True. So what do you want to call this new anthology monthly."

Dracula raised his hands and spread them out as if imagining a theater marquee.

"Worlds of Wonder."

Before Wanda could decide if she liked it or not, Carla was back with their meals. She was amused to see her boss splash ketchup on his meatloaf. She conservatively used a little salt and pepper. Both of them enjoyed the food and saved the rest of their conversation for when they were back at the offices.

It was quarter of two when George Dracula and Wanda Rawlings stepped off the elevator in front of the Wonder Press offices. Ever the gentlemen, he opened the door for her and followed her inside.

"Boss, can I ask you a question that's been bothering me for a while now?" Wanda inquired as he helped her out of her jacket.

"Of course."

"How on earth do you read through all those manuscripts we get in every week?" She draped her beret on the coat rack hook.

"I'm a fast reader," he grinned mischievously.

"No one is that fast." She put a hand on her hip. "Really. I want to know."

Dracula's expression changed. It was obvious she wouldn't be put off.

"Very well, but let's go into my office. What I'm going to tell you has to remain between us."

"Alright," she agreed, though at the same time she couldn't help but be curious as to why his answer had to be so mysterious.

He had her take the seat in front of his desk, then went and dropped into his own. He folded his hands together atop his desk blotter and then brought them up under his chin. Wanda could see he was mentally debating whether to reveal his big secret or not.

"Look, if you don't want to tell me, Boss, I'll under…"

"I'm a Muse."

At first she wasn't sure she had heard him correctly.

"A what?"

"A Muse. You know, the Greek spirits that inspire people." He opened his hands as if to reveal himself sans disguise. "I am a Greek Muse."

Wanda cocked her head wondering if Dracula was merely joking with her. And yet there was something innocently sincere about his declaration.

"You're not lying to me, are you?"

"Wanda, I am incapable of lying. To you or anyone else for that matter. It's not in my nature. I was made to inspire others to create. In my case, stories."

"But I thought all the Muses were women?"

"Ah, right, my sisters." Dracula sat back and began counting off his fingers. "Clio, Melpomene, Arche, Erato, Mneme, Aoide, Melite and Euterpe. I think there were a few more, but I really never got to know any of them all that well."

"Okay, but to my point, you're a man."

"Ah, right. Sorry for the digression. You see, over the centuries my sisters have done a fairly decent job of promoting all the arts among the human race. Whereas Dad was content with letting them run the show."

"Dad as in…?"

"Oh, of course. As in Zeus, the All Father."

"So Zeus is your father." Wanda was beginning to wish she was anywhere else but in that office by then.

"Oh, I'm sorry, Wanda. I can see this might be a little much for you to take in all at once."

"That's putting it mildly, Boss."

"Hmm, maybe it's time I showed you," he finally admitted. Reaching across his desk, Dracula opened the lacquered teakwood cigar box and withdrew a cigar. He stuck it in his mouth, lit a match and then began puffing away.

"Just give me a second, please," he spoke around the stogy. "This will just take a second." Soon the cigar tip was glowing and Dracula was sending forth plumes of white smoke.

"That should do it." He stood up and walked over to the wall table. It was as always covered in envelopes containing unsolicited manuscripts.

"So you wanted to know how it was I could read through all these stories. Let me show you."

He picked up the top envelope from the nearest stack and then, holding it in front of his face, he blew a cloud of cigar smoke over it. As the wispy tendrils began to wrap around the yellow manila, they began to take shape.

Wanda blinked to clear her eyes.

The smoke was now floating in the air in the shape of an old World War One bi-plane.

"Ah, an aviation adventure," Dracula beamed. "I was hoping we'd get one of those soon. I love aviation tales."

He turned and handed Wanda the envelope. "Go ahead and open it up. My letter opener is right there on my desk."

Still perplexed, she did as he asked. Once she'd ripped open the envelope, she pulled out the typed pages and inspected the cover page.

"It's from a Walter Hogan of Cleveland. He says it's based on his experiences in France as a pilot during the war."

"Great. Let's see what else we've got in there."

Before Wanda could say another word, Dracula had dug out another envelope, this one in the center of a pile. "Don't want you to think I'm cheating," he chuckled as he once again held up the unopened submission and blew smoke over it.

This time the white tobacco fog morphed into the shape of a horrid head, with most of the skin missing, and the eyes enlarged as if in death.

"Well, I'm going to bet that's not a romance," Dracula said dryly as he once again passed the envelope to Wanda. "I'm thinking we've got a zombie thriller in that one."

Sure enough, the enclosed manuscript from one Paul Montang of Wisconsin was about ghouls that haunted a small Midwestern town back the early 1800s.

Dracula repeated his unveilings two more times and the smoke correctly revealed the story contents before the envelopes were opened.

"It has to be a trick," Wanda muttered, still unable to grasp what it was she was seeing.

"It's no trick, save for my being what you'd refer to as a kind of super-natural being."

"But...how...why?"

Dracula left the manuscript table and moving past the lovely young woman, leaned back against his desk to be close to her. He put his cigar down on his desk ashtray and then folded his arms over his chest.

"As I was saying earlier, Dad was satisfied with how things were going here on Earth and my Muse sisters were doing a good job as the human race progressed along its evolutionary path. From cave paintings, to the printing press, telling stories remained the purview of a select handful. Mostly the educated and not so much the masses. Then along came all this."

Dracula swept his arms out. "The magnificent twentieth century and suddenly more and more people from all walks of life were able to read... and more importantly wanted to read. All of which led to right here and now, Wanda. So seeing all this coming about, Dad decided it was time he had a Muse son. This whole explosion of literacy and the knowledge that accompanied would be a task a bit more robust than my sisters could handle. Thus, thirty years ago he convinced my mother, Calliope to ... ahem...join him in creating that baby. Mother wanted to call me Vlad because of those famous Transylvanian fairy tale chroniclers, but Dad was a big fan of George Bernard Shaw and so they comprised with George Vladimir Dracula.

"And ta-ta, here I am. At your service. The first ever male Muse with one singular task, to make the pulps as great as they can possibly be. And that's just what I've been doing these past few months. With your help and that of the rest of the crew."

Thus did Dracula conclude his own whopper leaving Miss Wanda Rawlings fairly dumbfounded. For a few minutes she merely sat there in silence. Then she looked at the manuscript table and those still on her lap.

"You're telling me the truth, aren't you?" Even her own words sounded alien to her ears. Maybe she was at home having a dream?

"Every single word, Wanda." His smile was incredibly sincere. "But I really can't do it alone. That's why I had to tell you..."

She jumped out of her chair, grabbed his face in her hands and kissed him hard. It was no time for talking. Wanda Rawlings wanted dreams to come true and at long last, she had found the one person who would do that for her.

Six weeks later.

To – Mr. Robert E. Herwood
Crosscreek, Oklahoma

Dear Mr. Herwood,

I'm happy to tell you that I loved your adventure story, "Demons of the Desert" starring your barbarian hero, Crom. In fact, it is going to be the lead story in our newest monthly, *Worlds of Wonder,* which will debut in January. Thanks again. We expect more great yarns from you.

George Dracula
Managing Editor

Of course by now you know the rest. Dracula turned Wonder Press into the most successful pulp publisher of them all. He and Wanda were married in 1938. Together they introduced dozens of talented writers to the world. From Robert Heenline to Isaac Asitov, Sax Rhumer to Jack England. All of them got their start in *Worlds of Wonder.*

After World War Two, with the pulps dying out, George and Wanda moved to Hollywood where they started WanDra Productions and began producing series for that new fangled toy called television.

But that's really another story. I hope you've enjoyed this one as much as I've enjoyed telling it to you. Oh, and let's wrap it all up shall we? Who am I? I'm guessing many of you already know by now.

My name is Zeus. But like my boy, George, you can call me Dad.

Vlad the Imp

J. SCHERPENHUIZEN

"**H**arry! Harry!" Louisa Hargraves strained her eyes to search the bushes at the bottom of the garden a couple of hundred feet away. "Come back this instant!"

The seven year old had been there but a moment before, crouched down in the grass, doubtless deep in conversation with his imaginary friend, and now he was gone once more, despite her warnings he wasn't to go out of sight. Her heart in her mouth, she drew her skirts up with one hand and began to rush down toward the place where she had seen him last. The sky was grey as it had been for a week and the clouds were growing dark. She feared it might begin to rain.

The boy seemed strong, having recovered from his recent illness, but she did not want to risk its return. The wind picked up and the tall oaks which loomed over the slopes that covered the lower reaches of the valley below began to toss themselves about in a wild ecstasy of chattering leaves. Movement shivered over the lush green grass and wisps of mist swept out from between the great trunks and the sea of foliage to mingle with their cousins in the sky.

The breezes tugged at her jacket and her bonnet and whipped her skirts about her legs as she trotted on toward the boundary where the garden met the wild. In the rising concatenation of sounds issuing from the thrashing leaves and the whispering reeds she thought she heard an odd laughter, aimed cruelly at her distress. She should have had one of the girls from the house watching him, she chided herself. She should never have left him alone. Boys were way too wild and adventurous, or *real* boys were, so Edmund said. He accused her of hovering over and mollycoddling her Harry.

Edmund prided himself on the manliness of his line; soldiers going back to Agincourt and Poitiers; and no one could accuse her husband himself of being all talk after the way he had acquitted himself against the Boers. Sometimes she feared that he was already preparing her darling Harry for the front lines.

"Harry!" she cried out again, plunging in among the trees. The oaks were huge and ancient, their massive trunks encrusted with moss and crawling with ivy. The branches creaked as the wind continued to grow stronger and she heard a crashing sound only a little distance away as a large limb gave way under the weight of its own leaves and plunged to the earth.

Again she called her son's name, her voice rising to a scream now as she imagined him lying trapped beneath the fallen limb. Thunder rumbled in the distance and Louisa groaned. She turned about in confusion. Somehow she had lost sight of the house entirely and under the burden of the blackening sky a strange twilight had come to reign in among the trees. She strained her ears once more, thinking that perhaps he might be crying out to her, and she was merely too wrapped up in her fears and her own calling and perhaps if she calmed herself, above the susurration of the writhing leaves, the rustling grasses, the lashing vines and the beating of her own heart, she might capture his voice. But the only sound she heard was the cacophony of the excited wood and the rushing of her own blood in her ears, and again, that maddening suggestion of laughter.

It could only be the fever of her own anxiety, she told herself, and yet her reason spoke softly and another voice, one of ancient superstition spoke to her of other things, half-forgotten but lodged in her Welsh lineage. Things more ancient than Christ or Moses, things which predated the flood and were old when the most ancient of these venerable trees was not yet a seed.

"Harreeeeeeee!" she screamed, as much to drown out her own half-unarticulated thoughts as in hope of a response. She drew in another great breath, ready to scream again when suddenly she felt herself assaulted from behind as some creature of the forest hurled itself upon her and she felt herself captured in a rough embrace. Shrieking she stumbled forward, almost hurled off her feet by the force of the tackle, but she managed to stay upright and grasped the two small arms she felt squeezing her tight. Now, the yelled, "Boo!" which had sounded in her ears, registered in her mind and her heart cramped with an odd concoction of hope, anger and fear.

"Harry! Harry!" she cried. "You mad thing! Is that you!"

He only laughed. Of course it was him.

"You wicked child!" she gasped. "You wild thing. Are you trying to scare me to death?" She prised his arms away from her waist and pulled him in front of her, none too gently.

Harry. Harry. Of course it was him, with his laughing black eyes and his shock of black curls and his skin white as China clay and the devil of a smile on his lips.

"What on earth did you think you were playing at?" Louisa cried out. "Do you want to be the death of me?"

"You couldn't find me!" Harry exulted. "I was quiet as a Mohican!"

"Well, no more Fennimore Cooper for you, my lad, if that's the sort of behaviour such tales inspire in you. Goodness!" she cried, looking about. "How will we find our way back to the house?"

"Why go back?" Harry laughed. "Let's stay in the woods. We can eat berries and hunt game."

"And where shall we sleep and how shall we keep off the rain? Do you have a tepee or perhaps a snug cave? Stop your nonsense now. You are for the high jump as it is, my lad. If we get wet, I'll keep you inside for a week. Now, how do we find the way home?"

Her relief at finding him whole and apparently hale had begun to give way again to fear as the realisation that she had no idea of how to find the house impressed itself upon her fully. The gloom had continued to deepen among the trees and there was nothing in her surroundings that pointed the way. She had thought that the hill below the house slopped down a good distance beyond where the trees began and she could have found her path roughly by going uphill at the very least but the area where she stood seemed strangely flat even though she found it incredible to think she had ascended all the way to the valley floor in her search for her son without noticing how far she had strayed. It appeared to her that she had been nowhere near so long between the trees.

But there was something about the woods at times which seemed to bend the minutes into hours. Amidst the ancient giants it was easy to think that time had stood still and eons had passed with nothing to mark them.

"Come!" said Harry, apparently sensing none of her concern. "Follow me."

"How do you know which way to go?" his mother demanded. "Harry, we really can't afford to get lost, with you so recently unwell. A soaking simply wouldn't do and I fear the rain is not far away."

"Everything will be alright," Harry assured her, as if he were the adult and she the child.

"Well, if you are sure you know the way," Louisa agreed, for she had no idea of it herself and it wouldn't do to simply stand there helplessly as the darkness drew on.

Harry led her by the hand, walking with such confidence that she felt perhaps he did know the correct path and soon they would be home again, sitting before a roaring fire with cups of hot cocoa grasped in their hands and laughing over their adventure. Soon they came to a little stream and Louisa's confidence evaporated.

"This isn't the way, Harry," she said. "I didn't pass any stream and no stream runs near the house. You are leading us astray."

"No!" Harry insisted. "We need to go this way."

"No!" Louisa snapped, stopping in her tracks and holding him back by the hand. "You've made a mistake!"

"I know where I'm going," Harry insisted. "We'll be safe there."

"Where are we going?" his mother demanded. "We'll be safe at the house! We'll only be safe in the house."

Harry pursed his lips and puffed contemptuously. "Indians don't live in houses, nor do the foxes and wolves. They're all safe. What about the birds that nest in the trees?"

"Harry! We're not animals nor are we primitives. This isn't the place for us!"

"Of course it is!" Harry yelled and suddenly wrenched his hand free of his mother's and leapt away from her. "It could be! We could live here with the animals, we wouldn't have to go to the towns any more. I wouldn't go to war, which would please you, even though that might be rather fun!"

Louisa starred at him in amazement. Who was this child, she wondered. Could it really be her darling Harry? The boy had always been a little wild, but this was too much. Perhaps he was unwell again. Perhaps he had another fever, though in the gathering darkness there was no sign of a flush on his cheeks; if anything he looked preternaturally pale. He laughed at her, as if he could read her thoughts and skipped away through the trees, following some ancient path only he could see between the creaking trunks and the rustling bushes.

"Harry, come back!" his mother cried. "Harry, I'm *afraid!* Don't leave me!"

But the child paid no heed and she rushed after him, terrified he would lose her in the forest. A sudden crack of thunder drowned every other sound in among the trees and a flash of light followed all too soon thereafter and huge raindrops began to fall, crashing through the leaves like a meteor shower.

Suddenly she tripped and fell, landing heavily on her hands and knees. Something broke inside her then. She had never felt so small or insignificant in all of her life. She was a bug here, surrounded by the forest giants. She could feel them towering above her watching her grief with immense impassivity. Beneath her lay the forest floor amassed with fallen leaves and rotting vegetation and the huge body of the hills compared to which the forest was no more than the down upon the back of her hands, and above that, dwarfing the little beast that was the earth towered the endless ocean of the sky where the roiling clouds wept pitiless tears upon eternity. And beyond all that, beyond the torrent it unleashed upon the green hills of Wales, the immense emptiness of space, the freezing void within which the deluge seemed warm and she no more than a firebug, whose brief instant of flaming was about to be doused.

Grief heaved her chest and bitter tears ran forth to be lost in the rain. *Harry, Harry*, she thought, *what have you done to us, what madness has betrayed us?* An inhuman wail filled her ears and it took her a moment to realise that it was her own. The wail of a dying animal, she fancied, and a terrible sobbing broke forth.

"Don't cry, Mama," she heard a voice say. His voice. Harry's voice. Of course it was his voice, though she had been sure he had run away.

"Come," the voice said and she felt him tugging at her arm, and somehow she found the strength to get to her feet. The thunder came again and the lightning, closer even than before and she was moving, as if in a dream, no longer questioning anything, for she knew nothing and it was better to be moving, following her guide, who was now more mysterious to her than any stranger had ever been.

The thunder cracked once more and a tree burst into flame ahead.

"We're here! We're here!" Harry cried with glee and before her she saw a strange-looking outcrop of basalt overgrown with grasses and moss lit up in the flames of the blazing tree.

Louisa stared at the tumulus in amazement. "Come on, come on," Harry cried. "It's dry in there. We need to go in."

Louisa held back, though she did not know why. She was drenched to the bone and the covered dolmen looked dry. She suspected that the flames from the tree were strong enough to even provide some warmth. Yet it was all so improbable, and that disturbed her, because she was not dreaming and she did not believe that angels had provided for them thusly. And still she found herself without the power to resist her son's importuning. Like one destined for the scaffold she allowed herself to be led into the doorway of the tomb.

Louisa was lost in uneasy dreams, for how long she knew not. She struggled not to awaken, and even after she found it too hard to believe she still slept, she kept her eyes closed for a while rerunning the events she last remembered in her mind and hoping that they too were part of her dreams. The brightness of a fire gleamed beyond her closed lashes and it would have been nice to imagine that she had fallen asleep before the hearth in the spacious lounge of the Monmouth house. But that would not explain the scent of moss and vines or the soft breezes that she felt blowing and the sounds of the forest which buzzed and croaked about her; but it was the nearby hooting of an owl which caused her at last to give up the pretence of slumber and open her eyes.

The glow behind her lids transformed into the tree set alight by the lightning, still aflame. She had experienced too many wonders to wonder at another. Looking toward her feet she saw Harry, sitting with his back against the wall, watching her with his bright pitch-black eyes, a look she couldn't read upon his face. To call it sphinx-like would have been too definite. Continuing her survey of her surroundings she gazed behind her where she felt another fire burning and saw that Harry had somehow constructed a rack of sticks and vines upon which her heavy outer garments hung steaming slightly still.

In the roof of the tumulus was a hole through which the smoke from the fire disappeared. The floor beneath her was soft with leaf mould. For the moment she was comfortable enough and felt she should be grateful somehow to her son for arranging things thusly, even if it was he who had delivered them into their predicament in the first place.

"You've arranged things very well," she said. "I can see that rereading the *Swiss Family Robinson* so many times did not go wasted. You have created quite the palace for us, even if you did maroon us in the first place. I can't imagine how I was in such a stupor as to remain asleep while you removed my outer garments and went about all this industry."

"There's many a glamour in the forest," Harry said. "We can hardly expect to understand a great deal of what goes on here. Though Vlad has told me so much."

'Who's Vlad?' Louisa demanded. Something about the mention of this unknown personage disturbed her.

"I'm not supposed to tell," Harry said, biting his lip and looking around nervously. It was the first time since she'd found him in the forest that any distinct air had coloured his behaviour other than glee.

"You mustn't have secrets from your mother," Louisa told him. "It isn't right."

"Vlad is a secret," Harry said. "He's his own secret. It isn't right for me to betray him. He's not my secret to give away."

"But now you have," Louisa said. "So let's have no more pretence. Who is this Vlad?"

"He's my friend," Harry said. "My *best* friend. When I got better I found him down at the end of the garden with all the other fairies."

"Ah, I see," Louisa said, somewhat relieved. "So he's a fairy."

"Yes," Harry said, "but he's different from the others. He's not from around here. He came with the gypsies from a long way away."

"Really?" Louisa said. "Why would he do that?" It occurred to her that fairies were always connected to the land; the trees and the rocks and the waterways; it was not part of their nature to stray. Yet she could hardly expect her seven-year-old child to be overly well-informed on figures of fantasy.

"He's an adventurer," Harry said. "He's also a king. Vlad Imp."

"Vlad the Imp?" Louisa said. "Not the most kingly name I've heard, though I don't doubt a likely companion for a mischief like yourself."

"He's a conqueror," Harry said, "And when he's conquered everything around him he goes to look for another place to conquer. That's why the other fairies are afraid of him."

"They're afraid of him?"

"Yes, of course," Harry said. "He's the most powerful one, and he's come to be the king hereabouts, and I'm going to rule with him."

"I see," Louisa said. "Well, that will be nice, I suppose. And what about me?"

Harry shrugged. "I guess you'll be happy in heaven."

Louisa's eyes went wide with shock. "Harry, why would you say that?"

Harry shrugged again. "Well, you want to go to heaven don't you? You always said it was the best place there is. When I was sick and I thought I might die, you said that I wouldn't, I wouldn't for sure, but that I didn't have to be afraid because, even if I did, I would go to heaven which was better than this place here and I would be there with Granny and Da and Alphonse and baby cousin Greta and we'd be singing in the heavenly choir full of joy.

"And I believed you. In fact, sometimes when I had had a very great fever and the doctor came and you all looked so sad, even though you tried to hide it, I think I visited there and looked around and I saw everyone and could even hear Alphonse barking. But I wasn't meant to go there yet. But you can go there and it will be as wonderful as you said."

'But I don't want to go there anytime soon!" Louisa cried. "I have so much to do and see still and I have to look after you."

Harry laughed and the sound chilled her bones. There was something callous, even cruel in it.

"*I'm* looking after *you*," Harry said. "I brought you to this dry place while you were lost. I made you comfortable and dried your clothes and built another fire while you were sleeping."

"How?" The words left her lips unbidden and she wished she could call them back. How had he found this place? Harry had never been left to explore the woods without her. She didn't think Edmund had brought him here. Edmund never did anything with the boy. Nor did the servants go into the woods. The furthest Harry had been was the edge of the garden.

"Vlad told me where to bring you," Harry said. "He knows the entire forest."

"Why?" Louisa demanded. "Why?"

"He said it was your fate," Harry said.

"Harry! Stop talking like this!" Louisa said. It was all too much, all too insane. Why would she question him on such stupid fantasies? How did a little boy think of such wicked things? Unless he didn't…but that was too terrible to think of.

She wanted to get up and run but where to? The forest was black as pitch. The sky must have still been covered with clouds and not a trace of light penetrated the canopy of trees beyond the glare of the fire. It would be madness to go running about in the darkness, running from her fears and the ravings of a strange child.

He was a strange child. Her Harry, the little boy she had carried in her belly and nursed at her breast, sung to and read to and fretted over. She would gladly have given her life for him a thousand times over and yet now, for the life of her, she could not think why. Was it really him or some changeling? Had something in the deep Welsh woods taken up residence in the body of her boy?

"Harry," she said. "I'm scared. I don't like the way you're talking. Come to me. Come and embrace your mother. Let me hold you like I did when you were sick, because now I am sick with fear and sadness and I need you to hold me."

Harry smiled at her in a twisted sort of way.

"It doesn't work like that, mother," he said. "You should know that. It is a terrible thing for a child to precede their parent to the grave, but the natural order of things for the reverse to happen. Or do you wish it were the other way around?"

"I wish for none of us to die!" Louisa said. "Who even mentioned death? Why do you talk like this, Harry, when you know I am afraid and I ask you for comfort?"

"But I told you, you would go to heaven," Harry objected. "And Vlad says so and he's never wrong. That's why it will be alright."

"What will be alright?"

"That you will go to heaven and I will stay here with Vlad to rule in the forest."

"Harry, the way you are talking is mad. How can you speak of me dying without any sense of sadness? Do you not love me?"

"We cannot escape our fate," Harry said. "I said nothing of you dying. I said you would go to the grave and to heaven which is everlasting life.

That's what happens to the good people who live in the light, but there's another kind of life, under the ground and deep in the forests and places which are forever in the shade.

"Life is a battle between the darkness and the light and the slugs and the worms and other things that live there, and in the depths of the sea, those who are cousins to the snail and the dragons thrive and Vlad is a king in all those realms. Vlad *Imperator*. And the creatures of the light have eternal life in heaven if they live right on the earth, but for we others who live for mischief, that eternal life is denied. But there is another type of eternal life, for conquerors and lovers of adventure who don't have the meekness of Jesus within them, and that's what Vlad has offered me. So we will both be happy. You will have your heaven and I will have an eternity of adventure and conquest."

"You don't know what you're talking about," Louisa cried. "You're a little boy. What you speak of are abominations and horrors; you don't know what the reality is."

"Of course I do," Harry snorted. "Vlad explained it to me. No one knows it better than me. He showed me once, in fact, when I was at the bottom of the garden and I saw the cat had caught a mouse. The cat didn't kill it but toyed with it. There was terror, you're right, and there was blood, but it was only terrible for the mouse. The cat was full of joy and completely without malice. That is how we are, Vlad explained to me. We are the men for whom other men are mice, while we are cats. Their suffering is short and our lives are long and glorious, as are the lives of kings, which is why the Egyptians worshiped cats.

"And I have it in my veins. Where does our house come from? Don't we have it because *Papa* is awfully good at killing and staying alive? And haven't all our ancestors been the same all the way back to Agincourt? Grandpa and his grandpa; didn't they all come home victorious from battle to be richly rewarded for it? But I'm going to be better than all of them, Vlad explained to me. I'm going to be the best at killing that there ever was and live longer than all of the rest…"

And that's when Louisa began to scream. Because it was madness and yet she could not but see that it was true. These were not the words of a mere child. These words were given to him and by who if not the Vlad he spoke of, because who else had there ever been to indoctrinate him so? Surely he had not heard these blasphemies from a maid or a relative; they could have come from nothing but the unclean spirit who had somehow invaded their child's mind, his spirit, his soul.

Leaping to her feet she plunged out of the tumulus and into the darkness.

Louisa felt as if she had become two people, one of whom was crashing through the forest, bumping into trees and being clawed at by their low-hanging branches and clutched at by clinging vines. This primitive being was aware of these physical torments but paid them no heed. Its only interest was in getting as far away from the tumulus and the thing therein which had been impersonating her son. Yet even as this fleeing creature blundered about in the blackness of the night, another looked on slightly from above and wondered at its mad behaviour. She was a mother, that was all this other being knew. She was a mother, and her little boy was being left behind because of some mad panic of superstition which had overcome the creature in charge of her legs.

Where was her conscience, her duty, her prime directive? She had to go back, this entity insisted tirelessly, while the other blundered on until the passion that drove it gradually was worn away with exhaustion and finally she stopped to listen to what the passenger was saying.

And so Louisa stood swaying, half dead on her feet, darkness crowding in on her from all sides. She had always loved the prettiness of the woods but now she cursed its utter blackness and wished it was all paved over with cobblestones and lit with blazing gaslights or by the new wonders of Edison or any kind of cleansing flame. Cover it all with mills if need be, there could be none more dark and satanic as the forest itself and the horrors which hid within it.

She sunk to her knees in the detritus of the forest floor, soggy with the recent rains and now silent as the grave. She imagined she could feel the worms moving in the darkness below the mould and the snails and slugs exulting in the decay around her. The dragonflies hovering and the prehistoric centipedes crawling among the leaves and vines. The subjects of Vlad's vast domain, all the life that hid in the night and lived beneath the earth and in the depths of the seas, the leviathan and the kraken and all the horrors which sustained themselves from before the flood to beyond Armageddon and who would never be dislodged though all the world be made one great metropolis. If people somehow found a way to live without vegetation, those creatures would live on in the sewers and the vast caverns that honeycombed the world and the lochs and the rivers and the seas.

People were merely an infestation which had become too sure of itself and imagined that its brief ascendency was the unfolding of destiny rather than another momentary phase in a process which had seen trilobites and saurian's and a thousand species of insect and mammal rise and fall while somehow, so he said, Vlad would survive them all. And yet how?

How? her reason demanded, now. Now that she had finally ceased to flee. If he and his unholy kin had been on the earth for eons, so too had her race who had conquered the day and also she thought, taken rule of the night. They had built their vast metropolises. They had created their lighted thoroughfares and lighthouses to drive back the dark. Perhaps this Vlad was a mere idle boaster and relied upon that superstitious streak which he had awakened in her.

If he were so powerful, why did he and his kin hide in the darkness and lurk in the woods beyond the perimeter of the garden? Hadn't the Lord driven the unclean spirits out, legion though they had been, and sent them running off a cliff? If the belief of country folk were not mere superstition then did those beliefs not also contain a myriad of ways to ward off their evils? It was not always the dragon who won.

Presuming, of course, that there was something to all of this and she had not merely been guilty of the most despicable cowardice and superstition. Now that her rational mind had begun to finally make itself heard she wondered if she should not just let it take over fully?

But whatever else rationality demanded, it also demanded that one not deny the evidence of one's senses. Once more she ran over the events in her mind and found little comfort in them. She could not reconcile the image of her child and his cold manner, the words falling so glibly from his lips with their twisted sentiments. She thought of the improbability of the fire before the tumulus and of her child accomplishing all he had while she slept without some infernal aid. It was easier to imagine that he had had some help such as Prospero had received from Ariel while she had slept in the tempest than that he had accomplished all that alone.

In the forest around her, things crawled and fluttered. The croaking of a frog began and somewhere an owl screeched. She imagined that somewhere, far in the distance, she heard the howling of a wolf. She shuddered involuntarily and wondered if her newfound reason had any more value than the panic that had sent her crashing through the benighted woods; at least then she had gotten somewhere rather than standing impotently in the blackness full of thoughts but with no clue of how to proceed.

If indeed her son could yet be rescued and this fiend defeated, where would she find the means to do so? She had not so much as a pen knife to sharpen a stick with, though she had some half-remembered inkling that such an implement could be useful. And if she had one, what would she do with it? Thrust it into the chest of her son? He had spoken much truth and nothing more truly than that it was a terrible thing for a parent to see their child in the grave before them. She had thought she might face that horror with him already when he had been in the worst of his illness, and had thanked God ever since that she had been spared such a terrible fate. Now she found herself thinking, somewhat blasphemously, that perhaps the scenario Harry had painted was not such an unhappy one. If she could go to heaven and he could live on, happy after his own fashion, even as an abomination, would that be so bad? What profiteth it a man to gain the world and lose his immortal soul, was a deep question indeed, but not one to ask a mother faced with the loss of her child who might well sell her soul to avoid such a fate.

Now she felt only shame at the thought of her panic. Looking around her, as if awakening from a dream, she saw that some light had begun to illuminate the woods. Looking up she saw the clouds had cleared from the sky and a full moon could be spied through the ragged window in the canopy.

Touching her throat she felt the silver crucifix that always hung there and drew some comfort from it. Suddenly she no longer wanted to flee. Standing in the darkness she became aware of the sound of a stream nearby. She sought it out, and making her way to the bank stooped to wash the mud from her hands. Cupping them, she drew up a draught, and finding herself suddenly with a raging thirst, she drank long and deep. Finally satiated, she washed her face and her arms. Looking behind her she spied a few patches of dappled ground illuminated by the moonlight filtering through the trees. Here ran a little track such as might be made by the progress of generations of rabbit and deer. But the only prints which showed in the mud that night were those of two humans, an adult and a child and they all led distinctly in one direction.

Caressing the cross at her throat, she began to follow the tracks.

It seemed she had been crashing around in circles in her mad flight from her child, for she had not got very far from the dolmen at all, and soon, following the trail by the stream, she saw the uncanny glow of the flaming tree, still burning before its darkened entrance, though the second fire had died down and was little more than a pile of glowing embers now. She hesitated for a moment and called out the name of her child, but no one answered and she thought he might have succumbed to sleep. She grew silent and crept forward, wishing through long habit not to disturb his rest if he was once more embraced by dreams. But the little cavern was empty, so far as she could see.

Her clothes still hung on the makeshift racks and she couldn't help but admire her son's handiwork and industry. For the moment, she chose to banish from her mind the consideration that infernal help might have played some role in his achievement. Her clothes were quite dry now and gratefully she donned them once more. Feeling more like herself, she sat down to wait for the return of the prodigal and tried not to think of what kind of ghoulish adventure had taken him abroad in the moonlight.

Her back against the dolmen wall, she watched the burning tree and wondered idly if its seemingly perpetual flame was some infernal version of the one which had burnt on before Moses, or, a blasphemous voice whispered within, perhaps even the same. For had it not been said that one man's God was another man's demon and was there really anything in the division of beings of lightness and darkness? Wasn't Lucifer himself a being of light? There were those who said the faerie were themselves fallen angels. Once she had thought such talk amusing but now nothing seemed entirely amusing; but neither did it seem entirely awful and she wondered what kind of transformation the experiences of the night had wrought in her and feared that they were too alike to the ones that had turned her Harry into someone she could hardly recognise as her own child.

Somehow these thoughts morphed from waking ones to dream visions and the flames danced in her mind even while her eyelids shielded her sight. An owl sat in the fork of a great tree looking at her sagaciously before it hooted and flapped away as Harry himself flew down to alight before the tumulus' doorway. It had been his maiden flight and a little shaky, as had been his first hunt; but Vlad had been pleased, or so he told the boy as he sat perched between his shoulder blades. Now the dark fey sat astride one shoulder having slipped up to his new perch like a drift of mist as he was wont to do.

A shiver of pleasure went through the boy as it did whenever he saw his mentor display one of these uncanny tricks, because he knew, one day, he would be taught the same arcane skills. Already he could fly, but eventually he would be able to grow and shrink at will, become a rodent or a snail, stretch his limbs into tentacles and swim to the bottom of the sea. He would learn to live as easily in the crushing depths of the ocean, or the rim of a volcano, or in the ice of an asteroid as he once had in his cot. Of course he would not be able to bear the sun but he had grown an aversion to it already and wondered how anyone could ever prefer its harsh glare to that of his lady the moon.

He looked down on the sleeping woman in the entrance. He had known her as his mother once, but something ancient had awoken within him and such a recent attachment seemed like a small eddy of sentimentality in the great ocean of his incarnations. She had simply planted the seed of his soul on the earth once more but Vlad had returned him to the promise of eternal life on that plane upon which the angels so longed to exist that they forsook heaven for it. That realm where all the pleasures of the earth and of the flesh could be bought with a little bit of blood and the short suffering of multitudes. All of which they were supposed to trade for a song which lasted for all of eternity. He couldn't imagine that the heavenly choir were good enough to justify the choice.

He did love his mother, he realised, but simply in a different way to which he had before. The same way he loved his breakfast and flight and the hunt now and all else the earth had to offer which Vlad had laid out before him. He wanted her now – for his lusts had already become enormous – if not for the crucifix around her neck. He looked at her lovely throat and was surprised to see that the sigil was no longer there. Doubtless, he thought, in all her mad scrambling she had snagged it on a tree and lost it. So now there was no impediment to him feeding upon her once more, just as he had when he was a babe and she had first given him life, except this time he would not stop until she was drained. She could have her heaven, then, and he could have his.

Tenderly her knelt beside her and put a hand on her face gently to tilt her head a little more. He felt her arms go around him, embracing him, drawing his lips toward her neck as if she understood the gift he intended to bestow upon the both of them. Too late he realised the ruse as she slipped the crucifix she had secreted in her palm around his neck and fastened it deftly with her well-practised fingers.

He hissed like a scalded snake and strained to get away, but she wrapped her arms around him and trapped them by his side. A blood-curdling roaring escaped his lips but an even fiercer determination had possessed her and she held on.

"Help me!" Harry screamed, looking at his saviour, but the darkling prince had turned once more to mist, apparently discomfited by the flimsy bit of metal about his apprentice's neck. The flames on the tree flared more brightly and shone upon the silver cross and she wondered all of a sudden whose glamour it was; for if the Lord sent his rain upon the just and the unjust alike, perhaps he was also as generous with his fire.

"Let me go," Harry screamed, "Let me go! I don't belong to you! I belong to him! *You* belong to *us*!"

"No," Louisa said. "No, my boy, you are mine now, and so you will be, so long as life remains in my body. I didn't bring you into this world to lose you to a will o' the wisp that got stuck on the wheels of a gypsy's cart. I don't mean to be a snack."

She took the jacket she had been using as a pillow and forced him into it, then tied the arms around his chest, effectively making a straightjacket out of it. For good measure, she took the belt from around her waist and wrapped that around his arms. Throwing the boy over her shoulder she set out through the woods with a strength she would hardly have thought herself to have had.

That was the last time Vlad saw Harry. His mother had been quite determined to keep them apart. Yet there were plenty of other gardens which opened onto the woods and children who liked to play around their edges. Over the centuries, a thousand playthings had come his way and gone, and doubtless there would be a thousand more. It was the nature of the hunt that sometimes the prey got away. He rather admired the tenacity and cunning the woman had shown in thwarting him and his poor protégé who he suspected would be kept indoors and away from the damp, enticing places of the world where he might once more get a chance to follow the lower calling that was the glory of the earth and Vlad's delight to initiate new denizens into. Perhaps the boy would be locked in a seminary or an asylum; unless, of course, his father saved him and took him off to the glory of war, the roaring of which pulsed so strongly in the child's veins. Otherwise, he suspected, the poor child was destined for heaven and there was no help for that. He couldn't save everyone.

Draculhu

WILL MURRAY

For Edward Bransfield, the search for Draculhu began with the phantom fly.

He had been lost in a book one summer night when he felt the distinct sensation of a fly buzzing past. The fly made no sound. Bransfield heard no audible buzzing of wings. There was only that momentary sensation of something small and determined shooting past his left ear, a feeling of fleeting pressure so distinct that he flinched and looked around the room.

There shouldn't be a fly in this house, he thought with annoyance. The windows were closed and the HVAC was operating. It was nearly 90 outside his Midlothian, Virginia home, but a pleasant 70 in his living room.

Bransfield rose from his comfortable chair and searched for the fly for ten minutes, waving around a rolled-up newspaper in an effort to shoo it from wherever it had landed.

But he found no fly. Nor did it return.

The next time Bransfield had the experience, he was driving to work in Chantilly, Virginia. Stuck in traffic, his mind drifted off into the kind of reverie that was an occupational hazard for an ORV—operational remote viewer.

Again, there came that distinct sensation of a fly shooting past. A silent, invisible fly. Again, he flinched instinctively.

This time the hairs at the back of his neck lifted up. It was the dead of winter. The windows of his black Toyota CR-V were sealed and the heater was blasting.

It was not impossible that a fly could be loose in his closed car in the middle of winter. But it was so unlikely, he felt odd.

Snapping out of his reverie, Bransfield recalled the previous incident. Arriving at work, he searched the car thoroughly. No fly. Not even a dead one.

"Twice is coincidence," he muttered. "Three times will mean enemy action..."

The third time came only a week later.

He was wrapping up a remote viewing session, his mind returning to his physical body during the transitional point when he was emerging from a Theta state, when that snapping sensation came again. This time it cut across his field of vision. Except that he was lying there with his eyes closed.

Bransfield could almost see the fly in his mind's eye. He was not surprised when he sat up and opened his eyes in the dull gray room set aside for remote viewing sessions and found that he was alone.

"Something's not right," he muttered to himself.

He repeated that sentence to his superior after he finished transcribing his session notes.

"Three times now I've had the weird sensation of a fly shooting past my head. It's almost impossible for there to have been a fly in each instance."

Director Cranston stated, "You do this non-local work for a while, and you become hyper-sensitized to unusual stimuli. Sounds like you're picking up stuff that belongs to the astral plane. During extended remote viewing sessions, sometimes viewers have reported..."

"Reported what?"

"Oh, different phenomena. One viewer thought he had been followed back from wherever he was reconnoitering. We had to bring in an exorcist. Got rid of the thing, whatever it was."

"Wonderful," Bransfield said dryly.

"Another time someone came back from viewing some inhabited Exoplanet and another viewer had a weird sensation that the first viewer was on the planet Earth for the first time."

"Picked up a passenger?"

"Or an attachment. A parasite, possibly. We got him cleared out, too. In your case, I'm not sure what's going on. But it sounds to me like you're picking up passing critters belonging to some interpenetrating dimension."

"What do you recommend?"

"Treat it like you would a pesky fly you can't swat. If these things belong to another realm, they're on a different vibratory plane. They're not bothering you particularly. But just to be safe, keep a diary of these incidents. Just in case they amount of something."

Bransfield did that. But it was six months before anything unusual occurred.

On the morning of August 1, he woke up from a deep sleep. As he trained himself to do, he kept his eyes closed. Sometimes when you rise up out of the Delta State, you can pick up ambient sensory information. Some of it was personal; some of it was, well, whatever. Astral stuff.

Sometimes, Bransfield would see crystal clear images in his mind's eye. Often, they made no sense, as if he had been remote viewing something while asleep, something that his sub- or super-conscious had become attracted to. The act of waking broke the connection milliseconds before his mind returned to the waking state, and an image lingered.

Other times, he would see strange faces. On further occasions there were signs or words in a hieroglyphic language he could not read. Once he saw black ants milling around a cracked sidewalk. Many of these images were pedestrian and not worth recording.

The voices he listened to carefully. Usually, they made conversation that didn't quite make sense. Sometimes, they predicted things that didn't come to pass. Bransfield had learned to disregard the voices once he recognized that they were probably mischief makers from another plane of existence. He wondered if they talked to him when he was completely asleep and he simply didn't remember.

On this occasion, there was something very different.

Slowly returning from REM sleep, his brain began processing visual images that would normally stream from his opened eyes. With his eyes closed, his mind perceived something...*else*.

Crossing above him, apparently several hundred feet above his roof, yet visible in his mind's eye as if no solid ceiling structure lay between them, something black and silent glided past in the predawn grayness.

Its outline was that of a manta or a stingray. But it also reminded him of a great shadowy bat. Charcoal black and silent, it cruised overhead, and in the few seconds he had a mental lock on it, Edward Bransfield was struck by a cold feeling of deep dread.

The dark shape displayed two pair of wings. Behind the head that he could not see from the angle at which he viewed the weird cruising shape, was a great set of wings with ragged edges. Below them was mounted a second set of hind wings, much smaller, but also tattered like the burial shroud of a disinterred corpse.

There was a tail, like on a stingray. It was forked, whipping as it trailed behind.

In less than a minute, the apparition was gone. But the sensation it created of a cold, impersonal predator remained in Bransfield's mind long after it had glided out of range of his senses. The charcoal thing also felt ancient, almost impossibly old.

Clairaudiently, a single word reverberated in his mind: *Draculhu*.

That morning, he reported to work.

On the outside, the place was a rambling Victorian-era home whose first floor had been converted to a reading room. The sign said *Victoria Venkus Tea House*. Other signs proclaimed *Fortunes. Palmistry. Astrology*.

A licensed business open to the public, it was actually a front for the Cryptic Events Evaluation Section of the National Reconnaissance Office. Its mission was planetary defense. Its specialty, incursions from Outside. CEES was a classified program so black that Vantablack didn't come close to describing it. Congress didn't suspect it existed. The President was not in the loop, either.

Reporting to his superior, Bransfield described what he had perceived.

Director Cranston took his report very, very seriously. He lost a little bit of facial color as he listened.

"Have you ever heard that name before?" Bransfield asked him.

"No, never. Sounds like Dracula."

"That's what I thought," laughed Bransfield. "But Dracula is a myth."

"Draculhu also rhymes with...*Cthulhu*."

Now it was Bransfield's turn to lose color. "I hadn't thought of that."

Turning to his desk computer, Cranston punched up a file, saying,

"How do you imagine it was spelled?"

As Bransfield gave it to him, Cranston's fingers typed rapidly. "Nothing like that in the database of Old Ones," he reported.

"Should I feel relieved?"

"Wish I could tell you. I get a cross-reference to Dracula, which means 'Son of the Dragon' in old Romanian. The modern translation is 'Son of the Devil,' pronounced *fiul diavolului*. I'm going to assign a set of non-local coordinates to this name and run another viewer against it. We'll see what he comes up with."

"Let me know."

"I will if it's appropriate. If not, this is the last conversation we're going to have about this subject. Understood?"

"Perfectly," returned Bransfield. "The subject is closed until you reopen it in my presence."

Four days later, Bransfield was called into Cranston's impersonal office. Cranston looked grave; his voice was brittle.

"ORV #8 was tasked the Draculhu target. But we can't debrief him. His heart is beating, respiration is normal, but it's as if no one is home. We had to inject him with stimulants and slap his face before he returned to consciousness. But he's not himself. Can't talk. Doesn't understand directions. We can't get anything out of him until he snaps out of his trance."

"If he's not himself, what is he?"

"I don't know. The doctors can't explain it. But I'll be damned if I send another viewer against that four-winged demon, whatever it is."

"Where does that leave us?"

"We can't ignore this. This creature falls under the heading of External Threats. And it's invaded our segment of reality. We're going to have to take unusual measures."

"I don't like the sound of that."

"You shouldn't. You're going to be our scout."

"Dammit! What about not risking any more viewers?"

"I meant what I said. You have the ability to astrally project. You'll go that route."

"What do you think that will accomplish?"

"We need more data. A line of attack. Something. I'll have some of the public psychics working the floor look at it in different ways. Once we compile the data, we'll send you out there."

"If that's the way you want to play this, I'll stand ready."

Bransfield had an intuition what Director Cranston would do. Two days later, it was confirmed.

"I reassigned the target, but CRV-style this time."

CRV stood for controlled remote viewing. It was an entirely different method of obtaining non-local information. The viewer worked with pen and paper, sitting up, and not going as deeply. Some viewers got clearer information this way. Some of the floor readers were being trained in CRV in the hope they could be recruited as part of the operational team.

Bransfield was handed the session pages. He saw on the first page that the viewer decoded the target with the ideogram signifying a life form, a simple loop. But he continued looping reflexively, inscribing a mad vortex that grew darker and darker the more it spun inward. Like a black hole.

Looking at the Stage II pages, Bransfield picked out a lot of emotional information. Darkness. Dread. Wings. Hungry. The word Vampire came up more than once. The viewer categorized this term as an AOL—analytic overlay, thus dismissing it as a valid perception. However, it recurred repeatedly.

The word Abyss came up more than once, sometimes prefaced with the descriptor, Great.

The Stage III sketch was a stunner. Bransfield went cold inside when he saw it.

It depicted a dorsal view of what appeared to be a manta ray. Except this was no creature born of Earth's oceans. Along its sides were two staggered sets of wings. The superior started at the shoulders and an inferior set picked up directly behind them, where the body tapered down to the forked tail. The edges were frilly and torn...

There was no head. Only what appeared to be a ribbed neck, stunted yet wide.

The viewer had labeled some of the parts. The headless neck was labeled "Intake?" with several question marks.

Bransfield looked up. "It's almost as if he's describing a flying vehicle and not a creature."

"Go to Stage IV."

Stage IV sketches were more elaborate, and contained more data. There was also a word: *Draculhu.*

"Good target contact," Bransfield muttered. "What do you make of it?"

"Noticed the reference to the Great Abyss. That was a huge clue. It's the other name for the Underworld of the Dreamlands."

No one knew what the Dreamlands were. They were kind of a mirror image of Earth, but existing on the astral plane. People had been visiting it in dreams and astrally for centuries. Like any territory, it harbored safe zones and scary places. The Great Abyss was the worst of the latter.

"Interesting that the viewer said Draculhu was like a vampire," Bransfield murmured.

"Vampires drank blood. That's not what happened to the ORV #8. But his mind appears to be gone. It's two days later and he's wearing the same vacant expression, muttering the same inarticulate sounds. We have to feed him by hand and change his Depends. It's as if he's forgotten everything he ever learned from birth."

"Do you think this bat-ray-creature took his mind?"

"The medical team is operating on that assumption. Unquestionably, it removed every conscious memory his brain possessed. He's on automatic. He breathes, he eats and sleeps, but he's not any different from a newborn infant."

There was no point in stalling. Bransfield went right to the point: "What's the mission?"

"Astral projection is among your skill sets. I want you to penetrate the Great Abyss."

"No one has ever gone there. Not on our team, anyway."

Before Cranston could reply, Bransfield felt something dart past his right temporal lobe. Bransfield flinched.

"What's that?" Cranston asked.

"One of those damn astral insectoids. I just felt it shoot by me."

"I didn't see anything."

"Because it's not operating on our vibrational plane. But it gives me an idea."

"Go ahead. Let's hear it."

"Instead of plunging into the Great Abyss, why don't I follow one of these ghost flies back to its point of origin? It might be the same place where Draculhu dwells. My thought is this could be a soft probe."

"The astral fly, or you?"

"Both," I said.

"Fine. That's the mission. The two may not be related. But if they are, that's intelligence we need to acquire. Use Viewing Room #1. Get yourself together. Whenever you're ready, you go."

"Understood."

The viewing room was a neutral gray. It was circular in order to minimize any severe angles through which extra-dimensional intruders might enter. The only article of furniture sat in its center—a soft bed. The sideboard held a sheaf of paper, pencils, pens and a remote control for dimming the soft recessed lights. Even the domed ceiling was gray. All this was psychologically configured to prepare one to remote view from an emotionally neutral and objective point of view.

Bransfield lay down on the bed and dimmed the lights. He did this slowly to ease himself into the proper mindset. Psychonauts before him had mapped the Dreamlands in a general way. No one could explain what it was, in terms of our reality. Some believed the place was an ancient version of Earth that existed before recorded history, which persisted in a non-local way. Others thought it was a parallel other-dimensional Earth.

Wherever it was, whatever reality it represented, Bransfield would now penetrate it. Taking slow measured breaths, he went deeper and deeper into an Alpha state, then entered Theta, and finally drifted down into the Delta brainwave zone in which waking awareness cycles downward, ever downward.

But Ed Bransfield knew how to stay conscious in Delta. As he felt himself drifting off, he separated from his body, looked down at it, then cast his superconscious mind into the so-called Gate of Deeper Slumber, the metaphysical entrance to the Dreamlands.

Instantly, he translated. It was night over there. A half-familiar moon was shining down over the whole expanse of it, shedding a purplish light over all. Bransfield could see the ruins of Sarnath, and the distant city of Celephaïs, which was said to have been dreamt into existence by its ruler, and other known settlements. Mountain peaks reared up, some of which he recognized by sight, for they had been designated in classified NRO maps, the names acquired psychically and by other exotic means.

The Dreamlands was classified as a thought-responsive environment.

Once one entered it, all a traveler had to do was think of a place, and his attention went wherever he wanted, like the cursor in a computer database.

Bransfield moved closer to the ground, half flying and sometimes floating. He was hunting astral flies. But Bransfield didn't know what they looked like in this world, or in any other. He only knew their energy signature…

In time, he gravitated toward a cavern mouth below the lofty tableland called the Plateau of Leng. Around its boarded-up entrance, one of them was loitering. It was intensely black, a tiny cloud of malevolence. It possessed a solitary shimmering eyespot a little less black than the whole, like a decapitated Cyclops, but with no other features. It seemed to be hunting. Prudently, he maintained his distance.

After a while, it retreated into the cave, which showed indications of being an abandoned mine.

Bransfield allowed for some time to pass, then followed, passing through the weathered boards as if they were not solid.

Once inside the entrance, Bransfield left all light behind him. Fortunately, light was not necessary to see in a dream state. The walls of the tunnel shot past him, dark and furrowed, but Bransfield could not perceive them visually. He could only sense their substance.

The tunnel sloped into the ground, and then suddenly right-angled downward into a great smooth well. Up from this came a dark radiance that was not illumination. Bransfield hesitated before the shaft's gaping mouth, then dropped down slowly and cautiously, ready to shoot back upward if necessary.

When he reached an open space at the bottom, it was as if he had dropped into a great black womb. Bransfield could see nothing. He sensed nothing. There was only a terrible blackness that was disturbingly still.

Bransfield held poised in place, waiting for any images to resolve. But nothing did. There was no light down here. There seemed to be no *anything*. The little black insectoid had come down here, so he focused on it, seeking its energy pattern. Once he made contact, he crept toward it.

As Bransfield moved along, blind yet not blind, he became aware of vast shapes—malign consciousnesses, darker disturbances in the darkness. Congealed energies that were disturbingly negative.

Whenever Bransfield sensed one, he shifted his trajectory. Once something whipped out and almost struck him. In the dream state, he was immaterial, insubstantial, but this thing, this contact, frightened him to his core.

At last, Bransfield came upon something he could perceive in a blind-sighted way.

It resembled an obsidian pyramid with a flat top. Broad at the base, massive in its construction, and cyclopean in its architecture.

Holding steady, Bransfield directed his attention at it, attempting to divine its significance. Words clairaudiently came to mind, triggered by psychic impressions. Vault. Tomb. Crypt. Prison. Then, an alien name: *Zin*.

Whatever dwelt within those grim sloped walls, it appeared to be encapsulated therein.

Willing himself to move onward, Bransfield shifted in a fresh direction, seeking something else of interest.

Then he perceived the astral fly. It darted over his head, apparently oblivious to his presence, then arrowed for the front of the great vault. Zipping straight ahead, as if the weird flying thing was about to crash into the windshield of a speeding car. Except it went *into* the vault.

Bransfield perceived what appeared to be a fissure in the masonry front. The fly had gone into the jagged crack.

He would have followed, but Bransfield began sensing subtle waves emanating from the structure. They were negative, in the way you some-times feel a person's unpleasant emotions when they are just starting to become aroused.

Bransfield was studying the crack when *it* emerged. Not the fly this time. But the great charcoal-black shape of Draculhu. It floated out of the crack, and Bransfield moved swiftly to one side, until he found something that might have been a stalagmite, or some similar formation. He remained out of sight behind this form as the rotted-winged span glided past.

For the first time, Bransfield could see it head-on. Twelve feet from wingtip to wingtip, it seemed to be headless. The neck was an open gullet, like a chicken that had been decapitated, but which continued running in circles, its brainless body not realizing it had been killed.

As it glided by, Bransfield could feel the palpable waves of negativity radiating from it. Fear clutched at his gut. Bransfield sensed that if it detected him, he would enjoy no protection against it.

Bransfield waited a considerable time for the fluttery form to pass on. Then he fell in behind it. Bransfield feared to follow. But this was the mission. He was not about to shirk his duty.

Tattered wings undulating, Draculhu floated along until it came to the well's nether mouth. Up this, it vanished. Bransfield loitered until he was sure it could not notice him. Then he followed it upward and leveled off. Along the tunnel, he moved, and eventually emerged into the weird lunar light of the Dreamlands dreamscape.

The creature seemed to come alive in the moonlight. It rose into the night sky with increasing animation, as if somehow charged by the lavender lunar rays.

Bransfield wondered if it was about to attack one of the settlements below. Instead, it kept rising, rising, rising and then…abruptly, it popped out of existence.

Directing his attention, he surged where it had gone.

To his surprise, he found himself out of the Dreamlands. Before his consciousness reconnected with his body, he had a glimmering that Draculhu had crossed dimensions and was now in his own reality.

After slamming back into his supine body, Bransfield switched tactics. He again became a remote viewer, and began hunting it, even as dread took hold of his heart…

What if it hunts me in return? he thought.

More quickly than he thought possible, Bransfield located its foul energy signature and tracked it. It was moving through effulgent moonlight. Earth's silvery moon seemed to energize it even more than the alien orb that hung over the Dreamlands.

Bransfield watched it pass over a suburban tract, seemingly uninterested in its surroundings. Without warning, it gave a frilly flip of its triangular wings and shot down through a second-floor window of an unremarkable vinyl-sided house.

Bransfield was tempted to do the same, but something inside of him said: *Don't.* Instead, he moved nearer to the window pane. Through eyes that were non-physical but highly attuned, Bransfield saw it alight on the chest of a sleeping woman, settling as flat as a beached skate, its wingspan draping the bed. Slowly, its headless neck extended, and its terminal orifice plunged into her rising chest without breaking the skin.

As Bransfield watched, he realized the four-winged monstrosity was *feeding.....*

But on what? Energy? Life force?

Bransfield also sensed that the room was busy with astral flies. He was in no position to intervene. He had no physical presence here; he was a soul untethered from his body. The thing might be able to sense him, but it might also be too primitive to do so. Since it had no head, conceivably it also lacked a brain.

The feeding did not take long. Retracting its neck, which Bransfield realized was some type of natural siphon, Draculhu flipped up its ragged-edged wings, snapped them downwards and propelled itself aloft, melting into the ceiling and emerging from the roof, to sail back into the eerie moonlight.

As Bransfield watched, it flew about. Draculhu had fed. But was it... *satiated?*

Bransfield kept well behind it, trusting he would not be detected.

Then a cloud passed over the moon. Draculhu faltered. The cloud was thick and cut off all moonglow. Night clamped down. Only thin, spidery starlight remained.

Blocked from the recharging lunar light, Draculhu began to sink slowly to the ground the way an injured sunfish settles to the sea bottom.

In a little patch of grass, it alighted. It lay there, the triangular tips of its four wings rising and twitching, as if dying.

As Bransfield watched, all animation subsided.

Long minutes crawled by, during which he wondered if Draculhu was deceased.

The answer came when the moon broke through a ragged rent in the cloud banks. The superior wingtips began to rise and twitch as it struggled to lift off the ground. But it failed to take off. The moon was again swallowed. It sank once more, and the process continued.

Eventually, the cloud bank scudded on. And in the returning lunar light, Draculhu regained its strength and lifted silently back into the night sky. This time, it seemed to have a definite direction in mind.

It vanished. Bransfield had a momentary glimpse of the vastness of the Dreamlands. The unholy predator had returned to its den...

"The Vaults of Zin..." muttered Director Cranston.

"What?" Bransfield asked.

"You've discovered the Vaults of Zin—one of them anyway. One of the darker legends of the Dreamlands. Mentioned in the Pnakotic Manuscripts."

"What do they say about them?"

"That we don't know. The only known copy resides in the Dreamland city of Lomar. All we know are what psychics and lucid dreamers have brought through. There's a crack channeler in the Non-Local Affairs Department. I'll ask her to channel whatever the Pnakotic Fragments say about the Vaults of Zin. Maybe there's something about Draculhu, too."

"So I'm out of it?"

Cranston nodded. "For now. But stand ready."

The next day, Bransfield was called back in.

Cranston handed him a notebook in which someone had recorded several pages of dictation.

"This is what the channel produced. Go ahead and read it. Then I'm burning that notebook. Nothing contained in it must go beyond this room."

REPORT OF [redacted]

I was unable to decipher the portion of the Pnakotic Manuscripts related to the Vaults of Zin, which appears shielded from psychic probing. I next attempted to tap into the entity Draculhu itself. This is all I heard or received.

I sense no mind, no consciousness that I can convert into concepts understandable by humans. This creature does not possess a brain as we understand it. It does not have forbearers, or offspring. It is unique unto itself.

I intuit that it came into existence before man walked this planet. It was not created. It was dreamed into existence.

When I probed more deeply, I received the following:

"Ph'nglui mglw'nafh Cthulhu R'lyeh wgah'nagl fhtagn."

Translated, this means: "In his house at R'lyeh dead Cthulhu waits dreaming…"

I am forced to conclude that this is a dream entity conceived by Great Cthulhu, a byproduct of his unconscious brain which manifested in the Dreamlands, a sort of psychic twin inhabiting the Great Abyss instead of the Pacific sea bottom.

I dare not penetrate Cthulhu's mind for more data. I sense something scanning my own thoughts and must break contact now.

Looking up from the notebook, Bransfield said, "Sounds like this thing is one of the unclassified spawn of Cthulhu."

"A nightmare is more like it. Give me that."

Bransfield surrendered the notebook. "What's our next move?"

"The channel who wrote that is in diapers now. We think the act of scanning Draculhu brought her to its attention."

"I'd better lay low."

"On the contrary," corrected Cranston. "You're going to be the flame."

"The what?"

"The flame that draws the blackest of black moths to its destruction."

Bransfield felt his mouth go dry.

"One of the techs came up with a plan. I've approved it. It has a 99.965% chance of succeeding."

"That's an oddly specific number…"

"It's specific for a reason I'll explain later. Get your affairs in order. Be back here at 10 P.M. The moon will be high by then."

Ed Bransfield had dinner at his favorite Thai restaurant, eating alone. His thoughts were troubled. They kept going back to the bat-ray-dragon creature called Draculhu.

It was a vampire, all right. But it didn't drink blood. It absorbed souls, or at least the energy of souls. It was literally a nightmare. A nightmare conjured by sleeping Cthulhu, who might or might not even know it existed, depending on what level of consciousness produced the thing.

Bransfield reviewed in his mind what he knew of Cthulhu. Imprisoned in a sunken vault in the heart of the Pacific by the Old Ones long ago, the creature had been hibernating for eons, awaiting the proper time to awaken and rise in order to destroy the world of Man, just like the Kraken. Maybe the Kraken legend was merely an adumbration of Cthulhu, a distorted memory of a terrible cosmic reality. Who knew? It was a bottomless pit of mystery.

Although Cthulhu slept, it dreamed, and sometimes its telepathic mind reached out to weak-minded human beings, impelling them to do its incomprehensible bidding.

Did Draculhu also do Cthulhu's bidding? Or was it an independent entity, real in both the Dreamlands and in the more substantial dimensions of Earth?

While he pondered those questions, Bransfield navigated his meal. Once again, the passing-bullet feeling came again. One of the astral flies was present. It cut across his field of vision, only he couldn't see it. He just felt it darting past his forehead.

Trying to focus on it, he realized it was circling madly—orbiting him. He didn't like that. Before, the creatures just flitted by on the way to God knows where.

This one was *interested* in him....

Finishing his meal, he settled his check and drove off. As far as he could tell, he was alone in his CR-V.

Returning to headquarters, Bransfield entered via the private agent's entrance. Director Cranston's secretary handed him an envelope. She said nothing. She didn't have to. These were his sealed orders.

In the back of his mind, Bransfield wondered if Cranston had delegated the responsibility to his secretary because he knew this was a suicide mission and didn't care to struggle with a proper sendoff. Cranston was an odd one. His first name was classified. No one knew anything about him. Presumably unmarried, he wore only a Miskatonic University graduation ring with its onyx stone.

Entering Viewing Room #1, he removed his shoes and got comfortable on the working bed. Dimming the lights but not extinguishing them, he lay back and opened the envelope.

Instructions

Locate Draculhu. Engage his attention. Lure him to the attic of this address:
55/White. Remain on station until mission accomplished.
Return if you are able to.

"Encouraging," Bransfield muttered to himself. Well, that was Cranston. Bloodless and to the point.

After dimming the lights to absolute darkness, Bransfield lay back and began meditating into the proper brain-wave frequency which enabled him to return to the Dreamlands, a disembodied observer.

As he dropped off, he became aware that the room was swarming with invisible flies....

The flies met him in the Dreamlands. Were these different ones? It was impossible to say. The swarm was about a dozen strong.

Like beads on a string, they followed him to the boarded mouth of the abandoned mine, down the well-shaft and all the way to the shadowy Vaults of Zin.

Orbiting like tiny unseen insects, the swarm became a distraction. He realized that he had never apprehended their purpose. Now he wondered if they were satellites of Draculhu.

He waited within sight of the crack in the face of the great tomb-vault for Draculhu to appear. Time seemed to pass in this timeless place, but it was difficult to measure its progression in the darkness. No markers existed.

Finally, out of the great fissure, Draculhu emerged, its superior wings folded close to its upper and lower surfaces, propelled by its undulating hind wings.

After the devilish tail cleared the crack, the triangular wings uncurled, and the charcoal horror floated into view in all of its tattered majesty.

The sight made Ed Bransfield quail inside. A sense of conscienceless evil radiated from it. This radiation of negativity was what the Old Ones were supposed to be like. Beyond human concepts of good and evil, all but indifferent to anything but their incomprehensible needs.

Abruptly, the constellation of flies departed and swarmed in the direction of the manta-winged ray-demon.

Congregating around Draculhu, they formed a floating string of cloudy black pearls, turning in his direction…

With an inner jolt, Bransfield realized they were returning because they were leading Draculhu to him.

Well, that was the plan. Best to get on with it…

Turning about, Bransfield zoomed in the direction of the vertical mine-shaft while Draculhu and its insectoid satellites silently followed.

In the non-local environment of the Dreamlands, to think about an action was to execute it. Only flash seconds of delay intervened.

Bransfield broke clear into the diffuse violet moonlight of the Dreamlands before he looked backward.

Flapping its triangular wings, Draculhu emerged from the partially-blocked mine entrance and swooped up in his direction. Its progress was determined, although the four ragged-edge wings worked languidly. If it was sightless, it was not entirely blind. For it followed him as if it were tracking a radio signal. In the way, it was. It had homed in on his unique energy signature.

Crossing the invisible barrier to the Earth plane, Bransfield broke out into the starry world he knew and flashed through the moonlight-charged night air. He did not look back. There was no need to. He knew Draculhu was hunting him. There was no time to entertain fear. He must reach his destination.

The address he was given had been reduced to a version of non-local coordinates. It was not a street address. It was the color of the house and its street number only—55/White. That was all that was necessary. His intent and the intent of the tasker were all that was needed to enable him to navigate to the designated location.

When the white clapboard structure came into view, Bransfield saw that the attic had only one window, set at the gable end. It was a strange window. It looked like a mistake. It resembled an old-fashioned four-paned window, but much narrower and tilted over on its side, rotated at a 45-degree angle. Moonlight made the panes opaque.

He entered the peak-roofed attic through that off-kilter aperture.

Inside, there stood a great globe of blown bluish glass. It was about the size of a compact car, if cars were spherical. Inside clustered a mass of filaments, like cobwebs of spun glass. Bransfield could see these filaments clearly because a small hole in the roof permitted a ray of moonlight to shine down into the globe's interior, illuminating it like a strange natural satellite that had been deposed from the night sky.

Stealing himself, Bransfield entered it, and held himself in place. He looked down. The globe sat on some type of mechanized pedestal whose steely parts shone brightly, as if new. The rest was an impenetrable black.

No time to study it. He turned his attention back to the crazily-tilted narrow window. Before long, a triangular shadow loomed on the other side of the four cramped panes.

It was the headless form of Draculhu. It floated there, fluttering its tattered wings, as if hesitant to intrude.

Eventually, it slipped in, melting through the glass and pausing before the shimmering globe.

With a cold feeling of dread, Bransfield understood that it was aware of him. He also sensed that it did not care for the clotted darkness of the attic space. But the ray of moonlight magnified by the filaments of the glass globe attracted it like a moth to a flame, just as Director Cranston had suggested.

Pausing only a moment, Draculhu began extending its intake funnel and pushed it through the blue-glass skin…toward him.

Retreating to the shadow-clotted rafters, Bransfield willed himself into immobility.

Flicking its forked tail, Draculhu fully entered the globe.

Bransfield wondered if the filaments were somehow designed to ensnare it. But that hope was soon dashed. Like a manta ray inside a great aquarium, it swam about the interior of the globe, its ethereal substance unaffected by the glassy threads, which belonged to a different frequency domain than the Dreamlands nightmare. There, it hesitated, as if afraid to plunge into the darkness beyond the sphere's moonlit confines.

Feeling that he was safe in his dim corner, Bransfield watched. If he had to move, he would do so quickly.

Draculhu did not exit the moonlit shell. It floated in place, uncertain, cautious, yet unwavering in its attention upon him. It possessed not eyes, but he could feel its vibrational *regard*…

As Bransfield held his ground, astral flies swarmed around him. To his horror, they entered him. Fixing unseen appendages on his insubstantial form, they started dragging him inexorably toward the moonlight-shot globe.

The insectoid servitors were scouts of Draculhu! They were drawing him toward that slowly extending intake organ. Images of horror came into his mind. Corpse flies. Jackals. Vultures. Carrion eaters of all types. Opportunistic parasites, they fed on what the apex predators left behind. Predators such as Draculhu…

Willing himself to shoot up through the roof, Bransfield found that he could not exert self-control and break free. The astral flies had him firmly in their grip.

Draculhu floated in the moonglow-infused globe, charged by the lunar light, patient yet hungry for its hapless prey…

Bransfield felt like a fly being pulled into the spider's web… Nearer and nearer, he was dragged, and his mind began to rebel against the foul thing he was facing.

In his brain, he heard a voice. A human voice.

Say when.

When?

Say when to snap the trap.

This wasn't in his instructions. He instantly understood why. Cranston didn't want Draculhu to read his mind. Assuming that it could.

Snap the trap! he transmitted mentally.

Bransfield was not three feet from the illuminated blue globe when there came a violent actioning of mechanism, like a bear trap closing. It happened too fast for him to perceive the totality of it.

One moment he was being drawn to the lunar-lit sphere and the next, the attic went dark...so dark that he could no longer perceive the globe. In this astral form, it should have been possible to see what had happened.

Thinking that the aperture that let down that single ray of lunar light had been sealed, Bransfield turned his attention upward. But the silvery moon ray was still shining down. But where the globe had stood, there was only a deep, unrelieved darkness. Balked by something he could not understand, he was unable to penetrate the weird darkness that did not reflect the lunar light.

It seemed impossible. But the light simply stopped dead in space. It was as if the blackest of pits had opened up before him.

Could they have created a black hole to capture Draculhu? he thought.

No, that was insane.

The voice in his head said *Return to base.*

Bransfield wanted to scream that he couldn't, that he was trapped. Before he could form thoughts for transmission, the astral flies relinquished their grip. They swarmed toward the black singularity and disappeared within...*what?*

Released, Bransfield's consciousness returned to his prone body lying in the viewing room.

Snapping erect, he fumbled for the dimmer. Illumination returned. His body felt cold. The tips of his fingers tingled.

After Bransfield struggled back to normal brain function, he reported to Director Cranston's minimalist office.

C ranston's welcome was typically flat. "Congratulations. Dracuhu has been successfully encapsulated."

"In what? A black hole?"

"Two halves of a spherical shell casing that closed over the witch ball, sealing it irrevocably."

"I thought that was what it was."

"Did you also recognize the witch window?"

"No, sir."

"Back in Colonial days, it was believed that windows installed at 45-degree angles could not be entered by witches riding broomsticks. If one slipped through, they would become entangled in the filaments of a small witch ball suspended from the ceiling. We built a bigger version for Draculhu."

"You have me at a loss for words."

"The shell was coated in Vantablack, a substance created from nanotech, and so intensely black that it absorbs 99.965% of light striking it.

"Now I know where you got your odds."

"Once the trap snapped, all available light was cut off to the ball's interior. The tech boys figured that it would paralyze Draculhu instantly. It wouldn't have the strength to move, much less exit."

"Well, it didn't follow me back..."

"It can't. Probably in a coma now. The ball will be removed and buried in a hole so deep it will never know daylight. Maybe we'll drop it down an exhausted oil well and pour in concrete."

"Was it that simple?"

Cranston laughed in his chilly manner. He extended one hand, showing his Mistakonic U. ring. The onyx stone reflected no light. Now it resembled a small black hole in reality one couldn't penetrate. Vantablack coating.

"We expended half a million dollars to put our trap together on short notice," he said. "There was nothing simple about it. There was only the question of whether it would work."

"And whether it would get *me* before we got *it*."

"You were the flame, not the moth, ORV #4."

Bransfield allowed himself a tight smile. "Who was that who reached out to me while I was being dragged like a blood sacrifice?"

"I did the honors. I would trust no one else with an agent's life."

"I didn't know you were telepathic."

"I came up through the ranks. Forget you heard that. Have a full report on my desk by tomorrow morning. Then the subject of Draculhu goes into the Dead Matter file."

"Better it than me..."

"Dismissed."

Ed Bransfield did his best to forget Draculhu, and all he had experienced.

Three weeks came and went before the memory returned with all its shivering horror.

One warm October evening, he slept out on his screened sunporch, oblivious to the droning buzz of dog-day cicadas in the trees.

With a start, he jerked awake. At first, he wasn't sure what woke him. Then something skimmed past his head.

Sitting up, he peered about in the moonlight. Nothing moved out there.

Turning over, Bransfield tried to go back to sleep. And it happened again. A quick zipping pressure which he felt more in his soul than on his skin.

Sitting up again, he closed his eyes and tried to focus with his inner mind.

Therein, Bransfield perceived three tiny cloud creatures orbiting the bed. Orbiting *him*. Black. Cyclops-eyed. And thirsty in a way he struggled to grasp.

Focusing, Bransfield apprehended what they thirsted for. Not blood. Not ectoplasm. Not his immortal soul.

They thirsted for *revenge*...

The Angel of Death

ANDREW SALMON

A rash of deaths within London's anarchist circles drew the attention of Special Branch that unseasonably warm May in 1897 but was not deemed particularly significant. What was the loss of a few bomb throwers, cut throats and agitators in the grand scheme of things? For the Queen's annual summer vacation was at hand and this was always a time of high alert for the Branch and the confidential agents recruited to assist them in protecting the Empire.

Would Her Majesty head north to Balmoral Castle in Scotland? Or south to the Isle of Wight and stately Osborne House? This was a closely guarded secret. The sudden death of the Royal Equerry responsible for the safety of the Royal Train imperiled the trip.

Mina Hawker had been carrying out her duties as a confidential agent when she was confronted by the person responsible for her, and her associates undertaking Branch work. She dashed to rejoin Dr. Abraham Van Helsing, and Quincey Morris at the house in Belgravia that Arthur Holmwood had inherited along with the title of Lord Godalming.

"I saw Dracula," she blurted before the men were seated. "No more than an hour ago."

"Where?" growled Morris, fists clenched at his sides.

"Kensington. Off Holland Park. Services for Connor Williamson today out at Brookwood Cemetery. I was to follow on the Necropolis Railway but when I spied Dracula I came here instead. He is within our grasp at last!"

"You did not approach him?" asked Van Helsing.

Mina shook her head. It was all she could do to keep from rushing after the fiend after what the Count had done to Lucy.

"Should have put a bullet through his brain!" Morris sprang out of his chair and paced. He and Holmwood had both proposed to Lucy Westenra and were awaiting her decision when Count Dracula murdered her eight months ago. Holmwood had learned of the Count's ties to anarchism while seeking justice for Lucy's murder and they all had agreed to work as Special Branch agents to better hunt their quarry. Dracula's hasty flight to France had left them helpless to act. Next they learned he had been present at the murder of a Russian prince in Paris. No connection could be established between the Count and the assassins. This was not the first time Dracula had been present at such attacks and he was referred to as the Angel of Death by Special Branch. Mina's husband, Jonathan, had remained in Paris on the hunt.

"If Dracula's here in London, there's something brewing," Holmwood observed.

"Perhaps these dead anarchists..." considered Mina.

"What of it?" asked Van Helsing. "Not uncommon for such people to harshly deal with members of the Cause."

"The Angel of Death," Morris observed.

Van Helsing nodded. "Title well-deserved. However Special Branch has never turned up a scrap of evidence against him."

"With Lucy lying cold in her grave because of that monster!" said Mina, enraged.

"All hearts were broken when Miss Lucy murdered." Van Helsing's voice cracked. "Terrible it was."

"And pointless," Morris added.

"No. Worked for the Branch did she. Hunting proof supporting suspicions held against the Count. How she die?" demanded Van Helsing. "No mark upon the body, no sign of struggle. Lying peaceful on warehouse floor as though in bed and slumbering. As if her life had simply drained away. "

"She was after Dracula when she was murdered. He's responsible in some way," asserted Holmwood.

"And that is all we know, Van Helsing persisted. "His presence then and his presence today strengthen only his Angel of Death moniker. The deaths surrounding him now are our only avenues to investigate."

-2-

The death of still another anarchist, the eleventh in six weeks, spurred the agents to action. Ronald Griffin had supplied weapons and explosives to any group that could meet his price. The man's death was not suspicious as Griffin had been seventy years of age with decades of strong drink behind him. However he had been a high ranking member in the Cause and the agents agreed that a search of his house might yield something of worth.

Griffin's residence was held by the government as he had left neither will nor heirs. As Lord Godalming, Holmwood had the ear of the Home Secretary and was granted permission to conduct the search. It was decided he and Morris would do so while Mina and Van Helsing collected what information they could from their sources. There was one in particular the doctor was anxious to speak with.

With Griffin's associates and the Branch's investigators having already gone through the place, Holmwood and Morris did not expect to find incriminating material just lying about. No, theirs was a hunt for the overlooked. Griffin had dealt firearms and explosives from the house for three decades—there had to be places of concealment.

Open drawers and tossed beds bore mute testimony to prior searches. Quick soundings for hidden cavities behind walls and beneath floorboards revealed nothing and they proceeded smartly to the cellar.

They had brought along a bull's eye lantern and had instant need of it once they descended the steep wooden stairs to the musty, dark confines below. The ceiling light was not working and the lantern's light insufficient until their eyes adjusted, revealing details of the cluttered chamber.

A furnace roared, the heat stifling but welcome as the rooms above had been chilly despite the May sunshine. Holmwood cast the lantern about so they could get their bearings. Amidst crates and sagging cartons they distinguished pathways through the clutter. One led to a cast iron tub along one wall swathed in inky blackness. The metal gleamed in the lantern's beam. A wall of tools opposite the tub were rusty with disuse. A hatchet blade caught the light from its place among its dingy brethren.

The carton lids had been strewn about the floor by earlier searchers.

"Nothing but bones to pick over," observed Holmwood.

They separated. Holmwood guided his lantern into the dark recesses while Morris hoped to use the glow from the furnace grate.

A soft click drew the American's attention.

"Something, Quincey," Holmwood announced from the gloom.

Morris joined his friend. The light revealed a hollowed-out recess in the wall behind the paneling Holmwood had opened upon accidentally tripping the spring latch. The recess was in one black corner furthest from the furnace. The space was five feet high and as many feet wide. Short shelves on either side were indicative.

"Rifles" said Holmwood.

"Shelves for cartridge boxes," added Morris.

They had found Griffin's cache. The hidden compartment was empty however.

"Figure the Branch got this lot?" asked Holmwood.

"I don't know, Art. Perhaps he sold them before he croaked. Either way that's it for us. Dammit!"

Holmwood slammed the panel closed in disgust. "Let's get that dust off at any rate."

Lantern raised high, they made their way to the long, iron tub against the opposite wall. The bulb over the tub had been broken. The tub was a good four feet in length. Holmwood rested the lantern on one corner and turned the tap. Water thundered into the tub and both men placed their hands under the jet.

Morris closed the tap. Holmwood handed him the coarse scrap of towel off a wall hook to dry his hands. Standing over the tub, Morris noticed the water was slow in draining. It was not an unusual hiding place so long as the tap was not used.

"Hand me the lantern," said Morris. He passed it over the slowly draining water, opaque with dust.

"Something's blocking it." Morris bent over for a closer look but only the circular opening flush with the tub surface was visible. He had to lean directly over the opening with the light to see the obstruction.

He shifted the lantern and tilted it so the light shone down into the drain.

The water swirled down the drain and the light reflected off an eyeball with a cerulean blue iris staring back up at him.

-3-

There were many in the medical profession with anarchist sympathies and Dr. Van Helsing cultivated acquaintances with several of these men in his work for Special Branch. Dr. Henry Scott was one such contact, well established in anarchist circles, and Van Helsing believed he and Mina had an approach which should yield results with minimal risk.

They arrived at Scott's Harley Street office to find the stout Scott and his staff hurriedly preparing for his immediate departure. Van Helsing made the reason for their visit plain.

"I am at your disposal," said Scott "Only I'm for Brookwood Cemetery to pay my respects to Mr. Griffin and have not a minute to spare."

Van Helsing seized the opportunity and asked if he and Mina might accompany him. Scott agreed.

As the carriage navigated the crowded streets, Mina and Van Helsing were treated to a litany of Dr. Scott's woes which lasted until they reached Waterloo, abating only within one of the private waiting rooms on the second floor of the Necropolis Railway Station. Four men were carrying Griffin's flower decked coffin to the train. The loading took place after the mourners had boarded which meant the train would be departing shortly. Mina and the two doctors hastily boarded. It was only in the confines of the private compartment that the matter at hand could be raised.

"The Cause has suffered many losses of late. Lost am I in accounting for them," Van Helsing began. "One dedicated as myself cannot but wonder if we are being targeted. If I or my niece should draw such attention..."

Scott smiled reassuringly. "I've heard nothing along those lines. We are perfectly safe."

"What of Count Dracula's presence in London?" asked Mina. "The Angel of Death as he has been called."

Scott gave a surprised start. "Dracula here? Nonsense."

"I have seen him with my own eyes."

"You are quite mistaken. If the Count were here I would know about it. Word would have passed along before his arrival, I assure you."

Mina sought to press the matter but Van Helsing surreptitiously placed a hand on her forearm. Scott was quite correct in assuming word of Dracula's arrival would spread. Van Helsing did not doubt Mina's word and preferred to have the contradiction play out. "Your words are pleasing to my ears, Doctor," he said. "Safer I feel. You have assurances from our leaders that these losses are natural? O'Toole, Bennett, Griffin, Williamson - such numbers!"

"And more this last month!" added Scott. "Rogers, Sims, Smith, Carter. Signed death certificates until my hand's numb. Back and forth from Brookwood so often it's like a second home to me."

"My worry has returned at hearing this," prompted Van Helsing.

Scott went on to recount the nature of the deaths: a fall down a flight of stairs, food poisoning, death in bed, a fever - all perfectly normal. "Death watches over us all," he said in closing. "Ah, but such is our lot. Watched at every turn by the damned police, hounded to the grave. Only nailed into our coffins do we escape their scrutiny."

Arriving at Brookwood, the train reversed onto the spur line leading to the North and South stations. Non-Conformists utilized the North Station whereas Anglicans were interred at the South Station. Van Helsing thought the North Station would suit the anarchists and was surprised when the train continued south after two other caskets had been removed.

The unloading proceeded efficiently once the train had come to a full stop at the Anglican Station. Three coffins in all, each accompanied by an entourage of mourners who paraded solemnly by the train window. Dr. Scott adjusted his black suit coat and was about to stand when Mina's voice rang out.

"Dracula!"

Bathed in the sun's radiance, Dracula strode boldly past just outside the train window. He turned and glanced into the compartment as he glided past. Heavy moustache and thick eyebrows lent a Satanic cast to his aquiline features. The piercing black eyes seemed to tug at the souls of the Branch agents. Scott's reply broke the momentary connection.

"You do hang on to a notion," he said. "I can assure you Count Dracula is not in England."

This astonishing comment caused Van Helsing to turn a sharp glance in Scott's direction. He stared at the anarchist in mute appraisal. Mina did not press the point in the wake of Van Helsing's earlier signal. It was a significant development, though one neither could fathom presently.

"They'll be heading to the grave site," Scott continued blithely. "We'd best join the procession."

Van Helsing preferred to surveil the mourners rather than be in their midst. Feigning as much weakness as he could with his powerful frame, he struggled to rise then fell back on the seat. "I'm afraid my nerves combined with this sudden heat has gotten the better of me. An old fool am I. I don't believe I can manage the walk."

"I shall remain with you of course, uncle," added Mina, wise to the game.

"You are quite certain?" asked Scott.

"Indeed, sir," Mina replied. "He has suffered such spells before. With rest he'll be right as rain in half an hour."

Dr. Scott was through the compartment door like a shot. He left the door open, allowing the breeze to reach them from the open platform.

"Follow them, Mina," Van Helsing urged. "I feel we are at the heart of something."

"How did he not see Dracula?" asked Mina as she straightened her hat and skirts.

"Much have I to say on that. Only now is not the time to say it. Quick, my dear!"

Mina glanced along the platform, then stepped out of the compartment. Pausing at the exit she saw the deserted paths the funeral processions had taken.

Dracula was losing no time, she mused as she descended the station steps. Which way had they gone? She studied the path. To her right lay the Non-Conformist section and this seemed the most likely. That said, the section was quite close to the station which brought an element of risk. The path on her left was farthest away, good for privacy, but still uncomfortably close to the southerly running Bagshot Road. It was also the most crowded with a group of mourners gathered outside the chapel.

Assuming Dracula and his underlings would prefer privacy, she turned left and proceeded along Cemetery Pales Road as quickly as decorum would allow amidst the strolling visitors paying their respects. The cemetery was a jumble of gravestones in boggy black soil surrounded by heather and great trees.

Time favoured her action as it was just past eleven and the train would not depart until 2:20 that afternoon.

She soon learned she had chosen incorrectly when she spied a large procession up ahead. Dracula's party had been smaller. Whirling about she all but sprinted back the way she had come.

She had barely started along the path paralleling Bagshot Road when the procession led by Dracula appeared up ahead. Her blood froze. Mina cast her gaze about for a means of concealment and spotted a long, low crypt just behind her at the road's edge and darted for it.

The voices grew louder as the men drew near. She peered around one corner of the marble crypt, her face hidden by a bush.

"I cannot change your mind?" Dr. Scott pleaded. "In light of recent events, it would put our brethren at ease."

"The Cause determines our actions," said a tall man of athletic proportions and a head of blonde curls. Mina saw the man turn to Dracula who nodded slowly in mute ascent to some unspoken instruction. Scott seemed oblivious to this exchange. "We must remain here. I doubt any of us shall see London again."

"That is a shame," Scott whined as they moved up the road.

It was imperative she return to the train before they did so that Scott would find her and Van Helsing where he had left them.

Throwing caution to the wind, she lifted the hem of her skirt and ran for all she was worth over the grass between the tombstones. Her angle to the station gave her an advantage over the others following the winding path. She would reach the station around the front of the train before Dracula and the others approached at the rear.

Pitchers of water were set on stands outside the compartments against the day's heat. She snatched one up and was stepping into the compartment just as the Count and the others rounded the back of the train. They no doubt caught a glimpse of her but she was not concerned. By the time Dr. Scott rejoined them she had plucked two glasses from the porter's cart and she and Van Helsing were sitting quietly sipping water.

"Ah, you're back," said Mina, setting down her glass. "I could hunt up but two glasses. Damn these porters, vanishing the instant the train comes to a halt. And you must be parched."

Scott did not seem the least interested in what Mina or Van Helsing might have been up to in his absence. A bland recounting of the ceremony followed as the man seemed unfocused. "Shall we take luncheon before we head back?"

"Uncle is responding slowly in this heat," Mina said. She waved her fan in front of her hot face. "It is not doing me much good either. We have decided we'll spend the rest of today in Woking and head back tomorrow morning when it is cooler."

Scott managed faint protest but, ultimately, seemed eager to be shed of them. Mina and Van Helsing thanked the doctor for his hospitality before hunting up a carriage for the short trip to Woking.

-4-

The first order of business was to send a wire requesting Arthur Holmwood and Quincey Morris join them at their earliest convenience. Hopeful the interview with Dr. Scott might turn up something useful, the two men were prepared to travel and responded with news of their imminent departure. Mina and Van Helsing waited in the rooms they had secured. They were not idle.

"I find my thoughts returning to Dr. Scott's odd behaviour," admitted Mina. "I cannot understand it."

"Much thought have I given to this subject and there is only one possible reason for his blindness: mesmerism."

"Please explain."

"He could not expect us to believe his fraudulent denial. In Harley Street we might have been fooled but not when the subject being denied is standing before us. This leaves only one conclusion."

"You're saying he believed it."

"Precisely. I maintain a post-hypnotic suggestion blinded him to Dracula's presence. It would require an almost supernatural ability to so block off a mind."

"To what end?"

"That is the heart of the matter. Brookwood has been the epicenter of whatever is brewing. I can only conclude they did not want Dr. Scott to know what is in the offing."

"It must be significant if Dracula is here and such lengths are being taken to conceal it."

"That is certain. Anarchist leaders cannot remain in one place without drawing Branch agents like flies. I suspect a short timetable for their plans. Let us hope Arthur and Quincey have something to add to our deductions."

A lunch of cold boiled and lemonade was just completed when a solid rap on the door demanded attention. Arthur Holmwood and Quincy Morris had arrived.

"You saw most of Griffin off then," observed Holmwood with a wry grin.

"We got the rest," added Morris.

"Whatever do you mean?" asked Van Helsing.

They succinctly related the details of the house search, the finding of the eye in the tub drain and the ensuing investigation. "Who knew Griffin had a glass eye?" said Holmwood, summing up. "Gave us a bit of a fright."

"You confirmed it was his?" asked Mina.

"Branch files had the information."

"However did it get down the drain?" asked Mina.

"Search me," Morris replied. "It might have dropped out and he just left it. Box of four more just like it on his bedroom dresser."

"What did you uncover?" asked Holmwood.

"Precious little, it pains me to say," Van Helsing replied, his bushy eyebrows drawing together in a frown.

"Dracula and his fellow anarchists are remaining here in Woking," offered Mina. "At least for tonight. Why remains a mystery."

Morris pulled a rolled-up newspaper from his pocket and tossed it on the table where it flopped open. Mina and Van Helsing read the headline.

"It is decided then," said Van Helsing. "The Queen will summer on the Isle of Wight."

Which means she'll be passing through Woking tomorrow."

"The Queen couldn't possibly be Dracula's target," said Mina.

"Certainly not the Royal Train," agreed Holmwood. "A detachment of Royal Hussars guard the Queen. How many men did the Count have with him?"

"Four," replied Mina. "One of them Dr. Scott who returns to London in less than an hour."

"It's out of the question," said Holmwood.

"Why does Dracula remain then?" asked Van Helsing.

"Dracula has been present at numerous high level assassinations," said Mina. "If he is the mastermind behind these murders, and the current action we are considering, why risk being present at the attacks? What does he gain from such associations? Would it not be prudent to observe from a safe distance and avoid any connection to the event?"

"I have been considering this very thing," Van Helsing admitted. "I have only an inkling pulled from unlikely sources. I wish to discard it but cannot. I speak of a supernatural explanation."

"It's come to this then," said Holmwood. "Fantasies."

Mina spread her arms imploringly. "If anyone can explain why Dracula would risk so much, so often, for so little, please enlighten us. We've concluded the Queen is beyond his reach. So what is his aim? I'll listen to anything at this point."

"I am a foolish old man who studies the ancient myths for amusement. Dracula is nearby when powerful persons are murdered. He takes no hand in the act yet risks the light of suspicion and physical peril should an attack go wrong. The stray bullet. A too powerful bomb blast. And so on. Why?" Van Helsing met the glance of each agent seated around the table as if imploring them to furnish an acceptable motivation for Dracula's actions and forestall his next words. His gaze met only confusion. "Auras. Life energy."

"What is this?" asked Mina.

"At the moment of death, it is said the spirit, the life energy issues forth from the body."

"So what if it does?" asked Morris. "How could this interest the Count?"

"Count Dracula is an incubus," replied Van Helsing.

"A what?"

"A demon which feeds on the life energy of its victims."

Mina's eyes brightened with recollection. "Yes! I have read of such a creature. Demons who perch on one's chest as we sleep, hypnotizing the victim so they do not awaken while feeding on the life force until the victim is drained."

"That is the creature I mean," said Van Helsing. "In Romania such a creature is called moroi."

"It's too fantastic," observed Holmwood.

"Why else does the Count risk being present at such terrible events?"

"Why not just creep into bedrooms at night?" asked Morris.

"He risks discovery in the act," Van Helsing replied. "Dracula must have a penchant for the life force of powerful people. Royal blood as fine wine to him. Such people are surrounded with layers of protection. Difficult to penetrate these inner circles undetected."

"Are you suggesting he has allied himself with anarchists in order to feed on the life force from targets of assassination?" asked Mina.

"And remain an innocent bystander while others prepare the feast."

Morris shook his head. "No. I don't buy it. We're tripping these rascals up all the time. Some of them would have bartered what they knew about Dracula for a lighter sentence."

Van Helsing glanced at Mina. "Dr. Scott?"

"Couldn't see Dracula right in front of us."

"Hypnotized to blindness with regards to the Count. I say Dracula's past cohorts received the same treatment."

"It's crazy," said Morris.

"It is the only theory for all the facts," said Van Helsing.

"How does this help us?" asked Mina. "We have decided the Queen cannot be the target."

Holmwood started with a sudden thought. "Why, it would be diabolical."

"Out with it, Art," urged Morris.

"The Royal Equerry."

"He was killed in a riding accident," recalled Mina.

"Yes. But he oversees the preparations for the Royal Train," added Holmwood. "Or he did. Lived on an isolated estate. Dracula may have gotten to him. The accident. The house staff said the poor man seemed to deliberately drive his horse into the trees. Low hanging branch broke his neck."

"Hypnotic compulsion, certainly," said Van Helsing.

"This is getting us nowhere," said Mina in frustration. "Dracula and his cronies can't stop the train with all the security in place. Why they'd be spotted by the police lining both sides of the track."

Holmwood took up the explanation. "Yes. I rode the train last year, if you recall. Officers are placed every two hundred yards along the track."

"That's that," said Morris.

Holmwood slapped his palm down on the table. "Good God! The train will stop for them!"

"Not likely," scorned Mina.

"Not intentionally, no," agreed Holmwood. "But it will stop. The Queen. Forgive me. I must be indelicate."

"Lives at risk overrule such matters," said Van Helsing.

"The Queen will not use the Royal convenience on board while the train is moving. This is not generally known for obvious reasons. There are secret spur lines along the route where the train can stop - isolated areas well hidden. A perfect target as the track spotters are not told of these stops and do not watch the track in these places."

"An interesting nugget of information," said Morris.

Holmwood nodded vigorously. "The Count must have got it out of the Royal Equerry before planting the urge to commit suicide. The stop five miles east of Godalming is always used. A secluded spot for an attack."

Morris frowned. "You all seem to have forgotten the detachment of hussars armed to the teeth."

"Griffin's lost cache," offered Van Helsing.

Holmwood was silent for a moment, then shook his head. "Griffin's house was being watched. Couldn't possibly move a store of guns and explosives without drawing suspicion."

"Griffin's coffin would not be searched," said Van Helsing.

"Hardly room in there for an arsenal with the old man's body flat out."

"Exactly." Van Helsing paused. "How large was that tub you mentioned where you found the eye?"

A look of horror etched the faces of the agents.

"Are you suggesting..." began Holmwood.

"The eye was washed into the drain," said Morris. "And that tub was spotless compared to the rest of the junk down there."

"Good Lord! The furnace raging despite the heat of the day," Holmwood recalled. Burning what? The memory of the gleaming hatchet blade - as if recently cleaned - among the rusted tools sprung to mind and he shuddered.

"Ample room for weapons in an empty coffin," said Van Helsing.

"But where are the men to use them?" asked Morris. "This horror show does not produce an attacking force out of thin air."

"You forget the recent rash of 'deaths' amongst the anarchists," said Mina. "The burials all took place at Brookwood Cemetery. Trees abound there. Twisting, secluded paths. Plenty of cover."

"You have hit on it, my dear," said Van Helsing. "Look at the roster of the recent dead. Assassins, sharp shooters. A cache of weapons and explosives transported south on the eve of the Queen's journey. There's the reason Dracula is in Woking. They will attack the train. Dracula, an immortal moroi immune to harm from bullets or brute force. He will drain the Queen's life as he did poor Lucy last year. The seclusion ensures escape. No witnesses."

"How will they manage that?" asked Morris.

"Blow up the train of course."

"We must have proof to be certain!" said Holmwood.

A sudden thought hit Van Helsing like a thunderclap. He glanced at the time. "Heaven preserve us! The train departs in thirty-five minutes!"

Holmwood and Morris leapt to their feet. "What would you have us do?"

"The Necropolis Railway posts a man to guard the coffins stored aboard lest the wealthy dead be shorn of the funeral finery they are expected to carry into the afterlife. This man must be complicit if the transport of live anarchists is to be successful. You must question him."

"The cemetery is two miles from here," said Holmwood. "A carriage?"

The Texan's mouth twisting in a grin, Morris said, "Saw a stable up the next block. I'll show you how we get along back home. Let's ride!"

-5-

An hour passed which felt like an eternity to Mina and Van Helsing. The doctor sighed heavily when the clock showed 2:20. This was the point of no return. Tension squeezed them like a vise and only intensified when at last they heard the stamp of riding boots outside the door.

"You were not too late!" Van Helsing pleaded as the two men entered. "You found him!"

Morris tossed his hat on a vacant chair. "We did. Odd fellow. Name of Renfield."

"Believed us to be detectives," chuckled Holmwood. "We did not set him straight."

"What did he say?" asked Mina.

"Kept going on about doing nothing this time. We pressed him but he only babbled about flowers. How he hadn't touched them this time."

"Five pound note in his pocket," Morris continued. "Said that was for the flowers only he hadn't touched them."

"We got it eventually," said Holmwood. "He was paid by an unknown party to remove the flowers from atop the coffins once they had been secured aboard the train. And he hadn't been told to do it this time."

Van Helsing slapped his knee. "There is our proof. Don't you see? There must be small holes drilled through the coffin lids so the living anarchist inside can breathe. Once locked safely inside the rail carriage this Renfield has been bribed to remove the flowers concealing the holes to facilitate this. Renfield would then replace the flowers at Brookwood for the short trip to a private spot where the man might be released with no one the wiser. An empty coffin is buried."

"But he did not touch the coffin this time."

"Because the coffin contained guns and explosives, not Griffin."

"All right," said Morris. "They smuggled men and weapons out of London. Where did they get to?"

Mina recalled her earlier journey through the cemetery grounds. "The path they used closely parallels Bagshot Road also running south."

"Makes sense," said Morris. "They wouldn't want to cluster here with all the security around. Hiding in the woods, I say."

"Dracula must have established a rendezvous point," said Van Helsing. "He knows where the train will stop."

"We must alert the authorities," said Mina.

"With a tale of a Transylvanian incubus bent on the Queen's life force? They'd have us in straightwaistcoats in a heartbeat," said Holmwood. "I hardly believe it myself!"

"With concrete evidence we might fare better," said Van Helsing. "We shall have to make the attempt ourselves. I would only slow you down. You three will have to prevent the attack."

"How?" asked Mina. "If we believe Dracula to be moroi…"

"There is a Banishing Spell used as protection against this incubus," Van Helsing replied. "It is cast when spoken in the entryway one wants barred to moroi. I have used it when my studies have exposed me to forbidden knowledge. I shall arm you all with it."

"Three against how many?"

"Ten we know of," replied Van Helsing.

"I like those odds," said Morris. "We've got surprise on our side. They'll likely turn tail once our guns are added to the mix."

"They'll set out under cover of darkness, I expect," observed Holmwood. "Perhaps before dawn."

Two hours after sun down, the street urchin they had enlisted to watch the hotel Dracula and the others were using sent a message up to their rooms.

"He's gone!" said Mina, the note clutched in her fist.

"Should we light out after them?" asked Morris. "It'll be a tall order finding them in the dark. Still…"

"We'd give ourselves away clanging about the quiet countryside," concluded Holmwood.

Van Helsing nodded. "Their destination we know. If you depart before first light, you can still reach the spur before the train arrives."

"Won't be until after eleven. With the rails cleared of all traffic, the train will make excellent time despite its late departure. God willing we'll get there first."

"We got a trunk of Winchesters and revolvers," explained Morris. "Stowed away downstairs. Horses at our disposal."

Sleep was impossible though each tried over the long night. When the first rays of dawn cut a pink slash in the east, they were ready. Three were dressed for hard riding.

"Godspeed, my friends," said Van Helsing. "For Lucy!"

-6-

Revolvers and shells in their pockets, they carried rifles under their arms out the back of the hotel and up the alley towards the stable. Ten minutes later they rode their horses south out of Woking.

They stuck to the worn footpaths through wooded areas. They saw no one but still proceeded with caution once the sun had fully risen. Not knowing where Dracula and the others were concealed they stopped half a mile from the secret spur. There was no alternative but to wait for Dracula's group to move and give themselves away believing they were alone. Rifles clenched in their fists, they passed a tense hour on foot.

Finally low, distant voices reached them. They moved silently in the direction of the sound. They saw the track in a clearing fifty yards ahead but no sign of the anarchists. Of course they would not show themselves until the train had switched off the main line. The anarchists were faced with a delicate challenge. The forthcoming attack could not be a free-for-all with bullets whizzing about and erupting explosions, as either might kill the Queen before Dracula reached her.

During the sleepless hours, Holmwood and the others had concluded the attack would be diversionary, creating mayhem through which the Count might slip aboard. Once inside, his great strength and imperviousness to bullets would be all he needed to defeat any defense raised against him. Once Dracula had achieved his goal, a decimating explosive attack could be launched.

The first indication of imminent action was the faint chuff of an approaching locomotive. This resulted in the first movement from their hidden adversaries as a rough-looking man in a tattered peacoat appeared through the trees bordering the track. He held a bomb in one gnarled fist, the sun winking off the clock face indicating a timed device. Striding boldly to the tracks leading out of the spur he concealed the device close to one rail.

The hidden spur line had been neatly laid along the flat ground between two low grassy hills. This natural obstruction so near the main track rose high enough to conceal the train from view during the short halt.

The locomotive sound rose in volume as the agents silently checked their weapons. Soon the noise was deafening and there was the train at last. Having greatly reduced speed to accommodate the switch, the eight chocolate-brown carriages crawled by and entered the track between the low hills and was lost from view.

Immediately Dracula's men sprang into action. They burst from the forest and, using the hill for cover, closed on the train with weapons raised.

One of them broke right and headed for the switch the train had used to enter the spur to place a second device. With bombs at either end they hoped to block the train in. The man in haste stumbled on the rails and his infernal device flew from his hand into the bushes. Instinctively he lunged for it and exposed himself to the watchful eyes of the hussars on the train. There was a sharp crack and his blonde head snapped back. He fell lifeless across the rails.

All pretense of stealth was abandoned. The anarchists began firing on the train, using the length of the locomotive for their approach. The engineer and his mate were the first to fall to the guns and they were matched by the sharpshooters who bagged two of the anarchists.

The Branch agents broke from cover and dashed across the tracks. Bullets whizzed about their heads. They dove headlong into the foliage.

This fire alerted the anarchists to the presence of other actors in the scene. Two of them, protected in the gap between locomotive and coal tender, leaned out to fire at the spot the agents occupied.

Morris was ready and raised his Winchester, driving a bullet into one of the men who collapsed against the hot iron. He fired steadily at every target. "Gotta get that first bomb off the track! I'll tackle it first chance."

The remaining anarchists were content to remain behind cover and fire at every hussar who poked his head out. One lingered an instant too long and was drilled through the brain. He pitched out onto the stones. Another followed as barked orders roared from inside one carriage.

Holmwood shifted his position after a bullet struck a little too close for comfort. Raising his rifle to return fire, he caught sight of movement to his right out of the corner of his eye.

It was Dracula!

With a determined stride, the Count closed on the train. Holmwood shifted his aim and fired. The bullet struck Dracula in the shoulder. He did not react. A bullet from a hussar caused the lapel of Dracula's black coat to fly open as the metal burrowed into the Count's chest. Another struck his thigh. Yet another sliced through a lock of his curly hair. They had no effect.

The hussars in stunned disbelief leaned out the windows to be sure of their aim. Two more were struck from behind by anarchist bullets.

Holmwood drove shots into Dracula's side and back but nothing could slow his advance.

A momentary lull in the firing settled as both sides regrouped. Morris and Mina broke from cover simultaneously.

Morris dashed to the main track and, using the intervening hill as cover reached the bomb that had been placed earlier. He snatched it up and frantically stopped the simple stopwatch mechanism that displayed one minute until detonation.. He slid it into a pocket to keep the anarchists from giving it another try while dropping the Winchester for which he had no more shells. He pulled two revolvers from his belt. He was directly behind the anarchists and rounded the hill to fire at them. They whirled in surprise. One cried out and fell. Another grasped a shattered shoulder.

But it was Mina who dared all. The lull freed her to sprint along the train and hop onto the short stairs of a carriage. Dracula was within ten yards of her. At the top of her lungs she yelled the Banning Spell.

Dracula was stopped dead in his tracks upon hearing it. His eyes blazed impotent hate. Bullets thudded into his body.

A rifle barrel jutted out behind her as she stepped down from the train to face the Count.

"Mina!" bellowed Holmwood.

She flung herself to one side as the muzzle flashed. The bullet grazed the top of her shoulder on the way to Dracula's midsection. He grunted as he turned toward the locomotive. Mina collapsed unmoving.

Meanwhile Morris had dropped another of the anarchists and the last three gave up the fight and scurried into the woods.

Dracula leaped across the coupling littered with dead anarchists and faced Morris. "This action has cost me," he hissed.

Morris fired his revolvers. They were empty. He pawed at his pockets for shells to load. He found only the time bomb. Pulling the Bowie knife from the sheath at his waist, he advanced on the Count. "For Lucy."

Dracula visibly relaxed as he moved forward, a cold smile twisting his hard mouth. He fixed Morris with his bewitching gaze. "Drop the knife! I command it!"

Struck by the Dracula's compelling mesmerism, the knife slipped from his hand to clatter at his feet.

"That's better," said Dracula. "Denied of one prize, I claim another."

Morris stood stock still as Dracula closed the gap and placed his palm flat on the chest of his victim. Morris could not move a muscle.

The soldiers broke out of the carriage and fanned out. Holmwood could only throw down his weapon and fall to his knees. Others shouted at the two men beside the locomotive but there was no response.

Before the hussars could draw closer, the bomb Morris had re-armed in his pocket exploded with a flash of blinding light. Little of either man remained afterwards.

"Good God!" exclaimed Holmwood.

The force of the explosion knocked the soldiers off their feet. They recovered quickly and secured the area.

"The woman and I are agents of Special Branch," called Holmwood as he was roughly seized and searched for weapons. Four men propelled him from the forest's edge. "We carry documents confirming our identities."

"Shut it!" a hussar barked as they threw him to the ground beside Mina. A detachment went after the last of Dracula's men.

Mina stirred. She had only been stunned by the bullet's impact. Her eyes fluttered open and she sat up, dizzy. "What," she managed. "Arthur!"

"We were successful," said Holmwood with little enthusiasm.

"Quincey?"

"He has avenged Lucy. He is at peace."

Mina felt the reply like a hammer blow. The cold light of anger seethed behind her tears. "Dracula?"

"Destroyed. Morris blew the demon back to Hell with a bomb."

"Dracula is immortal. Can he be killed?"

"If not he'll have a damnable time reassembling himself, scattered about the forest. Today we are victorious. Tomorrow..."

The Mysterious Affair at Slaine

JACQUELINE SEQUEIRA & PHILIP CORNELL

At the time, in late October and early November of the year 1929, the alarming circumstances that transpired at Slaine Court were very much a cause célèbre that occupied the press, especially those newspapers more attuned to the public's taste for the morbid and sensational. As we move into a new decade and new events exert fascination on the people of Britain, I feel that the role an extraordinary gentleman played in unmasking the truth should be recorded if only to correct the many misconceptions that proliferate still.

But firstly, I ought to introduce myself. My name is Jonathan Harker, known to some as Captain Harker after my service in the Great War. I shall relate the events in chronological order, as I experienced them, although in hindsight, once the truth was unveiled, the whole affair moved far beyond my limited perspective.

I had not long returned to London after a sojourn of some months in Belgium and I was musing upon the need to find more permanent accommodation than the boarding house which was my current lodgings. Whilst strolling from the third potential new residence—none of which had quite satisfied my expectations—I encountered a face that struck me as somewhat familiar on the corner of Albemarle Street as we both waited for the bobby on point-duty to wave us through when the traffic eased a little. The man I thought I knew was a tall, spare figure in an elegant suit and a cape of a type one does not expect to see these days in the great metropolis, and it was this more continental attire that reminded me of how and where I had first met him, a decade earlier.

It was in 1918 that our paths had crossed in Paris while I was waiting to return from my service with my regiment, known as The Old Contemptibles.

I noticed a flicker cross the high brow of the imposing gentleman with the dark moustache and elegantly trimmed goatee when he turned to his right to glance at the oncoming automobiles and omnibuses.

"Captain Harker, is it not?"

"Indeed it is, Le Compte Parau-Tepesch, if I recall correctly? How good to see you again. I recall with gratitude your kind help when that pickpocket relieved me of my pocketbook in the Rue St Lazarre. The modest funds I could have survived without, but—"

"Your medal for gallantry meant rather more to you, did it not?" said the man, completing my thought. "It was propitious that I chanced to observe the miscreant abstract your wallet after his confederate contrived to obstruct your path. But please, call me Dracule, we are old friends, non?"

Dracule had indeed observed a duo of thieves rob me and with commendable promptness he'd followed the pair down a nearby alleyway and persuaded them—by bumping their heads together while lifting them by the scruff of their necks—to relinquish their ill-gotten gains. I had later wondered whether Dracule had spotted the villainy through keen sight or by familiarity with the less savoury habits of the underworld.

I shook my old acquaintance by the hand, and his remarkably firm grip again reminded me of our original meeting, and I invited him to join me for dinner at the Pungent Bulb, the restaurant at my club specialising in the fare of France and Eastern Europe which had been welcoming so many men returning home after the Great War.

So it was that evening we partook of a splendid *Steak Frite*, mine cooked well-done with a delicious garlic gravy, while Dracule preferred to eat his rare, and demurred when I recommended the infused sauce, saying that garlic had never agreed with him. I offered to pour him a glass of the delectable Bordeaux but again he passed. "I never drink… wine" he explained "although a gin with tonic water would not go amiss." Our gastronomic differences did not impede a most pleasant evening. I recounted my recent trip to Brussels while Dracule, who had originally been introduced to me as 'Compte Dracule Parau-Tepesch' gave me a brief account of his fascinating, and very impressive, ancestry which extended back many centuries to an area in the Carpathian Mountains known as Transylvania, or 'the region across the forest'.

"My name means, 'son of dragons' after the dissolution of the Dual Monarchy in the Great War", he said.

"The Austro-Hungarian Empire?" I asked

"That is right. *Osztrak-Magyar Monachia* to use the Hungarian term or, to quote the phrase preferred by our former foes *'Ostereich-Ungarische Monarchie'*." He spoke with a perceptible accent from his original homeland in Moldavia, from where he had inherited the title 'Count'. He had fled Bukovina and Romania and lived in Brussels and Paris.

Dracule was very well-educated, being fluent in Hungarian, German, French, and English. His English was fairly formal and on occasion my more colloquial turns of phrase left him a little perplexed. An intellectual he certainly was, but perhaps a bit out of touch with the common man. The fact that despite these differences our dinner together was so convivial rather surprised me. Dracule asked me many solicitous questions about my life in London after the war, about my lodgings, my friends and how I was settling into life after military service.

We concluded the evening with cigars, Dracule having persuaded me to try a *Carpati* from his fatherland, an unusually strong but not unpleasant blend of German and Turkish tobaccos. The Count offered to pay for the meal, but I insisted, reminding him that I still owed him for recovering my wallet and that I always paid my debts. He laughed, displaying strong white teeth beneath his moustaches (which he waxed in the continental fashion). We strolled together back towards Albemarle Street and at one point we passed a poster on display outside a cinematograph theatre.

"My word," said Dracule, "it is Bela Blasko, I knew him in Lugoj."

Seeing my confused expression, he elaborated. *"Timis Countes"*

Seeing I was none the wiser, he elaborated further. "In western Romania. I would be interested to see Blasko, or Bela Lugosi as he now seems to call himself, in this "Thirteenth Chair" talking picture. Since you insisted on paying for our dinner, would you permit me to reciprocate with this cinematic entertainment?"

He pronounced the work "kinematic", and before I could stop myself,

I repeated the word with the English pronunciation, but Dracule smiled. "It would perhaps help my familiarity with your native tongue. I see it finishes being exhibited on Friday. Friend Harker, is there perhaps some young person you would like to accompany you? I miss the company of young people."

"There is my friend, Miss Westenra, of whom I spoke at dinner. I should like to introduce you to her."

"Then she will join us on Friday if it is convenient." And so we closed our social gathering with a plan for another one.

So, at five o'clock on the following Friday, Miss Lucy Westenra and I arrived at the motion picture parlour where the Count, resplendent as ever, waited within. I introduced the young woman to Dracule.

"Dracule," said the Count with a bow, "for let us dispense with titles."

"I am most pleased to meet you," said Lucy with a charming smile. "Jonathan has told me something of your fascinating story. He tells me you are familiar with this actor." She indicated Bela Lugosi's name on the poster. "I'm afraid I don't recall seeing him before."

"He is quite well known on the stage in my homeland, and I can boast a small acquaintance with him. We shall see how he presents himself on— what do they say, 'the silver screen'?"

I smiled. "You are becoming more comfortable with our colloquial speech," I said, and again that white smile appeared, as his fingertip touched the waxed tip of his moustache. We entered the cinema.

The actor Lugosi's role in 'The Thirteenth Chair' was 'Inspector Delzante', and as the story progressed, I found myself attempting to solve the mystery the story presented to the audience. However, I could not help but notice that after about twenty minutes Dracule emitted an audible snort and seemed to settle back into his seat, even at those moments when the rest of the audience leaned forward in suspense.

When we all withdrew from the auditorium and gathered in the foyer, Lucy and I thanked Dracule, telling him we had enjoyed the film.

"Alas, I was able to solve the simple story after eighteen minutes," said Dracule, "but it was of interest because of my old friend Blasko… sorry, Lugosi, as he now styles himself. I wonder what his next cinematic endeavour will be. I will be happy to see one of my old countrymen again, even if through the medium of the silver screen."

I noted that his pronunciation was now the accepted one. "Well, I am impressed that you solved the film's mystery so swiftly. Perhaps *you* should become a detective?"

"Perhaps I should" riposted Dracule.

Lucy left us briefly to retrieve her wrap from the cloak room and returned to us in the company of two distinguished-looking gentlemen.

"Monsieur le Compte, Captain Harker, I would like to introduce you to my employers, Dr Seward of Purfleet, and Professor Van Helsing, who has recently joined the practice from Amsterdam."

The Professor was a man of just above middle age, of medium height, strongly built, with his shoulders set back over a broad, deep chest. He had the look of a man of deep thought and wisdom. The Doctor, by contrast, was not much above thirty, tall and lean, with the look of a man who spends much time indoors, and possessed of sharp blue eyes that denoted a keen intelligence and an enquiring mind.

We spent a few minutes standing on the street outside the foyer of the lovely theatre building making our introductions, when a magnificent Rolls Royce Silver Ghost pulled up to the entrance beside us.

"Ah," said Dracule, "this is my new automobile. Tell me, friend Harker, what do you think of her?"

"She is the most beautiful auto I have ever seen," I replied in awe.

"Dear Miss Lucy," said Dracule "please permit me to have my driver see you home. It is late for a young lady to be out."

"That is most kind of you, Monsieur, it has been a long day and I will be glad to see my Mama and settle in for the evening," replied Lucy.

Dracule beckoned to his driver, who alighted from the car. "My friends, this is my man, Renfield, a most capable fellow and he will escort the young lady home." said Dracule. Renfield was a man of short stature but appearing to possess great physical strength. He had a shock of black hair and a slight but noticeable tic on the left of his long, pale face.

Dracule turned to Renfield again and said, "Please escort my young friend to her home and ensure that she is given over to her mother's care."

Dracule then, with great ceremony and solicitude, settled Lucy into the car, and we watched as she was driven away.

"My old friend and my new acquaintances," said Dracule, "may I suggest we find a small dining house, sup a little and expand our friendship?"

The four of us found a little supper club nearby. No garlic or wine was selected this time and we dined on a good, hearty meal of roast meat and vegetables. We settled into a comfortable bonhomie almost immediately. We were told that Professor Van Helsing had been a teacher and mentor to Dr Seward and had recently returned from the Continent after many years and joined Dr Seward in practice. As well as the general practice, Dr Seward was also used by the local constabulary as coroner and had many a fascinating and morbid tale to tell.

"I was lucky that Dr Seward was looking for a partner for his growing practice once I had returned from Europe," said the Professor in his broad Dutch accent.

"The luck was mine," tendered Dr Seward. "My practice is so enriched by having such a polymath; a philosopher, a metaphysician, and one of the most advanced scientists of the day."

"Ah! Please spare my blushes, my friend!" laughed the Professor and turning to Dracule said "Your driver seemed a very interesting fellow, Monsieur, how did he come to be in your employ?"

"Ah, the mind of the professional. You noticed that small contortion of his face?" said Dracule smiling.

"Yes, usually psychological in nature, and occuring when a person is under stress; but they can be physical in origin, too," replied the Professor.

"There is no tale of interest to tell there, I'm afraid. I went to an agency looking for a man who could tend to me, my home, my car and of course, my stomach. He came with exemplary references and has worked all over Europe. I was fortunate to secure him," responded Dracule.

"Dracule," I ventured, "you said you were able to solve the mystery of the film in only eighteen minutes; perhaps you should be a detective like Inspector Delzante ?"

"Ah yes, mon ami, in truth, my friend Lugosi excelled as the inspector. I look forward to seeing what the director, Mr Tod Browning, and my old friend collaborate on next. I do fancy that I could make a good hand at detecting; it is a question of applying the grey matter: logic, psychology and deduction," responded Dracule, with no hint of false modesty.

"It is much easier to deduce the identity of a criminal when there is a script and a predetermined ending," responded Dr Seward. "For the detectives I work for, it is not always so easy. Determination, dedication and no small amount of luck are often required as well."

"Do you perhaps refer to this oh-so-terrible case of the murdered young woman that is baffling local law enforcement?" queried Dracule.

"It is a most concerning case, indeed," replied the Doctor. "The young woman was found in a graveyard by the diggers in the early hours of the morning. She had been killed, yes; but also, exsanguinated. I was called in to examine the poor wretch's pale body by the police and was horrified by what I saw. I fear that we can find no clue as to the killer or motive; it appears as if it were an opportunistic crime. The young woman was visiting the grave of her recently deceased lover. She had been grief-stricken since he had died and, on a whim, went to the cemetery in the still of the night. I was fortunate that the Professor was available to me; his questions and systematic turn of mind helped me to formulate my findings. She had been strangled and there were small holes in her wrists that had been used to release her blood—we suspect some of it may have actually been consumed by the killer. A most heinous crime indeed."

"There are legends of blood-drinkers going back to ancient times; the Greeks, Egyptians and Persians all had stories of the imbibing of blood, as did most of the ancient peoples. Even in my own country of Romania we have legends of blood drinkers: the *Moroi* or the *Strigoi*. There were believed to be many ways in which a person could become one, according to the stories. A babe born with its caul, the seventh child born where each of its siblings were of the same sex, all were doomed in this way, as were many others who were deemed unnatural," offered Dracule.

"I hope they find him; a person who could do that does not deserve any mercy!" I cried out.

"But what do you mean by this, my friend?" asked Dracule.

"Only that someone who could do this could strike again, and whether insane or evil, young women should be safe from such a creature," I responded hotly.

"Do you think you could perform this 'justice' yourself? Dr Seward, Professor Van Helsing, what say you learned gentlemen?" asked Dracule.

"Ahh, I am an officer of the law in my capacity as Coroner and therefore believe that the machinations of the justice system must play out. If we allow for vigilante-style retribution without the test of law, then we risk descending into anarchy," countered Dr Seward.

Van Helsing replied thoughtfully, "A person who does not have control of their own actions, who is a mortal danger to others…is it better to remove them and the harm they can inflict or leave it to the dictates of evidence and the good sense of twelve good men with no training or understanding of science? I don't know the answer to that one."

As the conversion became a trifle too morbid and unsettling, I attempted to change the subject and spoke of the need to find myself a more permanent set of rooms. Some of the lodgings I had looked at were less than suitable; one even had a railway line not twenty yards from the bedroom windows. I told my new friends that I was to inspect rooms at Whitby Haven Mansions on the morrow.

"I predict that it will prove satisfactory for you," replied Dracule with a smile. I appreciated his optimism, but secretly did not share it.

Whitby Haven Mansions proved to be entirely satisfactory. The landlady, Mrs Murray, gave me a lease to sign and, since I was not encumbered with a surfeit of possessions and effects, I was successfully ensconced the following Tuesday. I was rather taken, I confess, with the landlady's daughter when she kindly assisted me settling myself in.

"Wilhelmina Murray," she introduced herself "But please, call me Mina. All my friends do, and I hope that we shall come to be friends," she added with a kind smile.

"I trust that in time we may," I agreed.

In due course I acquired a modest collection of furniture to complement the few items I initially moved in with. I sent a few missives to a few friends and acquaintances to inform them of my new address. To my considerable surprise I got an immediate reply from Lucy Westenra.

"Jonathan," she wrote "what a small world it is. You are now residing in the same block of flats where my old school friend Mina lives. Her dear mother is the landlady. Our mothers were great girlhood friends, and she was like a second mother to me when we were schoolgirls together."

I could not resist showing the letter to Mrs Murray and her daughter, who clapped their hands together with delight.

"Dear Lucy," said Mrs Murray. "Such a sweet girl, I have always considered her another daughter. We must have her and her dear mother to tea to celebrate."

Slightly to my surprise, the afternoon post also brought a letter from Dracule, applauding me for finding agreeable and convenient lodgings, and reminding me that he had predicted as much. "Alas," he confided "I have not been so successful. But I am content for the time being as a guest at the hotel which styles itself as 'Slaine Court' here in Knightsbridge. They have a façade that rather pretentiously strives to mimic a mediaeval castle. I am not afraid to confess that I do not find this ambience disagreeable, for it brings to mind the edifice I occupied in my homeland before the war."

I was pleased to hear that he too was feeling content where he now dwelled and sent a reply to that effect. Thus commenced no infrequent communication between us.

The promised tea was arranged for a week later. Lucy attended, looking her usual slightly Bohemian self, with her hair combed in the fashionable 'flapper' style. Mina, perhaps so as not to appear too 'loose' for her mother's sake, had her short hair arranged in a more business-like fashion, as befitted her employment as a stenographer and typist—though she had for the evening curled dainty ringlets framing her brow. The women soon relaxed, laughing together about shared memories of their school days and of more recent circumstances; Mina at the legal practice where she was employed as typist and Lucy in the doctor's practice where she worked as receptionist.

Lucy spoke admiringly of Dr Seward. "He has recently become a consultant for the Coroner's Court. A very famous Professor of Medico-Legal Jurisprudence, Professor Van Helsing, had been his mentor and is now his partner. The good doctor recently examined a poor lady who had bled to death. Completely exsanguinated."

"Oh, how horrible!" protested Mrs Murray.

"That is NOT suitable conversation for young ladies," Mrs Westenra said, nodding in agreement.

In an attempt to steer the conversation to more convivial matters, I recounted how I had renewed my acquaintance with Dracule, telling the tale of how he had recovered my army medal for me.

"He is of a very noble family, and is a Count, in fact, of his native land."

This elicited murmurs of impressed approval from around the table.

"In fact, I had a letter from him this afternoon. He is staying at Slaine Court, that impressive hotel with the crenelated towers," I added.

"The one that looks like a castle?" gasped Lucy. "Very posh, though I am not surprised. His auto is one of the most beautiful I have ever seen; I felt like a duchess riding in the back."

"He told me it reminds him of his ancestral home in Transylvania, where he grew up," I said. "The comment surprised me, for I should not have thought him given to sentimental feelings, for he is very well educated, even scholarly."

"We are all affected by such thoughts," said Mina. "It would be inhuman not to be. Mama, may we invite the gentleman to tea?"

The other ladies nodded in agreement.

I offered to drive Lucy and Mrs Westenra home in my newly-purchased automobile, partly out of gentlemanly politeness to the ladies and partly, I'll admit, to show off. And impressed they were. "A 1928 Armstrong Siddeley" I said proudly.

"I should not expect to ever drive a car," Lucy said "though I certainly believe that a young woman of today should know how to."

"Perhaps," I ventured "I could give you some lessons, Lucy?"

"Oh yes, please" she replied in assent, her mother looking not as delighted by the prospect.

"Of course, this car is not a patch on the Count's Silver Ghost," said I, feeling suddenly self-conscious.

"Well," said Lucy, "it wouldn't do for a noble Count to take driving lessons, but I must admit I would have rather the Count drove me home; something about Mr Renfield did not feel right."

"Surely he did not take any liberties?" I gasped.

"Oh, no, not at all. He was perfectly polite and drove me straight home, and as instructed handed me over to Mama. It was just…oh, I don't know. I feel silly now for having given this foolish fancy a voice. Ignore me; what I need is some adventure, maybe behind the wheel of a fine auto," sighed Lucy.

I took the hint and promised to get back with arrangements about her lessons. It was now quite dark, so I escorted the ladies to their door. They invited me in for a cup coffee, and I was tempted, but declined. As I drove back to Whitby Haven Mansions, I tried to convince myself that it was so I would not disturb the Murrays if I returned late, but I secretly suspected that my growing feelings of affection for Mina might have been related.

Mina and Mrs Murray were just tidying away the crockery when I got back.

"Well timed, Captain Harker," said Mina with a hint of good-natured teasing.

I bade them both good evening and went to my room where I spent the next hour writing in my journal and replying to Dracule's letter so I could post it on the morrow and pass on the ladies' invitation to take tea the following week.

The next day Dracule's resplendent Rolls Royce drew up outside Whitby Haven Mansions, attracting no small measure of attention from passers-by. His chauffeur, Renfield, held open the door, and, clad in a dark cloak, Dracule ascended the stairs. He bowed formally to both Mina and Mrs Murray as I introduced them, kissing their outstretched hands in the continental fashion which elicited a barely perceptible snigger from the older lady.

"I am delighted to meet you Mrs Murray and to make the acquaintance of your so lovely daughter," Dracule said. Mrs Murray offered to take Dracule's cape, but le Compte himself took it off and, folding it, placed it over the back of a nearby rocking chair while we gathered around the table.

Mrs Murray poured cups of tea while the conversation touched on many subjects, until Mina broached the topic which she well knew her mother was eager to hear her guest recount in his own words. "If you do not find the memory a distressing one," she said to le Compte.

"By no means," he replied, recounting how he had left his homeland of Transylvania in the closing days of the war aboard the steam vessel Demeter II, then settled for a while in the region of Alsace on the upper Rhine in France.

"The views of the river were a little reminiscent of the Tisza in the old country," Le Compte explained. He told us again the story he had told me when we met of how he had made his way to Britain, all the way up to his recent occupation of Slaine Court. "This so splendid building is inspired, so I have learned, by a castle in the Boyne Valley in Ireland. There was a great battle there in the seventeenth century."

"You must all let me repay your kind hospitality by visiting me at Slaine," said the Count. "I do believe that you would all find it of interest. I have been so fortunate to reacquaint myself with the inestimable Captain Harker and for him to introduce me to such delightful company. I would like to invite you and all my new friends to a night of dinner and cards at Slaine Court."

The ladies enthusiastically thanked Dracule and he said he would send his man Renfield to collect us all the following Friday.

As Dracule prepared to depart I noticed him check the waxed tips of his black moustache as he looked briefly at his reflection in the full-length mirror in the hallway. He replaced his dark cloak with its burgundy-coloured lining and, with a tip of his hat, farewelled us.

It was a somewhat foggy afternoon with a bit of distant, rumbling thunder when the Count's chauffeur, Renfield arrived to convey us to Dracule's residence in Knightsbridge. It was not yet raining but Renfield held his umbrella over the ladies as we seated ourselves in the automobile. Slaine Court, as we drew towards it, did indeed look impressive, set back from the road, and surrounded by lawns through which the driveway curved to the front door. Once the vehicle had deposited us at that very entrance, a doorman in livery held the doors open for us, while Renfield saw to parking the car behind the building which must once have been a noble family's residence.

Dracule was awaiting us in the foyer with the rest of our party, Lucy and Mrs Westenra and Dr Seward and Professor Van Helsing, who had just then arrived. The Count beckoned that we follow him up the staircase to his rooms. They were lavishly, though tastefully, furnished as befits a gentleman of le Compte's noble Central European ancestry. His man Renfield, who had, it seemed, travelled up from the garages in a lift while we took the stairs, took our umbrellas and overcoats.

Also in the foyer, our host showed us a large portrait in oils, in which I could see in the subject a decided resemblance to our host.

"This," said he with pride, "is Vlad Tepesch, my ancestor who distinguished himself battling the Turks in the Ottoman Empire days of old. The original portrait had to be left behind when circumstances forced me to flee my homeland. I did, however, have a photograph of it and while in France, commissioned this new facsimile."

Beside the portrait hung a Coat of Arms which featured a dragon and a full moon among other heraldic emblems. A longcase clock, or 'grandfather' clock as the old song had it, stood near the painting as did a smaller portrait in an oval frame of a beautiful young woman who struck me as somewhat familiar. Dracule seemed to sense my interest and anticipated it.

"My bride," said he, "my late wife. I was, fortunately, able to include that picture amongst the few effects I was able to take with me."

It then struck me of whom the portrait so reminded me, for there was a strong resemblance to Lucy Westenra. Perhaps, I wondered, Dracule had, whether consciously or not, been drawn to Lucy for that very reason. I wondered whether the ladies might say something, but none commented. Rather, they feigned interest in a landscape painting of a castle on a cliff above a river, the waterway inspiring the women to speculate whether it might be the Danube.

"My ancestral home, overlooking the Tisza, which does indeed flow into the Danube," our host confirmed. "But, to our repast. Amongst his other abilities Renfield is a highly capable chef. He left luncheon ready for us to share when he drove to collect you. He is currently performing the last touches to the repast as we speak."

We examined some of Dracule's other decorations, amongst them a Broadwood upright piano which boasted a magnificent inlaid case and countless curios, some in cabinets and some on little ornamented tables. We were served a deliciously modern cocktail from America called The Bee's Knees, gin served with honey and lemon. The mood was gay, and my friend Dracule seemed to be relishing his role as host.

We were eight for dinner, a perfect number to enjoy fine food and fine company. Renfield, it transpired, was a very accomplished manservant; besides his duties as chauffeur, he also served the magnificent meal with such a quiet manner as to be almost invisible.

The food was progressive in the American style, being light and tasty. We started with an exemplary cold tomato consommé, a clear light soup with a delectable flavour of fresh tomato. I saw Mrs Murray looking quizzically at the offering and as an aside to her daughter Mina, asked whether they had forgotten to heat it. Mina blushed and quieted her mother. The next course was a broiled fillet of Scottish salmon with parsley butter, followed by chicken breast à la rose which was accompanied by a Waldorf salad. The dinner was rounded off by the lightest and most delectable lemon chiffon cake.

The conversation over dinner was amiable and flowed easily, our wine glasses were kept topped by the silent but observant Renfield with a *Mustoasă de Măderat*, a delightfully delicate white wine from our host's home country. We were quietly digesting both the meal and the stories of our host family's past in the region 'beyond the forest' as Mediaeval

Monks christened the regions known as Transylvania.

After dinner we all retired to the drawing room and Mina sat down to the beautiful little upright piano and began to play a few notes. She was soon joined by Lucy, and the two young ladies began to rummage about in the piano stool. They eventually found some pieces of music they both knew, and with Mina playing accompaniment on the piano, Lucy sang in a clear, bright voice and serenaded the group for some time. After a while, the delightful young ladies put their heads together, and with a whisper and nervous giggle started up another tune, a current Music Hall classic 'Never trust a sailor an inch above your knee'. The gentlemen laughed but the two admirable mothers blushed, and Mrs Murray, who had raised her kerchief to her face said, "Thank you girls, I think that may be enough now."

Our host suggested that we had the perfect number to play Bridge and that we break into two groups of four. On my table sat Dr Seward, Mina and Mrs Westenra; and the second group comprised Dracule, Professor Van Helsing, Lucy, and Mrs Murray.

We played cards for more than an hour when we realised that we each had empty glasses, so I offered to go to find Renfield and ask him for refills. I walked through to the kitchen and could not see him, so thought perhaps he was performing some duties in the butler's pantry. I knocked once on the closed door and entered.

To my shock I saw Renfield slumped on the floor. I bent over him and took his wrist but I felt no pulse. I swiftly returned to the drawing room and addressed the room. "Gentlemen, I am in need of your assistance. There appears to be something amiss with Mr Renfield; I have just found him on the floor, and I believe he may be dead."

The ladies cried out in fear, but the Professor showed himself to be a man of action and was up on his feet and racing to the kitchen in an instant. The Professor leant over the supine body of the man and performed checks upon the prone chauffeur. He stood up from the body and turned toward us all, sombrely intoning, "You are correct, Captain Harker; Mr Renfield is indeed dead. There is a small dagger in his heart and judging by the temperature of the body, he has been deceased for approximately one hour. Please, Dr Seward, would you see whether you concur?" Dr Seward then approached and, leaning over as the Professor had done before him, he finally announced "Yes, I agree, about an hour ago; must have occurred whilst we were all at cards. We must call the police immediately. Everyone must stay as the police will wish to ask each of us questions. Monsieur Le Compte, do you have a telephone?"

Dracule excused himself and went to the foyer of his flat where his telephone was situated. I could hear his muffled and earnest voice as he called for the assistance of the police. Dracule returned to the sitting room and immediately poured everyone present a small sherry to calm their nerves as we waited for the police to arrive. The women were most obviously affected and were settled into the armchairs and sofas near the fire so they could give comfort to each other.

After nearly half an hour of tense waiting there was a loud knock on the apartment door. We had all been silent, reflecting on the situation and trying not to think of the dead man still laying not far from us in the pantry. The only movement in the room was mine, as I paced back and forth, unable to sit still and unable to talk.

Dracule went to answer the knock and returned to the sitting room with a very large and somewhat simian-looking man, dark with deep set eyes under a heavy brow and a moustache to rival that of Dracule. He looked more like a pugilist than a detective. He was introduced to us as Detective Cotford of Scotland Yard. The detective had with him two obviously junior officers who were looking around in awe at the opulence of the rooms. There was also a tall and handsome man, with a calm manner and a reassuring air; this man was Doctor Holmwood.

"Please everyone, I will try to make this unpleasant ordeal as easy for you as I can" boomed Cotford in a deep-toned, sonorous voice, "however, I must ask you to remain until I am able to release you. I will need to question each of you in turn. As Dr Seward is so closely associated with this case, I have brought with me Doctor Holmwood to examine the body and to advise me."

Doctor Holmwood nodded to the room, his eyes travelling over the company until he came to Lucy, where his gaze rested. Then excusing himself, he and one of the young officers went out the door and through to the kitchen and pantry.

"Firstly, I will talk to the group as a whole. Can someone please explain to me the reason for this evening's gathering and how you are acquainted?"

As the host of the gathering, Dracule volunteered himself to answer the detective's questions. "Tonight was a dinner party that I hosted to celebrate friendship. Captain Harker, I met around ten years ago at the end of the war; the rest of the party are more recently-acquired friends."

"Thank you, we will go into more detail later," interrupted Cotford. "The deceased, how is he part of this gathering, what is known of him?"

"Renfield is my man, I employed him some two or so months ago. I had arrived in England and decided to settle. I quickly realised that I was in need of a servant and went to the Massey Agency. They recommended Renfield as one with all the skills I required and with excellent references. He had worked all over the Continent and so was able to adapt well to my foreign ways," replied the Count. "I know little of him; he has not been in my employ long. He was a cheerful and competent fellow and performed his duties well. He is a single man, and to my knowledge has no close family still living."

"Excellent. If you do not mind, I would like to contact the agency and gain more information," said Cotford.

"Of course," responded Dracule. "I have the details of the agency and also the references I was supplied. I will get them for you."

As Dracule was about to leave, Doctor Holmwood re-entered the room and went over to talk to Detective Cotford. His voice was not loud, but carried in the still, quiet room such that we were all able to clearly hear him say, "The man has been dead for no less than one hour and no more than two. His heart was pierced by a small dagger that is still in situ. There is nothing more that can be gleaned from the body here, so I will have it removed immediately to the morgue." Then turning, he addressed Dracule, saying, "Monsieur, will you permit me to use your house telephone to call to have the body removed?"

Dracule nodded and left with the Doctor to show him to the phone.

"Now," said Cotford, "I will need to interview you each separately. I must ask that you do not discuss amongst yourselves what is said so that you do not influence any others' remembrance of the night's events."

Dracule returned and Cotford again turned to him and asked "Monsieur, is there another room where I may conduct private interviews?"

"Yes," answered Dracule. "You are welcome to make use of my study. I will show you to it."

"Thank you. Then if you do not mind, I will interview you first," responded Cotford.

The pair exited the room with one of the constables who had been beckoned by Cotford, leaving the rest of us in the sitting room whilst the remaining constable and Doctor Holmwood took care of the body of Renfield in the pantry.

After what felt like an age, Detective Cotford and Dracule returned. "Due to the youth of the two ladies, I will interview them with their mothers present. Please remember, do not discuss any of tonight's happenings amongst yourselves. Mrs and Miss Murray, will you please accompany me to the study?"

Whilst Mina and Mrs Murray were thus occupied, the rest of the medical team arrived and the body of the unfortunate Renfield was quickly removed. This unfortunately meant that the body was brought out through the sitting room as the key to the locked back door of the flat could not be found. Upon seeing the large bag and the outline of the dead Renfield, Lucy let out a scream and collapsed into her mother's arms. Doctor Holmwood went immediately to the young woman's side to attend her.

Lucy's cry brought Detective Cotford from the study to see what had brought this cry of despair. He looked enquiringly at the gathering, and I could see Mina's pale face just behind him, her hand clinging to her mother's.

I explained, "Poor Lucy has just seen the body being carried through and it has justifiably upset her nerves."

Turning to the morgue team Cotford enquired "Why would you do this? Surely, the back door and stairs would have been much more appropriate."

"Sir," replied the clearly shaken and intimidated morgue attendant, "we tried, sir, but the back door was locked. I sent young Harris here," he said, nodding at his assistant "to try from the other side, but it was of no use; the door was not to be opened, and Monsieur the Count did not have the key."

Detective Cotford then turned to Dracule. "Is this so? When was the last time you saw the key? Did you know this door was locked? Is it always kept so?"

Dracule looked coolly at Cotford and replied, "There are two keys, my own and Renfield had one. The door is never locked except when I retire of an evening. Your men asked me for my key, but it was not in the entryway console where I keep all my keys. I told them that it would be on the set that Renfield kept, but they checked and his keys were not on his person."

The detective looked bemused and said more to himself than to the room, "So, did our killer enter and exit through the back and lock the door behind him? But why?"

Then he shook his head, as if clearing his thoughts and looked over toward poor Lucy and Mrs Westenra. "Please ladies, if you would accompany me to the study."

The two trembling women rose from their seats and followed. They were quickly replaced by Mina and Mrs Murray who sat quietly on the settee looking ashen.

After what seemed like an age, Detective Cotford returned with Lucy and Mrs Westenra. "The ladies have now provided all the assistance that I think they can. Doctor Holmwood, could you please escort all the ladies home? I will see you back at the station in a few hours." Then turning to the two older ladies said, "I thank you for your clear testimony. I am sure that as mothers your most immediate concern is that of your daughters. Please take them home and comfort each other as much as you can. I hope I may call on you if I have more questions and you will find me not so frightening as you have tonight."

"I hope to not be too much later" I said to Mrs Murray. "I will do my utmost to not disturb you when I arrive."

"Thank you," replied the good woman. "I am unsure of whether we will sleep tonight, so you will not disturb us." And so saying she nodded to Dracule and said, "I thank you for your hospitality; until the last, it was a most enjoyable evening."

"Madam, I am so sorry that you, all of you, had to bear witness to such an event in my home. I am desolate," said the Count, rising. He then accompanied them to the front door of the flat and saw them into the lift with Dr Holmwood.

Dr Seward was called next into the study and after a good half hour the Professor followed. The two worthy gentlemen were dismissed after their interview and then it was just me left with Dracule and the attending constable in the sitting room.

"Captain Harker, thank you for your patience. I hope you were not too discomposed by the wait," said Cotford, beckoning me toward the study.

I followed him in and looked around. I had not seen the study previously. It was a dark but comfortable room with many shelves of beautifully-bound books. A great, neat but very ornate desk took up a lot of the space and was positioned so that the occupant could sit at it with his back to a large window so as to maximise the daylight. In front of the desk was a comfortable armchair of forest green and it was to this chair that Cotford pointed. I settled myself and Cotford walked around the desk and sat facing me.

Cotford seemed to be most interested in my friendship with Dracule; he wanted to know all the details of how we had met on the continent, how we had reconnected here in London and then how he had become acquainted with the other guests.

"I thought you would be asking me about tonight," I said. "Do you not wish to know what I heard, what I saw, what I think?"

"Patience, Captain. All in good time. Did you see or hear anything that you wish to tell me about?" replied Cotford.

"Well, blast it, no. I mean that's the thing. I saw nothing, I heard nothing and if the back door were locked, then that must mean it was one of us."

"Why do you think so?" Cotford asked

"The door was locked. No one could have gotten in or out, so it must have been one of us," I stated.

"Hmm, my conclusion would be different," he mused.

"But, I say, how? What do you mean?" I enquired.

"Well, if the door was locked and the key gone, my first thought would be that someone had taken the key and locked the door on the way out," he replied

"Oh, well of course. My mind must be more addled by the evening events than I thought," I said, feeling foolish.

"Now, Captain Harker, please tell me your recollections of the evening."

I told the detective everything I could remember of the night, and he sat and listened closely, occasionally referring to the notes he had made in his policeman's jotter.

"You say you were all together for the whole of the evening. Are you sure of this?" he enquired. "Please think, during the dinner, during the little concert, during the cards, did no one leave the group at all?"

"Certainly not during dinner. During the concert, I could not say for sure. I was close to Miss Mina and Miss Westenra and most of the company were at my back. During the cards, again I cannot be sure. I have to concentrate hard when I play; I am not such a natural as Dr Seward. I played with him and Miss Murray and Mrs Westenra. What happened on the other table I cannot say, I'm afraid. I find myself wanting as a witness," I finished.

"Ah, can you tell me your impression of how Renfield was found?" Cotford asked.

"Yes, of course. We had been playing at Bridge for quite some time. Miss Murray, who is quite an impetuous player, bid Misère and so I was sitting the hand out. I heard a voice from the other table mention that we were low on drinks," I recalled.

"Can you remember who said it?" asked Cotford.

"I believe it was the Professor. I am almost positive. It was definitely either him or Dracule, but it does not make sense for Dracule to have said it, as it is his home," I responded.

"Please, go on," prompted Cotford.

"I realised at that moment that my glass too was empty, and as I was sitting out, I offered to go to the kitchen and chase up Renfield. He was not in the kitchen, but I could see the door to the pantry was a little ajar, so I went to look in. It was then that I saw Renfield on the floor. I bent over him and could feel no breath, so I took his wrist but could feel no pulse," I explained.

"Did you move the body at all? Please describe the position you found it in," Cotford asked.

"He was lying on the floor, facing toward the door. He was positioned exactly as you found him." I offered.

Cotford nodded for me to continue.

"I returned to the company and asked immediately for help. There were two men of medicine present. Professor Van Helsing was the first into the room; he agreed that the man was dead," I said.

"Please describe what happened as exactly as you can remember," asked Cotford.

"Well, the Professor knelt on the floor beside the body. He had his back to me, but I saw him reach out to touch the body, then he stood and declared him to be indeed dead. He said that there was a small dagger in the heart and that he had been dead for at least an hour," I said.

"So, you could not see what the Professor was doing, or the torso of the body at this time?" asked Cotford.

"Not exactly. I mean, I could tell that he was checking for signs of life, of course," I offered.

"Of course," agreed Cotford. "Had you seen the dagger earlier?"

"Well, no. I mean, the man was dead, and the dagger was small. I had certainly not noticed any blood and had not needed to move his coat," I answered.

"And then," prompted Cotford.

"Well, then the Professor stood up and moved aside and beckoned for Dr Seward. Dr Seward then knelt down in much the same way and pronounced that he agreed with the Professor, saying that he believed Renfield to have been dead for around one hour. Then Dracule went and called for the police and we all waited in the sitting room until you arrived."

"I thank you, Captain Harker. I am sorry to have kept you so long. You may return to your lodgings now and I will be in touch should I need more information," said Cotford.

And thus dismissed, I returned to my host and bade him goodnight. I drove my auto back to Mrs Murray's and entered the house as quietly as I was able. I could tell the ladies were still up but did not wish to disturb them, and so retired to my room.

The following week passed slowly. I did not hear from either Dracule or Detective Cotford. The papers were full of the story and there were some wild theories being expounded, the most common of which seemed to be a robbery gone wrong or that the murder was a case of mistaken identity, that the killer had mistaken Renfield for Dracule and killed him in error. Many of the papers expanded on my friend's mysterious past and his coming to London. Of course, to the London paper anyone not from England or London for that matter, was a mysterious stranger; and after the war, anyone with an accent was immediately suspect.

By silent and mutual agreement, the Murrays and I decided to spend most of our time at home. We did not discuss the events of the dinner party amongst ourselves and none of us wished to face the polite but earnest enquiries of our friends. This suited me perfectly and I found that the friendship I felt for Mina deepened. With her mother's blessing we went for long walks together in the nearby park and talked of trivialities. We were just the three of us at dinner and I felt a comfort and strength in their company that I had not felt since before the war. I found my heart most at peace when I was with her.

After the end of the week, I received a small, hand-delivered missive from Dracule. It read, "Please friend Harker, I am in need of a friendly face. I am not able to leave Slaine Court for the newspaper men are camped on my doorstep. I dare not go out for fear of being accosted. I am hoping you could come for tea at your earliest convenience." I paid the delivery chap and replied that I would come by at around three that afternoon.

At the appointed time, I drove up outside Slaine and saw the throng of reporters outside just as Dracule had described. I parked my auto and pulling up my collar, braced myself to walk through the mass outside the foyer. Unfortunately, one of their number recognised me and then they all descended, shouting out questions, tussling with each other to get close.

"Captain Harker, Captain Harker!" they called. "Tell us what happened? Who is that old foreigner? Was it you who found the body?" they yelled.

I pushed my way past and into the safety of the foyer, then called for the passenger lift. I alighted and found Dracule waiting to greet me. He led me through to the sitting room.

"May I offer you some tea?" he asked. "I have not yet replaced my man; it seems wrong to do so whilst there are still questions as to what happened. I will make it with my own hands."

I nodded and waited for Dracule to return with the tea. I am not a man who disapproves of foreigners, but it must be said that they cannot make tea. I sat with the pale imitation and sipped. At least it was hot and there was some nicely-made little sandwiches.

"It is impossible, my friend. You see how it is, I cannot leave my flat. They hound me, they follow me if I try to go anywhere, and they make up stories because they do not know the truth of what has happened. They call me Johnny Foreigner and say that I am not to be trusted. My neighbours now avoid me, and I am desolate," he moaned.

"Chin up," I said. "This will blow over. These newspaper chaps are always after someone. I have every faith in the detective. He will find our killer and set your name to rights."

"Do you believe so?" he asked. "What do you think happened?"

"It seems obvious to me. Someone broke in to rob you and surprised Renfield in the pantry. He stabbed him and then took his keys, locked the door and escaped down the back stairs before we happened across the body," I answered. "Believe me, this will be a very simple case and once broken by Cotford, the press will forget all about Dracule, Le Compte Parau-Tepesch," I reassured him

"Yes, yes, of course, you are right, and I think maybe you are correct about what happened here. I have many objects of art that are highly valuable; a robbery gone awry is surely what it was," said Dracule. "Is this the direction of the good detective, do you think?"

"He was the one who pointed out to me that the killer would have left through the back door. I got a bit muddled in my thinking to begin with, but yes, I am sure this is the way he is leaning," I said.

After this exchange we lapsed back into our old ways and talked for an hour on this and that until it was time to leave.

"Friend Harker, why do not you leave by the back stairs, the servant's way, and then those bothersome reporters will not accost you," said Dracule.

"Oh, so you found your key. Where was it?" I asked.

"Alas, no, my own key could not be found. Of course, I so rarely have need of it that I don't know when I mislaid it. I had a locksmith come and make me a new lock, just in case the criminal still had the key he took from Renfield and came back," he said.

"A wise move and I will go down by the servant's stairs and take my leave from the back of the building, thank you. Next time we meet, we will be able to put this horrid business behind us."

I departed Slaine and drove home, thinking of my friend and his predicament.

Two weeks had passed. I was at my breakfast when I received a message from Detective Cotford. It read, "Captain Harker, I have come to the end of my investigation and would like to gather everyone together tonight to let you know the outcome. Could you please bring Mrs and Miss Murray with you to Slain Court tonight at seven? Doctor Seward and Professor Van Helsing will be in attendance and Doctor Seward will be bringing Miss Lucy and her mother."

I must admit I was curious to know the outcome and surprised by the invitation. I went at once to see Mrs Murray to advise her of the request and she seemed as anxious as I to know the result of the investigation. I sent a man with a response in the affirmative to Detective Cotford and tried to settle myself whilst I waited for the hour to come.

At seven we arrived at Slaine Court. Professor Van Helsing arrived at the same time, and we met in the street, in front of the hotel. There were police in front of the building and so the reporters were kept at bay. They still shouted their horrid questions, and the ladies shrank a little from the noise. The Professor and I quickly bustled them inside to the quiet and safety of the foyer and then summoned the lift to take us up to Dracule's flat.

Dracule met us at the door and once again ushered us into the sitting room. Mrs Westenra and Lucy had already arrived, as had Doctor Seward and Detective Cotford. Two constables remained in the entrance hall of the flat. The ladies seated themselves and we men stood around the room. Detective Cotford stood with his back against the fireplace, his dark eyes watching us all.

"Thank you all for coming tonight. I suppose this seems a bit unusual, but then so is this case," started the detective. "From the beginning there have been some unusual elements to this case that at once seemed so straightforward."

We all of us looked around at each other and then fixed our attention fully on the detective as he carried on.

"The case looked at the outset to be a murder targeted against Mr Renfield," began the detective, "a case of intruders coming in through the servant's entrance at the rear of the flat, possibly admitted by Renfield himself, so therefore known to him. Which may explain why Renfield did not cry out. But then, why take the key? The murder was silent, the house guests were occupied. Our killer was someone with no small amount of nerve, to commit this crime in a place so full of potential witnesses. Whilst it is true the guests were occupied, any one of them could have entered the kitchen and surprised our killer in the act. The killer was therefore more concerned with the need to kill than the possibility of being caught."

We all listened intently to this and not one of us uttered a sound.

Detective Cotford continued. "There are so many baffling angles to this crime. If the perpetrator was known to Renfield, as I believe, why choose a night when there were so many in the home. Why not chose a time when Monsieur Le Compte was not home? My conclusion here is that it had to be this particular night. Again I asked myself why? Also, why did not Captain Harker notice the blood when he examined Renfield's body?"

"But, I say" I interjected, "the position of the body, the small size of the dagger, surely that is the explanation."

"Possibly," responded Cotford. "From the start, I could see that this was a premeditated crime, and that the killer was a member of the dinner party. The key was taken so that Renfield could not exit the flat. As part of my enquiry, I was also obliged to investigate the background of the victim. Renfield was an Englishman and had been living in Europe for ten years or more. He had travelled extensively working as an English butler for many upper class European families, who viewed him as a symbol of their high status. He did not stay more than two years with any one family and gained excellent references from each of them. He was an exemplary servant, as I am sure you can attest, Monsieur." he said, nodding to Dracule.

Dracule inclined his head in response, his keen, intelligent gaze focussed intently on Cotford.

"I know you are each aware of another case that is gripping our city at the moment, the young woman killed and drained of her blood."

Lucy gasped and clutched at her mother's arm and Dr Seward exclaimed, "Surely you are not suggesting a link between the two?"

Cotford nodded. "Upon deeper investigation I noticed that Renfield had been in the same cities as many killings of the same nature. There had been no linking of the similar cases as they had been carried out in different countries, and there had been no collaboration between the police forces as they were considered to be the one-off crime of a madman within their own country. Then Renfield returned to London and another young woman was murdered."

Lucy let out a small scream. "I was in the car, alone, with him! I said to mother when I returned home that I did not like the feel of him!"

"Yes," replied Mrs Westenra. "My Lucy was quite agitated when she returned home, but I put it down to the moving picture she had seen with the gentlemen. She did not sleep well that night."

"And talked about it with Doctor Seward, no doubt?" asked Cotford.

"Well, I did say that he gave me a creepy feeling to the Doctor and the Professor, but they too told me it was just nervousness from the picture," replied Lucy.

"And you, Mrs Westenra, did you discuss Lucy's fancy with anyone?" asked Cotford.

"Well, of course I mentioned it to Mrs Murray," replied Mrs Westenra.

"And there is nothing fiercer than a good mother defending her child," retorted Cotford.

"I say, surely you cannot be suggesting that one of these estimable women committed the murder? It is an outrage!" I interjected.

"Peace Captain, I make no accusation against the ladies; it is merely an observation," responded Cotford, and nodding to the two mothers, continued. "I meant no disrespect, rather the opposite. A mother would do anything in defence of her child."

"You are correct, detective, but I did nothing to that man," replied Mrs Westenra hotly.

"Of course, madam, of course," soothed Cotford. "However, one of your group did. As we know, when that unfortunate young woman was found Doctor Seward was assigned to the case," he continued.

"I knew nothing of these other cases," protested Doctor Seward, "and further had no reason to suspect that the Count's man had any hand in it."

"No, you didn't, but you consulted with your mentor and partner, did you not?" asked Cotford.

"Well, of course. When one has access to the pre-eminent scientist of our day, it would be folly not to consult," replied the doctor.

"And you, Professor Van Helsing, recognised the pattern of the man's mania immediately, did you not?" asked Cotford.

All eyes now turned to the Professor, who sat passively observing the detective.

"You had seen such cases before, as a consultant. You had travelled throughout Europe giving advice on complex cases. As I say, you recognised the pattern of the slaying and of the victim. The young, slender, and fair-haired women; the same marks upon the wrists from where the blood had been drained. I put it to you that you were on alert after talking with the doctor and when you saw Renfield that night after the pictures, he reminded you of a description that you heard of a man seen in the vicinity of the murdered woman in Amsterdam. You observed him and noticed his unusual behaviour in the presence of Miss Lucy and came to the conclusion that you could not allow this man to kill again and decided to take justice, nay vengeance, into your own hands," continued Cotford.

The Professor turned to the Count and said, "Do you mind if I smoke? Ladies? I am in need; I find this quite alarming."

The Count nodded and rose to fetch an ashtray.

"May I continue?" asked Cotford.

Van Helsing bowed slightly.

"We know that Renfield came up to the flat through the servant's entrance at the back and so he must have had his keys about him then. When the young ladies were putting on their little concert, you took the opportunity to slip into the kitchen and under some pretext or other sought out Renfield. At this point you dropped a sedative into his drinking glass and removed his keys from their hook near the back door so that he could not leave. And then you waited. You returned to the group and after an hour when the drugs were in full effect, you mentioned that there were no drinks, knowing that someone would find the body unconscious. Captain Harker found Renfield and called out. Being ready for this you were able to ensure that you were first on the scene. And then whilst leaning over the unconscious body, you stabbed him with the small dagger. You pronounced Renfield dead and then called out to Doctor Seward to corroborate your statement. Given the cold of the butler's pantry and Renfield's having been lying on the tiles for some time, stupefied, Doctor Seward agrees that he may have been dead for up to an hour."

All eyes were now focussed on the Professor, who was sitting impassively, smoking his cigarette. Quietly he arose from his chair. "I have done the right thing by removing this monster, but I am sure your twelve good men will not agree."

Detective Cotford motioned to his men, "Please take him." And then turning to the rest of says "This is a hard case. There is no doubt that the Professor believed himself to be doing the right thing and I think knowing that you, Miss Lucy, were in possible danger prompted his actions. I will say good night now." And then following his constables from the room he left.

We all sat in stunned silence for some time and then the Count, remembering his duties as host said "I will get the brandy, I think we each of us need it."

We sat with our drinks but said little as the enormity of what just happened sank in. After a short while the Doctor rose and turning to Lucy and Mrs Westenra said "This has been too much for me to take in. I have known the Professor for many years and cannot yet believe what has happened. Please let me escort you home now." And the three rose and left.

I then rose and turning to Mina and Mrs Murray said, "I think we should follow the doctor's lead. This has been a hard thing to hear. Count, I am so saddened that this happened in your home. I will message you in a few days."

As always happens, even after such a fateful occurrence life slowly returned to normal. I found myself spending more and more time with Mina and realised that I wished to spend the rest of my life with her. It was the fulfilment of my greatest wish when she consented to be my wife. I asked her mother if I might have Mina's hand and that wonderful lady took my own and shook it, saying, "My son, I am so happy." Not long after this Doctor Seward and Lucy let it be known that they too were engaged to be married and Lucy left working in the practice.

Whilst we had corresponded, I had not spoken to Dracule in some months and feeling remiss, I sent him a message to meet me for supper so that I could catch him up on all that had been happening.

I arrived at the restaurant and found that Dracule was already seated and waiting for me. He rose when he saw me approach and shaking my hand said, "It is good to see you, my friend."

We talked about small things and enjoyed our dinner sitting by the window watching the fashionable world walk by. Things were not as easy between us as they had been once, and we each made efforts to keep the conversation going. We were just at one of those stalls in the conversation when I looked out the window and saw Detective Cotford walking by. Without thinking I raised my arm in greeting. Noticing me, the detective stopped and then turned, entered the restaurant and approached our table.

"Well, gentlemen, this is a surprise. But I always say, London can be a small city," said Cotford.

I indicated a chair and said, "Please join us."

"If you are sure I am not intruding," he replied.

Dracule nodded and Cotford pulled over the chair and joined us.

"I have been wanting to see you. Your case was a difficult one and I don't feel that it was fully resolved. I cannot prove it, but this is what I know. That you, Count, set all this in motion," Cotford said looking directly into Dracule's eyes.

"The more I looked into this case, the more coincidences there appeared to be and as a detective I do not believe in coincidences. I believe that you knew who Renfield was and what he had done," he said.

I jumped to my feet. "This is appalling, please leave us!" I cried, but Dracule just waved his hand and said "No, please go on."

Cotford nodded. "I will say that there is nothing you have done that is criminal and nothing that I could do to prove your involvement. As I said, you knew who Renfield was and what he had done, and you also knew about Professor Van Helsing. You came to London after Renfield and then hired him as your man. You were also aware of Professor Van Helsing joining into the partnership with Doctor Seward and observed his lovely young staffer who so well fit the profile of Renfield's crimes. Your observations led you to see Captain Harker whom you remembered from a brief incident in Europe when you interfered on his behalf with a gang of thugs. You orchestrated to meet him and to then in turn be introduced to the professor and the doctor. You arranged that the professor should see Renfield in the company of Miss Lucy which would raise his protective spirit. You seem to have a power of mesmerism almost; you suggest and infer and plant ideas into the heads of your friends. You did not know how this would play out, but you made sure it would. As I say, I cannot prove any of this but I want you to know that I know and that I will be watching you." And so saying, he rose and left.

"Why, of all the absurd poppycock!" I retorted.

Dracule looked at me sadly and took a locket from beneath his shirt. He opened it and there was the picture of the same young woman who was in the frame in the parlour on that fateful night. "My wife" he says, "Taken from me most cruelly. The police could do nothing, but no other young women will die at that fiend's hands." Then he too rose from the table and walked away.

That was the last I ever saw of the Count, but I often look into the face of my beloved Mina and I recall the look on the Count's face when he gazed upon that small portrait. And I think, what would I have done?

Pied

JULIE DITRICH

There is a phenomenon known as the Black Sun where starlings synchronise and swoop in myriad patterns across the sky at dusk.

It is unnatural; that is me.

There is a story, a lamentation, about lemmings, suiciding collectively. Leaping from cliffs into ravines. It happened once or twice.

But it was unnatural; that was me.

And as folklore decrees, there is an old tale about charmed rats, scampering through the streets of the old town only to plunge into a river and drown.

That was also unnatural; and it was me.

Or rather it was *causal nexus*.

The result of the unholy tune I conjured from my pipe. Sometimes to fulfil an expectation or a contract. Sometimes to test my limitations. Sometimes from vexation or a fit of pique. And always to redress an imbalance or injustice.

I sit now, black leather-covered legs splayed in invitation in my trailer behind the stage of the Fiend Festival, scratching my Van Dyke beard. We're about to be called. My band—my three "goth rock brides", as they like to call themselves these days, and to whom I have been married for over 800 years—can see by the look in my eyes that I'm planning something. There is trepidation in the air. They smile gingerly and caress my shoulders with their pale hands, and I feel their anxiety rising. But they are responsive to my whims and will adapt accordingly once we're performing.

We trekked over eighteen hundred kilometres to be here. It took nearly fifty days. We carried nothing, except our costumes. No water. No food. No tents or sleeping cocoons. Not even our instruments, except for my pipe, which always hangs from a leather thong from my neck. It is always on me…in light or in darkness.

We usually always travel by foot or by water to our gigs. Last year we journeyed to Whitby, England. The year before to Varna, Bulgaria.

On this occasion, I confess, we did occasionally hitch rides on the back of hay-filled horse-drawn carts through some of the Romanian back-forest roads before we traversed through Hungary, Austria and then finally to Lower Saxony in Germany.

We were four in number and went unrecognised without our face paint. The people who picked us up were docile peasants with bad teeth and with no trace of guile. Generous. Not braggarts like some of our fellow musicians or the impresarios we've worked with. It was refreshing. When they set us down and bid us goodbye, they occasionally presented us with some *sărmăluțe*, or *jumări* and raw onions, or a bottle of the traditional plum brandy *țuică* to fuel our travels.

When they weren't paying attention, I, in turn, slipped an old guilder into their pockets. It will change their fortune if they use it wisely.

In our everyday lives we reside in Transylvania. In my crumbled citadel in the Carpathian Mountains. It is heavily fortified by a nearly impenetrable forest of ancient oak and hornbeam and linden, with beech and spruce higher up on the alpine range.

Although the site could presumably be spotted from the air, you would not see turrets and barbicans. Rather, you would merely spy ruins, overgrown with weeds and infiltrated by thorns on the edge of a precipice. Just as I like it.

But even if prying eyes did penetrate our woodland defences, they would not guess what lies underneath…a subterranean vault with myriad passageways and stone bricked rooms with a complex ventilation system. Inside, we draw mineralised water from a deep well. There are six hidden entries or exits, depending on your point of view.

We still use our old weaponry. Bows and arrows, knives sharpened like fangs. We train daily. We share our roles. We are sentries and sharpshooters, fighters and survivalists, skilled in camouflage. My army. My family.

Our first line of defence are the chamois—goat-antelopes that graze around the periphery of my home. They are comfortable with us but skittish with strangers. The villagers have learned not to hunt them. When they are disturbed, we know about it quickly and we respond accordingly.

From the outset there been several attempts to discover our lair. In the first few hundred years after our pilgrimage, it was the Tatars and Ottomans and an occasional witch-hunter. After the last big war, it was the Russians who held siege in neighbouring castles to perfect the art of torture. In recent times it was an archaeologist or two.

We disposed of them quickly, leaving their bodies in the forest for the brown bears and lynxes. By the time the carnivores were done, all that remained was a bone fragment or two scattered indiscriminately in the leaf litter.

During the centuries it has been our manifesto to lay a trail of false clues and create a mythos of blood-sucking demons that could transmute into wolves and bats. The ploy has been successful. While the curious eyes of tourists and paranormal investigators turned to other Transylvania castles, we escape their probity. It was a deliberate deceit that succeeded beyond our expectations.

We tour for six months and we nest for the other six. We sleep, ravish each other, and also rehearse and record in a padded, sound-proof, two-room bunker powered by an old generator we stole from the Communists during the Cold War. Our musical instruments and tastes are now modern, except for my sacred pipe.

By the time we reached our destination we were lean and hungry and aroused. It was my brides' home of origin.

Hamelin, or, in the mother-tongue…Hameln.

As we entered the town, my wide-eyed brides held hands and skipped through the cobbled streets as I sauntered behind them in a paternal way. Their brethren are long dead. Plague, starvation, shattered hearts… My brides were amongst the original one hundred and thirty children I liberated from here.

We needed an excuse to return and the Fiend Festival gave it to us.

We are Pied and I front our band.

The twins are exotic…dark eyed and dark haired. One plays the electric guitar and the other the bass. My fair-haired blue-eyed beauty plays the drums. I play the pipe. As is my trademark.

We were the headliners in previous years as we were to be this time. What better place to be all that and more, than where it all began?

Hamelin is the same town and yet it is not. The buildings are old and opulent but not of the era I remember.

As we meandered the streets, it dawned on me that I had acquired a level of infamy that preceded the notoriety of my musical vocation. I didn't know how I felt about it. Confused. Thrilled. Invaded. Superior.

My legacy was on display for all to view. Rat pastries in the *konditoreien*, my likeness painted on stained-glass windows, mementos of all manner from drinking vessels to attire to stuffed rodent playthings in shop windows.

I don't shut out the new age…I just can't reconcile it with my memories of the penultimate event that had undulated through the ages from the 13th century to now.

My brides were still dancing when we arrived at the Street Without Drums. A stranger cautioned us not to sing or frolic while we traversed its length. The story says this is the last place the missing children from 1284 were sighted and so music has been forbidden here as a sign of reverence and grief. I have no memory of the date or of those specific circumstances. One fetid street looked and smelled like another back then.

It was on the street that demanded silence where I spotted the first Fiend Festival bill poster plastered on the side of a building. I wanted to feel the thrill of reading our name in the largest of letters and the most stylish of typography. It took a moment before the shock sunk in…and then I ripped the poster from the wall and offered up a blood-curdling howl to the sky. Passers-by glanced at me in horror at this indiscretion and raised their fingers up to pursed lips. But I was livid. Yet again, I had been cheated.

The Fiend Festival occupied a large field near a forest, west of the township. The organisers had set up barricades around the perimeter, as well as an enormous trellised and roofed stage at one end.

Beyond that were the artists' trailers. I found ours quickly.

I stormed inside, with my brides traipsing in behind me. They instantly threw themselves on one of the beds, giggling and rolling about sensuously while Renfield, our English manager, paced the floor.

"You bilge packet!" I bared my teeth. "What is this abomination?" I said, shoving the scrunched-up poster into his face.

"I know. I know. I'm sorry," he sniveled. "I rang the Festival producer to complain and he shut me down. He switched out the acts at the last minute and there was no way to warn you."

Renfield ran his hand through his lopsided doss-house hair. Sweat dribbled down his pale face, steaming up his spectacles. His tie was skewed, and his expensive shoes were scuffed. I could see hairless skin on his sockless, freckled, skinny white ankles.

"Why wouldn't Pied get top billing? Especially in this town. It makes no sense!" I continued my tirade. "One wouldn't exist without the other!"

His contrition sounded genuine, as he crumpled onto a luxury leather armchair.

"I negotiated with the organisers last year. It was a no-brainer until one of the support acts recorded his new song and it went to No. 1 on the Billboard charts, and then they gave your spot to him."

"You mean that imbecile who can't even write original material…"

"Yes. But he's an imbecile with charisma and a No. 1 Hit!"

Renfield sat panting for a few moments and then regathered his thoughts.

"He eclipsed you," he said, "You've been the headliner at this festival from the beginning and I've begged you… Let's break out. Let's tour America! Let's tour Australia! Let's tour Japan and South Korea! Let's get more exposure. Other gigs. But nooooo…"

"I've already visited those countries."

"Not under my management you haven't."

"We visited those places long before you were born, and they were not to our liking."

"I don't know how to respond to that," he countered. "You need to stay off the mead and get real. Your popularity has slipped, and you've no new album the year, so you've lost all your musical momentum."

"I left you the reel-to-reels and the sheet music at Whitby last year. That should have been enough."

"You left me nothing. If you had, we might not be in this position."

"Now you listen to me… I put the bundle in your car with our instruments before we left, just like you asked and just like I have in previous years."

"I'm telling you it wasn't there. And I would've told you that if you had given me your mobile number."

"You know my position on that," I responded.

He sighed. "I'm finding it increasingly more difficult to represent you when I have no address, no email and no phone to reach you. You come and go as you please. You rarely ring me. It's like you mysteriously vapourise and I'm left to be your voice for six months of the year without instructions. I just can't take it anymore."

"You make plenty of money from our labour."

"But at what cost? Every time I deal with you, I have a full-blown anxiety attack!" he blurted out. He began flopping around, loosening his tie and hyperventilating.

It had never happened before but in that moment Renfield silenced me. I began to deliberate and turn over details from our last encounter a year ago.

Although my musical style had changed considerably over the centuries in line with the natural evolution of modern music, I still wrote my compositions on staff paper. Fountain pen on parchment. There was nothing better. It was a remnant from the discipline of scribing instrumental scores for the likes of Mozart and Beethoven who had taught me everything I knew.

I poured Renfield a glass of honey mead—one of our artists' perquisites, which came in a customised gift bag of gourmet cuisine and wine. Then, under the guise of getting in some practice, I gently blew a few notes on my pipe, which calmed him down immediately. He went silent while I sat pondering.

That evening my brides and I sat in a restaurant, fortifying ourselves for the following night. We would need an abundance of vitality and stamina to perform. Renfield came with us and was no longer lachrymose but ebullient. He was not perceptive enough, however, to recognise that I was still brooding.

We sat in a booth, eating *Leberknödelsupper* and *Leberkäse*, mustard and sauerkraut on semmel, and drinking beer.

In the middle of a random conversation, snatches of music drifted in from the outside and spirited themselves into my ears.

"Bloodied red shoes at the cathedral."
I sat up. Rigid.
"Hobbled horses at the pier."
There it was again.
"The tinkle of bells on ankles
As the iele scorch the earth in the glade."
My song.
"Diablerie... Diablerie..."

I threw money on the table and ran outside. The others were accustomed to my impetuousness and didn't pursue me. I heard them clink beer glasses behind my back.

A teenage busker in a grey crocheted headpiece, stood on the street corner, strumming an acoustic guitar. He played my chords. He sang my lyrics with a husky voice. I did not understand. Why was this hapless hopeless youth decapitating my music? And even more importantly, where did he get it?

History might have labelled me as cruel, but I was not a monster. The children I lured away centuries ago remained untouched. Many people testified I took them by forceful supernatural means, and yes, that was true, but they stayed willingly. They trusted me. I never starved or maltreated them and indeed, over time, we founded a secret nation together in the Transylvanian foothills. Soon their memories faded. I gave them a choice to be self-reliant or to stay with me. Those who wanted offspring fanned out and divided into the *Siebenbürgen*. Then there were the few who stayed.

The flute determined my immortality. Every time I played, it imbued me with lifeforce. While the children grew up and gradually withered, I did not. Nor did my small army or my brides. But I had to feed them to sustain them...my blood, my breath, my saliva, my semen, which transferred its potency to them and kept them youthful.

I give. You give. They give. She gives. He gives. That is how we resided in our enclave. There is harmony just in the ideology.

As far as this impertinent teenager was concerned, ordinarily I would have pinched his cheek or mischievously tapped his hindquarter. That night, after he had moved to a deserted cobbled laneway to count the coins in his guitar case, I broke his neck and dumped his body into the Wese.

In less than two hours the Fiend Festival will begin. Twelve goth rock acts in twelve hours from noon to midnight. Forty minutes a set. A twenty-minute break in between for the stage to be undressed and redressed. Ten thousand robust fans, converging from all over the continent and beyond.

Pied has two sets of instruments. The first never leaves our stronghold and, as part of his contractual obligations, Renfield takes care of the second set, delivering them to our gigs whenever we perform.

Truth be told, I had not seen this marauder coming. It signaled my complacency. Had I sensed him, then I would have stopped him earlier. But now that I knew who **HE** was, I quietly observed him from the wings.

I watched him with disdain, with contempt, as he swaggered around the stage in his sunglasses, wearing his supreme braggadocio like a coat. I do not bother describing him here because **HE** does not deserve it. I do not want to name him because that would leave his imprint or residue upon the ether and I want to rob him of his power. The speakers on either side of him reverberated with my song. Every now and then he patted and adjusted his earpiece and nodded to the sound engineer and the lighting guy who sat in the middle of the arena in their black cube.

There was nothing original about him.

HE wailed the verse.

HE destroyed the chorus.

And yet, the gathering crowd outside the barriers began hooting and whistling in excitement.

HE knew I was there, of course. **HE** was putting on this show for me… gyrating and flaunting his masculinity because he knew he could get away with it. Tonight, he would amp it up and attempt to seduce my devotionals away from me.

When the front- and back-of-house sound engineers were happy with the clarity and sound levels of each instrument and vocal, **HE** sauntered towards me, lifting his sunglasses and meeting my gaze in a surly manner, as if **HE** had won a contest he hadn't even entered. His lips curled upwards at the corner. I blocked him and then leaned in, put my mouth to his ear and whispered, "I know what you've done, you pretender. You'll never get away with this."

"But I already have," **HE** said simply, then pushed past me and laughed.

I contained my need to inflict harm in that moment…the timing wasn't right and there were a number of roadies in the vicinity. I needed to remain an eagle, hovering above an unsuspecting prey and just waiting patiently for the right moment to extend my talons.

I saw him approach his bodyguards, murmur something and then point in my direction. Their faces hardened and they locked their eyes onto me and tightened their fists. Later on, when nobody was about, they sidled up and threatened me for threatening him. Fools. They will pay.

Hours before, I had asked Renfield to investigate how my song had been registered and attributed in the music world. He scurried about, making phone calls, and checking his electronic device. When he had the answers he needed, he scribbled some notes on a piece of paper and thrust it in my hand. He then apologised, blaming himself again for his lack of attentiveness. In this respect he was blameless, and I let him know it. That piece of paper told me everything I needed.

HE had registered my song as his. His name was emblazoned as both the composer and the lyricist on the single and on the sheet music and all over something Renfield cited as "streaming services". **HE** was now a phenomenon, ready to funnel my riches and establish his reputation as a musical prodigy. He also had fourteen other songs of mine to support him in that quest.

As Renfield and I surmised, **HE** must have quietly shadowed me when last we met and witnessed me placing my parcel into Renfield's vehicle. Then, envy and curiosity had driven him to steal it.

Undoubtedly, when **HE** saw that my music was written on paper all **HE** had to do was transcribe it onto his electronic device to establish his claim as its creator. In the interim, my reel-to-reel had vanished…probably destroyed. I had no recourse. I had no proof the song had ever originated with me.

Parasite.

I take and I also restore. I am balance personified.

But if you steal from me without compunction, then there is only one possible finale…you must pay the piper.

It all begins and ends now.

We are the second to last act to perform.

The night is warm. We are about to play under a full moon. I see the shadowy firmament beyond the stars. And my pipe, which hangs down my chest, imbues me with the confidence I need to finish this job.

My origins do not matter in this grand tale. I cannot remember anything before I found the pipe, wedged in the stonework of a well into which I had been thrown. I sat shivering in that dark murky freezing water for three winter days and nights without sustenance or warmth, shouting and begging for rescue. I knew what it was to suffer. With chattering teeth and quivering blue fingers, I had tapped over the crevices in an attempt to find a crack big enough for me to get a hand or foothold. My attempts to climb out had been in vain.

Somehow, I scratched and widened a small fissure and that was when I found it. My hand closed around its cylindrical wooden surface. I liberated it, as it did me.

I had no musical training, yet somehow, after I had examined it in the sunset's waning light, I realised it could be my providence. I raised it to my lips and began to play, as if the pipe itself was willing my frozen fingers to thaw and dance over its tone holes.

That evening I played what I thought would be my final melody. It flowed out of the well and made a sound like a trapped and injured feline, caterwauling for rescue from the underbrush. The melodic scream reached the ears of a passing Romani family who hauled me to safety and nursed me until I recovered and it was time for me to roam free again. They presented me with a pied coat to stay warm on my travels.

Later, as I fortified my role as the pipe's caretaker, I realised I had only to usher a thought, and the pipe manifested a tune of its own accord to meet that intention.

Now, I hear our introduction over the speakers. The male emcee booms firstly in German and then in English, "And now a band that needs no introduction, especially not in Hamelin. In this, their seventh magnificent year at the Fiend Festival. Please join me in welcoming…PIED!"

We run on stage. I applaud the audience as they applaud us, and they love me for it. The chanting begins. I see a group of our devotionals close to the stage, eyes blazing, mouths beaming, foreheads dewy with excitement. No matter what I do they will adore us. But tonight, even they will not be spared.

I grab my microphone and gaze upon my brides with heartfelt appreciation. Their hair has been caressed and uplifted into bounteous mounds on the tops of their heads. They wear black tulle tutus with black laced boots over black lace stockings. One wears an orange satin belt, the other a red satin belt, and the third a yellow satin belt of differing styles. Their pouting lipstick-stained mouths match their belt colours. Smoky grey hues and elongated black lashes accentuate their eyes. Their pupils dilate in anticipation.

I walk downstage and cast my eyes over the audience. I have forty minutes to win them and an entire night to cull them.

We begin playing our first song immediately. It is a bit more up-tempo than our usual fare. I do not play my pipe; I just sing.

I strut around the entire stage, catching the intimate gaze of the individuals in the front and the mass at the back. My hair is glossy and slick around my neck. I have three streaks of war paint on my cheek bones in our three signature colours. I wear a black leather armless jumpsuit with a sharp V on the chest. My muscles are accentuated and my skin shiny. I brandish my pied cloak...a cloak of many colours...orange and buttercup and scarlet with a lining of ruby satin. After I finish the first song, I acknowledge each bride and they counterpoint the introduction by playing a few chords from their respective guitars or with a drum roll.

We segue into our other songs of different themes and rhythms, and I pour my melancholy and trembling darkness into them. In certain choruses, the audience sings along, and they break into applause as we move towards the finish. At certain moments my brides shift into their brief instrumental solos and I step aside, let them take the spotlight and blow them kisses.

In between, I banter with the audience. I don't plan what to say. It just rolls out automatically from my tongue, but on this particular night, I feel resentful and disconnected from them. Hardened and dispassionate.

We bridge to the final song. I glance off-stage and see him getting ready to go on, leaping up and down on the same spot, shaking his arms and hands, working up his energy to dazzle them and take the festival into its death throes at the midnight hour. Ha!

I break every rule of musicianship and indicate to my brides to let the musical interlude fade out. The sound reduces to the pinpoint of a sinister hush.

"This is a little song," I say to the unsuspecting audience, "I wrote just over a year ago."

Their attention pricks up and there is ripple of disappointment mixed with a hint of curiosity. Ordinarily, they want an artist's biggest hit at the very end of a performance, and now they feel I will deprive them.

I glimpse him again in the wings, spinning towards me. I am pleased. I have his attention.

"It's a song born in the heart of a mountain."

I begin to chant the chorus softly… a capella.

"Diablerie… Diablerie…

That's the only melody you'll unearth from me

Diablerie… Diablerie…

That which is unnatural is inevitably linked to me."

I sashay across the stage to the front, as the music begins to rear up behind me. My brides understand what I am about to do and improvise accordingly.

Except for my devotionals, I am not greeted with the usual cheering and applause. Rather, I see the remaining faces register shock and confusion. Then the air changes and they signal their hostility. They think I am stealing what is already mine.

"Diablerie… Diablerie…"

"Boooooooooooo!" they jeer, "Booooooooo!"

Now, it is they who must face the music.

I see him in the wings, pacing and tearing at his hair. It brings me profound pleasure.

"BOOOOOOOOOOOO!" they roar.

I have now lost the crowd in its entirety except for a mere handful. The only thing that will soothe the others is if their shit-spinning, song-stealing hero takes over. But I will not give them or him the satisfaction.

He runs on stage, feigning that we are his support band, warming things up for him. He attempts to take my microphone. I break his arm in one move. He falls to the stage and I kick him as the cruel might kick a dog. But dogs are innocent. He deserves it. Infiltrator. Fake. Moaner.

He begins to crawl away. His bodyguards run towards me from all sides but once I reach for my pipe and press it to my lips to play the first few alluring notes it is too late. They are in my thrall and succumb before they even reach me.

The sound of the pipe travels like a melodious breeze to the edges of the field. I see the looks of horror on the audiences faces, shifting to a disconnection between brain and body, manifesting in the first instance as a sway in the hips, to closed eyes, to feet shuffling.

I glance over at my brides. They smile sweetly at me and keep singing while I continue.

"Bloodied red shoes at the cathedral

Hobbled horses at the pier…"

The audience extends their arms to the heavens. All the while their feet are moving side to side to the beat of the music.

"Damsels dressed like petulant dolls
Swishing petticoats on the melting floor
I ensnare the wallflower in a spin to hell
As the Terpsichorean lyre plays at the door"

It doesn't take long. Ten thousand people are now gyrating.

"Diablerie… Diablerie…
That's the only melody you'll unearth from me
Diablerie… Diablerie…
That which is unnatural is inevitably linked to me"

Ten thousand people are now dancing feverishly like bacteria in a pustule.

"The tinkle of bells on ankles
As the iele scorch the earth in the glade
I am instigator I am witness
Impervious to the thrall of the invisible maid"

Rivulets of black and purple mascara pour down their faces and they are exultant.

"Diablerie… Diablerie…
That's the only melody you'll unearth from me
Diablerie… Diablerie…
That which is unnatural is inevitably linked to me"

Hair-sprayed hair begins to wilt, and clothes begin to droop from sweat.

"Fragments of my stony soul
Unholy and profane
Longing to be temperate and whole
Lie in the lapidarium of Earth's dreams
Unfettered vagabond
Resisting the urge to conjure
Yet I continue to command the instruments of my instruments
Rarely to stop and wonder"

Their crazed eyes light up in euphoria. A handful will be immune and will drop on the spot and fall asleep. If they are not trampled, they will wake up believing it was a dream, but the evidence will lie strewn across the field ten-fold to what happened in Guyana with spiked drinks and a madman at the helm. Except I am not insane, and they are not drugged.

"Diablerie... Diablerie...
That's the only melody you'll unearth from me
Diablerie... Diablerie...
That which is unnatural is inevitably linked to me
Diablerie... Diablerie...
Languishing in the shadows of my melancholy
Diablerie... Diablerie...
Turning my back on mercy and chivalry
Diablerie... Diablerie...
Balancing the inhumane in humanity
Diablerie... Diablerie...
Condemned like this for eternity"

I play the song on a loop and my brides sing...

While my pipe plays, the crowd dances. They rave frenetically until their feet bleed and their blisters pop, or their soles wear out or until they drop. No one is spared. Not the *polizei*, the *sanitäter*, or the concert management who come to intervene, except for Renfield who I had lulled to sleep earlier in our trailer.

"Diablerie... Diablerie...
You cannot vanquish it from the depths of me
Diablerie... Diablerie...
Diablerie... Diablerie..."

They danced frantically. I see terror convulsing across their perspiring red and swollen faces.

The treacherous ones, the fickle fickly ones...

I hear their femurs pop and their fibulas crack. I hear their tendons rip. I watch them collapse onto grass, sloppy wet with blood. I see them beg for water, as their throats parch, and their lips crack. And I did not deviate from my resolve.

"Diablerie... Diablerie..."

I wanted their love. I wanted their ardour. I wanted their adoration. That was the contract between us, and they broke it.

I play my pipe till dawn as the bodies piled up. Some were insensible and some were lifeless. Occasionally, I would kiss each of my brides when I saw them fading. My breath was an elixir that restored their vitality and they quickly recovered and kept on singing.

When the drone devices did a flyover at noon to see why the hordes were not returning home or to their tents or hotel rooms, we looked at each other and ended the song suddenly mid-verse. A lone couple remained dancing, cheek to cheek with their arms enfolded around each other. The only thing sustaining them was the reverie of their bonded love. When we stopped, they dropped and joined the fallen.

Those who survived, well…my song will be the only thing they will remember, spinning like a vortex in their haunted minds for weeks to come.

As Pied walked away, leaving everything behind, it suddenly struck me… Fairy tale after fairy tale. Fable after fable. Parable after parable. And still, they do not learn.

I impaled him with my pipe, through his vocal cords. I retracted it as soon as **HE** finished gurgling and perished. Then I slung him over my shoulder and began walking home with my brides. I don't know how long or how far we traversed but once I found a power pole in the countryside, I hoisted him over the electrical wires and angled his arms behind him. I gazed up and admired my artistry… He looked like a quaver. I called in the starlings with my blood-soaked pipe and they occupied the wires beside him. Music notes on a bar. I wished I had a camera.

Now we continue our journey back to our citadel. We want to feel mellow again.

We will resume our normal ways of life, and once the fuss dies down and perhaps when five…ten…twenty-five…fifty years pass, Pied will re-emerge and make a comeback. I believe our next appearance will be at Eurovision.

AUTHOR'S ACKNOWLEDGEMENT

I wish to thank musician Alex Moss for his guidance in helping me understand the gothic rock genre and ensuring that my song lyrics were on point. I truly appreciate you sharing your expertise with me, and your extraordinary generosity and support.

War Against the Mafia

BY ALAN PHILIPSON

The metalflake-gold Buick Electra swerved from the highway onto a narrow desert track. It accelerated out of the billowing dust cloud, pushing past 60, then 80. In Ray-Bans, ventilated gloves, his black hair slicked back, the driver looked like a Gran Prix racer or a test pilot—but he was far too pale to be either. Through the windshield, soft morning light burned his skin, sharp, stinging like lemon juice in a fresh cut. As the sun climbed higher, the pain would intensify, becoming almost unbearable, but he couldn't turn back.

Arriving home the night before, he'd found the compound's security gate broken open, the house trashed, and his four family members missing. A note stuck to the wall with a butcher knife made no mention of ransom. It said if he wanted to see them again he should check the bone yards—mob body dumps spread over hundreds of square miles of desert. He'd hit the closest ones first, then spiraled out the search.

Fifty miles from Vegas, and well past daybreak, a miracle was the only hope left.

What looked like a low boulder shimmering in the distance morphed into the ruin of an abandoned well—the dumpsite's marker. He cut his speed and when the road branched, turned right. After a half mile on the odometer, he stopped. The track continued across the plain, with no cover in any direction save scrub and sagebrush. Before he got out he took a wide-brimmed hat from the passenger seat and put it on. Head lowered, grimacing, he moved away from the car and focused on the road in front of him.

He didn't have to go far.

With no hint of wind to disturb them, three mounds of soft ash lay where they'd fallen. From the edge of the nearest pile he picked up Zenobia's ring—white gold with diamonds and emeralds. Half-buried in ashes was her black negligee. The personal effects in the other two mounds belonged to Hannah and Peter. From the length of stride and the depth of the footprints leading up to the ashes, they'd been running hard right up to the end. The fourth set of prints didn't stop in a heap of gray fluff. It kept going, back the way he'd come.

He followed the impressions to the car, then k-turned and drove along their trail, driver door ajar, looking down. They stopped at the old well. He left the Electra running and hopped out. Some of the loose boards that covered the opening had been shifted to one side.

He peered down through the gap. "Johannes?" he called.

A familiar voice echoed up from below. "*Capitano!*"

Because of the morning sun's shallow angle, the lower half of the well was veiled in deep shadow; he didn't dare move the boards to let in more light. "Are you injured?"

"A little bruised and scraped," Johannes Vilnes said. "The water was deep enough to break my fall. I can barely touch bottom."

"Can you climb out?"

"I tried, the bricks crumbled under my fingers. Then they caved in on me, I had to stop."

"What happened, Johannes?"

"They took us by surprise," he said. "We were just waking up. Before we could fight back we had hoods over our heads, and our wrists and ankles were bound with wire."

"Did you see who did it? Did you recognize any of them?"

"No, it happened too fast. They sat us on the floor, with our heads covered, while they went through the house, breaking things."

"How many were there?"

"I counted six. Could have been more. We didn't have a chance."

"Did they say anything to you, or to each other?"

"Not a word, the whole time. They put us in the back of a van and drove us out here. Dumped us, hooded, tied up, in the dark. They were sure we'd never get free. Wanted us to suffer. They didn't know how lucky they were—if they'd attacked five minutes later we'd have been fully awake and had ourselves a feast."

"They had no idea?"

"No, or they would've tried to kill us in the house. Once the hoods went over our heads, they couldn't see our fangs."

Johannes didn't ask about the others. He knew they were dust.

How had he alone escaped destruction? Either he'd taken off running the moment he'd gotten free, or abandoned the others as dawn threatened to break. He was faster, stronger. They couldn't keep up his pace.

"You're going to have to stay where you are until after sunset. I promise I won't leave you down there. I'll come back with a rope and pull you out. I've got to get out of the sun now."

"*Grazie molto, Capitano.*"

"*Arrivederci.*"

He repositioned the boards to cover the wellhead and returned to his car. Pulling the door shut, he sat motionless, eyes closed, letting the air conditioning hit him full blast in the face. It did little to relieve the stinging pain, and nothing to soothe the shock of his loss. Zenobia, Hannah, and Peter were gone forever, finally free of their unholy curse. He wasn't the monster who'd devoured and corrupted them, but he could've released them seventy years ago—if he'd wanted to.

Dropping the Buick into gear, he retraced his route to the highway. With no speed limit and a land yacht that cruised at 110 miles an hour, he rolled into the compound near Red Rock Canyon forty-five minutes later, pulling under the carport beside a sprawling, single story house.

Slatted steel shutters on all the windows were battened down tight—they always reminded him of Palermo, as did the hostile landscape and breathless heat. In his haste to begin the search he had left the tall double entry doors ajar, but it was still cool inside—and dark. Out of the sun, his skin stopped burning; though agonizing, the reaction never left marks.

Furniture and furnishings had been torn to shreds and scattered over the white marble floors and sunken living room. The knife in the wall and the affixed note had become the only decoration. Why rip the house apart? A crude demonstration of power? Or were they looking for something?

He went straight to the hiding place, which he hadn't taken time to check the night before. Under a sliding panel in the floor was a safe set in concrete. The contents were intact: fat bundles of hundred-dollar bills, a dozen forged passports, bags of diamonds and Krugerrands, and a pair of stag-handled, Sicilian switchblades—a gift from the first Mafia don he had pledged fealty to, in 1898. He closed the safe and slid the panel over it.

The bedrooms of Zenobia di Schiani, Peter Moresby, Hannah Kruger-hof, and Johannes Vilnes had been likewise ransacked, boxes of grave dirt hidden under their beds thrown against the white walls. Their tragedy had begun the night they met his progenitor, the creature known as Dracula; his began an instant after awakening underwater in a remote Transylvanian lake. As he struggled, naked, against the formless, suffocating cold, his mind seethed with memories that were not his. The details of bloody crimes, vile sensations repulsed and terrified him.

Though created from a fragment of Dracula's persona, he was a separate entity, born without stain. He'd never lived before, of that he was certain. He'd never tasted blood. Never killed anything. Crawling out onto a muddy shoreline, he realized the torrent of alien memories had to be somehow countered, contained, or they would consume him and history in all its horror would repeat itself. As a defense against what he feared he could become, he'd gathered Dracula's final victims, murdered and transformed before that monster had obliterated himself in the lake. He'd turned the small clutch of vampires into his shield, a constant reminder of where the dark path led, where he could never allow himself to go. He did not drink blood; they did. He did not take lives; they did. He did not turn innocents into vampires; they did. Though it involved compromises, he'd found a way for them all to survive, to function together, wants, needs, and defenses intermeshed.

He walked across the sunken living room to the glass wall and pulled aside its sliding door. Parting the steel shutters a crack, he peered out at the sun-blasted atrium. Encircled by the house, completely blocked from outside view, the kidney-shaped swimming pool was empty, faded blue walls angling down to a silver drain. Affixed to the grate was a pair of shackles. A garden hose dangled over the diving board.

By any other name, a bone yard.

Satisfied that nothing had been disturbed, he closed the sliding door and freed the knife and handwritten note from the wall. Instead of a dot over the "i" in family, the author had used a little heart—a sadistic and juvenile flourish. It wasn't the first time someone had tried to damage him. But it was the first time anyone had succeeded. He crumpled the note and let it fall to the floor.

The phone rang. And rang. He finally found it under the slashed couch cushions. When he picked up, Carl "The Sausage" Fiorelli was on the other end.

"Johnny L wants to see you," the underboss said. "Penthouse, by the pool."

"Now?"

"Now. There's somebody he wants you to meet."

When Don Lupo demanded an audience, you showed up, day or night. Pain or no pain.

"Be there in ten."

He hung up without mentioning what had happened. He couldn't admit to anyone how badly he had failed to protect his own. Something the kidnappers were no doubt counting on.

In daylight, without the distraction of blazing casino lights, Las Vegas was gritty and bleak. Nothing hid the crazy web of overhead power lines, the potholed parking lots, faded signage, shabby liquor stores and gas stations, the surround of desolate brown hills. It was a wasteland in the middle of a wasteland, nested like a set of Russian babushka dolls.

Nested farther down in the pecking order was the Le Mystique Hotel and Casino. Twenty-two stories of curving, iridescent-green tinted glass. Paid for with blood.

He pulled up under the wide awning between concrete pylons and got out. The parking attendant gawked at the Buick's enormous engine compartment. Hand extended to take the keys, still grinning, he said, "That's the new '72 model, right? Three hundred-seventy horsepower?"

"No faster than thirty, clear?"

His tone wiped the smile off the attendant's face. "Yes, sir. Of course. I'll be careful."

Bypassing the entrance to the casino, he cut through the hotel lobby and took the elevator to the top floor. He used his key to unlock the elevator doors to the penthouse.

Down a short hallway, through a glass door, he stepped back out into blistering sunshine. He kept to a strip of deep shade along one side of the huge, rectangular pool. Well-tanned and oiled, long-legged showgirls in string bikinis and high heels balanced trays of mixed drinks, serving a handful of connected highrollers in deck chairs. Under a striped canvas canopy, a man sitting at a table waved him over, cigar in hand.

Johnny Lupo's round, bronzed belly spilled out of an unbuttoned, powder blue lounge shirt decorated with tropical fish. Matching shorts, a pair of flipflops, and heavy gold chains completed the ensemble. From the way cards were laid out on the table, he was playing solitaire. A guy half his age in mirror sunglasses sat in the chair opposite, dark hair carefully sculpted into a pompadour. He wore a tight-fitting, white disco shirt, open at the throat to display a gold medallion nestled in chest fur, and knife-edge-creased, brown bellbottom trousers.

The don wagged a finger at him as he approached the table. "You should sit out by the pool, get some sun, you look like a mushroom."

"*Non sono una persona diurna.*"

Johnny L laughed, shooeing a fly from the rim of his tall, iced drink.

The younger man shifted uncomfortably in his chair. "What's so funny?"

"He said 'I'm not a day person.'"

"So?"

"He only works after dark. That's why he's called Captain Midnight. *Capitano Mezzanotte*. His father, and his father's father, back to the old country with the Mustache Petes, all took that *nome di guerra*."

"Took what?"

"A fake name they fight under," the don went on. "You know, like the French Foreign Legion."

The younger man shrugged. He didn't know, and didn't care.

Johnny L gestured at the newcomer. "This is Adrian Lupo, my nephew," he said. "Adrian, this our magician. He makes people disappear."

The nephew raised a hand from his lap and instead of extending it in greeting, set a stainless steel, semi-auto handgun on the table. "That's a .44 AutoMag," he said, biting off his words for emphasis. "It makes *heads* disappear."

Midnight barely gave the massive weapon a glance. He and his family had seen the new *Dirty Harry* film, so he recognized the paraphrase of the movie's punch line. After Zenobia, Peter, Hannah, and Johannes had fed, when they were tipsy and mellow in the afterglow, he often took them down to the Strip for an airing. Movie theaters were much darker and more discreet than casino shows, so that's where they usually went.

Johnny L jabbed at the AutoMag with the lit end of his cigar. "Too messy and attracts too much attention. Mezzanotte kills you so dead, it's like you were never even born." He raised his glass. "*Salute, Capitano.*"

Midnight nodded minutely, acknowledging the compliment.

"If you're such a hotshot magician," Adrian said, "why don't you do us a trick?"

"Have some respect," the don cautioned. The fly was back, buzzing around the rim of his drink.

"Not a problem," Midnight said. He reached over the table for a playing card. As he straightened, the card in his hand vanished. It reappeared, spinning like a miniature buzz saw as it skittered across the pool deck.

Adrian slow-clapped in mock approval. "That's what I call a showstopper. Haven't seen a trick like that since—grade school recess."

A soldier Midnight didn't recognize, pattern-bald, thick-set, stepped up to the table and whispered something in Adrian's ear. He immediately scraped back his chair. "Gotta run, Uncle Johnny. Some business needs attention." Scooping up the pistol, he said, "It's been real, Captain *Kangaroo.*"

The pair hurried off toward the elevator.

"Excuse my nephew's manners," the don said.

"Nothing to excuse."

"Adrian's the closest I got to a son. My brother in Philly asked me to take him in. Things got too hot back there—blowback on some work he and his crew did. The kid's looking to start fresh in Vegas. He's a real go-getter, smart as a whip, but needs direction. I was hoping you'd take him under your wing."

"*Io lavoro solo.*"

"Yeah, I know you work alone. I thought you might make an exception."

Midnight said nothing.

"Doesn't matter. He doesn't want help from anybody. You can lead a horse to water, right? A goddamn, hard-headed pain in the ass, but I love him."

Johnny L looked down at his highball and swore. Waving at a passing showgirl/waitress he pointed at his drink. "Bring me a fresh one, baby.

There's a fly in my glass."

Midnight could see it floating next to a slice of lime.

Half a fly to be exact.

Midnight found "La Salsiccia" in the casino's eye in the sky, a series of one-way glass panels set in the second story floor that looked down on the gaming tables. Tall, broad-shouldered, with big nose and ears, Carl Fiorelli pushed back from the catwalk's steel rail.

"So, *Capitano*," he said, "what did you think of the nephew?"

"Not my type."

"Not Philly's type, either, or so I heard."

"Yeah?"

"A little too eager beaver. He and his crew tried to set up business in a spot run by another outfit. Moved in pushers, girls, the usual. Did it without checking with Daddy first. Things got messy fast."

"So messy he had to leave town?"

"Adrian used hand grenades."

"In that case, Vegas may not be far enough away. How long has he been here?"

"He and his pals arrived a couple days ago. Johnny L put them up in a house in Paradise Palms."

Midnight knew the spot, a development near the Stardust. "He brought his whole crew?"

"Four of them. They're supposed to lay low for awhile and let things cool down."

"From the way Adrian talked, it sounded like he already had some action going."

"In Vegas?"

"Yeah."

"If Philly finds out where he is, things are going to get dicey. But I don't see us taking it to the mattresses, no matter what happens. Johnny L can't protect—or avenge—his nephew without blowing up the truce between the Vegas families. Money beats blood, always has. The kid has no value here. We're sewn up even tighter than Philly. No place for him to squeeze in…"

Unless he pushes somebody out, Midnight thought.

As he drove back to the compound he worked through the other possibilities. He could have been targeted by Vegas insiders, another outfit making a move on Johnny L's turf, or someone in the Lupo mob looking to climb the ladder.

Fighting within and between families had always been part of the territory, held in check by fear of retaliation. His reputation in Sicily after the turn of the 20th century had kept a lid on usurpers there. No one had dared raise a hand to him or his. When he had moved the family to Chicago in the 1920's, one step ahead of Mussolini's anti-Mafia campaign, he had been immediately challenged by a rival in the Capone outfit who decided the old country reputation belonged to his "father," the previous Mezzanotte, not to him. One of the mixed blessings of his ancestry: he didn't seem to age. Which meant after a few decades passed in one place, he had to relocate or face closer scrutiny. Twice, Captain Midnight had retired to distant parts and passed the torch of his profession to a "son" who popped up elsewhere, equally distant.

The challenger in Chicago had vanished without a trace, along with all of his soldiers, never to be heard from again. An object lesson that had held for almost thirty years. When people again started to notice he wasn't getting any older, he and the family had to move on. This time to Vegas, where a Wild West attitude stretched an already tenuous moral code to include the heroin trade.

That had been nearly a decade ago, so what had happened at the compound wasn't a matter of someone mistaking his retired father's reputation for his own. Everyone in town who was connected had heard of him. Someone you talked about in whispers, if you dared speak of him at all.

Because of the longstanding truce between the Vegas families neither of those alternatives seemed likely. Taking down a don's most trusted enforcer was an attack on the don, himself. A first step to a hostile takeover. A risky play for another family, even riskier for a member of the Lupo outfit. Failure meant extermination.

So it was back to Adrian—the outsider whose best chance at survival and advancement was making himself indispensable to his doting uncle, and doing that as quickly as possible. He needed bait to get the person he intended to replace in his crew's crosshairs, so he had taken hostages.

Adrian was cunning, but not all that bright. He'd left a trail of breadcrumbs.

The crew that attacked the compound knew where it was and who he was. They had been confident he'd be gone; otherwise, they'd have entered with guns blazing. They knew about the existence of the others if nothing else, and had come prepared to take them captive. They'd left them in one of the Vegas mobs' dumpsites.

There had been no car tail on him in the days or weeks prior; of that he was sure. That didn't rule out more subtle surveillance, maybe less direct, carried out in stages over time, or even tracking from above by helicopter. If the kidnappers weren't locals, it was dead certain a local—for money or some other consideration—had given them a leg up. Even Johnny L had motive to do it: by clearing space in the outfit for his beloved nephew, making him an important component, he could protect him from retaliation.

Back in the trashed house, Midnight started sweeping up Hannah's bedroom, gathering her grave dirt and pouring it back into its small, brass-cornered casket. He went from bedroom to bedroom, collecting soil that had crossed an ocean and two continents. He carried the boxes one by one to the carport and put them in the Buick's spacious trunk, along with a shovel, a length of heavy rope, a flashlight, and a lantern.

He spent the rest of the afternoon cleaning, shifting the larger bits of wreckage to the shaded part of the patio. When he was finished, he sat in the darkened living room. As he waited for the sun to set, his memories of the others and those of his infamous progenitor intertwined like a nest of snakes.

Hannah, a seventeen-year-old music student, had been set upon by the monster in 1895, on a side street in Salzburg, Austria. She had been too frightened to make a sound. Dracula had taken Peter in 1893, in Amsterdam's De Wallen red light district. A British lost soul, he sought meaning—or oblivion—in the sensual, and found something less poetic. Two years earlier, Zenobia had been attacked behind Boboli Gardens in Florence, Italy, her beauty, wealth, and social status proving no defense. Johannes died at the monster's hands in 1896, near Grindelwald, Switzerland, and was reborn a vampire on the trail below a moonlit Jungfrau.

Dracula's recollections, although replete with grisly detail, ended there, a shadow passing over sprawled corpses, victims discarded to face an unthinkable fate. His family members' recountings of who they had been were untrustworthy, by turns grandiose and deprecating. When hungry, they were tigers. Pacing the cage. Fighting each other. The most ferocious had been Hannah, always the first to the blood.

Because they sensed the infinitesimal part of him that had created them, because he provided their sustenance, they regarded him as their Master. He was, in truth, their Keeper, and they his. The supplying of fresh victims, the draining of blood, the transformation of victim to vampire, and then to untraceable ashes was a perfect symbiosis—a balance in which damage was contained, and no new monsters were released into the world. By offering up his still-living, mob-contracted targets he protected his charges—and flocks of the innocent from them.

And from him.

At sundown he drove the Buick out of the compound. If daylight humbled him, darkness did the opposite. As the first stars of evening appeared over the desert, he felt his power building, crackling like electricity deep in flesh and bone. It made him want to tear open the Electra's roof with his bare hands so night could pour down over him.

When he reached the highway turnoff, he switched on headlights and followed the rough track to the abandoned well. In the high beams' glare, he saw boards scattered on the ground around it. He skidded the heavy car to a stop.

Someone had uncovered the top.

Midnight left the engine running, headlights aimed at the well, and approached it with his flash. Fresh sets of footprints and tire tracks marked the dirt. He leaned over the opening and shined his light into the hole. At the bottom, on the surface of black water, a film of ashes floated, along with Johannes' half-submerged clothing.

Even though he'd steeled himself, the sight jolted him. He should have anticipated the kidnappers might return before he did. Should have rubbed out Johannes' footprints and his own, and swept over the Buick's tracks.

As he circled the well, eyes focused on the ground, the flash beam reflected off something lying under the edge of one of the discarded boards. It was a spent, brass shell casing. "* —* 44 AUTO MAG" was stamped on the butt. A rarely seen cartridge designed to fit an equally rare pistol. The rimless shell had, upon ejection, ended up twenty feet from the low cirque of bricks.

He examined the inside of the well top more closely with the flash. The mortar had been loosened all around and in places had completely fallen out. There was no similar damage to the outside of the structure. That was consistent with a tremendous muzzle blast and multiple shots fired, and a weapon held below the rim, aimed at something down the hole. The other ejected casings had likely hit the walls of the well and fallen into the water, or had been picked up.

He clicked off the flash.

This was the important business that had pulled Adrian away from the meet at the Le Mystique. His crew had returned to the dump to check on the captives and found three missing, probably rescued, and the fourth alive down the well, so they had recalled the don's nephew to the scene. Whatever the original plan was—extortion or an ambush with family as bait—it had gone up in smoke. To silence a witness, or simply for the sport, Adrian had opened fire on Johannes, not realizing that .44 Magnum bullets were useless, and that the midday sun overhead was doing the job for him.

Midnight slowly poured Johannes' grave dirt down the well, stomped apart the wooden casket and tossed in the pieces. After replacing the boards on the rim, he drove down the side road until he reached the remains of Hannah, Zenobia, and Peter. Their mounded ashes had been driven over, flattened and spread by tire tracks. He shoveled their remains into their caskets and by lantern light buried them in a row of shallow graves well off the track.

He put the shovel and lantern in the trunk, closed it, then leaned against a back fender. The equilibrium he had fashioned and nurtured was no more, the barrier between himself and his progenitor swept away. And the companions to whom he had been devoted were lost, destroyed by ignorance and greed. Without Hannah, Peter, Zenobia, and Johannes, his existence—and his resolve—had no function and no meaning.

He looked up at the spray of stars. He knew the pain twisting his insides was something that Dracula had never felt. All Dracula cared about was his own pleasure. He was not the beast who'd spawned him, and could never be—even though that beast lived in his head.

He hadn't tasted blood, hadn't raised the dead, but he had subdued hundreds of victims and delivered them to the chopping block. He had watched every murder, witnessed the resurrections, the subsequent destructions, and dispersed the residue. For his companions and himself, he had created *una vita fatta dalla morte.*

A life made from death.

And in so doing had proved he was a monster in his own right.

He turned the Buick around and headed for the highway. Across the dark valley, he could see the distant glow of lights on the Strip. The others had despised Vegas, its hollow flash, its grinding barrenness. And now, they rested in it, unhappily, for all of eternity.

Back at the compound, Midnight removed a stiletto from the safe. When he pressed the trigger button a double-edged blade flicked out, razor sharp from tip to heel. The weight was so perfectly balanced that it felt like a feather on his palm. Midnight closed the knife.

The sun's rays hurt but couldn't destroy him; apparently neither could time.

Was he immortal?

That question was about to be put to the test.

The Paradise Palms safe house was a single-story on Raindance Way. Eight foot-high concrete walls and a steel-plate gate blocked view of the entrance and concealed the rest of property. Two cars and a van sat on the sloping flagstone apron out front.

He parked the Buick a few doors down the street, facing the way he'd come, and trotted back, keeping to the shadows. When he reached the edge of the driveway he ducked behind the vehicles and moved along the high wall. He could see where the ranch house's roofline ended and the back yard began. In a single bound, he jumped over the wall and landed in a crouch on the other side. A strip of flagstone pavement ran between the house and the inside of the wall. Lights blazed from nearly all the windows. Behind the house there was a patio and a swimming pool with no one in it.

When he tried the rear door, he found it unlocked. He took off all his clothes and piled them neatly on top of his shoes, then entered, closed knife in his fist. He faced a long hallway with doors on either side. Out of sight at the far end, the blare of a TV was accompanied by loud shouts and laughter. As he advanced, from behind the first door on his right he heard a noise. He turned the knob and looked in.

Under bright ceiling lights, a man in a bathrobe knelt on the edge of a king-sized bed. It was same guy who had come for Adrian at Le Mystique. Beyond him two women wearing nothing but eye masks and high heels sat against the headboard, their handcuffs looped through it.

Kinkus interruptus.

Like seizing a cat by the scruff, Midnight grabbed a handful of skin at the base of the man's neck, swinging him off the bed and into the wall, driving his head through the Sheetrock past his nose.

The knife flicked open.

As its edge arced from left to right, a chasm opened under the stubbly chin. Midnight released his hold and stepped back from the wave of red flowing down the wall to the floor.

"What's happening?" one of the blindfolded women said.

He lightly pressed a finger against her lips and she shut up. They were safe where they were. Someone else would have to free them.

Midnight continued down the hall, checking the other rooms one by one. When a beer commercial blasted from the TV, someone muted the sound. As he approached the end of the hall, he could hear a heated conversation.

"Forget the goddamned plan, Adrian. You let him find three of his people, you'll never get to them or him that way again."

He knew the voice; he'd heard it for years. The local leg up, the sixth man in the kidnapping, wasn't Don Lupo after all.

"Then how do we kill the fishbelly motherfucker?" Adrian said.

"I'll call him to a meet someplace private, where you can catch him in a crossfire. Once you start shooting, he'll know I was the one who fingered him. So don't screw it up. He's got to die."

"You get him there. We'll do the rest."

Midnight looked around the corner into the living room as the boxing match returned to the color screen. The three men on the sofa started yelling for someone to turn the sound back on. Adrian Lupo and Carl Fiorelli sat in armchairs on either side.

Knife in hand, Midnight swept across the back of the couch. The men pitched forward onto the floor, falling one after another in rapid succession, their blood spurting across the white ceramic tile.

Adrian rose to his feet, eyes wide. Midnight grabbed him from behind and with the switchblade pressed against his jugular, twisted him around to face the underboss.

"Don't do it, *Capitano*," Carl warned, reaching under his jacket for a shoulder-holstered pistol.

Too late.

Already done, ear to ear.

Midnight shoved Adrian away. Vocal cords severed, he could not make a sound. As his knees buckled and he toppled, his blood and that of his crew mingled in a widening pond.

Carl said, "Hands up, Midnight."

He raised them, one empty, the other holding the dripping stiletto. "What is all this about?" he said in a calm voice.

"Nothing personal, *Capitano*. Just business. Johnny L's brother set it up. The Philly territory wasn't big enough for him. He wanted control of the Vegas pie, too. Tricked Johnny L into taking in Adrian. A wolf in black sheep's clothing."

"Money beats blood."

"Yeah, always."

"And you?"

"Saw the opportunity. It was now or never. Not getting any younger." Carl frowned. "Time to for you to go, Midnight. Sorry…"

Fiorelli fired once, at close range, and apparently missed. The bullet slapped into the wall behind. Faster than an eye blink, Midnight closed the gap between them and spun past.

At the rasping tug of the blade, Carl grabbed for the side of his neck. "What the fuck?" he said, blood jetting between his fingers.

The underboss reeled away, fumbling as he tried to find and squeeze shut his severed artery. He wobbled towards the hallway then crashed to the floor on his face.

Blood.

It was everywhere.

All over floor, walls, ceiling, TV screen.

It was all over him.

He found a bathroom, and as he showered off he examined his chest. He had never been shot before. The bullet had hit him; he had felt it pass through, just under his breastbone. If there had been a wound, it was already healed and had left no mark, going in or coming out. Good to know, but it didn't answer the question of immortality. There were many other ways to die.

After drying himself, he crawled out the bathroom window. At the rear door, he put on his clothes, then jumped the wall and returned to the car. He turned onto Desert Inn Road, went past the Stardust in the wrong direction, then circled back towards Red Rock.

He was cleaning the stiletto with bleach and a toothbrush when the phone rang. It was Johnny L, a man who rarely talked on telephones—for fear of wiretaps. The don was so beside himself Midnight couldn't understand what he was saying at first. Then he got the gist: he was wanted at Paradise Palms, pronto.

There were now seven cars parked out front, filling the apron, blocking the driveway. Soldiers stood guard at the steel gate, weapons in hand. They let him through.

He could smell the reek of slaughter before he stepped over the threshold.

A liquid carpet covered the living room floor. Red, with purpling edges.

In a camel hair top coat, his face ashen, the don furiously puffed a cigar to mask the stench. "They killed him, Midnight," he snarled. "They butchered Adrian. Jesus, they did Carl, too."

A pair of women huddled together against the far wall, wearing silk bathrobes. Eye make-up and lipstick smeared, they looked shellshocked.

Midnight nodded in their direction. "Who are they?"

"They were here when it went down, but didn't see anything. When we found them they had masks over their eyes. Cuffed to a bed in a backroom."

"The killers did that?"

"No, the girls are pros. Specialists. Brought their own gear."

Midnight looked at the human wreckage sprawled on the floor. "Maybe you should pay them something extra."

"Sloppy work, *Capitano*. Not like you. They made this mess on purpose, to shove it in my face. To shame me in front of the other families. To weaken me." For a second, tears brimmed in his eyes. "I want you to find who did this, who ordered it."

"The trail could lead anywhere. It could start a war."

"I don't give a damn. Adrian was my brother's only son and the bastards killed him like a pig. Hunt them down, Midnight, and make them pay."

"Revenge is a bitch."

"Make it an *ugly* bitch."

He left the compound with hours to go until daybreak. A couple of turns, a few traffic lights and the Electra 225 was humming along the highway at 100 miles an hour, heading east. On the floor on the passenger side sat a briefcase packed with the contents of the safe and the stilettos.

When he glanced in the rearview, the lights of the Strip had already become an indistinct glow. Soon to wink out. In the highbeams, the road ahead was straight and deserted.

Johnny L had ordered him to follow a trail that led to him, and only him. To kill himself in the most unpleasant way possible. His family would have gotten a laugh over that.

The impending war of vengeance was not Don Lupo's; it was his. It would turn outfit against outfit, fathers against sons, leaving lakes of blood behind. And it would never end.

A life made from death.

Una vita fatta dalla morte.

Note for Readers of the Previous Story

Plans are underway by this publisher for Midnight to return in a graphic novel series from Alan Philipson, Nancy Holder and John K. Snyder III: **THEY CALL ME MIDNIGHT.**

The House of Dracula

I.A. WATSON

"There are mysteries which man can only guess at, which age by age may only solve in part."
–Bram Stoker, *Dracula*, Chapter XV

D o not be frightened, beloved. Those at death's threshold need fear no more.

Be calm. Relax. Lower your nightgown. Lay back. Let us sup together. I shall tell you a story as we feast, to help you to your rest.

The mortal Dracula, Voivode of Wallacia, his people's hope and defender, died on Christmas Day in the year Fourteen Hundred and Seventy-Six. His Moslavian retinue were outnumbered, cut down one by one in a running battle through the snows. The coward collaborator Basarab Laiotă, who had sold himself to the Ottomans, came upon him with overwhelming numbers of Turks. *That* Dracula fought them to the last, like a madman, like an angel of destruction, until he was cut to pieces on their sabres. He died damning them, and in their hatred and their fear they hewed his fallen flesh for hours.

Thus ended the soldier that had stayed the invasion of Christendom for a generation, whom some called monster and others hero. His hacked head was sent back to the Ottoman Sultan Mehmed II to be cursed forever.

The *immortal* Dracula awoke that same Feast of Christmas, at the very moment that the Ottomans did their worst. I was dazed and uncertain, unsure of where I was or what I was, or even who I was.

All I knew was hunger and thirst.

I rose from the dark vaults of my far castle near the Borgo Pass. It had been taken by my enemies. They revelled in my halls, soiled my women, doled out my treasure. I came against them by night, a vengeful shadow, and destroyed them one by one. None escaped to boast of their deeds. Their bones rattle still in the oubliette wells beneath the courtyard.

One day their ghosts may cease their screaming, but I am not renowned for mercy.

You must understand, beloved, that in those first days of my birth I was not fully aware of what had happened. It was many years before I realised the truth. You have been very clever in your researches, coming to it so quickly. That is why you are worthy to join with me, worthy to become my bride.

Subject: Dracula Country
Date: Tues, 4 May 2023 21:18:07 +0100
From: Samantha Caine
Reply-To: Hommi_Beg@janusnet.com
To: Lizzie_B_17@zoommail.com

Hey, Liz!
How our definitions of distant spooky climes have changed in a century and a half. Jonathan Harker came to the Borgo Pass by horse-drawn coach packed with worried unhappy travellers who feared the coming of night. The young solicitor in Stoker's book felt utterly separated from the civilised world he had known, his ordered world of train timetables and postal services. He journeyed amidst superstitious peasants into a dark gothic nightmare.

I came on a tourist package, with a luxury bus. My hardship is that wi-fi is down and I can't e-mail this report to you yet. The only folks in peasant dress are the ones who want to sell me Dracula postcards, t-shirts, or—heaven help me—plastic fangs.

I'm staying tonight at the Golden Krone Hotel in Bistritz, which is where the novel says Jonathan slept over. There was no such inn in real life back then (Stoker never visited Transylvania) but there's a quite nice tourist place now that is happy to cash in on the name. It even serves the 'robber steak' dinner and other food mentioned in the book. Slivovitz is the local plum brandy and it is rather nice.

Bistritz is quite a big town now, with about 70,000 residents, and it goes by the Romanian name of Bistriţa (complete with the keyboard-challenging t-comma character that is only found in that language). It has a lot of English-speaking people because the local 'Dracula' industry gets plenty of American and British tourists. I could actually see the locals pegging me as 'single gap-year film-student girl comes to make another micro-budget documentary on the legend of Count Dracula'. I reckon they must get around ten a month.

Evidently quite a lot of these film-student-girls must be up for gothic adventures with the local lotharios, going by the number of come-ons I've had and the amount of slivovitz that they wanted to pour down me. I gather that the local cemeteries are locked at night, not the restrain the unquiet dead, but to keep courting couples off the graves.

Anyway, tomorrow I'm getting picked up by the developer's people, hopefully not in a calèche with midnight black horses but in a nice air-conditioned 4x4, and I'll head out to the property and get a proper look at it.

And since I'm finally getting a bar on my phone I'll send you this while the signal lasts.

The world ever changes, beloved. Empires rise and empires fall. But also the world is always the same. The old days of blood and war seem to pass, and then they blossom anew. Men kill for land, for power, for hate, for God, or for no reason they can speak save that human desire to fight.

And always there is fear. When I returned in my present existence, the superstitious said I was 'Dracul', the devil, 'stregoica', witch, 'vrolok' and 'vlkoslak', vampire or were-wolf. They whispered that Hell itself had rejected me for my crimes – the crime of loving my land and fighting for it!

They spoke of the curse that the Sultan's necromancers had laid upon me, of bargains I had made with fallen Lucifer, of how I had murdered and devoured my own soul.

Those old beliefs burned me. I discovered myself unable to go forth under the sun's light, compelled against crossing water save at its highest or lowest flow, repelled by the instruments of faith. I discovered a different kind of taste for blood. Blood is life.

I was owed. Owed for my service to the people, owed for the sacrifices I had made, owed for the eternal sundering from grace that I now endured. Was I not *voivode?* Was I not master of these brief mortals, born to hold their days in my hands, to end them at my need? And if I was become a creature of half-life and dark shadow, was I not destined to rule over all others things of my kind? The meaner creatures were mine to deploy, the blackened hearts of vile men mine to command, the very tempests of the air and pestilences of the soil instruments of my will.

Was I not, I told myself, Dracula?

Was I not?

Hey, Liz!
I should have appreciated the phone reception in Bistriţa while I had it. I have passed beyond the rational world of cellphone signal towers and you're just going to have to wait for my wonderful reports and travelogue.

First impressions: the countryside is stunning. I got picked up about noon and we travelled the spectacular high route over Carpathia's Bârgău Mountains – Stoker's Borgo Pass – along one of the highest paved roads in the world. At some points we were looking *down* on the clouds in the low valleys. It was easy to pretend that beyond our car the land had not changed since the 1890s. We drove under the shadow of the spectacular Caliman caldera, one of the highest peaks in the region. My driver said that it is less-climbed than Mount Everest.

We passed Hotel Castel Dracula, by the way, on the way up the Pass. It's made up to look a bit like some of the genuine old buildings, but it was put up in the 1970s. It has three stars and free wi-fi for guests.

From there we branched off on one of the bumpy side-roads, climbing up through the thick national forest, blurring past little settlements of only a few houses and some walled farms. The road became a steep switchback with no passing points and a treacherous drop on one side, insufficiently barriered. My driver didn't bother slowing down.

I asked the driver about accidents but he just gave me the usual tourist chaff about "The dead travel fast", which Stoker quoted in *Dracula* from

August Burger's 1774 gothic poem 'Lenore'. It's about a young bride being taken away by her undead husband to a marriage bed in the tomb.[*]

And yes, I got my 'Lenore' facts from Charlotte. And yes, I'm mentioning her. Is this progress, do you think?

The final climb up to the version of 'Castle Dracula' I was aiming for had the four-wheel-drive taxi straining. Having survived the drive up the cliffside, I got my first proper view of Castel Bârgăului – that is, of course, 'Castle of the Borgo Pass' according to the material from Domnule[**] Wachsmann, the site's curator. Yes, the material he sent to Charlotte.

I don't see why this site isn't promoted more in the local tourist information (unless, of course, the primitive and superstitious Szekely peasantry prefers not to mention it!). This castle more closely resembles Dracula's home in the book than anywhere else I've seen in person or online. It looks to be one of the old line of fortresses built in the twelfth or thirteenth century as bastions against the encroaching Turks, intended to dominate a strategic mountain crossing. There is a big trapezoidal central block with wings coming out at right angles, surrounded by cliffs on two sides that provide sheer walls right down to the seething river at their base. The courtyard has a high curtain wall around some crumbling outbuildings. The site must once have been very near impregnable before the advent of gunpowder.

And it has *presence!* Oh, this place was built to lour. Even now, derelict as it is, it has a severe, gloomy authority, a silhouette against the grey sky that says 'This fastness is built for terrible war and more terrible deeds', rather more than 'Enter freely and of your own will.'

It's very likely that this *was* a castle of the historical Vlad Tepes, Transylvania's serial-murderer champion whose story has been stapled to

---

[*] German author Gottfried August Bürger's 1773 poem, first published in *Göttinger Musenalmanach* in 1774, is sometimes converted into English as 'Leonora', 'Leonore', or 'Ellinore'. William Taylor, the gothic ballad's first English publisher, claimed that "no German poem has been so repeatedly translated into English as 'Ellenore'." The work was a powerful early influence on the sub-genre that would later be classified as "vampire literature".

[**] Romanian for 'Mister', abbreviated as 'Dl'.

that of Stoker's vampire Count.* But Tepes had a lot of castles during his turbulent lifetime.

Anyhow, here I am at last, at ground zero, just like I planned with Charlotte, except without her. I'm camped out in the last bit of Castel Bârgăului that is relatively waterproof and habitable, having met with the local day caretaker and been settled in some partially-refurbished guest space above the main entrance (for partially refurbished read 'doesn't leak too much and includes a DIY camp-bed, water tap and chemical toilet'). The best views are actually south-westward over the valley, but evidently those chambers are now considered a bit unsafe and the glazing is long gone.

Tomorrow Dl Wachsmann will arrive to meet with me to discuss the possible refinancing of the site for commercial reuse. Tonight I get to sleep in the ruins of Castle Dracula, may God have mercy on my etc.

Y ou see how I hesitate, beloved. You lie before me, ready for my kiss, but I pause.

There is more to tell, you see. A bride learns all upon her wedding night. Death's secrets open to she who enters death's domain.

I was Dracula, reborn in darkness, more terrible, cleverer than I had ever been. I dwelled in this fortress, once one of many strongholds of my realm and now the sole refuge whose graveyard soil sustained my sleeps. I slipped from history into legend.

Ah, how they feared me! How they avoided travelling abroad after sunset, shunned the crossroads, shuttered their houses with rosary beads and garlic buds.

So it was for many years. I amused myself. I took what I desired. Some I made like shadows of me. You shall understand that soon, my dear. Do not tremble; the night seems very different past the veil.

---

* Stoker's inspiration for the vampire Dracula is most often held to be Vlad III the Impaler (1428/31 – 1476/77), three-time Voivode of Wallachia. *Tepes* is the Romanian word for 'impaler', a soubriquet won for his mass-execution impalements of between 40,000 and 100,000 men, women, and children, amongst other war crimes. He is considered a Romanian national hero for holding back Ottoman invasion.

Other scholars prefer different origins for Stoker's character.

Decades piled on decades, and that change of which I spoke came upon the turning world. My attention was caught by the rise of a kingdom to the northwest, your island race of Britons. They grew from tinkers and raiders to engineers and empire builders. Edirne, Constantinople, Venice, and Rome faded, and Paris and Berlin rose – and London most of all, the beating heart of a vast new empire.

How I yearned to taste of it.

I laid my plans and came to your England.

Liz,

You're going to think I'm pulling your leg, but I had a *weird* dream last night. I mean, a Castle Dracula-appropriate weird dream, in a way. It was so personal I'm only writing about it so that I can delete this stuff and never send it, I guess.

So there I am, lone Final Girl in ruined gothic Transylvanian castle etc. And it is a spooky, gusty, spidery old place, so fill in all the classic gothic details for yourself.

But that wasn't bothering me, to be honest. I was just missing Charlotte.

You know why. I can say it now. Che should have been there with me. This deal, it was her plan, ever since she read my great-granddad's journals etc. She was the one who put the effort into researching it, who made the contacts, hooked the investor, talked us into the chance to launch our dream business in a really spectacular manner. You *know* how much she worked at it, Lizzie. It was her vision, her quest.

And now here I was, doing it, but she wasn't there.

So yes, I drank a lot of slivovitz and I cried a bit and I huddled in my sleeping bag on my creaky uncomfortable camp-bed and I cried a bit more. At some point I drank myself to sleep.

So to the weird dream. Let's face it, if you camp out in Castel Bârgăului then you dream what you deserve, and nightmares no extra charge.

It wasn't a nightmare, exactly. It was a lucid dream, I suppose, feeling like one of those out-of-focus art movies or something. A voice woke me up, calling. After a while I realised that it wasn't the wind through the broken chimney or the shrieks of hunting bats. It was a woman, and she was calling my name.

She sounded just like Charlotte.

I followed the voice into the castle proper, into the further, higher part of the ruin, down corridors at Dutch angles and up Moebius stairs. I called out Che's name and hastened after the echo replies.

She awaited me in one of the grand, rotting chambers above the river ravine, where stars shone through broken windows as clouds scudded between earth and sky. It looked just like Charlotte, and she knew me and she smiled. She was dressed in a long flowing white nightgown, like Ingrid Pitt in that old Hammer film – and oh how I desired to be her Madeline Smith!*

I said so, and we laughed, but then I got serious and said, "But you are dead, Che."

And she said, "Love transcends death, Hommy," and she kissed me.

Hommy-Beg. That was what Che always called me, Lizzie, after Stoker's nickname for my namesake, author Hall Caine, to whom he dedicated *Dracula.***

Charlotte kissed me, Liz – and then the dream turned very erotic, and vivid, and detailed, and explicit. But Che and I were together again, and her hands were on me, and her lips and teeth, and the dream went on and on. I wish it could have lasted forever.

But it didn't. I woke up this morning cold and sore from the camp-bed, and Charlotte must have quite exhausted me because now I feel very drained and listless! Well, if I was going to get preyed upon by a vampire in Castle Dracula they sure picked the right one to send. I have no complaints.

Anyhow, I need to dress and get ready for curator Wachsmann. Game on.

---

* This would be *The Vampire Lovers* (1970), loosely based upon the story 'Camilla' by J. Sheridan le Fanu (1872, five years before the publication of *Dracula*).

** Sir Thomas Henry Hall Caine CH KBE (1853 –1931), though mostly forgotten now, was one of the most successful British novelists, dramatists, short story writers, poets, and critics of the late nineteenth and early twentieth century. Caine was far more successful as an author than Stoker in their lifetimes, but from 1878 Caine and Stoker became close friends, each commenting on and even collaborating in the other's writing and researches. It was Caine who first directed Stoker to some of the materials he used in *Dracula*. The dedication to 'Hommy-Beg', Caine's affectionate nickname, appears after the title page of the novel.

I set my war into motion. I laid my traps against the human race, from Varna and Whitby to the very streets of your capital. Such an exotic vintage from your ladies there; I admit to acquiring quite a palate for the ichor of Englishwomen. You are not the first such bride to try and thwart my objectives.

They came after me, those modern hunters who sought to protect their realm. They armed themselves with blades and guns, with crosses and whitethorn, and they armed themselves with lore. Professor van Helsing knew much of the vampire; his scholarship was inexorable.

We fought, your Empire and I, and though they outnumbered me millions-to-one I was not defeated. Weak modern civilisation cannot overwhelm the savage primal dark. They were cunning and hardy, but I was Dracula! Denied my first assay I returned towards my home to renew my strength and prepare my next gambit. Campaigns are more than a single battle, and I have ever been a tactician.

Van Helsing was clever, though. You should know, for does not his blood also pump in your veins, Fraulein Caine? Did you seek to emulate your forebear and challenge the immortal?

It was well done, his assault. The lawyer, the lord, the physician, and the landsman were his tools. They fought back my gypsies and took my coffin as the day's light failed. You must know of this, of the last desperate struggle to prevent my waking, to destroy me by the superstitions of my people; of the stake and the Bowie knife, and my crumbling to dust.

They ended me, I thought; but the old man from Amsterdam and I had one more battle to fight.

Hey, Liz!
Dl Wachsmann wasn't *quite* out of spooky central casting, but I think he'd have a shot. He turned up late, a little after noon – but of course he couldn't phone or text me here to warn me that he was delayed. He was a stick-thin old man who should have been a family lawyer in a *Scooby-Doo* episode. His spoken English wasn't as good as his written stuff suggests, but we got on alright in German.

He was hard to convince. I've never missed Che more, and not just because of my lurid fantasies last night. She could have won the old fellow over much quicker than I. But I laid out the case, the marketing possibilities for converting parts of the castle and the slopes for tourism, the merchandising opportunities for high-end designer visits.

We walked the site, as much as was safe to visit. We even got down into the old family chapel and crypt, down a narrow flight of stairs I hadn't spotted before that led to a tiny open graveyard that was almost overwhelmed with weeds. "I used to keep the marker stones bare, but it doesn't seem to be important now," old Wachsmann told me.

The curator did know his history, I'll give him that. He was able to fill in gaps that my researches into the castle had failed with (my German's not *that* good, and Transylvanian Saxon is to German what Chaucer's English is to our language today, and the rest is Romanian or Latin—and hardly any of this stuff is online at all, even now).

It was from Dl Wachsmann that I was able to trace the line of usage of the site. It had been a minor seat of Voivode Vladislav II until Vlad Tepes killed him in combat in 1456 and claimed the voidvodeship (for the second time of three—they really passed that title around in old Vlad's day). It was rebuilt by hand by Vlad's captured enemy boyars and their wives and children who preferred slavery to impalement.[*]

Vlad's little brother Radu the Handsome claimed the voivodeship *four* times, but never ventured near Castel Bârgăului. That might have been because of the vast number of enemies that ended up on Vlad's spikes here, or for the other reason that Charlotte speculated about.

I pressed Wachsmann about the castle's legal ownership and who might need to sign off on Che's proposal. Evidently the place has been in the care of a trust board since the end of World War II and they keep a rather

---

[*] This story is usually told of Poenari Castle on Mount Cetatea over the Argeş River valley, one of several preferred candidates for the 'true Castle Dracula'. Accessed up 1,480 steps onto a mountain plateau, it was effectively impregnable. In 1913 a landslide dropped parts of the castle into the valley below.

Poenari Castle has a reputation as being haunted; during the Communist era in Romania visitors who camped there overnight allegedly experienced nightmares and sickness. The location has appeared as 'Castle Dracula' on TV shows including *Ghost Hunters International*, Da *Vinci's Demons*, and *The Hardy Boys/Nancy Drew Mysteries*. A hidden lookalike site is included in the video game *Fallout* 3.

hands-off approach. They've never been very interested in getting into the Dracula industry—the curator reported that Vlad the Impaler *was* here for about five minutes back in the day but it wasn't really an important site for him. He's only recorded as visiting once, in 1475, two years before his death, at the time when he'd just been released from long imprisonment in Hungary. They'd let him out because he had converted to Catholicism and was needed to fight the Wallachian ruler Basarab Laiotă, who had submitted his nation to Ottoman rule.

At one point, the curator broke from his detailed presentation of the ruin's past and spoke more frankly. "This is not Dracula's castle, Miss Wolfe. It is not to be a playground for thrill-seeker tourists. It is not a safe place."

I explained that there was finance earmarked for some essential maintenance works and health and safety measures on site.

"Dracula is not how you imagine him," Wachsmann objected. "His story has been…conflated, it is? Crushed together. Vlad II was Drăculeşti, that is Dracul, which then meant 'the dragon' and has now means 'the Devil'. He was so-named as a member of the Holy Roman Emperor's chivalric Order of the Dragon. His second son was Vlad III Drăculea,[*] the Impaler, one of four of Vlad II's heirs who ruled in turn in Wallachia. After that there were many Draculas, legitimate and bastard. They are a family line still, the Uzunovs. Your Western books, they like to simple things—"simplify?"[**]

"You indicated in your e-mails and letters that you and the owners would be open to investment here," I reminded the old man. "Historic monuments are expensive to maintain. A steady income stream would help to shore up the property and ensure its longevity."

"The castle is already long. Ancient. But as you say, I will take papers to the trustees and see if they say yes."

I wanted to meet with these mysterious decision-makers, but Wachs-

---

* Literally, 'the son of the dragon'.

** Cecil Kirtly proposed in 1958 that Stoker's Count Dracula was based on Vlad the Impaler. The idea was popularised by *In Search of Dracula* (Radu Florescu and Raymond McNally, 1972) and has since been embraced in fiction and tourism, though literary scholars are often sceptical of how deep Stoker's researches went or whether that identification was one he intended.

mann was adamant; he would return tomorrow with their views. He would call again. Did I require transport to return to the hotel?

I chose to camp in the ruins, and got some great promo video footage of the site and its surroundings with my 'gap-year film-student girl' kit. The sunset over the Pass was spectacular, and I got it all recorded.

I hope to dream of Charlotte once again.

I awoke in my native soil, in the chapel graveyard below the towers of my castle. I rose wounded and confused, as I had once before, when Mehmed's barbarian Ottomans had ended me more than four centuries earlier.

"You are, I think, perplexed at your condition," van Helsing told me. He stood no more than two strides from me, on the native loam that had spawned my rebirth.

I could not reach him. He had drawn lines of chalk and salted water, had laid grains of white rice, had used all the cowardly tricks in his books to hold me fast in a ring of mummery.

"It gives me no pleasure to do this to you, Count," the old man told me, and I believed him. "You are a remarkable being," he went on. "What conversations we might have, what things I might learn from you. But alas, that is not possible."

"You have been a worthy foe," I told him. "When you are dead I shall remember you." He was a mortal man, with mortal frailty, and he was growing old; but I intended to kill him in that hour.

I wondered whether he had come alone to my ruined chapel to plead of me eternal life as one of my kind, but he seemed to read my thoughts and shook his head. "I have come to destroy the vampire," he told me.

Okay, Liz, I admit that I was going a bit odd. I got ready for bed like a bride preparing for her wedding night. I brushed my hair, washed as best I could in the primitive sink, fixed my make-up, swallowed another fifth of plum brandy, and tried to go to sleep; hoping for Charlotte.

I got a screech owl that wouldn't shut up, and a sharp edge of camp-bed in my back (the damn thing was trying to kill me!), and then I had to get up in the dark and find what the outbuildings called a bathroom. It was bitter cold on the way to the porta-privy and my feet froze in my socks. My torch wasn't happy either, maybe because of the damp fog outside. I *swear* a wolf howled somewhere, and there aren't any wild wolves around this part of Europe anymore so it must have come a long way to spook me.

With the temperature and the miserable accommodations and evil toilets and nowhere to charge my phone it was less of a horror film than flashbacks of Glastonbury Festival. Or so I told myself as my teeth chattered.

On my way back to bed (or the torture device that claimed to be a bed) I spotted a light up in the western tower. At first I thought it was a reflection of my torch, but when I shut that off there was still a glow for a few seconds, like an oil lantern or candle guttering before it was doused.

That *did* scare me. Not monsters, but humans. Old Wachsmann, ready to play his part in a slasher flick. Or some of those ardent young men from the hotel bar, knowing I was all alone out here where nobody could help me? I didn't like the scenarios.

I found a broken chair leg. Yes, it was like a stake, but mostly it was the best weapon I could find for thumping would-be rapists.

I'm not brave like Che was, but looking for the intruder felt a damn sight safer than laying down in my sleeping bag and waiting to be assaulted.

There were vermin in the deserted rooms. They scuttled away when I walked into the old chambers, but there were bright beady eyes reflecting my torch-beam from the crannies. Some corridors were choked with old webs, festooned with spiders. Of course, Dracula could pass through such barriers without breaking them, but I took it as a sign to keep out and not get covered in spider-bites.

I found a stair into what I thought was the tower where the glow had been. The tight spiral caused odd patterns of light and shadow as I circled upwards.

I saw flickering flames in the room above, the yellow glow of a blazing hearth. I was convinced that there had been no such fire there a moment before.

I climbed into a circular turret chamber that was shuttered against the night. The heat from the hearth was warm on my back, on my buttocks and legs. There were rugs on the floor, perhaps bearskin or wolfskin, soft but hairy under my feet. There was some old furniture: a writing desk, a high-backed chair, a stool, a water ewer, and a vast four-poster bed with hanging canopy.

And on the bed, my Charlotte.

I wanted to run to her, to embrace her again, but something prevented me. There was a gulf between us. She did not notice me.

She was looking behind me.

"Am I dreaming again?" I asked, pleaded with Che. "Let me come to you." I wanted her to reach for me, to call me 'Hommy', to take me in her embrace.

Then, like the audience of a children's pantomime, I knew: *It's behind you*.

I turned, afraid of an intruder. But it was no intruder. This was his home.

"Come," the Count murmured. I knew it was the Count, because he was exactly what the Count should look like: Christopher Lee and Max Shreck and Bela Lugosi merged into a compelling tall, dark figure with widow-peaked hair and sharp green eyes that could pierce my soul.

At least that's what it felt like, in that impossibly-refurbished tower with the instant blazing hearth, and Charlotte laid out on the canopy bed.

But the Count had not called to me. Charlotte rose, glided over to him, kissed him, embraced him. "You don't like men!" I tried to object, but Dracula was not a man, or not just a man, and his sexuality was undeniable. I wanted Charlotte to kiss him. I wanted her to embrace him. I wanted her to yield to him.

Then Charlotte was kissing me, and it was good, and we were together.

And then *he* was kissing me the same way, and I've never been kissed like that by…well, by something shaped like a man anyway, and I'm not into that, but…

I can't describe it, Liz, except that I wanted it even as I hated it, needed it even as I knew it was wrong. But Charlotte was there, with him, with me, and he was with me, and it was all part of the same thing. It was erotic, it was perverse, it was, what, a dream of necrophilia? A threesome of the damned?

He was Dracula and we played his brides, and sometimes he was a man and sometimes he was a wolf or a ghost or a corpse or a swarm, and sometimes so were we. That's all I can say.

And even as I type this now, in the grey dawn light, it's all fading away, like bad slash-fic, like a Halloween letter to *Playboy*, like José Ramón

Larraz's *Vampyres** refilmed by Frederic Fellini. Maybe it was just too much *mamaliga***—or more likely the slivovitz!

Except that I have some cuts and bruises that I can't remember getting, and I ache all over, and I don't want to go out into the bright sunshine.

This castle is getting to me.

P.S. I just had a visit from one of the locals with a message from Wachsmann to say that he won't have a decision from his trustees until the next day. Might I be so kind as to await his visit tomorrow, and would I indulge him by staying a third night in Castel Bârgăului?

I faced the old scholar and found no fear in him, only a tired sadness. All enemies fear Dracula, so why did he not? Did he think that thin line of virgin chalk and holy wafers could hold me long?

This was my domain, my home. My present brides were gone, but I was far from helpless. The very shadows belonged to me. The mean dwellers of the castle, the rats and bats, the spiders and fleas, were mine. My power was bled into the walls and floors, the arches and towers. Over centuries this had become the very House of Dracula!

And I had returned here again upon my apparent death.

It occurred to me that all I had believed—that I had been taught by the ignorant peasants that I devoured—was wrong. Whitethorn and blade had not ended me. What other prohibitions were caused only by my lack of understanding? And without them, what bounds did I have?

Why should a circle of chalk and wafers hold me from my enemy's throat?

"You begin to see it," Abraham van Helsing said to me, 'but you have not yet followed through to the conclusion. If what you believed of yourself as a vampire was in error, everything else you believed might be likewise false.'

---

* Spanish exploitation director José Ramón Larraz's cult 1974 lesbian-vampires film *Vampyres*, starring Anulka Dziubinska, Marianne Morris, and Murray Brown, was censored for gore and sex, but its success spawned a sub-genre. In the US it was distributed as *Daughters of Dracula* and *Vampyres: Daughters of Darkness*, and internationally as *Blood Hunger* and *Satan's Daughters*.

** Romanian maize-flour breakfast porridge.

"What falsehood?" I asked, sickened as I had not been in all my immortal years.

"You believed yourself to be Vlad Tepes. To be Dracula."

"I am Dracula."

The old man tilted his head. "Are you? How much of the Impaler do you remember now, beyond the history books? How much did you ever recall? A mother's song? A father's advice? A childhood jape? A first love? Or are those things merely facts, as if you were told them by another? How much detail of your former days in the sun can you truly call to mind?"

"It has been a long time, Professor. Even you, with your diminishing mortal span, must be forgetting the details of your youth as your final years come upon you."

"You do not know those things because they never happened to you. You were never Tepes. Shall I list the historic contradictions? Or can you sense the problems now that you look for them? Shall I remind you of the bloody bargain that the Impaler made while he stayed in this fastness? Of Dracula mixing his blood into this graveyard dirt, along with the blood of she whom he murdered here?"

He stared at me. And I, who am glory and death, whose gaze beguiles and terrified—I looked away.

Van Helsing saw it. "Recognise the truth: You were never Dracula."

I sneered at the old scholar—and trembled. Some part of me, beloved, some deep core of my essence was shaken by the revelation.

"You were never vampire," he went on.

"Then what do *you* say I am?" I challenged the old man. "A ghost? A revenant? A berserker wolf-warrior of the Northern steppes?"

"Our definitions are probably insufficient, but you are none of them as the conventional usages would admit them. All of the things you mention were living souls once, were men before they were monsters. To be undead one must first have been alive."

"I was alive. I was…"

"You thought you were alive. That you were Dracula. That you were the Lord of Vampires. Now I believe that you were never any of them. Only that you thought it so."

"Then what am I?"

The old scholar set aside his cross. There was neither need nor use for it. "I have read the letters that passed between Vlad III Dracula, Voivode of Wallachia, and Francesco della Rovere, Pope Sixtus VI, between the years 1472 and 1474. They are preserved in the closed section of the Vatican Archives—an institution which Sixtus formalised and organised into its present incarnation. Do you have memory of the correspondence?"

"It was long ago."

"The Impaler was losing his wars. He was imprisoned for treason, on forged evidence.* He feared invasion, that the Turks might exploit the weakness caused by faction-fighting amongst Wallachia's defenders and overwhelm all. In his desperation he was ready to do a deal with the devil—that is, with Sixtus, one of the most corrupt Bishops of Rome to have ever darkened the Papacy.** He sought help from that founder of the Spanish Inquisition, from the forbidden texts closed away in the Vatican's library of proscripted books. And Sixtus sent him the means, the method, by which Dracula might turn the heathen tide. The means but not the materials."

"The means…" I began to apprehend then what it was that had been performed, what I only vaguely recalled through a filter of shadows. "A Black Mass. A virgin sacrifice." I looked to the ground in my chapel graveyard in my stronghold castle. "Here. She died here. On this spot."

"Do you remember her name?"

I did not want to remember. That Dracula was a patriot; he would render any price to triumph over his foes. A beloved virgin, an intended bride, one

---

*   Most historians agree that three letters purportedly from Vlad to Mehmed II, Mahmud Pasha, and Stephen of Moldavia, offering to join forces against Hungary, were crude forgeries made to allow Mattius Corvinus, King of Hungary, an excuse to imprison his political rival. Vlad was held in Belgrade and then Visegrád from 1462 to 1475.

**   Sixtus VI was Pope from 1471-1484, in a reign noted for its nepotism, persecution of 'heretics', and his part in the infamous 'Pazzi Plot' that tried to eliminate the House of Medici. He confirmed and promulgated the Papal Bull authorising the taking, transport, and sale of slaves "by force or trade". But he was also a patron of the arts and sciences, sponsoring the Sistine Chapel, the Sistine Bridge, and the *Via Sistina*, founding the present version of the Vatican Archives, beginning the papal art collection that would eventually become the Capitoline Museums, and authorising the foundation of Uppsala University in Sweden. Upon his death, a Medici envoy pronounced this epitaph: "'Today at 5 o'clock His Holiness Sixtus IV departed this life—may God forgive him!'"

bright angel in a pit of fiends, was not too much to pay to change the world. I did not want to think of Josephine.*

"The text was called after its opening words, '*Lapides exciba sanguine*'," the Professor told me.

"'Wake the stones with blood'," I translated.

"The bargain was not what the barterer intended," Van Helsing declared. "Vlad the Impaler won and lost, and finally one snowy Yule he came to an end. Heaven or hell awaited him, or maybe bleak oblivion. One cannot win a deal with the Devil."

"Then what? If I am not Dracula damned, am not vampire, am not all that I thought to be…then *what am I?*"

The Professor leaned down painfully and rubbed the graveyard loam through his fingers. He ran his hands over the ancient black stones of Castel Bârgăului, of Castle Dracula, of my home…

I knew then. Van Helsing saw it in my face, paler than pale.

"You have destroyed me," I told him. "Surer than a stake through my heart."

"Why?" the terrible old man challenged.

"Because I have no heart. I never had one. I was never alive. Only the blood sacrificed to the soil. Only the fear and the memories seeped into the stones. I am…the castle. 'Wake the stones with blood'. I was woken as Dracula ended."

"You became what you were told you were," Van Helsing said, each word a nail in my coffin. "You shaped yourself by their beliefs, a phantom

---

* The *Dracula* variant *Makt Myrkranna* (*Powers of Darkness*) was serialised in the Reykjavik newspaper *Fjallkonan* from 1900 – 1901, loosely translated from an even earlier and probably unauthorised serialisation in Swedish newspaper *Aftonbladets Halfvecko-Upplaga* in 1899 – 1900, allegedly drawn from an early draft of Stoker's story. These versions differ significantly from the regular novel in language and content, devoting much more time to Jonathan Harker in Transylvania, omitting many of the incidents in Britain, and adding a police investigation.

One key difference is the more prominent role played by the blonde vampiress at Castle Dracula to whom the other brides defer, and who has a much more protracted and erotic relationship with Harker in the Nordic versions. Her name is given as Josephine. Other scholars have speculated that Josephine was also the fair-haired vampiress at the tomb of Countess Dolingen of Gratz in Stoker's posthumously-published short story 'Dracula's Guest' (a tale often claimed to be an out-take chapter from an earlier draft of the novel).

of someone you never were, a building that had a nightmare it was a monster. You projected your dark dreams wherever your soil was taken. For a while, you convinced everyone that you were the *nosferatu*—even yourself."

"Until now." I shuddered, as no un-living thing should.

"Until now," the Professor told me, almost kindly. 'Now you know what you are. Now you believe the truth. You are a castle, not a king. You cannot rule the night. You are carved rock and piled stones, raised by tormented slaves. Nothing more. Return to that now. Buildings do not speak, do not scheme, do not hunt. Buildings do not imagine and buildings do not dream. Goodbye."

I was not Dracula, Lord of Vampires. I was not what I had thought to be. I never could be.

I was overcome by an old man with words of simple truth.

I became the castle and nothing more.

I was defeated.

"**Y**ou weren't defeated for good, though, were you?" I asked the Count, or the Count's Castle. "You always come back for a sequel."

"I slept for a while," he told me, looking down on my nakedness. "Then I woke."

"Yes. And what people believe about vampires now is very different from then. They don't care about whitethorn or running water. They want capes and sex and returns from ashes and dark reboots. And so Castle Dracula Is Risen From The Grave!"

"I *am* Dracula," he told me, and his nails were sharp as they traced across my breast. "I know that now. There were once Wallachian voivodes of that name. One of them committed an atrocity in this place, one of many, to win diabolic favours. His truelove's blood spilled on the graveyard soil where now you lay. He slaughtered thousands and was slaughtered in turn. He was damned and he was lost. I am not him."

"My great-grandfather told you that."

"Yes. And thereby destroyed me. But then I was remade, as you say."

"Stoker's book. And all the copycats. The plays and the films, the video games, the tropes…"

"So much belief. These stones drink it like blood. The belief is the life. You think me nothing, a pile of stones, but what is a human except a bag of meat? And yet we are more, you and I, than the materials of our construction. We are ideas. I am the House of Dracula. You are my bride."

"Charlotte?"

"She is mine also. You saw that. If she is dead then something better remains, by my will. Immortal Charlotte, improved and obedient."

"You killed her?"

"I knew when she researched me. I smelled her. I knew when she began to discern the truth from your patriarch's notebooks. It was no difficult thing to have her sent a small souvenir, a tiny stone from Castel Bârgăului. It was simple then to claim her."

"Where your substance goes, so can you."

"It *is* me. Before I understood that, in a different age, I shipped fifty boxes of my graveyard soil to England. Now, by the wonders of modern postage, by the power of UPS, I have shipped thousands of grains of myself across the world. I have gifted them to publishers and producers, to statesmen and scientists. I have seeded myself. I have taken the high ground." The Count grinned. I saw his fangs. "This time, beloved, the war is won before it begins."

I trembled as his hands roved over me, as he leaned towards my neck. Whatever else he is, Dracula is a traditionalist.

"Our third night. Our final encounter," I whispered. Were they my last words?

"Surrender to me, beloved. Life is short but passion makes it bright. Let me drink your days and feed you mine. Then you may serve me forever."

"A question..." I choked, though his will almost smothered me by now. I was not caught *in* his castle, he *was* his castle.

Charlotte watched me struggle, and behind her were shadowed other slaves, and Dracula thought that it was good.

"A question, Dracula. That rite that woke you, that made you...that turned dumb stone to consciousness and intellect. *Lapidibus whatever.* Where did it come from?"

I knew from Charlotte's researches: there had been a tome from the Vatican, a forbidden rite, something from the collection assembled by wicked Sixtus IV.

"But where did that tome come from? Who wrote it? Who made the rite? What was it originally meant for? When was it first performed?"

The Count saw that I was trying to distract him. He saw the wooden stake that I had concealed beneath my discarded gown. He saw me trying to raise it in my trembling hand as I defied his beguilement.

"Foolish, beloved," he chided me. "You know the truth of me. Such superstitions cannot hurt me now. I am the Ancient! I am *Dracula!*"

"Whatever you are, you are not the first place to be awoken," I told the Lord of the Undead. "You can project your power anywhere your substance goes? There are older powers than you!"

I screamed in rage, in revenge, and I finished my mission. I plunged the spike of Vatican wood into the monster's chest, where his heart should have been.

Dracula sneered at the stake. Until he understood a last truth.

I felt the power of that ancient, scheming Forbidden Library in distant imperial Rome, its jealousy and intelligence and eternal arrogance, as it seethed into the Castle's avatar.

I do not know if the Vatican spike was holy, but it was enough to kill a castle that liked to play at vampire.

Stones screamed, then fell silent forever.

I glimpsed Charlotte one last time, or whatever memory thought it was her. She crumbled like Dracula, both dust. The stones of the old fortress creaked and cracked. The stronghold weakened and began to fall.

The world changed. Dracula was a character in a novel, in movies. Castel Bârgăului need not have survived into the modern age. Herr Wachsmann and his trustees were not required.

Charlotte was avenged.

Oh, Liz, you'll never believe this. I had to write it once, just to clear it from my head before I delete it. I woke this morning, starkers in the wreckage of a long-collapsed hill fastness. It took me two hours to find my pack and clothes, half a day to hitch a lift back to Bistriţa.

It will take me a lifetime to forget what I have seen, what I have experienced.

In my pocket is a pebble from the ruin, and that is all I shall take with me if I can.

DELETE ALL.

"As we looked there came a terrible convulsion of the earth so that we seemed to rock to and fro and fell to our knees. At the same moment with a roar which seemed to shake the very heavens the whole castle and the rock and even the hill on which it stood seemed to rise into the air and scatter in fragments while a mighty cloud of black and yellow smoke volume on volume in rolling grandeur was shot upwards with inconceivable rapidity.

"Then there was a stillness in nature as the echoes of that thunderous report seemed to come as with the hollow boom of a thunder-clap - the long reverberating roll which seems as though the floors of heaven shook. Then down in a mighty ruin falling whence they rose came the fragments that had been tossed skywards in the cataclysm.

"From where we stood it seemed as though the one fierce volcano burst had satisfied the need of nature and that the castle and the structure of the hill had sunk again into the void. We were so appalled with the suddenness and the grandeur that we forgot to think of ourselves."

Excised original draft of the concluding scene of Bram Stoker's *Dracula*.

BIOGRAPHIES
(IN ORDER OF APPEARANCE)

DAVE ELSEY is a 'creature shop artiste', make-up artist, writer and film director, known for Award-winning special make-up effects, creature effects and animatronics in films such as *X-Men: First Class, Ghost Rider, Star Wars: Revenge of the Sith, Hellraiser, Alien 3, The Wolfman,* amongst many others. Alongside colleague Rick Baker he won the 2010 Academy Award for Best Make-Up for *The Wolfman.* In 2020 the BBC released a modern interpretation of Bram Stoker's *Dracula* written by Mark Gatiss and Steven Moffat that Dave and wife Lou created an array of dazzling practical special make-up effects for. In recent years he has directed award-winning short macabre films, *Keep the Gaslight Burning* and *Stay Alert.*

VICKY ADAMS, born in Sydney, is a former Graphic Designer working primarily within the music and film industries. She is the proprietress of Pan's Apothika, an Occult-Apothecary Shoppe based in East Hollywood, California. She loves all things archaic, vintage and dark, and has held a life-long interest in alchemy, herblore and the esoteric. Vicky lives in Los Angeles with her constant companion, Italian Greyhound Vincent Lucien.

CHRISTOPHER SEQUEIRA is a writer and editor who specializes in mystery, horror, fantasy, science fiction and superheroes. He writes scripts for various media formats and devises, edits and contributes stories to prose anthologies. Notable works include comic-book scripts for *Justice League Adventures* for DC Entertainment, and *Iron Man* and *X-Men* stories for Marvel Entertainment. Anthologies of his include *Sherlock Holmes and Doctor Was Not* (IFWG Publishing), *Sherlock Holmes: The Australian Casebook* (Echo-Bonnier), *The SuperAustralians* graphic novel (Black House-IFWG Publishing) and, in collaboration with co-editors Steve Proposch and Bryce Stevens, the three volume *Cthulhu Deep Down Under* anthology series and *Cthulhu Land of the Long White Cloud* (IFWG), as well as *War of the Worlds: Battleground Australia* (Clan Destine Press, with *H.G. Wells' Time Machine: Australia-Bound* being set for release in 2022 with that same publisher). For 2023 through 2025 for IFWG he has *Nosferatu: Horror Beyond Century; Cthulhu-Literary: Lovecraftian Tales Set in Other Fictional Universe;* and *FrankenStymied: The Monster by Other Hands* coming. A graphic novel for Outland Entertainment ('the ultimate Sherlock Holmes crossover') with artist Cristian Roux is also currently underway, first episode expected late 2022.

LESLIE S. KLINGER is considered to be one of the world's foremost authorities on Sherlock Holmes, Dracula, H. P. Lovecraft, Frankenstein, and the history of mystery and horror fiction. He is the former Treasurer of the Horror Writers Association and serves as Co-Editor of The Haunted Library, a series of horror classics published by the HWA. He lectures frequently on Holmes, Dracula, Lovecraft, Frankenstein and their worlds, including frequent panels at the Los Angeles Times Festival of Books, Bouchercon, NecronomiCon, StokerCon, World Horror Convention, World Fantasy Convention, VampireCon, Comicpalooza, WonderCon, and San Diego Comic-Con, and he has taught several courses on Holmes and Dracula at UCLA Extension. Klinger's work has received numerous awards and nominations, including two Edgar®s, an Anthony, two nominations for the Bram Stoker Award® for Best Nonfiction book, and a nomination for a World Fantasy Award. He has consulted on a number of films, novels, comic books, and graphic novels featuring Holmes and Dracula.

NANCY HOLDER has written over 90 novels and more than 300 short stories, role-playing games, comics, and pieces of nonfiction. She has been on *The New York Times, The Wall Street Journal, USA Today,* and *The Los Angeles Times* bestseller lists. A recipient of 7 Bram Stoker Awards, she was honored with the Lifetime Achievement Award from the Horror Writers Association (HWA) in 2022. She was also named a Grandmaster by the International Association of Media Tie-in Writers. She has written fiction and episode guidebooks for TV shows such as *Buffy the Vampire Slayer, Teen Wolf, Angel, Sabrina the Teen Age Witch, Beauty and the Beast, Wishbone,* and others, and for novelizing movies including *Wonder Woman, Crimson Peak,* and *Ghostbusters.* She is the writer on Kymera Press's comic book series, *Mary Shelley Presents.* She and Alan Philipson write pulp fiction and comic books for their original series *Johnny Fade, Green Hornet,* and *Kolchak the Night Stalker* for Moonstone. She serves as writer and editor at Moonstone for projects featuring The Domino Lady, The Avenger, The Phantom, Zorro, Sherlock Holmes, and other characters. She and Moonstone publisher Joe Gentile co-created The Domino Lady's daughter, Domino Patrick. She has served as VP and a trustee for HWA, and has been a judge for the Shirley Jackson and World Fantasy Awards. She was a faculty member for the Stonecoast MFA in Creative Writing Program at the University of Southern Maine for 15 years. She is a Baker Street Irregular, and has written many pieces about Sherlock Holmes, co-editing *Sherlock Holmes of Baking Street* with Margie Deck. She lives in Washington State. Find her at www.nancyholder.com and @nancyholder.

LEVERETT BUTTS teaches American literature and horror at the University of North Georgia. Besides his work with Dacre Stoker, he is the author of several short stories and novels, including the *Guns of the Waste Land* series, retelling the King Arthur legends as an American Western. He lives in Carrollton, GA, with his wife, son, hyperactive dog and apathetic cat.

DACRE STOKER is the great grand-nephew of Bram Stoker and the international best-selling co-author of *Dracula the Un-Dead* (2009), the Stoker family endorsed sequel to *Dracula.* Dacre is also the co-editor (with Elizabeth Miller) of *The Lost Journal of Bram Stoker: The Dublin Years* (2012). Released in October of 2018, *Dracul,* a prequel to Dracula, co-authored with JD Barker, was the UK's # 1 Bestselling Hardcover Novel in Horror and Supernatural in 2018, and a top 5 finalist by the Horror Writers Association for the Bram Stoker Award® for Superior Achievement in a Novel. Film rights for *Dracul* have been optioned by Paramount Studios. Dacre's recent work includes *The Virgins Embrace* (2021) with Chris McAuley, a graphic novel adaptation of Bram Stoker's short story *The Squaw* (1893). Additionally, short stories with Leverett Butts: *Last Days,* appeared in *Weird Tales Magazine, The Tired Captain,* featured in an

FX Sherlock Holmes anthology, and *Enter the Dragon* in *Classic Monsters Unleashed Anthology*. A native of Montreal, Canada, Dacre taught Physical Education and Sciences for twenty-two years, in both Canada and the U.S. He has participated in the sport of Modern Pentathlon as an athlete and a coach at the international and Olympic levels for Canada for 12 years. Dacre has consulted and appeared in recent film documentaries about vampires in literature and popular culture and hosts Bram Stoker-centric tours to Dublin, Ireland; Whitby, England; and Cruden Bay, Scotland; and Vlad Dracula III-centric tours to Transylvania.

RAMSEY CAMPBELL was born in Liverpool in 1946 and now lives in Wallasey. *The Oxford Companion to English Literature* describes him as "Britain's most respected living horror writer". He has been given more awards than any other writer in the field, including the Grand Master Award of the World Horror Convention, the Lifetime Achievement Award of the Horror Writers Association, the Living Legend Award of the International Horror Guild and the World Fantasy Lifetime Achievement Award. In 2015 he was made an Honorary Fellow of Liverpool John Moores University for outstanding services to literature. His latest novel is *The Wise Friend*, and PS Publishing have brought out *Phantasmagorical Stories* in two volumes, a sixty-year retrospective of his short stories.

JIM KRUEGER is one of the top-rated writers currently working in American comics. Significant successes include the prestigious *Earth-X* Trilogy from Marvel Comics, and *Justice* (a *New York Times* Bestseller, and winner of an Eisner Award) from DC Comics, with colleagues Alex Ross and Doug Braithwaite. In addition, he has had notable projects with *Avengers, X-Men, Star Wars, The Matrix Comics, Micronauts,* and *Batman*. With Ross again, and others, he did *Avengers/Invaders,* and *Project Superpowers* for Dynamite Entertainment. He has been a creative director at Marvel Comics, and is also a freelance comic book writer/property creator whose original works include *The Foot Soldiers, Alphabet Supes, The Clock Maker, The High Cost of Happily Ever After* and *The Last Straw Man*.

BRAD MENGEL is a lifelong reader and pulp fan so it was only natural that he would turn to writing. His book, *Serial Vigilantes of Paperback Fiction*, was the first major work on the paperback heroes of the 70s, 80s such as The Executioner and The Destroyer. His fiction work includes new adventures of Sherlock Holmes, Domino Lady and Senorita Scorpion. He is the author of the novel *Australis Incognito*, a new pulp novel set in Australia with a team of multi-generational heroes.

LEE MURRAY is a multi-award-winning author-editor, screenwriter, and poet from Aotearoa-New Zealand, and a USA Today Bestselling author. She is a Shirley Jackson and four-time Bram Stoker Award® winner, an NZSA Honorary Literary Fellow, and a Grimshaw Sargeson Fellow. Lee's debut poetry collection, *Tortured Willows: Bent. Bowed. Unbroken*, is a collaborative title with Christina Sng, Angela Yuriko Smith, and Geneve Flynn. Read more at www.leemurray.info.

CHRISTOPHER FOWLER is the multiple award-winning author of almost 50 novels and short story collections, including the award-winning Bryant & May mysteries, the latest of which is 'Peculiar London'. His books include 'Roofworld', 'Spanky', 'The Sand Men' and 'Hell Train', 'Paperboy' (winner of the Green Carnation Prize) and 'The Book of Forgotten Authors'. In 2015 he won the CWA Dagger in the Library for his body of work. He lives in London and Barcelona.

JASON FRANKS is the author of *Bloody Waters* and *Faerie Apocalypse* and the writer of the *Sixsmiths* graphic novel series, which were finalists for Aurealis, Ditmar and Ledger awards, respectively. His short fiction has previously appeared in *Aurealis, Deathlings, Midnight Echo*, and many other anthologies and magazines. He lives in Melbourne, Australia, with his wife, his son, and a brace of electric guitars. Find him online at www.jasonfranks.com.

RON FORTIER Comics and pulps writer/editor best known for his work on the Green Hornet comic series and Terminator – Burning Earth with Alex Ross. He won the Pulp Factory Award for Best Pulp Short Story of 2011 for "Vengeance Is Mine," which appeared in Moonstone's *The Avenger – Justice Inc.* and in 2012 for "The Ghoul," from the anthology *Monster Aces*. He was awarded Pulp Grand Master in 2017 by the Pulp Factory. He is the Managing Editor of Airship 27 Productions, a New Pulp Fiction publisher and writes the continuing adventures of both his own character, Brother Bones – the Undead Avenger and the classic pulp hero, Captain Hazzard – Champion of Justice. (www.airship27.com)

J. SCHERPENHUIZEN is a writer, artist, editor and publisher. His work as author and illustrator ranges from cute picture books like *The Wild and Crazy Dinosaurs* to the gritty horror graphic novel *The Time of the Wolves*. His short fiction has appeared in *Bloodsongs Magazine, Sherlock Holmes the Australian Casebook, Cthulhu Deep Down Under, Sherlock Holmes and Dr Was Not* and *Sherlock Holmes of Baking Street*. His novels include *What on Earth, The Secret* (co-plotted with Bruce Walshe) and *Profile of Evil*. In 2022 he received a Doctor of Arts degree from the University of Sydney where he teaches writing and critical thinking. Currently he is working on a horror novel for a well-known Australian publisher. His websites are www.janscreative.com and www.jscherpenhuizenillustrator.com.

WILL MURRAY is the author of some 75 novels, including two dozen in the *Wild Adventures* series, which features such classic characters as Doc Savage, The Shadow, The Spider, Tarzan of the Apes, John Carter of Mars, King Kong, and Sherlock Holmes. His acclaimed crossover novels include *Skull Island, The Sinister Shadow, King Kong vs. Tarzan* and *Tarzan, Conqueror of Mars. The Wild Adventures of Cthulhu* is forthcoming. With legendary artist Steve Ditko, Murray created Marvel's Unbeatable Squirrel Girl.

ANDREW SALMON has won several awards for his Sherlock Holmes stories and has been nominated for the Ellis, Pulp Ark, Pulp Factory and New Pulp Awards. He lives and writes in Vancouver, BC. His novels include: *Fight Card Sherlock Holmes: Work Capitol, Blood to the Bone* and *A Congression of Pallbearers* (collected in the *Fight Card Sherlock Holmes Omnibus*) *The Dark Land, The Light Of Men*, and *Ghost Squad: Rise of the Black Legion* (with Ron Fortier) and his first children's book, *Wandering Webber*. His work has appeared in numerous anthologies covering multiple genres. His tales from the *Sherlock Holmes Consulting Detective* series were collected in *Sherlock Holmes Investigates. Ace of Devils*, the first novel in the Eby Stokes series featuring the female pugilist turned Special Branch agent, will be released in 2022. To learn more about his work check out: amazon.com/Andrew-Salmon/e/B002NS5KR0

JACQUELINE SEQUEIRA first appeared in mass media as the Bride of Dracula in Australia's first real-life wedding conducted by a celebrant in the persona of Elvis Presley. This took place when she and husband Chris' nuptials required that all the attendees be dressed in costume; the bride and groom taking the parts of the Count and Countess Dracula, flanked by Gotham City villains and leading ladies of the golden age of cinema. Jacqueline's interest in genre has continued since then; with a many-year membership of Australia's leading Sherlock Holmes Society, The Sydney Passengers, and she performed for that group's theatrical activities in one of the titular roles in 'The Merry Wives of Watson'. Her first published writing was for the Passengers' journal when she co-wrote a piece on Sherlock Holmes' connection to Wilkie Collins' *The Moonstone*. She recently picked the pen up to contribute to Nancy Holder and Margie Deck's 'Sherlock Holmes of Baking Street'; an anthology where Holmesiana meets recipes, and, she has another culinary crossover work underway.

PHILIP CORNELL is an internationally respected Sherlockian writer and artist. He has written and illustrated countless articles over decades for *The Passengers Log*, the journal of the premiere Australian Scion Society, The Sydney Passengers. With Christopher Sequeira and Dave Elsey he worked on the comic-book series *Sherlock Holmes: Dark Detective*. He has written short fiction, including for *Sherlock Holmes and Doctor Was Not* (IFWG Publishing); and *Sherlock Holmes: The Australian Casebook* (Echo-Bonnier) which he also provided some illustrations for). However, an unmatchable claim to Holmesian fame is the fact some years ago his illustrations were used in public signage in a park adjacent Reichenbach Falls to commemorate Holmes's fateful visit to the area in 1891.

JULIE DITRICH is a fiction writer and comics creator. Julie has a BA in Professional Writing (University of Canberra) where she majored in freelance writing and scriptwriting. She is the first official Australian female comic book writer to work on *The Phantom* (Frew Publications) with the release of *The Adventure of the Dragon's Leg* in 2021, as well as *The Return of the Golden Circle*, which will be published in 2022. Julie was also a co-writer on *ElfQuest: WaveDancers* (Warp Graphics) and the *Dart* mini-series (Image Comics) in the USA. Julie recently introduced a new superhero character "Djiniri" in the *SuperAustralians* graphic novel (Black House Comics / IFWG Publishing). Julie's prose writing credits include short stories in *Sherlock Holmes and Doctor Was Not* (IFWG Publishing) and *Sherlock Holmes of Baking Street* (Belanger Books), as well as a horror story in *Cthulhu Deep Down Under Volume 3* (IFWG Publishing). Julie is currently writing her third *Phantom* story, as well as several children's graphic novels.

ALAN PHILIPSON sold his first novel in 1974. He's written 130+ since, working primarily in series men's adventure and science fiction adventure. He only recently started writing short stories, and by an odd turn of fate, comics. A series of three short stories that he co-wrote with Nancy Holder—all in the same 1940 pulp horror noir universe and soon to be published in a single volume by Moonstone Books—has been expanded into *Johnny Fade*, a five-comic graphic novel currently in production by Moonstone. The short story he wrote for this *Dracula Unfanged* anthology is being turned into a four-comic graphic novel by IPI Comics: *They Call Me Midnight*. Co-written with Nancy Holder, it's pulp horror noir, too. Although set in 1970, its story-time spans the previous 75 years. Both series are being drawn by the stellar comic artist, John K. Snyder III. Additionally, he and Nancy Holder are working on a number of projects set in the world of Kolchak the Night Stalker, also for Moonstone. Mr. Philipson lives along the shore of the Salish Sea in Washington state.

I. A. WATSON first encountered Dracula in the graveyard atop Whitby cliffs when his girlfriend presented him with a copy of Bram Stoker's most famous novel there. Many years later he now dwells in a large gothic house and shuns the daylight, obsessively laying his plans and drinking… coffee. This is because he is a writer. His eclectic list of published work in the genre of what-publishers-pay-for includes "The Angel of Truth" for this present volume's companion edition *Sherlock Holmes and Dr Was Not*, historic swashbucklers in five volumes compiled in *The Legend of Robin Hood*, reworked myths such as The Labours of Hercules, The Death of Persephone, and St George and the Dragon, occult fantasy (most recently *Vinnie de Soth and the Exorcist's Union*), science fiction (*Blackthorn – Dynasty of Mars*), and non-fictional essays in *Where Stories Dwell*. He has written almost forty Sherlock Holmes stories, including the anthology *The Incunabulum of Sherlock Holmes*. His dark secret is that he loved writing them all. A full listing appears at http://www.chillwater.org.uk/writing/iawatsonhome.htm

I. A. Watson's 'The House of Dracula' (artist Vicky Adams)